BEYOND DESIRE

"Ah," Mark moaned gutturally, his voice thick with wine, "you are lovely to kiss — whoever you are?" He tried to see Rosette in the dark. "Shamara? Is it you?" he asked, mistaking her for one of his concubines.

He did not give her a chance to answer. Rosette felt as though she were drowning in the sheer male power of his passionate kisses as they continued. Melting, she was conscious of the hardness of his cheekbones. He sensed the yielding, and his hands moved more caressingly, one raking through her heavy, rich weight of hair, the other moving to stroke the bare shoulder beneath her robe. He seemed to be drawing her very self into him, deepening the kiss he gave until her entire being was dissolving in a molten heat of desire. Whirling in a fiery tumult, she slowly began to submit to his increasing physical domination of her body. Beneath these primitive forces, his gently forceful kisses soon had her gasping for one tiny breath, but still he didn't cease. He seemed to be caught up in something beyond his own man's desire. . . .

Sonya T. Pelton

Bittersweet Bondage

ZEBRA BOOKS
KENSINGTON PUBLISHING CORP.

ZEBRA BOOKS

are published by

Kensington Publishing Corp.
475 Park Avenue South
New York, N.Y. 10016

First printing: May, 1984

Printed in the United States of America

For John, the personification of all my heroes . . . and more.

And . . . in appreciation of the best editor a novelist could ever have — Leslie Gelbman.

Part One

In the Wind

The best of Prophets of the future is the Past.
— *Lord Byron*

Chapter One

The Sahara Desert, 1874—From a heat-shimmering ravine the Arabian stallion appeared. . . .

Undulating waves of desert sand deformed everything, even the darkly handsome sheik in billowing robes astride the snowy white stallion, El Barq.

"So, now he comes. Ahh, he will be angry when he learns his beloved sister is not here," moaned Hadji-ben-Haroun.

Although the sheik and El Barq were yet a commingling blaze southwest of the kasbah's encampment walls, Hadji-ben-Haroun with his keen, black eyes had been able to identify Hasan al-Shareef, sheik of Kel Numair.

"There is no other who rides with the wind as his companion," Hadji muttered to himself, "and no one who owns a half wild horse named after the lightning in the sky. Ah, the sheik must be half savage himself!"

Hadji was already down from the lookout tower as the white spectacle swept through the entrance gate. Like enfilade, at sight of Shareef the sentries around the kasbah had leapt to attention; the man nearest the gate still bawled out in a lusty tone of authority, that is, until Sheik Hasan al-Shareef held up a lean, tanned hand to quiet the man.

The well-preserved gardens here in the vast desert oasis were wild and sweet, with feathery palm trees; the fountains from Roman times were lovely though crumbling.

Now the sheik had passed through a massive arch and into a wide, paved courtyard surrounded by an enormous, sprawling building complex. The kasbah, with towers and crenellations which gave it the look of a castle, was a combination of massive blocks towering to a height of several stories.

El Taj was somehow threatening and severe in its ancient majesty, looking as if it could defy the strongest enemy, even though a section of the kasbah lay in ruin.

The magnificence of El Barq delayed Hadji's reaction to the man on his white back who sat as if born there. The sheik appeared aloof and little mindful of the splendor of his ancient surroundings. But the children dashing here and there drew from the sheik one of his rare smiles. A smile that lifted a long, thin scar that slashed down his taut right cheek.

"Hasan, Hasan," the children cried happily his name which meant "handsome" in Arabic; and handsome was he indeed. Who cared about a little scar when all else on the man shouted pure male perfection? Cringing was for cowards, which there were hardly any of here in this desert stronghold.

The sheik was draped all in white, save for the black of his thick turban and the touch of red and gold in his caftan which showed through the deep slash of his airy *djellaba*. He rode easily for all his hugeness and height, lean but deep in the chest and powerful across the shoulders, very tan with long, flat cheekbones and wide jaw that tapered to a squared-off chin.

Even from across the inner courtyard, Hadji could see the glitter of the dark, viridescent eyes and the well-recognized slant of arrogant eyebrows.

His caftan billowing in a rare breeze, the huge sheik dismounted just as a short man ran breathlessly from out of a tent to catch up to the sheik. After the sheik had eased his tall frame to the ground, the squat Arab took the stallion's bridle and led the magnificent beast from the courtyard.

Plump gentlemen in white, fluttering robes moved from out of the interior, followed by a handful of servants clad in spotless shirts and white, billowing breeches. They bobbed and bowed in their humble manner, looking like so many waddling ducks.

The scene of habitation here was incongruous, for at first sight the kasbah, with its white, crenellated ramparts of old, appeared unlived-in. This had been the thought of Mark Brandon when as a lad in his teens he was first brought captive here.

This was the desert that Baron Tremayne Rawen chose for his odyssey in 1859, going so far even as to prepare for the desert crossing by subjecting himself and his children to severe bodily privations: minimum food and water, and exposure to the relentless sun. It was said that the blooded Spanish lady knew her end to be near, thus she sent her children from England's shores with the baron.

The baron and his children and guides didn't even reach the Tanzerouft of the Sahara he had hoped to traverse. The baron's impetuosity had cost him much; he and the guides were first robbed and then slaughtered outside the Tanzerouft.

When the captive children were taken north to the ancient desert encampment of Kel Numair—the Panther Tribe—they were in a wretched state, covered with crawling, biting vermin and clothed in nothing but rags. Mark Brandon and Rozelle Modestia Rawen, the young lord and lady—they who had been raised at Oakland Manor in England—were in 1860 ruthlessly captured and then forced into a relatively barbaric life deep in the Sahara.

Mark Brandon soon became the adopted son of the childless Moorish chieftain, now deceased three years. But now he, Hasan al-Shareef had become a powerful man here. He held the reins and ruled here; no one dared duel words with him on any matter that arose—even though some would have liked to. He possessed no Arab blood, but this fact had been lost in the light of his compelling leadership.

Displaying an almost childlike eagerness, Hadji-ben-Haroun stepped forward. "Hasan al-Shareef," he greeted warmly, looking into the mesmerizing face of the sheik. *"Ma-t-toulid?"*

But there followed a moment of abrupt, breathless tension before the sheik returned the greeting.

"Hadji-ben-Haroun. Peace to you." He nodded, then answering the question asking how he fared, he said, "All is well."

Hasan al-Shareef clamped the slighter man by the shoulders, his fingers curved steellike around Hadji's robed flesh. "Has my beloved sister arrived yet? I am very eager to lay eyes upon her beauty after two long years of men and fighting."

The sheik had said this with a threat and demand in his deep tone.

"Ah . . . I have sad news," Hadji murmured with a hint of apology.

Sad news! "What is this?" Hasan demanded, sorely displeased even before the Arab went on.

"You will see Rozelle Modestia by evening on the second day from now—if all goes well," he added reluctantly.

A hush fell over the inner courtyard. The sheik glanced from Hadji to the plump gentlemen and finally back to Hadji. In the midst of that hush Hasan heard the flutter of female tongues above them in the shady terrace.

"So handsome and rugged is he!" So disturbingly male that this did strange things to so many female pulses.

Hasan heard them too, and turned about slowly to stare up at the screen where he knew the veiled and shrouded beauties stood peeking through. The whispers were suddenly stilled and the sheik came slowly back around to face Hadji. There was a sudden expression of deep-seated amusement in the glittering eyes of the sheik, despite his disappointment at learning his sister was not here to greet him.

Slyly, Hadji could not think of anything that would suit the sheik better than to relax with a few concubines — few indeed! Here was only a whisper of the harem of long ago — concubines fluttering in their gossamer robes about him and a well-rounded form laboring atop the sheik for his pleasure.

"You have done your work well, Hadji," Hasan said indicating the exotic females he could imagine above with a nod of his turbaned head. "Though women have not pleasured me much in the last two years, I hope now that you have not done your work too well. I am weary from the long ride and . . ." The sheik would not say what he thought, weary of women in general. He waved a long, brown hand, asking, "What is it, Hadji? I see you are eager as usual to speak."

"Three weeks ago I received your message and have done as you commanded, that is all," Hadji replied.

"All but for Rozelle Modestia."

Hadji gulped, feeling the full lash of the sheik's words.

Hasan al-Shareef turned languidly in the direction of the screen, as if by a wish from his lips Rozelle would suddenly appear there. He stared hard, almost seeing her standing there. But, like the mirage he had seen in the desert, her image wavered and vanished. How lovely she had been in his mind's eye, fully blossomed into the beautiful woman she must surely be by now, like a white-fleshed houri of allure and loveliness with a playful smile on her rosy mouth. Hasan knew a great desire to hear her delightful laugh ring in his ears, and toy with an auburn curl. How did she really look now? Would she be thinner? Fatter? No, not Rozelle, that slender, taut body would still carry its virginal freshness. She had better be yet untried! Ah, the tales he could spin for her now. Mostly truth, indeed, for he had been far and wide.

Hadji hesitated, for even though his neck might depend upon it he could not answer that so quickly. "All but for Rozelle Modestia." Hadji could not be certain just how far the sheik's vexation and disappointment extended this time.

Hadji-ben-Haroun was never more aware of the man's imposing height than right now. Hasan al-Shareef watched over the El Taj like a hawk; no, like a panther—Kel Numair, the Panther Tribe he was chieftain to. His brooding eyes took everything in at a glance; and when their leader was away, a thousand eyes of men watched and were responsible, preparing lest an attack would come from another warring tribe. Thankfully, El Taj stood impregnable to attack.

This region of the Sahara, the most isolated and primitive area of the desert, having neither roads, houses or anything resembling a city, is practically all desert. Here live the seminomads of Berber origin. No one ever travels here, except those desert travellers who cut across it to reach the Atlantic Coast. Some who had tried to make it there had ended up enslaved on the Mauretanian Coast. They would be taken inland to various tent villages. There were ancient ruins of old castles, and kasbahs like El Taj, but these numbered very few and only one of two were in even the last vestiges of habitation.

Hadji's position was suddenly made more comfortable for him, for the moment. "Tomorrow evening," Hasan said, his tone intense and thoughtful. "So be it. But I shall hold you, Hadji-ben-Haroun, personally responsible that she arrives then, by sunset, and safely. Nothing must happen to Rozelle." He would not add why this was so important to him.

He fingered his short sword and lowered his long, sweeping, tawny lashes. To conceal the emotion running through him at the moment.

But for Rozelle, Mark Brandon Rawen would not have lived as long as he had. He seemed to breathe danger and to thrive on it. For Rozelle Modestia he had been cautious while fighting. Who else was there to live for? What did other women matter but for the moment's pleasure they gave to him? He couldn't put a name to such dreams of Rozelle as he'd had. But he acknowledged this one thing, her future was all-important and he felt somehow responsible for her welfare, even though Rozelle was a gorgeous, independent creature. In as much as she was all that remained of his past life in England, of their parents and how they came to be captured by the old Moorish chieftain who had eventually, after fiercely defying opposition from the group of elders, adopted them. But mostly the chieftain had desired a son, for he had impregnated his women with nothing but daughters. So Mark Brandon became that son.

Rozelle was grown up now and it was up to the sheik to choose her a husband. If Rozelle did not reach El Taj by sunset of the second day from now there were those who very well might not live to regret this.

Hasan al-Shareef frowned darkly for a moment, unconscious that a housemaid walked by with a beautiful brown-eyed baby in her arms and smiled at him timidly. He seemed to be looking clear through her, but Andra knew the sheik had much on his mind after being away for so long.

Hasan was quite conscious though, as he hadn't been before this day, how thoroughly Moorish his thoughts had become. He was no longer an Englishman in his mind. How long had he quelled this truth? he wondered but only briefly.

"My son comes." Hadji-ben-Haroun dispelled the sheik's reflections.

Shareef nodded, stared off into the far distance beyond the walls with his forest-dark eyes, and then went off to meet Tarek, his deputy.

The lurking of a scheme shone in Hadji's jet-black eyes as he turned and unbridledly hurried off in the opposite direction. *"Fissa! Fissa!"* he muttered to himself. I must hurry.

Chapter Two

Morocco, 1874 — The city reared on banks of low hills huddled in the northwest corner of a wide, sandy bay.

The blaze of myriad-colored flowers which lit up the gardens of Morocco shone in and around the town and greeted the weary traveller coming ashore.

Rosette Forrest, with a face so fetchingly beautiful, had gazed breathlessly upon this jewel of a city when first she arrived here and was impressed by the mixture of African and European life. King Charles II of England had once called Tangier the "brightest jewel."

Now, a week later, the night was warm and quiet, without a breeze, as Rosette lay in her room at the Tangier Hotel. She yawned in boredom, absently studying her long fingers, this way and that held aloft. Her arms fell back to the bed and again the sigh of reigning boredom.

She could still feel the motion of the sea. The passage had been a long and perfectly dreadful one. With the storm raging, the ship had pitched and rolled almost incessantly for thirty hours or more. Rosette and her faithful maid had experienced seasickness for the first time ever, despite the comfort of the luxury suite.

"Oh, poor Lucie, she is only just beginning to recover," Rosette muttered against the big, silky, orange pillow, her cheek pressed to it.

Having come loose from its soft chignon, her hair now spread across her pillow like luxurious, auburn silk. She shut her eyes. Her lashes lay very long and still, spiky against her camellia-fair skin. She could still hear the chanting of verses from the Koran, in nasal tones. The voices floated up to her room. She was reminded again of all the white-turbaned, coal-eyed men she had seen milling about in doorways and in streets that day. Involuntarily she shivered.

Heavy eyelashes fluttered open. Rolling onto her stomach, she stared at the brick floor on which stood various trunks marked by the officials. She caught her lower lip with her teeth.

My lord, we still haven't gotten them unpacked.

She rolled onto her back, plopping her arms on the hard mattress. Burning steadily, the candle at her bedside drew her gaze.

"Damn him," she said softly.

The fire swam in her dark, almond eyes that filled suddenly with tears. Why do I have to be reminded of England again? Why did she have to be reminded of *him?*

Shifting her head on the pillow, candlelight caught the sheen of her hair causing it to shimmer like fine brandy. From her velvety cheek Rosette dashed aside a bitter tear.

"Bloody damn Perry Marland anyhow!"

Lifting her head, she brought up her fist to punch her pillow in frustration. Forget it, Rosette, forget Perry Marland. He isn't worth a tinker's damn!

The night was ink black. Smelling of rich and deep, cool greenery, altogether foreign to her senses. Exotic, tropical and alluring. That hot, surging blood of freedom was singing in her veins again.

"I wanted this. . . ."

The great winds, the hot sun shimmering radiance, the entrancing indigo and purple nights of Africa. "I shall forget Perry Marland!" she vowed with vehemence. "I shall . . . oh yes, I shall!"

But Rosette could not deny it was there.

Desire, aching in her heart once again. She desired . . . more than she could express, more than she knew. It was here, perhaps, in the nomad's fires, the sultry winds, the scents coming up from the hidden earth. Carrying her soul away as if . . . as if on a magic carpet.

She shivered again. But this time with an unexpected and unknown emotion.

She was just twenty and had recently been presented at court in England. A lot of good it did me! For then—oh, *then* her mother's escapade had ruined it all!

How can I ever show my face among all those aristocratic ones again? Lady Louise had thrown all her principles to the winds and had run away with that horrible nasty Frenchman. Him with the sinister, curling mustache! Ugh! How, oh how could Louise run away with him?

Lady Louise Forrest, Rosette's mother, had been a great beauty of the gypsy type, daughter of a Romany mother, Sir Henry Sutcliff her sire. Sutcliff had been one of the most prominent Englishmen of his day. Her grandfather, he was gone too.

Her father, Lord Alfred Forrest, had recently passed away—following the scandal that rocked London. He had left Rosette, who was their only child, a large fortune. Southend. Her home. Sad to think she didn't even miss the manor and its beautiful surrounding grounds.

Sadly Rosette reflected back. Her father had become one of the most cynical, embittered and despairing of men. And Rosette had quivered beneath the shock and shame of her mother's guilt. Took it all upon her own shoulders.

Those happy, sunlit days, where had they flown to?

Rosette pounded her pillow, once, twice, three times. "Damn them all, to be sure!" she snarled through gritted teeth that shone like polished pearls and lips that curled up in a cynical mood.

Perry Marland, oh yes, whom she had above all others of her many suitors loved and trusted, had cruelly broken their engagement of two years standing.

"I *shall* not have my life tarnished, Rosette, by your mother's shocking conduct. I *am* sorry!"

All her pride in being a beautiful, charming, kind, gentle and sweet (so she had been told countless times) young woman had been trampled in the dust Perry's horse had kicked up and tossed into her lovely, agonized face.

After that fateful day she had felt little of the inner glow of love she had known for two years with Perry Marland. Friends, and her maid especially, noticed that Rosette was changed and slightly hardened by the triple tragedy she had undergone in the short space of seven months. They were neither surprised nor shocked at her unusual behavior.

The wreck of Rosette's parents' lives plus the desertion of her fiancé had rendered her mistrustful of any and all human relations. She had witnessed a portion of the terror love could inflict, what it could do to humans. Unlike other young women her age, Rosette could not regard love as security and sweetness any longer.

"What *will* she do now?" Lucie had buzzed along with the other maids at Southend Manor.

One had answered, as maids often do, "She'll put it from her, Lucie, and strive to fill 'er life with all the lesser things men and women take hold of sooner or later." She brandished her duster like a sword. "Love ain't all it's cracked up to be, you know!"

Jayne, the upstairs maid, took up. "She has not grieved sorely for her dead pa. Though these last years they've been far apart anyway, if you ask me. And after that shocking thing which her mother did—" Jayne made a smirk with her pale mouth—"Rosette had come to think of Lord Alfred rather with pity than with love, if you ask me again.

"Oh but his death was a shock to poor, dear Rosie. I think she was remembering—when he could but only lie still in his bed—just what he had been before her mother's flight from the manor with that nasty Frenchman! Ah, how she wept for the poor, broken like of her pa then."

Lucie sighed with much sadness. "I wonder

often what Rosie might've been like now had her mother been true and her pa happy to the end."

"She would've been married to that Lord Perry Snobface, that's what, if you ask me!"

Still in a spirit of sadness, Rosette had left England behind. She had taken only Lucie, her trusted maid and companion. After a short but miserable tour in the south of Europe, with which Rosette was all too familiar, she had crossed the sea to Africa.

"Here I am, running away just like a broken man to join the French Foreign Legion." A wistful smile had crossed her lovely face.

Bit by bit, Rosette realized a brand new experience. She had never been to Morocco or seen the Sahara. She had chosen it because she liked the exotic-sounding names, because dear Lucie had pointed on the map to the Sahara Desert.

Rosette had come face-to-face on that paper spread out on the table with a vastness of which she had often dreamed.

Idly Rosette had fancied that in the sunny solitude, far from all the flighty friends and acquaintances of her old life—of twenty years only—she just might learn to understand herself better.

To find herself again. That was her goal. But how, she did not seek to know. Not yet, her heart told her. A wild sense of excitement swept over her, though. Here was a vague yearning, a hot, shimmering place, a journey for the searching heart that knew not what it sought.

This was the wildest, most fascinating adventure, not knowing what lay ahead.

And so now, as Rosette lay in the dark of her room, smelling the perfumes rising from the Moroccan earth and sand, dreaming of the faces she had seen that day in the fabled port of Tangier, faces of copper, bronze, olive and some white, she felt that the unknown was very near her.

Chapter Three

From many parts of the world people gathered in the one small, romantic city of Tangier, this tiny Medina clinging to a steep hillside sloping down to a perfect natural harbor.

The first Phoenicians arrived from their home cities of Tyre and Sidon around 1000 B.C. When Carthage was destroyed by Rome the Romans moved in. When Rome fell under attack from both northern tribes and Saharan nomads from the south, Byzantium tried to take over but was crushed by the Vandals. Arab invaders streamed overland and took possession. Spain and Portugal made attempts to gain footholds on this coast. Portuguese hopes were crushed at the Battle of the Three Kings in 1578. And more than once Moorish refugees and Jews flooded back into this territory from Andalusia's towns.

Britain entered briefly into the picture for the twenty-three years it ruled Tangier in the seventeenth century, having been given to Catherine of Braganza as part of her dowry when she married Charles II. English withdrawal came in 1684. When Moulay Ismail established his court and capital at Meknès in 1793 he wanted no Christian ambassadors intriguing around the place, so Ismail made them remain in Tangier.

"Kasbah means a fortified castle—" Lucie, finding friends where she might, was already picking up a smattering of Moroccan Arabic—"Islam is the Mohammedan practice . . . and means submission to the will of God."

"What are you mumbling about, Lucie?" Rosette entered the bedroom at the same time her maid did.

Lucie shrugged. "I've packed clothes suitable to the warm climate, Rosie, and was just in the process of pulling out a ribboned hat, a straw one, from its bandbox. Do you think you'll be wearing this one today?" Rosette was finicky at times, and no matter how hard Lucie tried to please Rosette, her efforts proved futile on days like this.

The coquettish angle at which the little, blue

hat with its long, curving feather was set on Rosette's head seemed absurdly inappropriate to the climate and her mood. "Not this one!" Snatching the hat from her auburn head, Rosette tossed it aside carelessly. "Where did that dreadful little thing come from!" she snapped, in a peevish mood at the moment.

"Here, try this one." Lucie, looking sheepish about the blue hat, offered the straw one instead.

"Uh-uh."

Even at the straw one Rosette frowned in dissatisfaction and shook her head, causing the light from the window to pick up the accents of fire in the thick strands of hair.

Rosette had not slept at all the evening before. She felt as if there was a gritty dryness close behind her usually luminous eyes. Perhaps some witch hazel on a cloth over the eyes would help.

Rosette stared ruminatively out the window. I feel very alert and enduring . . . but not in the least bit natural. Her eyes snagged on some distant spot outside the window. Had some extraordinary event occurred, had she been taken captive by some dashing sheik, for instance, she was convinced that she could have managed to be neither surprised nor alarmed. That would be exciting—her eyes glowed momentarily. Then, no, that would never do. For some inexplicable reason, though, she experienced frustration at the moment.

"Rosie, dear, are you tired? We can go another day and rest this one?" Lucie asked, tentative, worried about the barely perceptible bluish tinge beneath the amber eyes.

"No, indeed not. I'll not miss an outing on this day!" For some reason today seemed important—like the start of something?

Rosette, Lucie decided by just looking at the younger woman, was not in a very convivial mood this morning. Or was she? Her moods were like quicksilver, she could change in an instant.

"We'll go to the *Socco* today," Lucie chirped, "I mean the *souk,* oh well—"

"Hmm, what's that, Lucie?"

"Oh—" Lucie shrugged—"nothing much, the native market, that's all." She stood, cocking her head in admiring the young woman.

Like her mother, Rosette was of a gypsy type. She stood five feet seven, had thick, wavy, auburn hair which she usually wore parted in the middle of her small, shapely head. Thick hair, lots of it framing a face with almond-shaped eyes of that same color, and she possessed a clear, warmly white skin, unflecked and unflawed. The young lady never flushed under the influence of excitement or emotion—at least Lucie hadn't seen Rosette do this in a long while now. So too did Lucie notice other things just now. Strange she hadn't noticed before how long and level

31

Rosette's eyebrows were — thicker than those of most women possessing fair skin. The shape of her lovely face was oval, with a straight, short nose, one that sometimes looked pert and up in the air at the tip. Lucie smiled when she came to the mouth. A very expressive mouth it is, not too small, and slightly depressed at the corners — like dimples tugging at her lips when she smiled. Perfect, white teeth shone between dusky rose lips that seemed unusually flexible.

Rosette stepped back from the mirror. "Do you think I have put on too much weight, Lucie?" She eyed her figure critically.

"Heavens no! You're slim as a gazelle, Rosie, you lost your baby fat long ago!"

Indeed Rosette's figure was remarkably athletic, with a naturally pinched-in waist. In her face, as now when in thoughtful repose, there was that expression of cool indifference that reminded one of opposition. Rosette appeared younger than her age, perhaps eighteen, and still had not used a powder puff on her face. But there certainly was nothing puerile about Rosie; she was all woman.

Rosette laughed and sent Lucie a warm smile. "You are a darling, Luce, and I'll bet you would compliment me if I had a face full of blemishes!"

"You're a natural beauty, Rosie. And you've never even had a pimple!" Lucie shook her head at the very idea of her Rosie being anything but perfect.

Yes, Rosette could smile easily and become just as easily animated. But in her animation there was a certain brand of fire. Timid people were generally disconcerted by Rosette's unusually fresh and lively appearance. For a moment Lucie thought of another young woman, wondering where she could be at the moment, if she were still alive. She shook her head, chiding herself for even having thoughts of that other one. It wasn't healthy to be reminded of the past, otherwise she might begin talking about what was better left unspoken.

"This dress is nice, Lucie. *N'est-ce pas?*"

"*Oui!*" Lucie agreed readily in French.

Rosette spoke fluent, musical French. She attracted many admiring males just hearing her speak the language. The gentlemen and not-so-gentle men flocked around her with noisy offers of assistance with her baggage. Lucie had watched Rosette remain unruffled, even faintly amused by their impudent prying into her affairs.

Pausing to study her reflection in the mirror, seeing Lucie behind her in it, Rosette musingly said, "What do you suppose those evil-looking men were doing with the two, frightened women we saw yesterday? When we returned from the gardens overlooking Tangier Bay?"

"Oh yes." Lucie finally came out her staring

daze. "I'm not sure I even want to know."

Unusually for her, and for the second time this week, shivers ran along Rosette's spine. "It made me angry inside just watching those two men treat those women so boorishly," she snapped brittlely.

Lucie shrugged in answer to the question. "Those two men were indeed nasty-looking devils, to be sure." Lucie would not add that she had overheard just this morning of more women being kidnapped, even French girls. She didn't want Rosette fretting when she had just begun to enjoy herself a little. At least this seemed to be the way of it.

"Yes, they were." Rosette turned her head to catch the profile of her figure. Her brow furrowed a bit as she wondered again, not being able to shake a sudden uneasiness that had come over her just recalling the scene of what looked to be an abduction to mind.

The two women, wearing gossamer draperies and spangled veils, had hurried by like floating wraiths in the dark. Their somber eyes stared out from circles of kohl. With stained henna hands, fingernails painted a brighter red, they had clasped their light raiment to their prominent, brown-nippled breasts. They were rudely escorted by a gargantuan man, almost black and with a zigzag scar slashing across the right side of his face. He wore a brown burnous over a short, gray jacket. He pushed and shoved the women hurriedly into the cart as if he had been stacking hay bales, and climbed in after them, showing as he did enormous, bare legs with calves that protruded like slabs of dark iron. The other man looked as skinny as a rail, but he moved with the power of a giant.

"Fissa! Fissa!" he had been hissing in a low roar.

"I wonder what that word meant, Lucie, the one that sounded like a command," Rosette wondered out loud now.

"Oh, that means hurry!" Lucie instructed, proud of having learned so much in a short period of time.

Pushing the incident from mind, Rosette turned to what she would wear that day. She chose a turquoise-blue muslin dress with full skirt. Though it was simple, at the same time it was very fashionable with the Europeans. A suggestion of her creamy bosom showed beneath the inset of white chiffon where the dress dipped low at the neckline. She would carry a white parasol, frilly and pretty, besides the straw hat to shield her from the hot sun.

She turned from the mirror. "Ready, Lucie?"

"Ready."

What's to worry, thought Rosette, reminding herself that she wasn't really afraid of anything today. As they stepped from the hotel, though,

Rosette wondered at the new sensations and feelings she was experiencing. What did this mean? Everything was crowding in on her at one time—her past, her hazy future, and her bewilderment over these strange sensations, like thrilling premonition. Premonitions she couldn't put a name to.

"There," Lucie said after a time, walking, pointing, "where the trees offer shade in the square. I see some tiny shops we can go into."

Leaving the fragments of Portuguese and Spanish buildings and the narrow streets behind, the two women entered the square where the streets were wider. The shop signs read in French, Spanish, or English and all the buildings had European flavor.

In the distance on the hill, Rosette could see Moorish houses with their whitewashed walls gleaming in the sun. Tall eucalyptus trees and gardens were visible behind wrought iron. The fragrance of the blossoms wafted down to cover the less pleasant odors stealing from the waterfront.

Looking up there toward the houses, Rosette knew another strange moment of premonition. What had caused her to gaze up there, mesmerized? The chills ran up and down her spine. But the sensation soon passed and she was back to her normal self again.

Here and there, judging from the quality of

their clothes, were well-off merchants of many trades. The complexions of the crowd varied, running from startlingly blue-eyed, though tawny, saddle-colored Arabs and darkening through the Negroid mixtures to the pure black of the peoples from far away to the south of the great Sahara. There were even the red-haired Berbers of the hills. Wound about some heads were tightly snugged, small, white turbans, a startling contrast to their black faces. Ancient, long-skirted coats were brilliant scarlet, their cross belts meticulously whitened with pipe clay. Below this were the white, baggy trousers. Huge, bare, black feet stuck out as they walked.

As Rosette walked along the street among the fruit sellers, the tiny foreign-looking shops, the turbaned men and staring children and the thronging, ragged wanderers, she couldn't help thinking of the desert to which she was now so near. It lay, she knew, just beyond the walled city. And this time the premonition returned and was nearer.

And so it was that Rosette started when a low voice spoke to her in French, and, turning around, she saw a fairly tall Arab dressed magnificently in pale blue trousers and a jacket braided with gold. He stood much too close to Rosette for any comfort. But she was indeed struck by the color of his skin, which was the color of *café au lait,* and impressed even more by the contrast between his dark look and his languid, almost too gentle manner. She at once decided, even before turning about, that that voice held a note of danger. She wanted to avoid him. Should she grab Lucie by the arm and make a run for it? crossed her mind in a panicky moment. Yet, when she finally worked up enough courage to turn, he smiled at her calmly and he lifted one hand toward the wall of rock beyond the city. All the while as he spoke he looked at her as if she were a beautiful ghost.

"Have you seen the desert, mademoiselle?" he asked in French.

"No," she answered directly, "never."

"In the desert one forgets everything," he said, still in a low, cryptic voice. "Even the desire of one's own soul," he added in French again.

Puzzled and a little wary of this strange dark man, Rosette said, "How can that be?"

"In the desert," he repeated, again mysteriously, "one remembers nothing when captured by its spell."

Remembers nothing? Rosette noticed that the dark eyes gripped her in their own special spell for a moment before she shook herself mentally from out of the trance.

"What is your name?" Rosette boldly asked, this time in French.

"Hadji-ben-Haroun, mademoiselle. You are going to Meknès on the morrow?"

38

Intense, dark eyes delved into her soul, it seemed to Rosette. She had to get away from this man and whatever he was doing to her. He seemed to have some power over . . . Preposterous! she told herself next.

"Oh." Rosette quelled a shudder of dark premonition. *"Oui,* but h-how did you know?"

"I have made inquiries at the hotel. But mostly I guessed this beforehand. When first you arrived, I was with another party at the time," he said with a faraway look. He shook himself and returned to the present.

When first . . . a week ago? She hadn't noticed *him.* Now Rosette stiffened and bristled at his outright boldness. A dull flush rode high on his cheekbones, but he attempted no apology. She decided that the flush was from something other than embarrassment. Excitement? In a hurry to accomplish some deed? Evil or otherwise? She also came to the conclusion that this Hadji fellow's thin face was quite homely indeed.

I'll certainly not answer any more questions he puts to me. Why should I? She looked to Lucie and the woman seemed to be offering silent agreement to Rosette.

Lifting her chin haughtily, Rosette paid no more attention to Hadji-ben-Haroun. The acute irritation with him was already beginning to fade. There was a thrilling moment, though, in which Rosette shut her eyes, like one expecting a blow that cannot be avoided. She hadn't cared for the look in the man's eyes. He seemed to have tried mesmerizing her with some strange power he possessed. She felt like one borne upon a wave, to the wonder, to the danger, of a murmuring unknown. What is happening to me? Again, that magic carpet ride through time and space.

"What a boor!" Lucie was clucking.

After the passage of only a few seconds, Rosette opened her eyes but she didn't see the tall, dark man lose himself in the crowd. All around her was a flood of gold, out of which the face of a darkly handsome man — a Moor? — looked. A vision: dark, viridescent eyes searching, looking from the vastness of the desert. But she had never been to the desert. Eyes that waited . . .

"Lucie!" Rosette gripped the maid's arm. "Back to the hotel, quickly!"

"I knew it." Lucie looked the trembling girl over. "That Hadji character tried putting you under his black spell. I'll just bet he's what they call a *djinn* here, a genie or a devil. I'm not sure which *he* is!"

Chapter Four

White robes fluttered in the wind. One man, who stood out from the others, sat astride a magnificent Arabian stallion that minced its way amid several white riding camels. The handsome beasts stretched out their long necks, blinked and ruminated while chewing their cud, arrogantly avoiding the white horse.

By sunset the amethyst-blue mountains had turned to a most spectacular mass of blood-red and gold that blazed in the west, and the lower reaches already had sunk into purple depths of coming night.

Sheik Hasan al-Shareef dismounted and strode into a huge tent.

Here the luxury was sparse. Several mats and huge, clay bowls for washing, carpets spread on the ground, Oriental in design, brass lamps hung here and there on hooks. Only one table took up space in the tent. Spread on the table was a map, drawn to scale, with detailed sketches of the Sahara.

A beautiful girl moved about the tent, walking in a languid fashion with a bowl cradled against one hip. When Marid saw Shareef enter the tent, she flushed a deep, dusky rose and greeted him with a soft Arabic word. At this hour, Shareef wore a white haik on his head. He was so handsome that her young heart turned over and she had to draw several deep breaths to keep from trembling. She was filled with an unbearable virginal desire for Shareef.

"Marid, you may go now," Hasan al-Shareef told her gently, unaware of the tumult he caused her by just standing inside the tent.

He is so tall and powerful, she was thinking. Marid wished she could learn to please him. But this was only for the concubines to do.

Tarek entered a moment later, but the girl couldn't budge in her thrall. Like the sheik, Tarek looked like a leader. But he was not exactly that. He was Shareef's chief *caid*. Like a bird of prey, Tarek's black eyes followed the brooding sheik, but ignored the enamored girl completely.

"You wished to speak to me, Shareef?"

Shareef nodded. "A matter of importance I would rather discuss away from the others," he murmured suavely.

Tarek, too, nodded. He desired not only to be leader here, but he also wanted Shamara, Shareef's most favored concubine. He knew he would have Shamara one day, not as Shareef had her—merely an amusement now and then to dispel his boredom. Tarek wanted Shamara forever.

The girl Marid's eyes were still fixed only on Shareef, with dark intensity. He had grabbed her arm just yesterday, to save her from being trampled by a young horse running scared. There had been rifle shots on the firing range just when the horse broke loose from his master. Marid would never forget the delicious shivers and the hot feeling that shot through her. She was snared in confusion, though, between the knowledge that Shareef desired her and his refusal to acknowledge her flirtations with him. When she was older, she decided, then he would look at Marid closer.

The sheik spoke in Arabic to her, in a clipped tone this time, and Marid jumped, starting involuntarily.

Shareef smiled to ease her jumpiness. "I did

not mean to frighten you, little Marid." He smiled in a way that was devastating to her worshipful heart. "But, as I said, Tarek and I have matters to discuss."

"The tea?" she offered timorously.

"No refreshments. Unless . . ." He faced Tarek.

Tarek glowered at pretty little Marid. "No."

Marid knew Tarek was a man of few words. He was also nasty and mean.

With one other deputy allowed inside, the three men gathered around the table. "We are having more than our share of trouble from the Ajjer tribe," Shareef was saying. "They overstep their bounds and slip between the fingers of both our army and our Touareg brothers."

Here Tarek exchanged a swift glance with his true Arab brother but he remained silent. His day would come, for the nobles of the Touareg tribes considered him the true chieftain of this region. But what could he do? Hasan al-Shareef fought like a lion, led like a lion, and ruled El Taj and Kel Numair like a handsome lion-king.

"The trouble began around the water hole again," Shareef went on, his voice like black velvet. "The nomads stopped at the water hole and began to argue with the Touaregs of the Hoggar. They began to quarrel over—" he waved his hand in a helpless gesture—"the same old story." His eyes darkened to a hue of deepest jade. "A boy of only fourteen, of Touareg, was impaled right to the ground with the Ajjer's lance. The Chaamba told me this, and there's nobody the Touaregs hate more."

Tarek and the other deputy broke out immediately into enraged babbles, shaking their brown fists and tossing their turbaned heads. Tarek paused in his fury to look toward Shareef. He blinked black eyes. Those eyes were just like lightning, ready to strike the enemy at any moment. How could Tarek even begin to compete with such a man!

Outside, Marid's heart fluttered and her small bosom sighed as she floated from the tent after the warm smile Shareef had given her. Marid was certain she was in love for the first time ever. All the way to her father's tent she rolled her dark eyes and mooned over the handsome Shareef.

"Do not be a fool over him!"

The voice sibilated close by, and Marid whirled to face whoever owned it. "Rida!" Marid exclaimed. "You frightened me. What do you want?"

Rida, older and wiser (at least she thought she was wiser), repeated the warning. "You make a fool of yourself over the sheik!"

Marid tossed her head. "You have been spying

on me again. Who puts you up to it, Rida?"

"No one does this but myself. You are my cousin, did you forget? And I look after you. You are promised to Harith."

Marid made a repulsive sound. "He is a poor man. I would rather be concubine to Shareef. I am in love with him!"

"Love!" Rida spat. "You do not know the meaning of love. And Shareef's concubines, hah, they have nothing much to do all day but be bored — and night too!"

Marid frowned. What is this? Shareef did not pleasure himself with those females set aside especially for his taking? Rida does not know what she talks about. "What about Shamara? I would like to be in her place someday. I will, too!"

"Hah, again, I say! That day will never come for you." Rida's voice went lower yet. "Hasan al-Shareef will be gone — like the wind. He will take his beloved sister and go back to England where he was born. That day is not far off. Everyone here knows it — all but Shareef himself."

He is going away? Marid trembled. He must not! Never! "You lie! I am going to go tell him all you have said!"

"No!" Rida grabbed Marid's arm in a fleshy pinch. "He will have you flogged, and me also."

"Another lie! He has never beaten one soul

here. He is gentle and does have a heart of love!"

Rida snickered. "Love he has not for any woman here. None but Rozelle Modestia, his sister. And that is a different kind of love."

"You are saying he does not love Shamara?" Marid's eyes shone with unshed tears.

"He does not. I tell you he loves no woman here. Only the one with the skin like a white dove's feathers. And I can show you his hate, the backs of some men, women also, in the house of Shareef. Those he has beaten!"

Marid stood still, waiting for Rida to retract that harsh statement. But Rida made no move to take it back.

"Ah! They are beaten by Hadji and his handful of sneaking wicked *djinns,*" Marid said, thinking she knew why now. "Shamara, Shareef's own favorite, she is in love with him!"

Bending over from the waist, Rida hissed back at her cousin, "You are the fool, again I say. Shamara is the harlot of the house. She sleeps around with everyone!"

"You are jealous, Rida! You only want Tarek for yourself and hate all who take up his time—like the sheik. What do you want with him? He is in love with Shamara. Rida, you are a fool!"

Now the girls charged at each other, scrapping in the sand. Robes came loose and long, gleaming, black hair flew about, fingernails flashing like tiny, wicked blades intent on injury.

"Enough!" came the discordant command.

"Shareef!"

Marid spun from the older girl and threw herself bodily at the sheik as he came up to stop the fight before one of them missed an eyeball.

Marid fiercely hugged the tall frame to her young breast, looking up at him adoringly with tear-damp, dirt-stained eyes. "Rida says you are leaving El Taj!"

"What is this?"

Rida scuffled her feet in the sand, looking sheepish and shy now that the sheik had arrived on the scene. He frowned down on Rida with a stern look riding his brown eyebrows, eyes beneath like black emeralds.

"Go to your father's tent now, Rida," Shareef said gruffly. Then, to Marid, whose sudden shyness mollified his anger, he said, "Go home, little Marid." His look told her he was angry no longer, so Marid scuttled off as gracefully as her disheveled robe would allow.

"We shall finish that other discussion on the tent raids tomorrow, Tarek."

With that, Hasan al-Shareef headed toward his white stallion. His robe and the horse were a blur of white in the evening.

Tarek snatched up Rida's arm before she could

move away from him. "Stay. I would like to talk to you."

He waited until Marid, too, was out of sight. "Who has told you this, that Shareef is leaving El Taj? Do you mean for good?"

"Yes," Rida answered shakily, afraid now that the man she desired was so near. "You know as well as everyone else." She batted her lashes in demure affectation.

"So. What do you think will encourage him?"

"He will follow his heart, the one he loves, from here."

Tarek lifted his turbaned head higher at this news. "When?"

"As soon as she comes and goes."

Tarek studied Rida suspiciously. "Is this the prophecy of your grandfather?"

"It is."

A sigh escaped her; tears stung her eyes. She should have remained silent in this.

"Then it is true. Tell no one else of this, do you hear?" His dark eyes bore into hers, making Rida quiver from head to foot.

"Yes, Tarek. I promise. No one else shall know."

She squeezed Tarek's hand before he could move away, and he dropped hers as if the flesh had burnt him. But repulsion lay nearer the truth.

Tarek watched as Rida walked away into the

dark. The torch from the tent behind him was at his back, anyway. There was none who could read the sly expression that flitted across his thin, dark face.

He will follow the one he loves from here. Did this mean Rozelle Modestia? Who else could the woman be? Shareef loves no woman. His sister is his only beloved. He takes a woman to his bed only when the need is greatest, otherwise he does not bother. Tarek's face darkened now. He takes Shamara to his bed. She is my beloved. Soon she will learn Tarek has eyes for her and no other. This does not matter to him that she has been used before. She is like a princess with her hair of midnight silk. Just thinking of her body made his own grow hard with want.

Tarek told himself, I will do all in my power to help this matter along when this mystery woman comes. If she is Rozelle Modestia who will lead him back to England, so be it. Tarek laughed in a nasty tone. He was the first to open Rozelle's virgin thighs. She had been like a white-fleshed houri. At first. He had been mistaken. She had desired him like the European slut that she was. She could not wait to take her pleasures to Morocco once she discovered the ways between a woman and man. Tarek spat on the ground. Never, he would never touch that white bitch again.

Tarek strode away from the spot he felt was

soiled just thinking about Rozelle Modestia. His direction was the kasbah. He thought, soon, Shamara, my love, you will know how my heart beats for you. You were destined to be mine, and mine alone.

Chapter Five

As the sands shift in an hourglass, so shift the sands of the desert; the third day was upon the brother who was in a fretted and vexed state of mind at the moment.

With morning's dawn there was no smile on Shareef's face. He had waited patiently for Hadji's promise to be fulfilled, but still there was no sign of the group that was to bring his sister to El Taj. "My God," he said, unmindful he spoke out loud, "something must have gone wrong."

He paced up and down the Persian carpets and the floors of fine mosaics. Rozelle, Hasan worried, could be in grave danger by now. But still he could not bring himself to go and risk missing her if the group came by another route. What to do?

What else could be keeping them except an attack? His viridescent eyes darkened. A girl as stirringly beautiful as his sister could be a rich prize for some fat oasis-dweller. This was the crux of the matter at the moment — where, in all the vast desert, could she be?

Hasan stopped his pacing to look for sign of riders — horses or camels — but saw neither.

His heart sank as he slumped into a nearby settee strewn with the skins of sleek animals. "I should have gone to fetch her back here myself. Fool!" he growled in irritation at himself. The thought was a deeply disturbing one — he should have gone and not left the task up to Hadji-ben-Haroun!

Shareef sprang nimbly to his feet. He was seething, longing for action, as if this was against his nature to wait or stand idly by, doing nothing in particular when something nagged and bothered him.

His countenance spoke, grim and foreboding. He was taut and still, like some lean marauder that had stopped its prowling and was prepared to pounce on anything that stood in its path.

"I am worried about Rozelle." He whirled suddenly. "Samein," he said to the swarthy man standing quietly off the raised dais. "I want her here!"

"If it will ease Shareef's mind, perhaps we can send out a party of men to see if they come — or not," he added carefully. Samein crossed small but strong hands low over his belly after he had gestured along with his words.

Shareef touched a sheathed blade lying across a low table. "If something has happened to my precious flower . . ." His eyes glowered dangerously as they stared at nothing in particular.

Staying where he was, Samein leaned forward. "Of course, many necks will lose their heads. And I know what you will do, my friend, my lord Shareef."

But Samein chuckled, attempting to ease the distressing situation with levity.

Shareef waved his hand in impatient circles, causing the huge, red ruby on his last finger to flash in the eerie, slanting sunlight.

"Have the men ready to depart in two hours' time. Go yourself to ready them, Samein. You've my authority to choose those you wish to ride out, and ready plenty of *guerbos* . . . they may have run out of water and —" He cut off his next words and frowned, looking out the opening toward the desert. He just now recalled the story to mind, that of King Solomon. He was said to have discovered the retreat of Balkis — Queen of

Sheba—by means of a plover bird which he dispatched in search of water during his progress through Arabia.

"Shareef?" Samein caught the sheik's attention finally. "It will be as you command."

Samein had not seen what Shareef was watching so intently out the opening. Outside the sun was becoming obscured by the dark haze creeping over the land. At the same time, genuinely delighted at this opportunity to choose the men to ride out, Samein's leathery face beamed proudly as he bowed out of the chamber.

Half an hour later Hasan still paced the room like a caged panther. It seemed as though twilight had fallen across the desert and the oasis encampment. Without warning, the sandstorm had started up.

Shareef's nerves were on edge. His eyes flashing like black emeralds brought to surface, he tried to see through the haze of sand.

Before the storm descended, there had been no sign announcing an arrival of riders, not even a distant plume of dust across the terrain of sand dunes.

He, Hasan al-Shareef, possessed a very well-developed visual memory for topography; through his powers of observation, he had attained the proficiency of the true desert people. In his mind was every journey's landmark, engraved and recalled in succession. As he went his way, he could call them up.

Several long moments passed before he exclaimed: "Why do I stand here and tarry like a crippled old fool!"

Shareef snatched up his blade and tucked two pistols inside his red sash. He tore from the apartment and strode along the corridor, unaware that dark eyes watched with a kind of bewildered sharpness.

The howling of the wind had so increased that one could barely hear the low groans the nervous horses and camels made.

Slowly, carefully, the party started off toward the north, with the mounted white stallion El Barq II in the lead. This is insane, Shareef began to tell himself. How could they ever find Rozelle and her guides? He comforted himself with the thought that perhaps this storm would be short in duration.

As Shareef rode, he recalled what he had been taught starting at an early age. The desert must become as familiar as home, the problems of travel here second nature. Navigation was a necessity for survival, he learned from an early age. Particularly observant of traces of each other's groups or caravans, he must know how to tell with incredible accuracy just how many camels and horses have passed one direction and how long ago they passed. In the sand-free, pebbled surfaces, though, even the caravan tracks and *medjbed*—camel—tracks become obliterated. A track in the Sahara's desert gravel lasts for years, but not so in the sand.

Shareef squinted his dark eyes through the opening of his burnous. He watched the behavior of the sand and any animals he could see—the two special keys to desert navigation.

Riding along at a slow pace, he finally began to relax, allowing his mind this time to reflect back—way back—to when Mark Brandon had only been at the encampment for six months. It was then his training and schooling had begun. He was schooled in the rudiments of Moorish warfare. For tradition's sake, he was trained in the use of the ancient *kandjhar,* the *kumiya,* the long, curved scimitarlike saber, and more modern short sword, and the broad-bladed, double-edged knife.

Then there had been the rifles. Shooting had been no novelty to the fifteen-year-old. And so he quickly demonstrated his ability with the long rifle. Hasan es Said, as he had been called back then, also proved that it was not by chance he had been able to gentle the wild, white Arabian, El Barq. Hasan would not have liked being held captive but for the horses he fell in love with.

Back in England, Mark had grown to a saddle by the age of seven. There seemed to be some kind of an understanding between Mark and all horses. His skill was such that he was not a month with the regiment before he, Hasan, was named official trainer of the horses. Since he was the only one who could break the white horse he eventually named Lightning—El Barq—he was given the stallion as a gift from the old sheik.

He stroked the silky mane of El Barq I's offspring now. He turned his mind to women of a sudden. Now the vague yearnings and urges he'd known all along and had no particular trouble dealing with were becoming stronger and widened in his loins. What invisible witch had this power to plague him this way? Shamara? Jamila? No, not one of them, his concubines.

He went back to safer ground in his mind-wanderings. Back again. At the end of two years he had been abruptly elevated to the rank of sergeant, *mukaddem,* and was sent out into the field. South of Meknès in the region of Khenifra. He went with an army of some fifteen thousand—all the tribes of the Kel Numair banding together to suppress the uprising there. How long ago that seemed now, Hasan mused.

Hasan al-Shareef soon developed a curious sort of liking for this sere, barren land, so wild and rock-strewn in places. So majestic the Sahara, so austere. By age twenty-three he had become the sheik of the second Kel Numair and was transferred to El Taj Kasbah.

If Hasan left the desert for any length of time—as when he visited briefly in England—it

58

soon lured him back. Would it always be this way? he wondered now. Was there anything, or anyone, who could keep him away? There was no woman outside the Sahara. Not even at his home in Morocco. He doubted if Rozelle Modestia could even tempt him to leave this place.

Rozelle Modestia, on the other hand, knew a great desire to return to England, one that had grown over the years as she herself had blossomed into a beautiful young woman. He called her the Desert Rose, but Rozelle held no particular love for the desert as her brother did.

Hasan began to earnestly pray that soon he would find her, as he watched the desert pigeons in their low flight now. Usually the pigeons or doves drink twice a day—at daybreak and early evening. Never do they drink during the heat of the day.

The sandstorm showed signs of moving on, the haze travelling swiftly to the north. Hasan grew more alert, watching the pigeons. Where there was water . . .

Part Two

The Adventure Begins

Give me to drink, Mandragora,
That I may sleep away this gap of time.
— Shakespeare

Chapter Six

Lost in reverie, Rosette gazed outside. On the windows strange lights were glittering, the dining room of the hotel was slowly filling with the ineffable splendors of Western color.

Suddenly Rosette glanced up sharply at the sound of movement nearby. A man was changing his place and going to another chair, directly across from their table. Rosette gently nudged Lucie who dined quietly beside her, almost nodding in her *chorba*.

"Hmm — what?"

"Nothing, Lucie. Go ahead, take your time."

"Oh, oh yes." Lucie spooned her soup into her

mouth, never noticing that Rosette was slightly troubled over something.

Rosette suddenly felt very alone. Despite the glory of the sunset bronzing the stranger, there seemed to be a cold shadow in his dark eyes. His whole expression was fierce and startling. Rosette likened him to a criminal bracing himself to endure inevitable detection. So crude and piercing was this mask confronting her that she started and was inclined to shudder. This too went unnoticed by the sleepy maid who continued to slurp her dinner thoughtfully.

For a moment, the man's eyes held Rosette's and she thought she saw in them unfathomable depths purporting wickedness. Or was it fierce determination she saw there?

In the space of a few minutes, the spectrum of the sunset passed from scarlet through violet to indigo. And then came the sudden dark.

He was studying her all over again. Rosette swiftly looked down at her nervous hands in her lap. All the exquisite consciousness of freedom died out of her. The man was beginning to vex her. He does not look like an Englishman, she told herself. But his whole air and look, his manner of sitting and walking, were surely foreign. She considered his coloring. He had hair that shade of warm brown that looked black in shadows. His eyes were persistent hot coals, his face long and thin and morose. He was indeed ugly, she decided.

What a strange man he is, she found herself pondering for the third time since he had entered the dining room. And just when had he exactly come in? He seemed to have appeared from nowhere. Her attention was beginning to become strangely fixed upon this unknown man. His appearance and manner were so unusual, to say the least, that it was impossible not to notice the painfully thin man.

Somehow, Rosette concluded, he seemed to pose a threat to her and Lucie. But especially herself. Was she only being silly, imagining this? She hoped so.

Rosette quickly finished her dinner and hurried Lucie back to their rooms. While Lucie was packing their bags for their journey the next morning, Rosette strolled onto the broad terrace which ran the entire length of the hotel. Somewhere a camel made its sorrowful rumbling sound and a dog barked.

Her bedroom opened onto the terrace in front, and at the back adjoined with a small salon. This salon opened onto a second and smaller terrace. From here the desert could be viewed beyond the tall palms.

There seemed to be hardly any guests at the hotel. The veranda was deserted and the peace of the soft evening was profound.

Against the white parapet a small, round table and a cane armchair had been placed. A subdued patter of feet in slippers floated up the stairway. An Arab servant suddenly appeared with a tea tray.

Rosette searched her mind for something polite to say as he quietly placed the tea tray on the table with the precise deftness which Rosette had already observed in the Moors. Before she could thank him, he swiftly vanished.

Rosette was thinking, what mysterious silent people she had met up with since landing in Morocco. She sighed. One didn't have to run their tongue while here, that was for certain. Seating herself in the chair and pouring out tea for herself, Rosette leaned her left arm on the parapet and watched, mesmerized by the huge stars that had come out. One could almost reach out and touch them . . . make a wish. . . .

Lucie appeared at the door, stifling a weary yawn as best she could.

"I wonder whatever happened to that Hadji character who almost gave you a fit of the vapors?"

"I'd rather forget all about Haja-ben-Ha. . . ."

"Haroun," Lucie supplied, her memory for languages and names in her favor.

Rosette shrugged indifferently. "Ah, whatever. But if you do not mind, Lucie, let's not discuss him and whatever spell he seemed to have over me for a such short time."

The light that floated in beneath the round arches of the terrace was subdued. Rosette sighed wistfully. Two strange men she had met so far, one without a name. She hoped there wouldn't be a third. She might as well get accustomed to this breed of staring stranger, though, if she was to find any enjoyment at all. This hadn't bothered her in Europe; why should it now?

The evening star shone in a sky that still held on its distant western border some final pale glimmerings of day. Again the evening proved to be balmy.

At the signal of night falling, many dusky wanderers had folded their loose garments round about them, slung their long guns across their shoulders and prepared to begin their journey, aided by the cool night wind that blows in the desert when the sun departs.

But Rosette couldn't know about them. She felt the near presence of the desert and the feeling quieted her nerves. That this desert village of Meknès contained no acquaintances to disturb her—other than Lucie—was to know all the security and peace she needed for the moment. Rosette drank it in dreamily. She sighed deeply and leaned back.

What woman had more liberty than she had? As free as the wind, here on this lonely veranda, with the shadowy trees below? Yes, as free-spirited as the wind.

A noise from behind her made her start, then catch her breath in relief. Why am I suddenly so nervous? It's only Lucie.

"I'll be retiring now, Rosie."

Lucie yawned for the hundredth time that evening and rolled her torso to release the kinks from her back. Rosette smiled at her maid. "From that I infer you are bushed."

"And so I am!" Lucie yawned widely and swept her kerchief from her head.

"Good night, Lucie," Rosette said barely above a whisper, not even hearing when the maid went to her own room beside Rosette's.

Leaning her head back again, Rosette thought over her collection of memories. Strange, she could think of her father now. Lord Alfred had been a man of passionate temperament. Strong in goodness when he had been led by love, he had been equally strong in nasty temperament when hate had snared him. He had always been a slave, the slave of love. Influenced by Lord Alfred's example, Rosette instinctively connected love with a chain — bondage.

Love of man for woman, of woman for man, Rosette had come to think of only as imprisonment. Bondage.

A few figures moved slowly, stealthily in the

shadows below. But Rosette saw nothing in her moody reflections.

Was not Lady Louise a slave to the man who had wrecked her life? But had the Frenchman, truly? Yet, had not her father been a slave to Lady Louise also? What a mess! Rosette thought now. Love. Bah!

Rosette shrank from the idea of herself ever loving again. Come to think on it now, with Perry she had felt in rare moments something of that thing called love. And now, here, in this tremendous, conquering land, she felt a stirring in her. What was it? There had been a most definite demand made upon her since she had arrived here. From where came its source she wasn't entirely sure just yet. What was it she longed for so fervently, that which she could not see? Now, in this dreamy land, she was conscious of a latent excitement that was not lulled to sleep no matter how hard she tried.

"Sleep," she murmured, "I'm not sure I can sleep."

While the darkness grew in the sky and spread stealthily along the sandy streams among the trees, she wondered how much she held within to give in answer to this beckoning she felt? One thing stood out in her mind, though. Never would she surrender herself to anything or anyone again. No, never totally. She would always hold that part of herself that called for commitment locked away in the deepest recesses of her heart.

A sudden chill stole over her. She heard muffled voices below her under the arcade. Was that distant clashing she heard of weapons? No, how could it be? It must be all in her mind. Was she hearing something that had to do with the future then? No, again. There was no one she knew here who fought with the sword. In fact, she hardly knew anyone at all, but those few she had come in contact with.

Rosette yawned wearily. Despite the chillier air she felt and the far-off noises she heard, without being aware of it, she was nodding into sleep right there in the chair. Her arm draped over the parapet of the veranda. Her face cuddled her shoulder.

Chapter Seven

Rosette entered the dream, stepping back into the misty corridors of memory. . . .

The willowy child entered her father's study, her long, auburn hair washed squeaky clean and gleaming with red accents, her bright tawny eyes searching out his lithe form. Her voice when she spoke—which was not often—was as musical as the first bird of summer. She was shy today because she had donned her new pink dress, hoping Papa would compliment her on how pretty she looked in it.

"Papa, do you l-like my new dress?"

Rosette twirled, and when she came around

she saw he hadn't even looked up from the papers scattered busily on his desk. "Yes, uhm, very nice, dear."

"Papa, may I sit on your lap?"

"Not now, dear. I am quite busy. Later, maybe."

Rosette heaved her thin shoulders in dejection. There wouldn't come a later, she knew. Not now, not ever. . . .

"Oh oh, please, Papa, please! I shall be good and not squirm. Just hold me, Papa, for a time . . . *please.*" She almost ended on a whimper.

"God, I am busy, can't you see? Go find your mother."

"Mama is getting ready to go out to a tea party—again!"

"That's nice, dear."

"Oh!"

Little Rosette flew from the room, sobbing her heart out. She ran smack into her mother's rustling, silk skirts, but Louise, rushing to leave the house for afternoon tea, placed her daughter upon a high-backed chair.

"You will fall down and get your pretty dress all dirty if you scamper around like that, Rosie!" She shook her long-nailed finger at the child, warning little Rosette not to be so naughty. "And, *please*, try to contain your silly tears in the future. You are more grown-up than that!"

"I am *only* seven," Rosette murmured

forlornly, watching her mother bustle busily to the door, tossing over her shoulder:

"Stay right where you are and don't you move a muscle until I return, you naughty, naughty girl!"

Rosette hugged herself trying to find some warmth from within. But it never came, not then, not the next day or the next, only the pitiful lonesome sob that always tore from her throat when she was shoved from her parents' lives.

Rosette climbed the tortuous road ascending from her dream.

The sound of footsteps on the wooden veranda floor brought her fully awake. The sound was some distance behind her. "Lucie?"

No answer came.

The soft footfalls crossed the veranda and stopped. Perfect silence returned. The feeling of calm had deserted her though, and wisps of the lonely dream vanished. She was instantly troubled by this sudden presence behind her. Yes, someone was there. She could almost feel the breath of the intruder falling on her neck. More than one? What did they want? Rosette swiftly recalled the incidents of the day — and the ominous stranger in the dining room.

Her discomfort increased twofold. Below was a jangling of spurs, the snort of horses, muffled steps again. The voices fell hushed.

Tingling all over, with her instincts to

alarm. . . awakened, Rosette whirled to face the intruder she knew suddenly had crept up behind her. Her eyes dilated and she started as she fully recognized the thin man from the dining room. He had been clothed fashionably before, but looked much different now. Her darting eyes fixed themselves on his brown burnous flung back from his thin frame. Now she recognized him from another place. One of those rudely escorting the women in white into that carriage. The thin, dark man, the same from then—and now, today!

"What do you want?" she stammered, her heart filling her throat.

He watched the fear grow larger in her eyes with each passing second. Rosette made to scream for Lucie—or anyone to help—but before she could make the sound a hand clamped over her mouth. "If mademoiselle will permit me to escort you . . ."

There had been the rush of danger in that whisper. That was all she heard before a cloth was clamped over her nose, then the pungent smell that put her to sleep instantly. Before the dark descended, questions flew at her like angry bees: Why were they abducting her? Where were they going to bring her? Had her earlier indifference about so what if a dashing sheik should abduct her come true? Had her uncaring attitude now cost her this? Suddenly this was not all that exciting! rushed through her brain at the last, irreversible moment.

Before she sank into the labyrinth leading to a black void, she had seen another robed figure step from the shadows. The stranger from the dining room was one; Hadji-ben-Haroun was the other, the man who had asked if she had seen the desert.

Chapter Eight

Rosette Forrest reclined on a small rug, pressed down by a sense of inertia. There was only one pillow, dusty with sand from the storm. The tent no longer rippled and shook; all was quiet now, with only the sounds of men making ready to decamp.

She had been brought the drink again, the one that left a bitter aftertaste in her mouth and left her somewhat in a state of confusion, one that seemed to be growing with each sip she took.

Rosette rolled her head languidly. It was like looking through a translucent wall. There were people on the other side that she could not distinguish, but they were there, moving about in the misty cobwebs of her consciousness.

Hadji had come to visit her, and now he sat cross-legged on the sand. He was eyeing her closely and his smile was warm though mysterious, his words always cryptic to her ears.

"I am your friend, Rozelle, and you must never forget this."

Why did he insist on calling her Rozelle? She'd argued over this with Hadji, but he always shook his head and Rosette would scratch her memory—my name is Rosette, isn't it?

She was like clay in Hadji's hands, this she was conscious of. Hadji had power over her, yes, but she was unable to react and she wondered if she really had the courage to do as she wanted? But what did she really want? What was this power he was able to wield over her? Perhaps all was truly as Hadji had said.

They had talked at length before the sandstorm arose, so long in fact that the conversation had elicited yawns from her. She was always so sleepy. It was strange, but she couldn't remember much of what they had discussed the day before. He was her friend, of course, and like he said, she should always think of him as such.

Rosette sat up slowly now, tucking her long legs beneath her buttocks. He had given her soft, gold *babouches* with upturned toes to wear. For her own, he had said, and gotten rid of her old ones while she was ill. She had soiled them in her illness, he had added.

"Was I ill for very long, Hadji?" she asked him with trusting eyes.

He shifted slightly, placing his brown hands upon his jutting knees. "Not very. But remember what I have told you, Rozelle. You must not allow the sheik to discover this." He grimaced as if in pain.

She summoned the strength to smile playfully. "I know. You are my friend, Hadji-ben-Haroun, and my brother—" she rubbed her forehead—"my brother will have your neck if he discovers your lack of responsibility in caring for me. Hadji, how did I catch the fever? I don't remember." She yawned and repeated, "How did I?"

Hadji caught and held her eyes, keeping them captive as he spoke, like a snake charmer. Only she was not a snake, but a very beautiful young woman. He was glad that the drink had slurred her English accent somewhat.

"You had journeyed to Morocco. To the house on the hill." He waved his hand negligently. "But, of course, you would not recall the journey to the house. Your fever was bad after that." He stared beyond her then. "I had allowed you to roam the market place . . . I lost sight of you. When I discovered you later that evening, you . . . were very ill. You look so much, so very much like — " dark eyes watered and glazed over — "you did not . . . you almost did not make it. I feared for my own life then."

Hadji had one thought. This one has emerged from Rozelle's shadow.

"But you did not let me die, Hadji, so why fear?" She stared at the dark-striped *djellaba* he wore. "Please, do not look so sad. I am alive and well."

"Yes." His eyes roamed her countenance as if seeing her for the first time. "You *are* alive. And, Rozelle, you must promise to always keep our secret. This is between you and I, only. If Shareef knows this, I will surely die!"

"How can he be so cruel?"

"Such an explanation is quite feasible, you will soon find. When you again meet up with your brother."

In bemusement, Rosette looked down over the strange clothes she wore. She had longed for a simple dress yesterday, but he brought this change of clothes, foreign to her. She had on a jellaba of thin, amber silk with a sleeveless tunic, the latter woven with golden threads. She knew that if she moved a certain way, the full circles of her breasts could be viewed, and she tried at all times to keep them covered by the tunic.

"Ah, mademoiselle, you need not be so modest. Not here, not in the desert."

Rosette had colored — that was yesterday — but now she was becoming used to Hadji's eyes and there was no cause for alarm; mostly his eyes kept trained to hers.

The flaps had been tied back to permit circulation of air, and Rosette could feel the new, gentle wind caress her flushed cheeks. It was almost like a lover's touch . . . but she had no lover to daydream over. She stared at the unusual pattern in the rug she sat upon, reluctant to meet Hadji's stare.

"Will I ever completely remember all that has gone before in my life? There is so much missing from my memory. Hadji — I don't even remember what my brother looks like," she ended on a sad note.

"Look at me!" Hadji commanded firmly and gently at the same time. When she was gazing into his obsidian eyes once again, he went on. "When you look upon the sheik next you shall, I say, Rozelle Modestia, you *shall* remember him!"

"Yes . . ." she murmured, staring into those compelling black eyes.

"He worships the ground you walk upon. Hasan Mark, as you called him when you were a young girl. Say this now . . ."

Suddenly she was overcome by a feeling of lassitude, and muttered in a daze, "Hasan Mark . . . Hasan Mark."

"Rozelle Modestia, you love this man, your brother. His will is to be obeyed at all times. He is your guardian. Never defy him."

"I love . . . him," Rosette echoed, believing she was Rozelle now.

Chapter Nine

She awoke, startled, damp with sweat. The heavier clothes stuck to her and she kneaded the itchy red spots where sand fleas had gotten to her soft flesh. They had brought her fresh water.

Voices drifted to her as if from out of a fog. One of the voices sounded angry, deep and masculine, one she hadn't heard before.

Rosette sat up. How long had she slept? She had a feeling the passage of time had only been a few minutes.

"Where is she?"

The angry snap of that deep voice again.

"Is this the tent?"

Her long, tapered fingers brushed aside the tears that had slipped from her eyes in her short slumber. If only her brother would come, she wished. Then she would not be so frightened and confused. But would she? What did he look like? She didn't even know. Was he handsome? Hadji had said her brother was a sheik.

What am I? Who am I? Rosette wondered over and over again. She looked down at herself then. Someone had entered while she slept and placed a garment on her. Her head was covered with it too. Were all these clothes to protect her from the biting vermin? They didn't do a very good job, she decided.

"I do not like the feel of this thing," she said to herself, prepared to snatch it from her head. Her hand poised in midair, for they, and the one with the deep voice, were entering the tent.

Seeing her, Hasan al-Shareef sharply inhaled. She wore a litham, the face veil that exposed only her lovely almond-hued eyes. He stared hard, angry, saying, "Remove that thing!" He turned to the man beside him. "This is not a garment for women!"

Rosette's long legs were tucked off to one side and she gazed up at him, looking vulnerable and lost.

When the man hesitated only a moment. Shareef crossed the tent with a lightning gesture to sweep the litham aside. He sucked in his breath, thinking how beautiful she is. "Rozelle Modestia," he mouthed the name he adored, like a soft caress.

Rosette blinked up at him, her own breath caught in her throat and breast. Why was there nothing she could remember about him clearly? At the moment, she couldn't even return his greeting, much less still the mad beating of her heart.

The sheik found himself motionless, staring, absorbed in the breath-taking beauty of this young woman who was his sister. And her hair—it seemed to be lighted with a thousand flickering candles. Her amber bodice fell to her waist from a high young bosom, but Hasan al-Shareef dragged his eyes from the spot very quickly and reluctantly.

A shock had run through them both the instant his flesh touched hers, but Hasan only mouthed the name once again, "Rozelle Modestia."

The other man had fled the tent to escape Shareef's wrath when it would descend. But Hadji-ben-Haroun nodded furiously, pointed to Shareef's back and Rosette caught his meaning. Yes, I know, Hadji, I know you mean this is my brother. Her warmed gaze shifted back to the tall, handsome, compelling and powerful man standing before her, bent a little as if mesmerized by her countenance.

This is my brother? Why oh why could she not remember him? She decided to keep her thoughts to herself. But it was so difficult just trying to realize this man who was a dream was supposed to be her brother. Besides, she could not speak her mind. She had promised Hadji.

"Rozelle, why do you not speak?"

The sheik was addressing her, but waves of nausea built and washed over her again. This sheik frightened her, even though he was supposed to be her beloved brother. He appeared vexed over something, his brow dark and foreboding beneath the black turban, his eyes the color of a storm-ravaged forest, smoldering with hidden dangers. Was he angry at her? What had she done to make him look at her this way?

Shareef's gaze swept across her flushed face. "Are you ill?" he rasped out, his eyes and his voice suddenly full of concern, and something else she couldn't fathom.

Unmercifully he loomed over her as he swept back his caftan and, kneeling, he lifted the slender form to be cradled against his iron-thewed chest. He stood like that with her, his brown fingers threading in the long, silk ribbon of her hair.

"Please . . ." Rosette begged, unable to stand his nearness. She felt so miserably mixed up. She felt the raw masculinity he emanated, and she suddenly wished he would let her go. She was feeling strangely ill at ease. Her main concern was with the way her heart beat so fast and hard, even under this stupor. Was this the proper fashion to behave in the arms of one's brother? His breath came warm on her cheek, and helplessly her cheek moved—much too close to his face. She wrenched aside, burying her face in the folds of his throat.

"Rozelle, what is it?" he murmured. Unconsciously, Shareef's voice was hoarse with emotion. "My precious flower, I have been worried sick, out of my mind. Damn!" He turned with her in his arms. "What is wrong with her?"

But Hadji only shrugged with the innocence of a child.

Shareef drew back to study his sister's face, the creamy skin, the full-lipped mouth, not too big, but moist . . . oh God! His eyes narrowed into dark slits, verdantly alive. She is so very pale, he thought. "Were you frightened?" he asked her, finally putting his thoughts into words.

She shook her head, no.

"You have never traveled in a sandstorm. Was it so bad then?"

Hasan squeezed a caress at her back, only getting a handful of the concealing tunic she wore. "Curses, will you please say something?"

The warm, sun-brown eyes opened wide, adoring this man, oh yes, her brother: How could she have ever been afraid? She hugged him closer. "I love you . . ." She choked back a sob. From the first moment she knew this to be fact. She caressed his strong shoulders lovingly, trusting him implicitly. "Hold me!" Her sweet breath rushed out in a soft sigh, at last, oh at last, someone was holding her close, making her feel warm and wanted and . . . no, not this, from her own flesh and blood.

"My darling . . ." Shareef gathered her closer, inhaling the sweet fragrance of her long, sweet hair curling into tiny wisps that hugged her moist cheeks. "Ah, my precious flower, you have never told me of your love before. Dear Rozelle, say it again!"

He reached out to brush the corner of her lips where a tear had gathered after slipping along her cheek. Against his throat, where he couldn't see her, she said softly, "I love you so . . . my brother." As his fingers lingered there where her skin was soft and moist she frowned and wondered at the unfamiliar sensation he was creating. He had never held her like this before, she was certain of it.

There was a manfulness that shone in his eyes then and he drew back swiftly to look down and study her lips, her eyes, her nose, and draped back the curtain of her hair to see the tiny, shell-shaped ears. He wanted to . . . to hold her forever!

The signal rose outside that the caravan was

packed up and ready to leave. Only one tent stood and that could quickly be thrown on the back of one of the camels. The clear platinum afternoon hovered all around her like a mirage.

Shareef's face turned toward the open flap. A brown eyebrow lifted as he faced her again. "Will go now. You are ready?"

A frown flitted across his handsome features and she stared up at him in bewilderment. Something there in his eyes made her want to jump out of his arms and run. She looked down as his caftan swept back and she noticed his hard thighs. Rosette suppressed the disquieting feeling coiling through her insides. She was still in his arms and he hesitated, as if he couldn't bear to let her go.

What was wrong? What was he going to do—let her walk or carry her? I really want to be in his arms just now—and I do not. He frightens me, even though he is my brother. Why do these strange feelings plague me?

"Are you strong enough to walk?"

"I—I feel a little weak, that's all." She lifted a hand to brush pink finger tips across her forehead where tiny beads of sweat had formed. "I think I can walk," she murmured.

"Are you sure?" he asked abruptly.

His eyes slid down over her body, in a measuring regard, then up again, resting on her mouth and tracing every soft curve of her lips.

She flushed again at the unusual sensations creeping over her suddenly warmed flesh. "Yes," she said.

Again he frowned. "I have decided to carry you, Rozelle. You will ride with me."

The effulgence of the desert sun made her blink and squint, but she still noticed as he carried her that he wore pistols and a sword at his waist. The hilt of the sword had jewels, emeralds and tiny rubies. She could not see the blade which was hidden beneath the folds of his robe. But she could feel it, pressing against her hip.

The camel groaned as the additional weight of the tent was placed upon its back. The stallion waited, his huge, white head turned their way as the sheik approached with his bundle of femininity. He remained silent as the sheik placed the young woman on the saddle carpet and then leapt up behind her. The hard muscles of his arms pressed against Rosette's soft breasts, the outer curve, and stayed there while he tugged at the stallion's reins and set out.

Although she was again overcome by that feeling of lassitude, questions ran rampant through her brain. Her eyes fell and lingered on the brown fingers, so long and lean. She could not only see but felt the great strength they possessed. Everything about the sheik was disturbing to her. She couldn't fathom why. This was supposed to be her brother, but why were her worries about what lay ahead disturbing her so?

Rosette wondered briefly about the sheik and his women. Was he a gentle lover? Especially when he wanted something from a woman? Did he ask or just take? Do his women come to him and fall to his every whim and bidding? How can I think such things and at a time like this? She flushed and chided herself for admiring her brother in the fashion only a ladylove should. But she could not help herself when his dark fingers brushed so familiarly against her softness.

To be sure, the sheik's own mind-wanderings were shocking to him. At present he ached to seize her and clasp her to him in a warm kiss. What madness is this? he asked himself. He brushed the sensuous thoughts aside, telling himself that these warm, vibrant feelings were only due to happiness, that he had found Rozelle unharmed. He knew a glow equal to that following a victorious battle.

Her eyes grown heavy, Rosette stared down at the movements of the powerful stallion beneath them, at the tooled leather saddle of orange color with silver-studded harness and bridle. He must be a very important sheik, she decided drowsily. In a quiescent state, everything was hazy for Rosette as she drifted in and out of a languid doze. She snuggled closer, unaware of the sheer tumult she was causing the man who held her.

Her nearness was becoming unbearable to him, but he pressed on and strained at the leash of that something he would not — dare not, in fact — name.

Chapter Ten

Against the limitless sky and sand the camels stood out like huge, dark humps. They had been riding almost four hours when El Taj rose in the distance and stared back, a welcome sight to the dusty travellers with its feathery palm trees, a green oasis in the midst of the rock-strewn sand.

Hadji rode close by, watching the sheik and the young woman covertly as they neared the high walls. She wore the garment with its cloaklike hood, and her head continued to loll against Shareef's strong shoulder.

In the party that neared El Taj, there were twenty riders in all, nine of whom were mounted on horses and had outdistanced the heavily laden, plodding camels. Two riders had gone on ahead and preceded the others to have everything in preparation for the sheik's arrival.

Opening her drowsy eyes, nothing looked familiar to Rosette. As El Barq topped a rise, she saw a tree-dotted oasis and a combination of towering block-stone, three stories high, with towers which gave the appearance of so many castles fashioned of white stone. All this flourished in the middle of the desert, trees and flowers, shady terraces and walled gardens. Rosette felt as if she were being thrust back in time into an ancient unknown world, impregnable to any outside intrusion or influence.

What lay ahead here for her she wondered. She had no indication as to what she should expect next. The tears thickened in her sore, aching throat, and despite the haziness in her brain, she felt an extreme nervousness. Why couldn't she remember anything of this place? Had she been here before? Had Hadji said she had? She couldn't even remember much of their last conversation. It flitted in and out of her mind like an elusive butterfly she kept trying to catch.

"We are home," came the husky, succinct voice, so near her that she could feel the warm breath on her throat. "Are you happy?" he asked.

Happy? Rosette wondered how she could be happy while she dwelled in this hazy, dream world. "Y-Yes," was all she could manage. Was this a lie she told him? She didn't even know that!

A male voice rang out, announcing the arrival of Hasan al-Shareef and his sister. Shareef lifted a hand and tipped her fine chin upwards so that she could look directly at him. Her chapped lips parted involuntarily, her pulse raced as his gaze found hers and rested there. He seemed to be mesmerizing her.

"Your lips will need some—" he faltered, then went on—"your needs will be tended to immediately, but of course you know that."

Surprise entered his dark gaze when she looked up and their eyes locked for what seemed forever. She was the first to shy away and look aside, confounded by his delving regard. "Of course," she gulped, "I remember."

"My sister, what is it?" he asked in a strange, gentle tone. "You are quivering all over."

Oh, this would never do! Bewitched as she was, how was she ever going to be herself and keep him from seeing that he did wild, crazy things to her ardor? There were hundreds of butterflies jumping around in her belly and in the area of her heart, and if not freed soon she would . . . she would—how could she know? This had never come over her before. Maybe it was all that spicy food she'd forced herself to eat, or that damn drink that Hadji pressed on her. "Yes, that is it," she said, unknowingly out loud.

"What? Tell me," he said in a velvety tone that shook Rosette even harder.

"I — it is nothing, my — my brother. I-I've been away too long, I-I guess."

She appears dazed, Shareef again noticed, and put it down to her being overtired and hungry. She could probably do with a drink of something cool, too. He would put Hadji and one of the housemaids onto it immediately. Something cool and refreshing to drink, and then he would visit her apartments later. They needed to do some talking after she rested. It had been a long time in between their visits.

He murmured something Rosette couldn't catch, and when he swung down from the horse, reaching up to help her down, she kept her eyes averted. How long could this act go on? Who was this man really, and why did he do this to her every time he moved or spoke a few words? If she didn't know better she'd have thought she'd just met the love of her life.

Rosette's fingers were slightly shaky when she caught hold of the thickest part of his arms. When she was down and standing before him, the inner courtyard began to swim in her vision. But she fought down her weakness with every thread of strength left in her — which wasn't much to speak of.

"We are home," he murmured thickly.

Rosette's butterflies did somersaults. He had

already said that. Did he have to repeat it?

"Don't you remember the place? Have you been away all that long?" he fired at her unnervingly.

There was a lambent warmth in the gaze that regarded her and she still felt a tingle where his long, manly fingers had touched her skin. And branded them. A quizzical gleam grew in the depths of his dark eyes — eyes she couldn't tell the color of — and she wished, she bloody wished he would quit staring so! Coyly she looked down, sniffed and flushed.

"I must smell quite nasty," she blurted, and was suddenly overcome with embarrassment. She couldn't recall the last time she'd washed, hoping to dear God it had not been all that long ago. Shareef's own masculine odor, musky and not at all unpleasant, caused her already highly agitated brain to swirl.

"It is not that," he returned tersely. "A perfumed bath should remedy your soiled state."

She reddened to a beet color. "What is it then?" she dared go one further under the camouflage of her high blush.

"Your manner of speech has changed," he supplied. "I cannot recall you ever speaking with an English accent, not the last time — "

While Rosette frowned in bemusement, Hadji appeared like magic suddenly. "I am sorry to intrude, my lord. But you see, Rozelle has been much with Englishwomen since last you saw her."

His dark eyes competing with the flash of Hadji's, Shareef nodded. "Ah, tea with the 'ladies' in Morocco again. Is that what you did to occupy much of your time, dear sister?" he clipped out in a brisk tone.

"I—" She continued to frown. Hadji's dark eyes flashed before her, seemingly giving a warning. "Indeed, I think it's delightful to-to—" A hand flew to her forehead. "I forgot what I was about to say."

"Ibn Hakeem," Shareef barked and a man in busy robes appeared on command. He bowed before the sheik. "My sister needs quiet, a peaceful atmosphere. Take her to the upper room, instead of her bedchamber. Have the servants undress her and bathe her immediately."

I can undress myself, Rosette was about to blurt in objection. But she thought better of it, under the circumstances. There was something in Shareef's gaze that brooked no refusal of his commands.

"Up?" The fat man blinked, the whites of his eyes matching the gleaming *gandourah* he wore.

Shareef waved a brown arm sticking out of his caftan. "Well, then, bring her to the pool first," he said in Arabic this time, watching his sister coolly.

Rosette blinked in confusion as her brother

strode brusquely from her presence. As if she were no more than a bothersome child he wished to be done with.

But when Rosette went along with Ibn Hakeem, her robe molded to her hips in a swooping breeze, and the sheik watched momentarily there and his verdant eyes were appreciative. In the last rays of sun she seemed to have been carved of gold as she paused to glance over her shoulder before entering the building.

Shareef thought, indeed, she is living but she is in a daze. Perhaps this is merely a condition of weariness. Was she suffering from some form of amnesia? Had she been in an accident Hadji had failed to report to him? Or had they become so estranged after their separation that he couldn't read her moods any longer?

Shareef strode in the direction of his own rooms. If there was something amiss, he would force Rozelle to speak of this. He shook his head; that would not do. Cajolery, sometimes this is more successful than force. Especially where a delicate woman was concerned. Yes, he would trap Rozelle and coax her into telling him all that had gone on during their separation.

The delightful tinkle of a two-stringed mandolin filled the evening.

The white, cotton gondoura covered her like a

loose nightshirt, making Rosette appear vulnerable, like a sweet young girl in her teens. She could hear the mandolin, but it wasn't loud enough to break through her spellbound thoughts.

Rosette had been bathed and perfumed, but demurred at the gossamer drapery—a flimsy, mauve thing to say the least—that those dark, giggling maids tried to press upon her to wear.

She wondered at the manner in which her pulse raced even when Shareef was away from her. She hadn't seen him since he'd left her in the inner courtyard. Where was the sheik at this moment? What was he doing? Ever after leaving her side, Rosette had been unable to keep him long from her thoughts.

As she had lingered in the beautiful aqua pool—a warm, small pool with a ceiling above like twinkling stars at midnight—she had daydreamed. The sheik had been watching her and in the daydream she had seen herself as a dancer. She had swayed sinuously over to where he sat upon plush pillows, the jewel-studded bracelets at her wrists and ankles winking, and clinking out a delightfully sensuous rhythm as she danced voluptuously. All her passions and desires, her very hidden soul, were in tune, throbbing with the heartbeats of her watching lord and master. "Hasan. Shareef." She had heard herself whisper his name breathless and husky.

With the perfumed water swirling about her

naked waist, Rosette had made believe she could feel the mounting strength of his passion until, finally and with a groan of frustration, he reached for her. His fingers were hard on her slim arms. Right there in the pool her eyes widened as she in her magical mood had responded to the hardness of his imaginary touch. Raw, urgent desire rose in her, passions which threatened to consume her whole, they ebbed and flowed, and then white waves broke into shocking shards of disappointment.

A voice had intruded on her dream state. "I have brought you a cool drink, mademoiselle."

Rosette had blinked up at the handmaiden, surprised to see she had returned.

Following her bath, Rosette dined alone on delicious pigeon, saffron rice, and drank refreshing tea. Mint tea, she guessed it must be, but she had never tasted such before. The taste was somewhat like the medicine Hadji had pressed on her, but much sweeter and tastier. Date cakes she set aside for later. Suddenly she had developed quite a liking and a hunger for this exotic food.

Actually she was never all that alone, for the serving women continued to amble in and out with various dishes and trays until Rosette though she couldn't force one more bite even if she wanted it. "I shall grow fat!" she said with a mouthful of white meat and giggles. She was satiated—"I am stuffed!" was more like it.

One of the women smiled at her in genuine pleasure that the younger woman had enjoyed the feast so much and could laugh with her stomach full. The woman joined the other serving woman in laughing when Rosette belched and then appeared shocked and embarrassed.

After the earthenware had been cleared away, Rosette reclined on some pretty pillows, feeling bored and lonesome. Musingly she stared at the Oriental patterns on the carpets, turning her head this way and that, and nodding as if deciding on a purchase. Suddenly she grew stock still. "Who am I? What am I doing here?" She stared down at a pair of yellow *babouches* with the upturned toes, a fresh pair one of the handmaidens had brought her. She flopped onto her belly, then groaning she turned on her side to face the door leading to the corridor.

Rosette's soul cried out for escape, anything rather than this languor of monotony, this slow-motion walk to an ever-hazing horizon which moved further away even as she tried to reach it. She could rise herself and go in search of something to occupy her time, but she was without will or energy.

"Rested?"

If her mood had been other than laconic, Rosette might have gasped in surprise and sat up when the voice sounded from the opening to the terrace. A deep voice. And he was wearing a black turban tonight, fashioned around his head in an airy cloud that trailed down and contrasted with the full-sleeved white linen he wore on his back. There was a sharp mound beneath the thin trousers that attested to his manliness, but as soon as she swept her gaze downward she brought it back up. As it was, she was too sluggish to move a muscle toward greeting her brother. But she could speak, if a little slowly and huskily.

"I am," she answered, making room for Shareef as he came to kneel beside her on the pillows strewn all about the fluffy, high pallet. "You are very good to look at this evening, Hasan," she murmured, conscious of the fact that she felt emboldened.

Bended on one knee, Shareef took up the white hand that was slimmer and daintier than he remembered it being. He stared down for several moments before lifting his dark gaze.

"You have not called me that since you were a child and I a lad of fourteen."

"Would you rather I said Shareef?" She watched a strange expression cross his tanned face and she wondered briefly if he was fair-skinned like herself beneath it.

He tilted her chin up, studying her and then

seeming to decide on something. "Yes, more piquant, I think."

"Wh-What?" she stammered and looked swiftly aside. She shivered involuntarily, jarred by the impact of his staring eyes.

He shrugged, saying, "Never mind." A slight frown reared between his brows. "Have you been well, sister?"

He would not say her actions seemed strange, her manner of speech unusual. After all, he had not seen Rozelle in over two years. One could not expect a person to stay the same and not undergo any changes. Was she eighteen? Or twenty? He shrugged.

"I am well, yes. . . ." She had been about to add "lord and master," as she had thought of him in her daydream. A blush spread across her cheeks just thinking back to earlier.

She fiddled with the gold tassel of a plump pillow and murmured a question. "Why is it that I can't remember you, Hasan?"

Again Shareef turned bemused. "Have I changed all that much? Can't you see for yourself that I am indeed your brother?" He turned her hand over to study the smooth palm, and again his eyes flashed up in an intent study of her face. "Could you explain?" he asked.

"Sometimes—" she faltered and gazed across the airy room. "Sometimes I feel very lost, Hasan, and it's—it's as if I don't know myself—who

I really am, where I belong." That's enough, she told herself, Hadji told her to go no further. "Ohhh, Hasan! Hasan!" The frightened sobs tore from her throat.

Lightning fast, Shareef stood, dragging her by the arm up with him. "Rozelle, you must snap out of it! Now!" Her legs unfolded and he caught her when she stumbled over a pillow. The action brought them closer, dangerously close, but ineffable delight ran through her at their contact as her hands came up quickly to brace herself against his wide chest and she blinked up at him in shy confusion.

"Curses, what is it?" he demanded for the third time, his eyes staring into her questioning face. She had paled considerably. He ran a finger along the soft curve of her chin, and couldn't stop the shiver that ran through his arms. "Rozelle, damn but you worry me, for I have never seen you this way. So pale and listless. You appear half asleep most of the time. You said you rested, but you seem overfatigued. Has something happened that has not been reported to me?"

Shareef paled himself just then. His sister had always been guarded closely, by his order. The women in charge had informed him that his sister was yet a virgin. But she had been away to Morocco several times in the past two years. How could the women be certain her maidenhood still was intact? He himself was to choose her husband, and one suitable for his beloved flesh and blood had not yet been discovered.

"No," she whispered, "nothing is wrong, Hasan."

"You appeared alarmed a moment ago. I demand that the physician see you, Rozelle, and immediately," he snapped curtly, brooking no refusal in this.

"I will be fine in a few days, my brother." She patted his hand once, twice, then returned it to his side. Beseechingly she gazed up at him. "Just give me time? Please? I do not wish to see the physician."

When she begged like that Shareef could do nothing but relent. More than ever now Shareef noticed that she dared not look him directly in the eyes; her gaze instead skittered across the thick carpets as if she would like very much to run across them and away from him.

The air was sultry this evening, with hardly a breeze to cool the big chamber, even though it was airy in itself. Again Rosette peered up at Shareef in bewilderment, but never straight into his eyes. She would rather avoid their velvet depths and feel safer for it.

The *rhaita* was being played softly, the sound of the flute stealing plaintively across the grounds. She caught Shareef staring at some faraway spot outside the terrace. What could he see out there in the dark? she wondered. Or was he just avoiding her for the moment? Now she studied him. Shareef's eyes—gazing into them just briefly as she had dared a moment past was like losing herself inside a deep, dark forest. They were not black as she had first determined, but the darkest shade of green ever, and it was difficult to discern the color unless the light slanted across them just right. As the sconces were doing at the moment.

Silence was reigning golden.

Shareef moved a little away from her, as if straining at a leash slightly. He smiled at the dreamy look in her tawny eyes. "You've eyes like a cat," he remarked suddenly and a moment later his brow again drew together in marked perplexity.

"Do I?" she purred in affection. She looked aside swiftly once again.

It angered him greatly that she appeared so far away at times. This was yet another puzzle, for his sister had always communicated her mind and feelings by direct eye contact. Always bold. Never with her eyes chasing off to the nether to hide—as if she were frightened of her own brother!

"Oh, please sit!" he finally growled, "you make me frustrated when you just stand there gaping around the room."

"I'm sorry," she said in a little voice.

"No, it is I who am sorry."

As if on command they both sank back down onto the embroidered cushions and hot-colored pillows. Purple. Magenta. Scarlet. Heliotrope. Morocco caldron. Maroon. Ruby. Bittersweet.

"Has tribal war and the desert sun made me so ugly that my own dear sister shuns the very sight of me?" He peered down his front to his jodhpur boots. "Have I grown too much brawn from warring with my neighbors? Do I sport a wart I'm unaware of, my precious flower?" He smiled warmly. "Sister of mine?"

The way he put that made her start, but she quelled the emotion and kept him from seeing her reaction. Sister? Was she? Her head swam and her senses whirled, like she was on a merry-go-round.

"Do I get an answer?" he asked.

Her lashes brushed her hot cheeks as she let her eyes roam his powerful length, quitting before reaching the seat of his manhood. "N-No." Her chin sagged and her eyes shut.

Again he reached out to lift her chin. "Look at me. Don't you know me anymore? It has, I'll admit, been over two years, but you, you are the same to me — only far more bewitching than I can even remember."

Bewitching! Rosette's butterflies started flipping again. He said it and that's exactly how she felt — bewitched! Bewildered!

"Hasan . . ."

"Ah, that's better. I love it when you smile. What is it, love, your wish is my command."

Love! Love! she thought. No, it cannot be the sort of love she fantasized over. Not with Hasan. Why did he call her love then? How in the world, she wondered, could he be her *brother?*

"Walk me to my r-room? I am suddenly weary . . . Hasan."

"Beloved, I shall do better than that! I shall carry you—like I used to when you were nothing but a willow switch."

She made to back away from him, but again that odd, dreamy look entered her gaze. "Yes, Hasan, do carry me!" She summoned the strength to giggle delightfully.

Strong, white teeth flashed against his tanned features as Shareef swept his sister up from the floor. And why should this be a grave mistake to carry one's own sister, Shareef wondered a moment later. Yet, after he had lifted her into his arms and smelled the sweet scent of her hair and of her feminine flesh, he was indeed a worried man. Shareef tingled strangely with an emotion his senses only reserved for his women. Concubines.

But here and now an intoxicating warmth entered his body as he felt the outline of her firm breast through the thin *gondoura* she was wearing. The emotion went one further—deeper.

It was as if she was someone else, and not, dear God, not Rozelle Modestia!

Preposterous!

"Hasan?" She blinked up at him, clinging to his wide shoulders. "Did you say something?"

"Nothing. Go to sleep."

She murmured softly and snuggled against his throat.

Hasan swallowed hard. Why, he wondered, while his gaze travelled to her piquant profile, did she keep hiding her face from him? He saw that her face blushed, even now, dusky as a desert rose of evening. His hard, chiseled mouth formed a thin, grim line.

Carrying the sleeping beauty to her bed, Shareef gazed down at her hair spread out now on the scarlet pillow. The dark copper clashed with the silk material and he was startled out of his wits as the realization of what he suddenly desired filled his heart with unexperienced fear. He must be going mad, for sure, what else could it be?

Sheer nonsense! Rozelle Modestia was his sister and he was going to make sure his mind-wandering strayed no further than that fact.

She slept on, never aware that relentless devils clambered aboard Shareef's back and pursued him from her bedchamber.

Chapter Eleven

Outside, sentries with guns stood always alert, guarding the ancient Moorish kasbah.

On a stone parapet, Rosette could see, between the feathery tops of swaying palms, glimpses of the desert and the far-off land with its brilliant blue mountains. A refreshing sight from the sere, barren land just beyond the kasbah's walls.

Drifting inside, Rosette chose one of the low divans and, reclined, let her eyes take in the sight of the opulent gold-and-white apartment that was her own. The palm-wood door stood open to circulate the air in the hot, arid atmosphere in the room. Only a slight breeze entered by the opening to caress her loosened, sparkling hair with its dark copper accents.

Worry nagged her again. Something was sorely missing in her life — no, *someone* was missing. Reclining upon velvet cushions in various brilliant hues, she slowly closed her eyes. Was it a woman she missed so terribly? Perhaps her mother? She would have to ask Hasan about their mother. For some reason, she didn't believe her mother still existed.

Rosette pressed shaking fingers to her temples as images flitted in and out of her imagination. But she could place neither form nor flesh to the person. Is it truly a woman? Then, could it be she was only trying to remember her beloved brother, and how it was before she fell ill? Could this be the way of it?

Her eyes slowly closed and she rested. Images, tangled and blurred, swam before her eyelids. Hadji sprang into these visions, and it was his eyes, only his black eyes that swam there, mesmerizing her. He was again proferring her the *manasa* begging her to drink. Drink all, his eyes seemed to demand.

"Oh!"

When she reopened her eyes she saw before her a woman, bent over with a tray. She had uttered something, words that Rosette didn't understand. As she stared up at the equally bewildered

111

woman in white draperies, Rosette discovered herself looking back. But why did she see the woman being hustled into a cart by two men, one thin, one heavy set, in her mind's eye?

"Do you know me?" Rosette questioned the dark, handsome woman placing a tray down beside her.

The slightly older woman shook her head and shrugged. Then she pointed to herself, mumbling a word, a name that sounded like Zarifa.

"Zarifa?" Rosette tested the name.

"Hmm . . ." Zarifa mumbled again. Then pointing shyly to Rosette, she carefully said, "Ro-zelle."

"Yes." Rosette clapped her hands together. "You do know me." She decided that she'd better be more guarded with her actions lest her brother discover she had been very ill and had lost almost all memory.

"Oh, Zarifa," Rosette feigned, "I do remember you!"

Zarifa shook her handsome head and shrugged again. She seemed to be just as confused as the younger woman was.

Footsteps, hard-soled ones, fell upon Rosette's ears just then. A deep, male voice filled the chamber, resounding clear and stern.

"My sister, how could you remember Zarifa? She is new here."

Biting her bottom lip, Rosette shrugged this

off with an airy shrug, much like the one Zarifa had executed.

The women in name executed this time a hasty bow and then an even quicker retreat. Shareef watched her go, curious over where Hadji-ben-Haroun had unearthed that one. His frown followed the woman's exit all the way, even while he was amazed at Hadji's ability to coax women into coming to this isolated desert encampment. His jaw hardened now. Hadji had better not be bringing them here against their will. Shareef was not one who encouraged his men to take captives, even though he had taken a young girl or two against their will in the past. But that had been when he was a lad growing into man. The idea had excited him at that time. Those he had brought had long since found themselves mates and married.

Munching daintily on a date cake, a bit nervous, Rosette studied her brother's mood. He seemed overly interested in Zarifa, especially in her curvaceous backside that had swayed sensuously in the filmy drapery she wore today. Why should this trouble me? Rosette asked herself. Her brother, good-looking as he was, must keep many mistresses or whatever the name was for them here. She wasn't sure if he did, but soon she hoped to know.

"My God," she said softly, "I don't even know if he has a wife."

She gulped the cake down hard, too late to wish she hadn't spoken this aloud.

Not realizing until he turned sharply to face her that she had indeed spoken the words loud enough for him to hear, Rosette blushed furiously. She realized she had made a grave mistake by the dark look he was shooting her way. Her heart pounded and suddenly she desired very much to flee from the room. With relief, she saw that his harsh look had softened.

"I see you meant me," he began. "No, Rozelle, I have not found time to become a husband during the last two years." He centered his gaze on the dainty cake pinched between her fingers, crumbs falling to her lap clad in filmy trousers.

He snatched his eyes upwards but only found more frustration there when his regard ran over the transparent, amber blouse, making Shareef very aware of her creamy bare skin underneath.

"Since when have you developed a liking for the date cakes? I thought surely you hated them?"

A quick grin appeared on her prettily flushed face. "And I've found time to develop a taste for the cakes," she said, adding on to his history. "People do change, you know." She tipped her chin.

"How well I know this," he murmured,

cryptically, and stared somewhere above her forehead.

"Do you mind, sir?"

"Mind?"

"Do you mind, sir, that I have acquired a liking for the date cakes?"

A look of arrogance lifted his brow in the midst of his high forehead. He tilted his head to look at her more sharply, perhaps more than intended, his deep, forest eyes measuring her. "Sir?" he asked simply.

"Hasan al-Shareef, sheik of Kel Numair," she said humbly, bowing her dark head where she sat cross-legged, *"Salaam Aleikum."*

He returned the bow, concealing his reaction to her salute.

Rosette tried to think fast, as usual in his presence. If nothing else, she'd discovered the necessity of doing so. Why had this bothered him, her saying sir? His look had been so dark, so sullen and threatening, enough to wither a girl's heart.

"Would you disown me for a little mistake, my brother? I had not thought to recall you disliked the, uhm, title."

He waved a long-fingered hand. "No matter."

"You won't disown me then?" she said, a little imp in her sun-warmed eyes. "Give me a tongue-lashing I deserve?" she said with challenge, a husky purr in her voice, curving her pink mouth provocatively. The long, loose trousers, *serrouelles*, he had changed into, and a shirt of white muslin open at the neck to reveal his brown throat, created a virile picture of manliness for her to behold. "Well?" she went one further.

"Enough!" he snapped abruptly, his eyes blazing with emerald lights.

Rosette drew back in alarm, dropping the cake onto the couch. Her cheeks grew flushed, her eyes went wide. Shimmering amber tears hung suspended and quivered between thick lashes. "I—I am sorry if I displeased Hasan," she said childishly, not realizing how she sounded in her sadness.

"Forgive me!"

He moved fast to sit beside her, taking the white, trembling hand from her lap. "It is just that I've been with such hard-bitten, ruthless, cussing men for such a long time that I'd forgotten the sweetness of a woman's gentle manner, her charm —" his voice lowered — "and her seductive looks that drive men wild."

Her butterflies were doing crazy somersaults in her breast, and her pulse was pounding rapidly. She stared at his head, wrapped in yards of *cheche*, the ever-present turban he wore, one of them. Either black, white or blue, he was never without the turban or haik. This had begun to give her cause to wonder about his head of hair beneath. Heavens! Surely he wasn't bald.

Rosette pulled a long but pretty face, her eyes blinked innocently. "Do I do all that? Heavens!"

Shareef dropped her hand as if it had burned him. He stared at her long and hard, casually asking her, "How long did you stay at our house in Tangier? Did you have company, like our friends from Europe? From London?"

She thought quickly. "You believe I have become too civilized in "their" company. Whoever "they" are, Rosette thought with a mental shrug. But she did recall a crowd of haughty faces, just where she wasn't certain. She frowned delicately and said, "Why don't we just forget all about our friends and talk just about us, Hasan. Tell me what we used to do — I love hearing about the past. My favorite subject. Please tell me, too, what you have been doing these last two years away from me?" Hadji had said that Hasan used to derive much pleasure in relating to her stories, tall and true, of his conquests and victories. Conquests? she wondered now again. What had Hadji meant by that one? He must have gotten that mixed with something other than war, Rosette decided now. Or did she merely hope?

Finally, a boyish grin spread across Hasan's face. He was delighted, she could tell, and it made her joyful knowing she could make him feel pleasure in her company. She desired the best for her brother, realizing just now that she must have always felt this way about him. Her heart turned. He meant so much to her that it was frightening at times. If Hasan was ever killed during his warring with other tribes, she knew here and now, she would die, simply die along with him. Oh, she loved her brother so much this made her feel like weeping. She wanted him close, always with her. She wanted . . . her burning cheeks almost scorched her, fanned as they were by these wicked thoughts of him again.

"Rozelle?"

Before she turned she knew he studied her with a deep, penetrating gaze that made her quiver within, her limbs turn to jelly. "Go on, Hasan. Tell me, and please never stop talking!"

And so he did, for close to an hour, all the while stealing glances at her mouth that reminded Shareef of a rose with morning dew yet clinging to its petal-softness.

"Hasan? Did you love her?"

He chuckled. "The one with the flaming hair? Or the one with the shapely legs? How about the one . . ."

"Oh!" She feigned shock. "Were there *that* many? Did they all live in Fez as the others?"

He pressed her nose flat. "You know, Rosebud, you ask one too many questions!"

"Rosebud?" She frowned. "Why did you ever stop calling me that?" She laughed then to cover her nervousness over the childish question.

"Because," he said, "you have blossomed into a

rare rose of summer." He smiled secretly then. "There was yet another name I used to call you."

"Yes?" She was even more curious this time.

"Miss Stinkbottom."

"Aha. Let me guess why you quit that one." She looked sideways at him and then blurted. "When I stopped having accidents as a little girl."

"Correct." He grew brooding and thoughtful then, staring back in time, not too long ago, reflecting out loud, "And then my Rosebud became a woman. You were afraid you were bleeding to death that first time in the month."

He turned to face her with a suddenness that startled her, but only for a moment before her surprise recovered. Still, his look terrified those butterflies into reacting strangely in the pit of her belly. "Yes," she went on to cover up her embarrassment, "I guess I remember that. Most girls do."

"Damn if you aren't blushing again. When did you start that?" He narrowed measuring eyes in suspicion, suspicion that grew. . . .

"Oh." She shrugged as if that was nothing at all. "I'm not sure, Hasan. I suppose all women blush at some time or another."

"Not my sister!"

There followed a silence of poignant nature.

"I promise never to blush again." She crossed her heart while he watched closely. "If you promise to keep on telling me stories."

"That, my dearest, may take forever."

"I have forever, Hasan." She memorized every line and curve of his face. "Don't you?"

He laughed off the silly mood and growled low, "Shut up then and listen!"

"Yessir. I mean Hasan, lord and master."

Rosette snuggled into the pillows and looked aside to conceal a huge yawn from Shareef. It was not that she was bored, only she felt so tired. That's all.

The night was wonderfully dry, the temperature comfortable. The thickly growing date palms below the terrace barely moved. It was very still, very dark.

An ethereal vision in a thin, white robe stood alone on the stone terrace. She hugged herself, feeling very romantic this night. The subtle influence of the Sahara was stealing over Rosette's second sense, her spirit.

Big stars twinkled in the black carpet of sky. Lowering her eyes, she stared at the smoked amber glass of the lamp, mesmerized. Just then a great sand moth lighted to beat its wide, gossamer wings against the hot lamp. The moth drawn to the flame, Rosette startled herself by remembering the line. Poor thing. Doesn't it know destruction waits for those who draw too near the flame?

Rosette smiled happily then as the great moth took flight to freedom and away from the consuming flame.

Rosette had retired as soon as Hasan left her to go to his own apartments down the corridor. She did not remember his rooms, but had an idea where they were located. Somewhere at the . . . other side? She shrugged, thinking it unimportant anyway if she remembered or not.

Sleep had not come to her. Just before the moon fell she had heard someone pacing in the courtyard below. At first the step had been heavy, hesitant. Then it came and went, without pause, as if the one who walked did so in a fever of frustration. Only when she returned to her bed did the pacing stop at last.

Toward morning Rosette slept. When she awoke the room was full of soft gold which told of the sun outside. She left her bed at once, stepped into a pair of soft *babouches* and padded out onto the terrace.

Already El Taj was bathed in golden beams and aburst with bustling activities. A flock of white-robed men pattered out toward the edge of the oasis, becoming smaller as she watched. Small, black-eyed boys were lazily sweeping the narrow garden paths of flagstone. They wore loose, white garments and dark red sashes. The snarl of camels in the back yards was audible.

"What a day!"

Rosette laughed for the sheer pleasure the morning brought to her. She felt wonderful just being alive; the usual dizziness had left her.

Drinking in the desert air made her feel very clean, very pure . . . pure? Rosette paused as a disquieting thought struck her. Am I indeed pure, untried? she wondered. How awful, she wasn't even sure if she was a virgin or not!

"Who cares!" She sang then as she stood facing the sun. "I feel foolishly innocent," she giggled, "like a chick or a kitten!"

The radiant sky, the warming sun and the freedom of the coming day and of many coming days in the desert filled her young heart with an eager zeal, an almost childish sensation. Had she always felt this way about the desert? She instinctively acknowledged then that she'd not always lived here.

She frowned, knowing something to be amiss. If she tried hard to summon up the past, what would she discover? Was there something dark and sad she'd rather not remember? It seemed to her there was something. Many things, in fact. Don't think, she told herself, just live for today. Free, like the moth of the night. She would, something told her, be careful not to get too close to the flame, otherwise she was bound to get burned.

Her thick, dark copper hair, unbound now, fell in a silken veil about her healthy, active body. Her breasts rose tautly to brush against the soft fabric inside her saffron robe. She looked down at the gentle peaks of flesh, proud of their firmness. A swirl of desire shot down from the peaks and down through her belly. She shook herself free of the hot chains, knowing there to be no way to end the craving inside her but to dwell on other things in life.

Activity! She was suddenly conscious of her restlessness, that she was in need of some form of recreation. A ride in the desert before the air grew unbearable was just what her body cried for.

"Ro-zelle, eat now."

Inside Zarifa bore a tray laden with fruits and the usual bitter drink. Rosette stepped in out of the sun, eyeing the goblet with mingled suspicion and disgust. Zarifa slipped out as swiftly and silently as she had entered.

"Do I always eat alone like this?" she wondered out loud, a shrug following her words. Who cares if she had lost her memory; it should return soon enough. No, again, I'd rather not remember.

Zarifa came in on shuffling feet to remove the tray. *"Merci*, Zarifa."

After breakfast Rosette peered over the edge of the veranda and saw Asad and Hadji-ben-Haroun squatting together in the shadows of the garden below. Their conversation sounded violent to her. The accentuated words fell like blows. But she had not looked down for very long before the two noticed her and rose smiling to their feet. The skinny man, Asad, gave Rosette the creepiest feeling just looking at him.

"Rozelle Modestia," Hadji called up to her and nodded his turbaned head. "Come down, please."

Rosette nodded back, her hair cascading delightfully over her right side and one breast. She returned inside and searched for the golden-yellow caftan and the burnous to shroud her head from the sun.

Rosette really wanted to wander alone. But she knew Hadji would await her. She hardly had the heart to dismiss the man; he had been so good to her . . . in some ways. She wrinkled her nose. Even if he did force her to drink that awful medicine that made her forget what had gone before in her life!

Behind the complicated pattern of the grille, Rosette slipped out of the robe, allowing it to slip to her feet and remain there. For an instant the flawless perfection of her body was revealed, the next moment the golden-yellow caftan came down about her like an enveloping sheath. The caftan concealed her gentle curves and milky skin. After fastening the row of tiny buttons at the front with some difficulty, she founced out her hair from beneath the collar.

Rosette stared down at the floor, hesitating before stepping out. The hairs stood out on her arm, but as she could see that no eyes spied on her, she stepped out from behind the grille to examine herself critically in the tall mirror. Again she hesitated with a thought: Why is it the feeling of being spied on left her as soon as she was on the other side of the grille?

The caftan was a little short for her long legs, but Rosette shrugged, it was much more modest than the other gossamer draperies she'd worn during the day. Even so, this caftan was of a lightweight material, owning a faint translucency.

Satisfied and, with the light hood in place over her head, she moved toward the stone steps leading down into the garden. Hadji awaited her below. There was all that quiet dignity and determination of Hadji's to deal with. She resolved, though, to walk with him for a while and then on some pretext get rid of Hadji. Could she pull it off? There was hardly a time when she was left to her own devices. So she would!

As if by magic, Hadji appeared right beside her after she had descended the stairs.

"You have slept well, little Rosebud?" he asked as she came into the sun. He tried to capture her eyes.

"Why does everyone keep calling me that, Hadji?" She refused to look at him just yet, but soon she would have to.

"You are remembered as the little desert rose, that is why," he said simply.

"I am not so little anymore." She laughed.

"So you are not." Hadji agreed. "You slept well then?" he asked again.

"Well enough, Hadji."

Now she faced him squarely as she strolled the stone path flanked by exotically colored flowers. "Why does my brother call me Rosebud?" she asked, unaware that she stuck to the same subject.

"It is easy to see, to understand why. All names such as yours mean the Rose."

"I like that!" She laughed at herself, bubbling, "Of course." She whirled in the colorful caftan. "I am a flower, Hadji, just look at me open up!"

As she whirled, Hadji thought she looked much like a flower, or a colorful butterfly. He appeared pleased, and there was something childlike that crossed his dark face to gentle the hard, determined look he usually wore. Rosette came to stand still beneath the palms, looking up into the huge fronds. There was a steady shining in the gold flecks in her eyes, misty this morning. Then Hadji stared steadily at her face as she stepped out briskly to walk beside him once again.

They were just coming upon the high outer wall when there arose the clatter of hoofs. Rosette turned, shading her eyes from the building strength of the sun. Mounted on the tall, white horse, Shareef galloped past at a tremendous pace, holding his reins high above the orange peak of his saddle. She stared after him, with obvious admiration lighting her young face.

"I would love to ride a horse like my brother's!" she said to Hadji when Shareef had disappeared through the tall gates.

"You know how to ride?"

Rosette whirled to face Hadji. "You don't know?" She gaped incredulous at his question.

He laughed then, coughing under his hand as if embarrassed. "Of course, how negligent of me. You have ridden ever since you were a child."

"A horse with spirit such as the white one?"

Her eyes danced with ever-growing excitement.

He nodded, slowly, as if unsure of his answer.

"I will ride this horse then, if one such still exists. I want to go far out into the dunes!"

"Rozelle must not go alone!"

"And why not?" she blurted impudently.

"There are the desert bandits, the *Targuis* or *Hartanis*. You could be taken captive."

"I will take the chance," she tossed carelessly. But I shall go alone!"

Hadji now smiled with a softened grace that was next to feminine. "As you wish. "But first a cool drink."

He was staring deeply into her eyes again. She gazed back at him as at a deep mystery. She hadn't the will to tear her eyes away.

"Come, Rozelle," Hadji commanded.

She obeyed.

Part Three

Golden Pipe Dreams

Have you not heard of Prince Aladdin's palace, the greatest wonder of the world? . . . And, having seen the palace, knew that it had been raised by the Genie of the Lamp.

— *Arabian Nights*

Chapter Twelve

The drink this time was strongly medicinal and it filled Rosette's head with exotic visions.

She had forgotten that she wanted to ride. The magic carpet had been spread and she wafted into a far-off, imaginary country. Sitting on her haunches, she swayed to and fro and listened to a distant flute with the voice of a drowsy bee that hummed in the garden.

"I feel so strange, hmmm, floating," she murmured. In her languid state she was aware of Hasan as a man—just a man—not her big brother at all. Just Hasan. What if he is not my true brother, not kindred at all? Already Shareef commanded her will—but not totally—not as strong as Hadji who bears the magic cup. She must not, as Hadji pressed, allow Shareef to read her mind.

Why did she accept the drink that Hadji always insisted she drink? She'd wanted desperately to say no, but he had pressed the cup on her. She fluttered her long veil of lashes; she didn't even have to look to see on the right of her a shady place where old fountains existed, some unused, and stone benches. Above, terraced roofs and high towers ornamented with Turkey-red tiles, and not far off, among even more palms, were a number of low, flat-roofed tents. Palms, whose feathery tops swayed gently in the light wind that blew from all around the Sahara, fanned air down to where she sat in the shade.

Hadji had warned her that the potion was necessary, that if she denied its medicinal properties, she would fall ill again, worse than before. Maybe even fatally, he had warned in addition.

Rosette opened her heavy-lidded eyes. The desert sun flickered gold everywhere outside the shade, weaving patterns of enchantment and of burning beauty. Her willowy body moved, and was oddly anxious again. She desired to be up and about, but Hadji had warned her she must rest to regain all her strength. Besides, she hadn't the will to rise and be active just now.

"How very boring to remain so idle," she sighed, surfacing a little from her euphoric state.

If only Hasan would return and keep her company. Something about him had definitely altered since he had come to her after the sandstorm. Or had it been since their first long talk? His attitude was changing at a swift pace. Did he experience the same forbidden feelings as she did? The sense of pervading mystery she knew while with Hasan made her increasingly conscious — or unconsciously aware — of the pulsating warmth that swept throughout her veins. No, not conscious, she concluded, but more like awareness, a physical awareness.

"Rozelle . . ."

Slowly she turned to see Hasan. He was leaning in a laconic pose against the tallest palm. Their eyes met. Something in those forest depths heightened the flush already high on her cheekbones. He moved then, slowly, away from the palm. The hawklike sharpness of his eyes never left her. Every movement he made stirred something alive within her. She wasn't certain whether to be excited or afraid. His look, it seemed, was such that he was seeing her not as a woman of his kin.

His words of greeting were magnified twofold and lashed through her body like a bullwhip.

"What are you afraid of, dear Rozelle? It is only I, your beloved brother."

Shy though smiling, she peeped up at him from beneath long, spiky lashes. "Sit with me?" She held herself very still as he approached. She could not resist the fancy that if he touched her again he would burn her flesh.

She exclaimed softly, "This garden is beautiful." Childlike, happy, she added, "I could live right here forever."

"You shall, if you like."

A devilish smile curved his crisp mouth as he sat on the flowery carpet beside her. "The stone bench is not to your liking?" he asked out of the blue.

She moved a little. "I like the carpet."

A sort of ecstasy was waking within her. His mere presence again touched her soul and body, like a lover reaching out with the latent power to awake passion in her blood. Why did this not bother her as it should? she wondered.

His eyes slid down over her with an expression in them that made her body turn heated and shivery.

"You have lost some weight, I see. Not much, but today I notice this." Actually Hasan was damning the young woman for being so beautiful, unique and mysterious. More than ever, though, he felt that her happiness was all-important. He felt this, too, to be a weakness in himself. Just now, all manner of disturbing emotions and imaginings again came unbidden to him.

"It is hot," he remarked. She replied with a small, "yes." He looked aside, his countenance a brooding mystery.

Briskly Hasan loosened the sash at his waist to get more comfortable. He wore a haik on his head, flowing airily onto his neck. Beneath the full caftan he wore a thin lawn shirt and the trousers were loose about his strong thighs but tapered in the legs. Rosette took this all in, but she really hadn't the nerve to study his physique further. She shrank from what was really running through her mind, like one startled into awareness of man's form and unable to cope with the idea of how he functioned or why. What he could do to her if he so wished.

"Can you tell me why?" he went on, his tone very low and husky.

"Why?" She blinked up at him in bewilderment.

"You said that you haven't been ill, so then could a lover be the reason for your slimmer figure? In love, unable to eat, you know." He waved a brown hand. "Living on love, *dear* sister?"

Yet another fire seemed to come alive in her. She merely shrugged in answer, tucking a strand of dark-red hair behind her ear on one side.

Suddenly she grinned and laughingly said, "If I were in love, a person could not tell by my appetite. I eat like a pig! And I would never starve in the name of love, to be sure!"

He chuckled. "Now you sound like the girl . . . I used to know."

"Do I?"

Quickly their eyes locked again, and just as quickly parted.

Looking beyond the wall to the most silver part of the desert, Hasan said cryptically, "The sun makes men careless here, breeds a certain lawlessness into them."

"Women too?"

"They open their hearts to it," he went on, "become vulnerable, and one can see into the warm and glowing recesses." He said this with slow precision.

Rosette could feel that his eyes burned into her profile. "I know its spell," she murmured. "The heart of the desert envelops me, quietly, irresistibly." She turned to stare into the darkly tanned face. "I'm in love, yes," she rushed on then, "with the desert, with its murmuring of fierce and distant voices, its hot eyes and . . ."

"Go on."

She smiled and shrugged, as if these gestures said it all. How could she tell him that she contented herself with bold daydreams, those amazing flights of imagination?

His upswept eyebrows lifted even higher at their corners. "You never told me this before. You have always had the greatest desire to return to England. How long and how deeply has this love for the desert been buried in you?"

Two long fingers brushed absently over her arm, causing sweet butterfly torment in her breast and belly; even her toes were beginning to tingle. "Forever, Hasan, I just never realized it — until . . . it was while I was away from here." She found herself unable to move away from his brushing, burning, touch. "Away from . . ."

Hasan cleared his throat. "What did you do, I mean when you were away from El Taj?" His forehead wrinkled, as if with some worry. "Did you perhaps find yourself a man?"

"Oh, Hasan, quit fretting. I have never slept . . . I mean been with a man like that before."

"Do you think I'm unaware of that?"

Her breath almost ceased to flow when his brown fingers slid to her wrist, pressed there where the little pulse fluttered a sweet, wild tune. "I mean, sweet Rosebud, a husband. When will you find one? Shall I help you seek one out?"

"Oh, dear —" she appeared shocked — "I am in no hurry to wed!"

The grasp had tightened unconsciously on her wrist. "Oh, but you are, little *sister*. You have changed, I'm very aware, and it's high time we found you a suitable mate. We shall go to

Morocco next week and invite all our acquaintances there to a party at my Tangier house."

"No, Hasan, no, please! Wait a little longer?"

"Ah," came the murmur as he touched her chin with a finger tip. "You are so damnably charming when you beg, and look like you just turned sixteen, with your heart in your eyes, so sweet, so sweet."

Hasan's eyes flew wide, coming to rest staring at the delightful widow's peak; her face reminded him of a slim heart. A thoughtful frown entered his face, as if he tried to summon up something important. Something having to do with Rozelle — her face? What was this that he could not put his finger on?

"Forget the husband for now? Please? Hasan?"

He paused with what he'd been about to answer. A small, prune-faced man in fluttering caftan and robe had come to the doorway opening onto the garden. His beady eyes brightened as he finally made out the sheik seated on the carpet there with his lovely sister. He blinked rapidly then and brushed at his eyes.

Rosette loosed a giggle. "What is wrong with him?" she asked Hasan.

"It is Samein. Don't you recognize him? He has been with us since we were brought here to El

Taj." He said this calmly, but his eyes frowned in puzzlement.

"Oh." She brushed at her forehead as if just remembering who the man was. "Oh, yes, of course. And he is — nearsighted!"

"Ah, yes."

Brusquely Shareef stood, nodded curtly to his sister in a polite manner, and then took himself off to join his deputy. Samein, though small, was one of the fiercest men ever to come long ago to the encampment. When Shareef reached the man, all his towering height beside the smaller deputy didn't intimidate Samein's fierce bearing one bit.

During the long days which followed, Rosette felt as if she gazed at herself from a long way off. It was like looking at a stranger and not herself. It was almost frightening at times.

Shareef closely watched her. There was something near curiosity in his dark eyes. As if some magic spell had begun to blind him but had not completed its work.

In truth there was a spell upon Rosette. By turns she gave herself to it, consciously in the mornings, then strove hard throughout the day to deny herself its subtle summons. Each time she tried to withdraw, it seemed to her that the wondrous spell became a little bit stronger. Her power to act normal with Hasan was growing weaker. Part of it perplexed her, part was expectant.

Usually Hasan's voice was like velvet, dark and deep. But Shareef's voice had been particularly harsh that morning when he joined her in the garden for breakfast. It grated on her already frayed nerves, like an instrument with delicate strings upon a rough surface.

Rosette knew that she could never endure separation from Hasan. She craved his brushing fingers; and oddly enough she could find no horror or shame in this. Only it was frightening at times. Like when Hasan lingered so near her.

One night she awoke from a dream, of Hasan, and was almost dazed with the shivery wonder of it. This time was different, and she was almost ashamed to think of what she had desired in the dream, and desired still when awakening to morning.

Every day she saw his departure, for a camp nearby. Into the sun he galloped away on the white stallion. She thought she had detected a faint sound of warning when she told him yesterday of her wish to ride. This tone of voice made her react by feeling defiant.

Now, this morning, he laughed as he called her a desert spirit. "I *love* the desert," she did retort defiantly, "why can I never ride out into it?"

He darkened. "I prefer that you just watch it from here," he demanded gruffly.

"Am I a prisoner in my own brother's house?"

In answer he turned from her to stride over and mount his stallion. He sprang into the saddle and pressed muscled legs against the horse's flanks. El Barq reared up with a flash of hoofs.

In total dejection Rosette watched the horse. I will not look his way! She was too vexed with him. With a short, high-pitched neigh that was like a fit of temper, El Barq bolted and headed for the desert sun. Horse and rider disappeared in a platinum flash.

"Ro-zelle . . ."

Zarifa was waiting for her, and she felt like a naughty child going to her nanny. Nanny? What is this? Rosette shrugged without care of nagging remembrances.

"Yes! I am coming!! Yes, I know the sun is too hot for my fair complexion! Yes I must drink my abominable medicine! And, of *course*, I'd better not be late for my bloody afternoon nap!" She tossed slim arms in the air.

"B-bloody?" Zarifa said with a blink.

"Bloody!"

At the strong tones in the young lady's voice, Zarifa's mouth drooped in sadness. At the corners of her eyes the tiny crow's-feet just beginning to form there bent downward.

Defiant spirits blazed in Rosette as she trailed after the distressed woman. Too bad Zarifa had been placed in charge of me, Rosette thought

141

nastily. But with little pity for the other woman this day. All her pity had been reserved for herself. Rosette hung her head, trailing the servant.

"I'm pooped!" Rosette drew a long breath when she stood inside the cooler walls. She stared around. "What are we doing here?"

Zarifa did not reply, only stood aside so that the younger woman might enter. A corner of Rosette's mouth smirked. Disinterestedly she let her eyes roam. This section of the old Moorish palace was strewn with Eastern rugs of faint and delicate hues. Aged and worn by many footsteps, the colors were dim greens, faded rose, gray-blues, and misty amber and yellows. Against the white walls squatted broad divans, also white, covered with ancient rugs from Baghdad. Large cushions, elaborately worked in dull gold and silver thread had patterns of ibises and birds in flight. In the four angles of the hall stood four tiny tables of rough palm wood, holding hammered trays of bronze, and green-bronze torches for the lighting of lamps. Vases of Chinese dragon china, vases with patterns of gardenias, sprigs of orange blossoms, flowering peach, but mostly the roses that seemed to be the favorite pattern here.

"Whose rooms are these?" Rosette realized she might not receive a quick, clear answer from Zarifa, if any at all.

"Mean who is stay here?" Zarifa tried haltingly in French.

"Yes, Zarifa, who . . . stays . . . here?" Rosette was amazed. French! Someone must have been tutoring Zarifa no doubt for *her* benefit. "Who?" she asked again.

"Mostly Shareef, Hasan al-Shareef." She pointed to the archway and narrow passage leading to another apartment. "Shareef is sleeping there."

"Not at the moment!" Rosette said wryly.

Rosette moved slowly in the direction of the apartment then.

"No! No!" Zarifa said in Arabic, tugging lightly on the bright caftan.

"What do you mean?" Rosette demanded, though she understood the order. "I will see my own brother's apartment, if I want, and neither you nor anyone else shall not stop me!"

Zarifa moaned in distress, but trailed meekly behind. The Shareef's sister was like a stubborn ass at times!

Rosette swept through the archway and the narrow doorway. Hasan must surely have to stoop to enter, she thought, looking up as she halted just inside the dense walls.

She gaped then, awe-struck at the palatial chamber. He lived like a king! How was it that she remembered none of this?

Leather footstools, covered with Tunisian

threadwork, stood beside the entrance. From the arches of the window spaces hung old Moorish lamps of copper, fitted with tiny panes of colorful jewelled glass. From some hidden alcove close by, the sound of a flute showered soft, clear, whimsical music.

Subtly and yet powerfully, Rosette felt Hasan's presence, as if he stood here in the flesh: fierce and proud, full of meaning. Just like this his apartments. It breathed almost his name. Hasan al-Shareef. Sheik of El Taj. Her brother? How could this be?

"How beautiful that tune is." Rosette paused beside the divan to listen, unmindful she still spoke in French.

"It is desert song," Zarifa said tentatively, if not a little proud of the new words Hadji had been introducing her to.

"It is a love song, is it not?"

"Love song, yes. Shareef is always in love."

Zarifa watched closely as the young woman whirled to face her. Zarifa trembled a little.

"You speak almost as if you believe that!" Rosette challenged.

Zarifa shrugged. "They tell me," she murmured simply.

Rosette smiled sagely. "Who are *they?* You speak of women, don't you?" she snapped irately.

"Shamara," Zarifa murmured suddenly, looking alarmed.

"Who?" Rosette looked up. Her eyes were dragged tentatively across the room, as if she didn't want to see. She felt rather than saw the young woman, felt the presence with almost unpleasant acuteness.

The young woman across the room had been lazily nibbling from a bunch of grapes, but now halted as she saw the two.

Shamara was straight and supple, slender, though her hips and breasts swelled with promise of passion. Her belly was a tantalizing white against her thin, gossamer drapery. Her hair was black, blacker even than Zarifa's. The young woman's hair had been carefully groomed until it shone like a blue-black jewel. Her eyes, Rosette could see from here, were a deep brown and wide and tender. The small mouth was smiling faintly at the moment, as she knew her beauty was being observed. The line of her creamy tan cheek and jaw showed the purity of her Arabic blood; her skin tinged in places with a glow of dusky rose petals.

Bewildered, unbelieving of such feminine allure, Rosette found herself murmuring, "She is very beautiful." There followed a painful stabbing in the region of her heart, of jealousy.

"Shamara washes feet with henna to make them—" Zarifa seemed to be choosing her words carefully—"make them *pretty* for Shareef."

Next Zarifa eyed Shareef's sister with something close to amusement. Rosette pouted, looking as if she would burst into tears any second. She was startled to hear Hadji's voice come up behind her then.

"You may go, Zarifa."

The woman stood confused momentarily, afraid she had done something to displease Hadji-ben-Haroun. But when he repeated the dismissal more firmly, she scurried away in a flurry of robes.

Now Hadji eyed Rosette closely, sharply intent on her weepy mood. He hadn't considered this, what he saw happening to Rosette Forrest. It spelled jealousy.

"From a little girl she was bred to the ways of wantonness," he began, perversely enjoying the moment, the torment in the misty eyes. "She has been educated well in the arts of lovemaking and coached in the secret rhythms of passion. Before she was ten she was trained in seduction and flattery. Shamara knows the means to arouse a man's desire, how to satisfy his hunger. There is no one more talented than Shamara in the art of love."

Let this be a warning to you, Hadji almost added but thought better of it.

Unblinking, Rosette continued to stare across the chamber. The bemused girl, not understanding Shareef's sister and her strange mood, stared back. Ah, she had been correct in her earlier thinking, Shamara thought angrily. The bemused expression on Shamara's lovely face altered to one of narrow-eyed dislike.

Rosette could very well imagine Shamara's firm, young body pressed hard against Hasan, pulsing with young life, caressing him with her hennaed fingers, seeking, stroking, his own firm lips sucking her sweet-shaped mouth. Those sensuous hips of Shamara's would press his gently but with infinite promise . . . oh!

Her gasp bore evidence of the girl's effect upon her vision and what she imagined took place here every night on the wide, pillow-strewn bed taking up an entire corner of the chamber.

"But you will forget all this here, Rosette, all that I have revealed and what you have seen. You must never come here again. The sheik is very jealous of his privacy and knows great joy in Shamara."

"Is she the only one?" Rosette found herself asking fiercely, her bottom lip beginning to quiver.

Hadji pressed a long finger on the lip. "No. Do you think only one of them can satisfy an appetite as big as Shareef's? He does not own a harem, but several women await his pleasure, at any time of day."

"Well, I wouldn't know about that," she

snapped, "nor do I care!" She tore her regard from the lovely vision of exotic womanhood.

"Then it is time you learned more about your brother."

She turned a frown upon the Arab. "But you said yourself I should *forget.*"

"I have changed my mind. Come away from here, Rozelle. You have much to remember of other things. And I shall refresh your memory," he said in French.

But I shall not drink anymore of that horrible medicine! she promised herself here and now.

God, I want to feel! Oh, let me be aware! To remember!

Not until later would she be aware that such a prayer answered would turn out to be a living nightmare.

Chapter Thirteen

The slippery feel of the magenta robe rubbed her gently swelling breasts as she wound the belt worked with gold thread about her waist. Rosette's eyes were nearly closed, as a woman closes them when she has seen the lips of her lover descending upon hers.

Rosette's mouth seemed to be receiving the fiery touch of another pair of lips. Her eyes were heavy-lidded as she wondered if was she indeed capable of being vulgarly curious about a man? Had she ever been curious? Indeed she was now.

She laughed then. "I must learn that visions can never give a kiss!" Her sunny-brown eyes flew open. "Oh, damnation, what is wrong with me?" She pressed her lips gently with a tapered finger. "I don't recall if I've ever been kissed before or not!"

But a strange impulse arose in her. She could not resist it this time. Putting her feet into bright yellow *babouches,* she stole out into the corridor, her feet making a soft, shuffling sound on the marble floors. Her slim ankles flashed white. She felt all her senses seemed to be sharpened. She now saw better, heard better, as she hadn't till now. She smiled wryly. The drink had been brought to her, by faithful Asad this time, and when the emaciated man had slipped out of her chamber, she had poured the nasty concoction over the ledge!

All the afternoon she had rested. El Taj was enjoying a siesta in the heat. After Zarifa had gone with a pile of used draperies, no one had come to disturb Rosette. She had heard no footsteps, no movements in the halls.

Nearing the sheik's apartments she hesitated, but now was determined to go onward. She walked on hurriedly, looking to the right and the left, her heart pounding in her throat.

Rosette was not conscious that she even breathed while she stood by the narrow door, frozen there. She feared now her chest would cease to rise and fall, she held her breath so tight. Then she started, hearing voices from within, sounds that shook her body and set the pulses in her temples to pounding. She listened, still holding her breath.

"Shamara, come here."

The lazy-sounding voice of Hasan. She had never heard his voice sound quite this way! Rosette pouted and bit her lip in disappointment.

He, Hasan, was in there with that gorgeous, exotic Shamara. She felt that she was suddenly face to face with a wretchedness such as she had never encountered before. It was this, a loneliness that was cruel. She was weighed down with crushing agony. Hasan must not find her here, spying on him!

"Your brother is occupied at the time. May I help you with something, Rozelle Modestia?"

She whirled after recognizing the deputy's voice. "Samein," she said with a quickness that made all the breath she'd been holding whoosh out. He stared and she drew her robe unconsciously tighter about herself.

Samein appeared uncomfortable and anxious, and he began to frown till his thick, graying black eyebrows nearly met above his hawklike nose. The corners of his full, black lips turned down.

Her face grown suddenly hot, very hot, her throat dry and parched, Rosette longed to use her legs, to run fast, in a way not entirely proper considering the length of her lounging robe. But she couldn't move even should she decide to flee!

A fawning, servile expression replaced the dark frown of a moment ago as Samein tersely questioned, his black eyes fierce. "How long have you lingered here by your brother's door?"

"I — I only just now came to see my brother."

"Why, might I ask? You have not come this way before."

"I — I haven't?"

"Is something amiss?"

N-no," she stammered.

An undecided expression entered his face. "Will you return to your apartments now? Shareef will not find you here and become angry, little flower, if you go quickly now."

The prospect of Hasan catching her right outside his door drew from Rosette a startled gasp. Samein placed his hand gently upon her arm to persuade her to move as he had firmly suggested.

Shareef caught his breath in surprise. In the act of making love to Shamara he had looked down to stare at her ecstatic, dark face.

As delightful as it had been to hold lovely Shamara in his arms again, he realized he had been pretending. When he was done the shock hit him with tumultuous force. He had made love to another, Shamara's moans reminding him that he had been living and loving in a dream world.

When the love fires died down, Shamara noticed the pain mingled with surprise in her handsome Shareef's face. She became alarmed now.

"What is it, my lord Hasan?" she cried in Arabic.

Above her, perspiring, he shook his head. "Nothing," he murmured.

"You will not tell me?" she coaxed, moving beneath him sensuously.

"I am all right, Shamara!"

"So!" she burst out furiously, shoving his big body away. "You are anxious to be with Rozelle Modestia!"

"That is not true," he ground out, angry not with Shamara but with himself.

"I love you! I have always loved you!"

In her dark eyes was the deep hurt of a little animal kicked by its master.

He shook his tawny head, a light tan wave of hair falling to the side of his high forehead. The bitterness of his tone was about to cut into her heart even deeper.

"Just now, Shamara, I allowed myself to be carried away by an impossible dream." His face went stone cold hard. "We are here, each of us a prisoner in his own way — I especially."

"You . . . are a prisoner . . . But you are Shareef here!" she cried, never completing the question. "People here are your responsibility, they depend on you! The old Caid left you with this!"

He rolled to lie on his back, staring up at the stark ceiling. "When I was first brought here to this place there was hatred in me. If I could have escaped, don't you think I would have seized the opportunity?" He laughed grimly. "It is ironic — I was tempted. The chain that bound me here was first forged upon discovering the old sheik hid my beloved sister from my sight and thus thwarted any attempt I might have made to get Rozelle out with me."

"That is how much you love Rozelle Modestia!"

Shamara leapt to her brown feet, dark eyes afire. "You love her even more since you and she have returned. You are with her always! I have spied on you and her, and have seen how you make cow eyes over her!"

Shareef glowered at the naked girl standing there. At first he had to struggle with himself to keep from seizing her creamy tan throat in his hands and throttling her. But gradually, as he lay there with throbbing heart, with her glaring down at him hurtfully, he gained sufficient control of himself. He cursed himself for speaking so candidly with Shamara. Her kind could never understand; she was too uneducated to fathom explanations.

"My lord Hasan," she half-whispered, "why do you not take her to you and be done with the thing? You desire her greatly since you returned. Your body waits to burst as it has never done with me," she ended a trifle sadly.

He looked up at Shamara sharply, rising upon his elbows.

"How do you know that?" he demanded gruffly.

"It is no secret." She smiled lazily at him, in her simple mind knowing she had baited him finally. "Everyone knows she has bewitched you, lord Hasan. She is bad, a *djinn*, a witch!"

"My sister is not this what you say!" he growled temperedly. "And Rozelle has not bewitched me! That is absurd, unheard of!"

Shamara closed her eyes for a moment so that he could not see the pain that was in them—or the murderous hatred that had sprung up.

When she opened them, Shamara filled her dark gaze with the splendid virile form of Shareef, his naked, white buttocks as he bent to snatch up his billowy trousers and robe. But his feet were as calloused as an Arab's, like he had walked the desert sands all his life. He didn't face her again as he spoke.

"I want you out of my apartments before midnight," he said softly. "Tip the sands in the hourglass," he explained in Arabic.

"It will be as lord Hasan says."

Sad and reluctant, Shamara went to gather her personal belongings. For the first time since Rozelle Modestia had returned from Shareef's home in Morocco, Shamara began to puzzle over what it could be that was different about the Shareef's sister. Rozelle was the same and yet not the same.

When Hasan joined her, Rosette was still in the garden with its high stone walls thick with climbing vines.

Her face had paled when he entered the garden, for he wore a look of thunder between his eyebrows.

She had come out to the garden and gone over in her hazy mind the scene with Samein, and the odd look he had sent her before he mysteriously departed.

Already stars approached with the twilight and misty purples of the desert drew unerringly closer. Sunset again altered the attire of the desert as fiery clouds still lingered on the western horizon, the limitless horizon that was empty during the day, merely sand haze and platinum light.

"Here you are," Hasan muttered with an odd tone.

But Rosette thought his the most male voice she'd ever heard. Like the hands with their implacable grip, his voice seemed to be full of sex. His intrinsically male scent settled over her again and love of her brother rose up to cry within her. After encountering the exotically lovely Shamara, Rosette felt as if she fought a she-cat, must fight hard in keeping his attention. But why? Why did she feel this way about her brother? It was absurd! But oh so true.

Golden silence reigned as he sighed while he lowered himself to the carpet. Sideways, she glanced at him. But he looked straight ahead and spoke.

"Is something amiss?"

A furtive sigh emerged. "No," she lied while she toyed with a fold in her muslin robe decorated with intricate golden suns and curlicues.

"Well, what is it then? I've noticed you seem unsettled over something." His lean jaw tautened.

The intense heat of his hand lying so close to her own caused an upsurge in her already battling emotions. Dark rode the flush high on her cheekbones and flooded her forehead to her widow's peak. Scarlet now, her face turned to him. In her breast mingled both eagerness and fear. Slowly coming to her knees, she turned, bent forward quivering and presented her face to him.

Still he stared without moving. He barely

breathed in the utterly trembling moment.

"Kiss me," Rosette whispered to Hasan.

A heat grew as Shareef saw the desperate pleading that entered the almond-shaped eyes. Eyes that boasted their own odd-colored beauty, like he'd seen on a frightened doe long ago in England as a lad. Distorted by an expression half angry and half fearful of what he'd discover, Hasan's face was mostly tormented.

His lips curled as judgments roiled against her and emerged. "Has it ever occurred to you, my dear, that we are related?"

She laughed over his curt retort. "I know. Would it seem strange to you if I kissed your lips?" Her voice lifted impudently. "Even now?"

"Yes!" he exploded, "it would seem mighty strange indeed!"

His uncompromising masculinity urged Rosette to even greater peril. "Why?" she asked.

She appeared so innocent, so damn vulnerable, that — God! — Shareef groaned, not meaning for it to be out loud. The blood of passion tingled in his veins, fiercely, bitterly even, that for a moment he was clothed from head to foot in a fiery garment of shame.

"I will tell you." His growl met her surprise. "I love you. Everything in me loves you. All that I have been, all that I am, all that I could ever be, loves you. It seems that I have never been anything else and there is no room in me for anything but the love of you. You are passion, and I am that to which passion flows."

Shareef's burning shame of which he'd been conscious of earlier fled from him now. How could he be ashamed of love? Yet, there was something else that needs to be arrested. . . .

Lifting his gaze from her dewy, awe-struck face, Shareef looked into the garden with its misty sunset purples hovering about like wraiths in the air. The very idea of seeking her—her!—had never entered his mind. Until Shamara brought this to light. Curse the bitch!

"You are that which my flesh must not touch," he said precisely, staring away from her, "and you, Rozelle, must not touch my flesh."

With that he sprang to his feet. As he began to move away from her, she knew instant dejection wash like waves over her breast. But now she knew devastation, by his indifference. There was a glimmer of hope as he turned with a last word.

"I never knew how much until the moment I found you in the desert after the sandstorm."

He left her with those cryptic words and was gone.

As the gloom gathered, Rosette sat silent as a bronze statue with darkness creeping up from the bottom, shadows stealing through the garden like dark ghosts. What have I done? her mind whispered in shock. Has insanity rocked my senses? I feel all here, but when he walks away he removes a part of me each time. How long before there is nothing left of Ro—Rozelle? Rose—? Ahh! She clenched her hands into neat fists. Who the devil am I really? Did it matter anymore?

He had said he never knew how much until the desert, when he found her? Of course. The origin of all their turmoil, for indeed Hasan was involved, and even more so. Passions of men ran deeper and were harder to suppress than a woman's.

He loves me, Rosette's heart sang. What else mattered as long as her brother loved her? That was all she needed for now. Then, perhaps he was not her blood kin, after all. . . .

The next dawning of vibrant hues found Rosette watching Hasan ride away on his white stallion. Behind him rode five Arabs with *moukkalas*, heavily encrusted Moroccan rifles and pistols stuck into bright sashes.

Rosette reflected back to Hasan's earlier words. *There's an aura here that makes men love danger and flirt with it.* Had these been his exact words? Or had they implied a different meaning? She couldn't know for sure now.

Rosette lifted her gaze. They rode towards the plains that looked to her like snow, shimmering like drifts of white powder, beside a sea that was merely a mirage. Rosette turned back into the chamber. After she had lowered herself to a squat divan, she sat gazing at nothing.

Melancholy increased, until it became oppressive and lay upon her soul like a weight too heavy to remove. A dreariness of spirit arose that was rare in Rosette Forrest.

But she was Rozelle Modestia — the last name was unimportant. But who was this other woman inside her whose name she dared not utter?

What if the immeasurable sands snatched Hasan and never gave him back to her? What would she do? Go back to who she had been before? What she had been doing before entering the Sahara? Back to Morocco and that house in Tangier?

How long Rosette sat there in a confused daze she did not know. She slept some, mused some, ate, drank, all under the manipulations of some invisible master puppeteer.

It was toward evening that a weary and travel-stained party of three men, legionnaires by the looks of their white kepis, rode slowly up the sandy track from the dunes. Mounted on mules, they carried their baggage with them on two lead mules. The officer — if that's what he was — rode a little in advance of his men. She judged him to be handsome, as far as Rosette could see, a fair man of perhaps twenty-five. He sported a blond mustache, and his hair, as he drew closer, was much the shade of the sand dunes. Closer yet, she could pick out green eyes with amber lashes, no doubt bleached by the sun somewhat. His fair, delicate skin was burnt lobster-red by the sun.

Curious now, Rosette leaned closer to the parapet. Who is this man of fair skin and hair? His hair was full of sand and longer than most, she found, and he rode leaning forward over the mule's neck. The reins were clutched loosely in hands that seemed nerveless from fatigue.

It was evident that both this officer and his men were riding in from some tremendous journey. Perhaps from the Gold Coast, Hasan had told her some about, or the Hammada, the stony desert.

The officer was just about beneath her balcony and she could hear the clatter of his mule against the flagstones. The Akbar emerged from the interior to greet this legionnaire and question his mission. Akbar spoke French and when he was satisfied, he drifted back inside, never far away if needed though.

Feeling oddly faint, Rosette drew a slim hand across her brow. The green-eyed man caught the movement, looked up and was startled. She met his green gaze finally. Her momentary frown disappeared after a closer look. He was surprised to see a woman owning such fair skin standing there like an ethereal vision above him.

Or is she some desert goddess, this Frenchman wondered. He sat straighter in the saddle and took off his hat to her. With the hat in hand, he swung himself off his mule and stood. Catching the saddle with one hand, he seemed to be slowly straightening the kinks in his back.

"*Mon Dieu,* I can hardly stand!"

Rubbing his aching backsides, he grinned up at her sheepishly. "Pardon, mademoiselle." He took a good look, his eyes widening further than the first time he'd first sighted her.

Unsteadily she descended the stairs, clutching her white caftan so that she wouldn't trip over the hem.

With unrestrained interest, Rosette studied him and his men. "You look bloody pooped!" she exclaimed.

His sunburn paled to pink but he seemed to recover from his shock then. "Pooped indeed! We've been lost in the terrible dunes for three bloody days—" he coughed and recovered—"in a sandstorm at that. We hit the track here just as we were about to pass out from hunger and thirst. *Ma foi,* what a great place this desert is!" He sniffed the air. "Is that food I smell? I believe it's—*pastilla*. Am I correct?"

She nodded. "Yes, it's pigeon pie," she laughed. She could tell he spoke simply, but with a light touch of humor that was underlined with cynicism. His words attracted and moved something in her. She had been terribly lonesome, and now here was this nice legionnaire come along to keep her company. He certainly didn't appear to be French, though she wasn't bold enough to question his authenticity.

"Ah! Those terrible dunes!" he exclaimed again. "A man could drown in them!"

Rosette looked out over them. "My brother is out there." She thought: But not my real brother, but I must not . . .

"Your . . . brother?"

With narrowed green eyes he peered closely at her. He shifted from one foot to the other then, as if testing his strength. "I am sorry if I seem a bit surprised."

"After three days in the dunes your provisions must be exhausted," she said, choosing not to answer his inquiry.

"We have not been able to replenish them." A sidelong look took in the curious crowd that had gathered around him. "I do hope they are only curious —" he laughed nervously — "and nothing else."

"Do not let them disturb you. Come inside," she said faintly, waves of weakness washing over her, coming and going. "We'll have some *atai benaana*."

"Ah, mint tea, right?"

"That is correct."

They lingered for a few more minutes in the courtyard with its surrounding *djenina*. The twilight had rapidly changed and the dark splendor of the evening drew near. Rosette gazed toward the distant dunes forlornly. But she could no longer make them out. At once she thought of Hasan. Why had he not returned? He had informed her during one of their long talks that he had gone lately on punitive missions against recalcitrant tribesmen in the desert to the south. Also he had to visit the many Douars, and did not return for several days at a time. Rosette shivered, reminded of the desert dwellers in the oases subjected to continual raids by desert bandits, the riffraff of the desert. El Taj, unfortunately, sat in the midst of an oasis. But Hasan had as much as guaranteed her there was little danger of attack, El Taj was like Ksar, a fortified village.

Then, straining her gaze to see better, in her vision rose the flame of a freshly made campfire way beyond the walls of the citadel. He was out there . . . somewhere.

Small Arab boys appeared magically, it seemed, grinning dark and broad as they tugged the cords of the lead mules to urge them back out to the stables. Rosette shivered involuntarily, feeling eyes, dark and threatening, as when she'd been behind the dressing grille, stabbing into her back, watching her from some hidden recess in the kasbah.

Continuing to gaze at the lovely young woman with a sparkle of admiration in his green, inflamed eyes, it was all the legionnaire could do to shoulder the two musette bags he had dragged off the lead mules. Already weak, she added to this. But it was a different kind of weakness, he discovered.

"Permit me, how remiss of me. My name is, ah, Pierre Maudet."

She smiled. "In the desert one forgets," she began but trailed away. "My name is . . ." Rosette pressed two fingers to her throbbing temple. "My name is—" her eyes flew wide—"Rosette."

He inclined his head to hear better, but her voice had been pitched low and indistinct. "Here, what? . . .

As the Arab boys had done several minutes ago, Hadji appeared and rushed forward to catch the young woman just swooning. He bent, scooped her easily into his arms and carried her toward the door. He glared once over his shoulder at the stranger and then vanished within the walls.

"Good lord, do you suppose she's ill?" Maudet asked his men, they whose stomachs growled with one thing foremost.

Several dark boys rushed up to Maudet, speaking sharply in a drumming beat. "Ro-zelle, Ro-zelle. . . ."

Over and over they chanted her name, then the lads melted into the mauve shadows with eyes glowing red like wolf eyes.

Paul Moreland, alias Monsieur Pierre Maudet, frowned his confusion while he scratched beneath the dusty kepi he'd replaced on his head.

"Incha'Allah . . . Incha'Allah," came the chant from the shadows.

"Oh, go away." Paul, suddenly irritable, snapped around.

Ah, Rosette. Paul knew he must indeed see more of this glorious creature. He was tempted to even fall in love with her. She was even more attractive than his own half-sister. But love, Paul thought glumly, had no place in the affairs of a spy and a murderer.

Chapter Fourteen

Rosette knew Hadji yet studied her with intensity, but she kept her eyes downcast, on the drink he held. There was something in his eyes, something she felt she must not see. It was as if his gaze deliberately pressed her down into the uttermost forgetfulness.

"Look at me, Rozelle," he cajoled gently.

Tipping the glass, Hadji watched as she again drank thirstily, against her own will.

She had made the blunder of looking into the black, hypnotic eyes, drawn there by an irresistible force. Now she shrank into the deepest, blackest abysses of them. Just now she

168

saw Hadji as some strange and ghastly figure, that there lurked something in Hadji that could cause her to be terrified. Immediately she felt hostile toward him, detesting what he was doing to her again.

"You are better, Rozelle."

His voice modulated to humbleness. But she felt hard, as if ice flowed in her veins instead of blood. He surveyed her with steady, unflinching orbs. After handing him back the glass, she shoved his hand roughly away.

"No more! Do you understand, Hadji?" She wrenched her face aside. "Please leave now. I wish to be alone."

Hadji murmured a fierce, soft exclamation she couldn't make out. With undisguised annoyance, she pouted at him but forced herself to steer clear of his eyes. She refused to look into them!

He makes my flesh crawl, she thought and turned defiant. I thoroughly detest the way I feel after being around him and downing that obnoxious concoction—whatever it is! Medicine? Bah? More like poison.

I am not myself afterward, she mused. Furthermore, I don't even know who myself is anymore.

The oddest thing happened next. Hadji's eyes brimmed with woebegone tears and he shook his turbaned head and appeared brokenhearted.

"If Rozelle does not drink the medicine, Hadji

169

will suffer by the Shareef's own hand. He can be very mean and ruthless when he is deceived."

"I knew it — you are deceiving him!"

"Please, I beg of you, do not do this to me." He peered between slim, dark fingers that he had splayed over his nose and eyes. "Please?" he begged one more time.

Her lips quirked at their corners in the beginning of a smile that said she was weakening. In a wobbly movement Rosette sat and tucked her tapered legs beneath her, pressing her palms to her knees. Even in her growing bemusement and vexation with the man, she knew great pity for Hadji.

"Be merciful to me?"

"Oh," she moaned, "you are like a child, you know that?"

He nodded vigorously in answer, his eyes glowing marbles.

"You are the oddest man, Hadji. You are fierce and you are humble — and will you cease staring at me like that! If you again try to hypnotize me into being better, well, it won't work this time, do you hear?"

Again he nodded. "You are too kind to me," he muttered, patting her slim hand.

"I wish that weren't the case, believe me!"

Shifty and obsidian went his eyes, but he grinned for her benefit. "Drink a little more for

Hadji? Hmm?" he wheedled. "I want Rozelle to be over her sickness. Yes?"

"Bloody damn!" Her vivid eyes chided him. "All right, then, but just a sip. A sip!"

"Please, do not employ your English swear words? They pain my delicate ears." He put his hands there. "Oooh."

"Oh, your ears are always hidden beneath that homely turban!" She giggled then, hiding her face behind her hand.

"Drink, Rozelle. Then we will talk of England again. You were very little. Ah, a delicate rosebud when Hadji first saw you. You do remember when you were first brought here as a captive?"

"No." Her shoulders jumped with a shrug. "But tell me, and, Hadji, don't leave anything out with Hasan in it."

Hadji's head dipped in the familiar bowing pose.

Like the needle of a giant's sundial, the tower above cast its huge shadows across the garden.

Under Zarifa's imposed supervision, Rosette had dressed for dinner that evening in the open-air Riad. The Frenchmen had requested her presence, and at once Hadji treated the visitors with true Moroccan hospitality. He would be there to watch over her himself.

"You'd think I was a prisoner here, a captive, the way Hadji trails after me. Like a jailer, he is!" She took it out on Zarifa's delicate ears as the woman pulled out a dress to wear.

Zarifa shrugged. "This jailer, I do not know what this is."

Rosette searched her mind, but as usual there were so many words she couldn't summon up. All her memories were cobwebby things. "I guess it means a man who sentences one behind bars —" Rosette shrugged — "something on that order."

Content with that, it seemed, Zarifa crossed the chamber to a small box fashioned from thuya wood inlaid with ebony and mother-of-pearl. "Rozelle's." She dragged from the box a hammered silver chain, short in length, with a lapis lazuli rock hung by the center links.

Smiling over the piece of jewelry, Rosette allowed Zarifa to fasten it at her nape. In the wavy mirror, she could see the necklace positioned exactly at the hollow of her throat. Pulling her hair back from her face then, Rosette held it there at the nape with a narrow strip of amber cloth. She paused to stare, her arms slowly lowering to her sides. Her brother, she'd just bet he put Hadji on her tail. Men! At least the ones around here seemed to play both ends against the middle. She couldn't speak to Hasan about Hadji, and Hadji was reluctant to discuss anything to do with Hasan—that had to to with his private life. Sons of the desert, all those here. Hasan was the most arrogant and proud, of course, he being the highest pasha, and when he rapped orders no doubt he was instantly obeyed. At times she regretted her inability to understand and speak Arabic.

Zarifa waited on the table and Rosette was again delighted with all the Moroccan delicacies. There was *harira,* a thick, wonderful soup to start, and Zarifa had revealed that following that would be *mechoui*, mutton cooked over embers, and there was even a kind of savory *mille feuille*. Refreshments were the usual *atai benaana*. A variety of wines had also been set out, but Rosette declined even a drop, much to Hadji's great relief.

Flitting over the visitors, Hadji's eyes came to rest on Rosette Forrest. Watch her well, he told himself, for she must not imbibe any alcoholic beverage. She might become conscious of the state she has fallen into if she became at all drunk. She would begin to weep uncontrollably, or, if not that, she could take dangerous measures and harm herself, to escape from herself. He had been giving her small doses of borbor, yet her woman's spirit had great strength and he needed the added art of mesmerizing to aid him. Hadji was starting to panic, though.

How long could he keep up this dangerous deception? Now he needed for her to go away, disappear. Perhaps this Frenchman? . . .

"You are a lovely vision, mademoiselle," Pierre Maudet leaned to the young woman in pink and mauve, a Moroccan-style dress with gold embroidery throughout. "Delightful, if you permit me."

Rosette almost giggled, feeling in high spirits though she'd had no wine. "Permit you to what, monsieur?" She tipped her head, fiery in torch and candlelights.

"To say so, of course. You are toying with me, mademoiselle."

Back and forth volleyed the banter, and once in a while Maudet turned curious over the pretty mouth trying not to yawn, and the lazy-lidded sun-warmed eyes. Why she stiffened and came alert to her surroundings just when another woman, much younger, came to wait on Maudet's companions, he couldn't fathom. She was reed-slender, possessing a seductive body, long, jet-black hair and dark, melting eyes.

"Shamara."

Zarifa had spoken to the younger woman and Pierre watched the exchange, as did Hadji and Rosette. But especially alert were Maudet's companions, for they all but drooled over the exotic loveliness of the young Shamara. Pierre also became perplexed when this English beauty beside him glowered ungraciously at this Shamara's proudly erect back, tiny, swaying hips and boyish buttocks.

Just then, to compound the situation, one of Shareef's men entered and swept a bold, possessive look over the dark beauty. Shamara froze, posing for him in a provocative manner of sultriness, a summons that teased the dark, handsome deputy. His eyes deepened to heated black glass, mirrors of passion for Shamara held barely in restraint.

Unable to help herself, Rosette's gaze kept drifting to the far-off campfires. All conversation ceased for her then as Tarek announced that soon the sheik would join them. From suspicion to undisguised desire that switched with lightning speed, Tarek glanced at Pierre Maudet and then to Shamara.

Shortly Tarek moved to the fringe of amber light, meeting a man there to speak in hushed tones before he joined the others. The heartbeats in Rosette's breast picked up speed. Tarek was talking to Shareef. He must have just arrived.

Not a flicker of a smile crossed Shareef's lean face. His eyes, like chips of black emeralds, flicked over the gathered guests.

Hadji's shifty gazes bounced back and forth, never remaining long in one place or on one face.

Nerves quivered in the pit of Rosette's belly for she could feel the heat of Hasan's gaze hard on her, and Maudet, as that one leaned much too close to whisper a witty thing in her ear. She dared not laugh. She needn't look, either, to see if the sheik watched them: she knew his hawklike eyes saw all and then some.

Shareef finally detached his tall frame from the flickering shadows and Tarek, the deputy, strode off in the wake of Shamara's gliding feet.

The hot rush that Shareef's powerful maleness always brought to Rosette's cheeks did so now. "Hasan." She softly spoke the greeting, salaam, and Hadji swung about to closely regard the exchange.

"Rozelle, salaam," he greeted in return, turning her blood to ice at the chilliness in his tone. He turned abruptly to Maudet who had stood to shake hands Western-fashion with Shareef. "I see you have been keeping my lovely sister company," he remarked, disregarding the proffered hand.

No sooner did Maudet's green eyes narrow than they returned to normal. "She is delightful—" he smiled at her especially—"a rare jewel in this barren land."

Sparks hovered in the air all around and Rosette could feel them like tiny shocks up and down her slim, bare arms. Strange, haunting music from some hidden alcove floated into the

Riad like a mysterious lament.

"I find this hard to believe that Rozelle—" Pierre coughed once—"is your sister."

Rosette caught the tightening of muscles along Hasan's lean jaw before he said abruptly:

"Do you?"

"I mean," he couched emphasis, "when I first looked upon your lovely sister she didn't appear as if she belonged here, especially not a sheik's sister. Well, you can see where—"

"Yes, I can," Shareef interjected in a clipped tone. "The truth of the matter is, Rozelle and myself were adopted into the great pasha's family." But he frowned over to her.

With seeming difficulty, Maudet said, "I thought, or I began to think it might be something of that sort."

"What brings you to the Sahara, Monsieur Maudet?"

Pierre chuckled. As he retold the tale he'd given the Akbar, Rosette took the time to study Hasan from beneath the long spikes of her lashes. Hasan, for now, was not looking her way.

How dark and mysterious he is, how vital and full of life—and menace. As she covertly watched his every slightest gesture, beyond the arched doorway came the soft strains of music. It mingled with the low hum of conversation.

Hasan, my beloved. The words cried out from the very depths of her soul.

Finally he was looking her way. She feared her heart would cease to beat. Slowly slipping, his gaze came to rest on her low-necked dress. Knowing where he gazed, she, more unconscious than cognizant of her actions, covered the spot with a splayed hand. Eyes lifted to hers to jolt her, then boring; it was as if he read her every thought. Heated pink rushed to her cheeks, and she was thankful that Maudet spared her by dragging the reluctant Shareef back into conversation.

"Where are you and Rozelle from, I mean originally?"

"That is the past, and unimportant. My home is here now. My homeland can only best be remembered as a cold place, with equally cold and flighty people. Their ways confuse the mind. At a young age I felt an outcast among my own. We are simple people here."

Hasan sipped a light wine and stared broodingly straight ahead. He was thinking, this night Rozelle was very different.

"You and your sister were captured then?"

An awkward silence followed before Shareef chose to answer the question. A small spark of poignancy touched his eyes. "Yes, we were captured. But very soon the past was forgotten, the future of existing anywhere but the desert renounced. The wild Moors came to know me well and respected me soon. My wants extended only to the exotic, glittering pleasures of the Moorish world." His eyes shifted to tenderly take in the young woman.

Rosette gazed. The winking gem in his turban caught the light. Brilliant shafts sparkled in all directions, mesmerizing her with their cold heat.

"I'm sorry." Rosette drew a forearm wearily across her forehead. "Excuse me, please."

With that she graciously arose from the chair Maudet had beat Shareef to. Actually Rosette believed Shareef hadn't the idea to play the gallant tonight. Did he ever? She couldn't recall if he'd ever.

Rosette was aware of only one pair of eyes. Hasan's. Dark green mirrors followed her, and a fine tingle made its way up her spine.

"You cried out."

Strong, vibrant hands smoothed beads of perspiration from her forehead. Rosette looked up from her bed and saw Hasan in the glow of the brazier set in the room to extract the chill of night. "I am all right," she said, quavery. "It was only a nightmare."

He passed a hand with tremors in it over her damp face. As she nuzzled his warm hand at once she noticed the muscles tense in his long fingers. Brusquely but gently he brushed back auburn hair that was disheveled. Her camellia skin flushed and he dropped his hand.

But now there was something going on here to which he dared not put a name. For the first time in his life he was frightened, frightened of what would become of them. Didn't she feel the torment? He pulled himself up in a hassock and sat beside her bed. Didn't she realize the pain he must endure just being around her? He had been consumed by jealousy when the Frenchman's eyes lingered on her. A man could not react this way, unless . . .

In a hypnotic fashion, Rosette stared up at him. She turned her head so that her hair shimmered in the moonlight streaming in. Tentatively she reached out and touched her finger to his lips. "Your mouth is very sensuous, Hasan."

"Take heed," Hasan warned, watching her parted lips with infinite hunger, his aquiline features in deep shadow, unreadable.

But light glimmered between his thick lashes and his lips curved in the ghost of a smile. Rosette lowered her hand and stayed quite still, but could feel his warm breath as it stirred the thick tresses of her hair. He lifted her chin higher, handling her face like he held a delicate bird he was afraid to harm. She could not speak any more. At last that something of a wild and lawless nature, that was more than passionate, that was hot and even savage in his nature, rose up in its full force to face a similar force in her and it insistently called and answered without shame. She felt his body tremble, as if the vehemence of the spirit confined within shook it. In the night the breeze slightly increased and shifted to enter the opening, causing the orange flame of the sconce above the bed to flicker. The breeze was like a message that was brought to them from the desert by some envoy in the darkness. This secret messenger seemed to be telling them not to be frightened of this wonderful gift. Take it with open heart, with the courage of great joy, it said.

"Rozelle, did you feel that? In the gust of wind?"

"It is the night calling to the fire that is in us . . ." She trailed off. He is not my brother, *not* in the blood. She knew.

There was a long-suffering moan. His mind said he must not touch her flesh, but he couldn't help the forces in his body.

She saw now that his eyes were as hard as polished stone, an agonized hardness. "Why, oh why, Hasan do I find it exciting to touch you? Am I bad, Hasan, am I?"

His lips brushed her fingers in a kiss's barest whisper. This has got to cease, he told himself,

the thought almost forced through his mind. She
was not a child any longer, but a woman, and he
was a man now with a man's desires. Ah, but how
little she knew! "Rose, little Rose." Yes, it is bad!
his mind shouted.

The hard tautness of his belly moved and he
knew a great desire to bring the curve of her
softness against his thighs and chest. He was
mad, he knew, as mad as she herself was, but
why, damnit, why did this torment him, and *why
her*, for God's sake!

But the kiss, the kiss when it finally came
would be burned in both their minds like fire, fire
forever, branded there. She gave her lips
up to his in a kiss that swooped her away to the
stars. Seared her body in a fiery cauldron. A fire
coursing through his blood, mingling with hers.
A heat such as Shareef had never known before.

She gasped as the fiery-tender kiss ended when
he snatched his mouth away. "My God, what am
I doing?" He shook his head. "Sweet Jesus." Just
who is this woman? He stared at her.

She loved that kiss as he had. He knew the
greatest desire to revel in it and not worry for
what tomorrow might bring. Following that
thought emerged a low groan of torment, of
suffering. Shareef's spirit galloped like an
Arabian stallion across the sands toward the
glowing ball of sun. Toward the fire that sheds
warmth from afar, but one that devours all that

draw near its flame. "Like a moth," Hasan murmured.

But Rosette was not hearing him. She was staring off into a distant land, her eyes saucers trained on the ghostly patterns dancing over the ceiling. She moved restlessly then. Suddenly, Shareef exploded into action, alarmed at her staring trance.

"Rozelle, what is it?" His fingers viselike around her wrists, he lifted her a space from the bed, shaking her and she lolled like a rag doll.

"Perry, don't!"

Shareef felt his blood freeze. Staring down at her, he turned quite still as if petrified himself. All the passion was driven from his mind and his body.

"Perry, don't do this to me! Don't leave me!"

He started as if someone had struck him a heavy blow, hesitated, then, with a look of fierceness entering his face, his fingers curled as if he prepared to throttle her. Some sudden change of feeling, some secret and powerful resistance, checked him.

He thrust her aside, onto her back. Bending over her, his strong fingers manacled her wrists and Rosette had to bite her lip to keep from crying out. But tiny whimpers emerged, so soft as to be barely audible. But Hasan heard them.

A tiny voice inside her asked: What are you

doing, Rosette? You have to escape from this man, this stranger, for he is surely that — before the worst happens. You could fall in love.

Shareef didn't move, was speechless for a whole minute. His gaze fixed to her mouth, he finally managed to ask, "Who . . . is . . . Perry?"

Rosette twisted and jerked her arm and cried out. But his fingers only tightened until they bruised her wrist. She blinked, staring into the face she couldn't make out much of.

"Who are *you?*"

She touched her lips that yet burned from a kiss that had seared them.

Shareef strode along the corridor, with the mid of night all around, looking like Satan himself. Lines around his eyes, weathered by harsh winds and sun — not to mention wrath at this moment — gave him a look much older than his twenty-seven years.

Violently Shareef unwound his turban, yanking, wrenching, cursing as he loosed the mane of tawny lion hair. Who was there to see him but the kitchen maids perhaps, making preparations ahead of time for tomorrow's meals.

Shareef vowed silently to never make such a foolish mistake again. Curses! Just who was this woman who was driving him to the brink of madness? Sister or not, he would enjoy throttling the lovely witch at times!

Nevertheless, there remained yet plenty of need to proceed with caution — Rozelle was indeed not herself.

From Akila's kitchen, on the side of the kasbah, wafted not only the odors of baked goods but the muffled, cheerful chatter of women gossiping. As a name was mentioned, Shareef's steps slowed. They were speaking in Arabic.

"What is wrong with Rozelle Modestia?"

"She is not herself."

Suddenly the chatter dipped to low, intense whispers. But their excitement was real now. Shareef was about to move away, not an eavesdropper by nature. Once again he found the need to hesitate.

Akila was insisting on something, and the other had lifted her voice to object violently.

"Then why is it she is so jealous of Shamara?"

"Who has said this?"

"Shamara herself. She saw the look in Rozelle Modestia's eyes. And Rozelle does not know a word of Arabic. How is that?"

"She was an English captive. I have never heard Rozelle speak a word of Arabic."

"Ah, but I have!"

"Who is this woman then — an imposter?"

"Foolishness. But there is a way one might find out."

"How is that?"

"If she is indeed Shareef's sister, she has a rosebud, a birthmark — here!"

Chapter Fifteen

"All foolishness." Hadji sat unblinking after Shareef had verbally attacked him.

Shareef's attention remained hard and fixed on the man. "It has been your bounden duty to watch over Rozelle."

"I have, lord Hasan," Hadji nodded and declared.

"How do you account for her strange actions then? There are those who believe she is not Rozelle Modestia but an imposter?" He lifted a dark brow.

As Shareef studied the wily Arab closely for signs of pretense, Hadji jumped up from his prayer cushion as if he'd been stung by a bee.

"Not Rozelle Modestia? Again I say, all foolishness. The kitchen women gossip in want for nothing better to occupy their feather brains!" Hadji peered down at his hands a bit sadly. "I believe Rozelle is not—" he sighed as if pained to say it—"she is not feeling well."

"I've noticed signs of weariness." Shareef paced the confines of the Horm, place of asylum, then whirled back to face the man. "Who is Perry?"

"I—I know of no Perry," Hadji said truthfully, although worry lines etched his dark skin.

"In Morocco? Could she have met someone named Perry there?"

Hadji shrugged, his gaze sliding away. "It . . . is possible. Yes, there were many visitors at the house on the hill, mild acquaintances who came to call. There were many gentlemen, you see, come with their ladies."

With exasperation, Shareef said, "True, they have always flocked around my . . . around her."

Shareef's glance shifted to the carpet then back up to Hadji once again. "Who is my sister's attendant?" Abruptly he asked.

Hadji rolled black eyes over the decorative Zellig flooring and announced, "Ah, that is Zarifa. The woman does only what is best for our dear Rozelle Modestia."

"That's fine. But I want Rozelle examined as soon as she awakes. A bath—" he waved his arm—"whatever. But have Zarifa see Rozelle completely in the nude. If she does not see to this task, then I shall do so myself."

Hadji only blinked in bewilderment. "What is this?"

"Do you know of Rozelle's, ah—" Shareef blasted out the rest then—"of a rosebud, a birthmark?"

"Of course!" Hadji exclaimed.

"You do?" he asked, almost in disappointment.

"That is how you may tell if she is an imposter, you are saying?" Hadji saw what Shareef was driving at even if Shareef didn't himself.

"Well, where is it then?" Shareef finally blurted.

"On Rozelle Modestia's pretty bottom!"

Ah, Shareef thought to himself, then said out loud as he turned on his heel, *"Mezyan,* Hadji," his voice rumbled deeply, "make sure it is still there."

With robe fluttering behind, Shareef exited the Horm. Hadji released a long breath of relief. He would go at once to find Zarifa, and then to find some henna—Shamara always has henna. Eh? What has come to my mind? Shareef, he knows there is deception? What if Shareef had long ago decided to play along in this? Then?

*   *   *

Rosette did not feel the horse beneath her or the reins clutched in her hand, and she did not see the moon.

El Taj's partially ruined bulk fell behind her as Rosette looked down at her hands clutching the reins — she knew she looked at them, yet felt as though she were not seeing them.

"I *am* alive!" She was alive, yes, and the moon-lit desert indeed flickered around her.

At last Rosette's mind began to function as the cool air whipped at her hot cheeks; the desert wind was on her cheek and in her hair. The fiery copper tresses whipped out from her burnous and she hastily tucked the curls back inside. It wouldn't do if someone were to come along — that would in itself be bad enough — but to know she was female.

The mystical attraction of the desert — where was it now? The voice of the desert that had called her persistently was suddenly still, ominous, holding her in its sandy coils. She gazed up at the moon and saw it was if through a golden aureole and mist.

Here no longer was a desert, sand with a soul in it, blue distances full of summons, that music gone, and spaces that had been peopled with spirits of the sun. Here was only a barren waste of dried matter, and ghastly with the bones of creatures and humans that had perished beneath the relentless sun. Relentless!

Rosette tossed her head impatiently. Who was that man back there who had taken all the romance with him when he strode angrily from her chamber? Did they call him sheik? Is he the one who hypnotizes me and keeps me here against my will? Why? Who is he?

What does he want?

She heard the dogs barking by the tents of Shareef's men. Gradually she began to recover with a sharp, physical pain such as experienced by someone who has been almost drowned and restored to consciousness.

Slowing her mount to stare at the moon, she wondered, How did I get away with it, out this far from the kasbah without him, their leader, coming after me?

Rosette had put on the riding habit found in the wardrobe and over that slipped on the enveloping burnous. After the sheik — yes, that's what he is — after he had left her, she had known the greatest desire to be away. She longed to be in the saddle, riding at full speed across the desert, challenging dangers she had only tasted once before.

To escape from the danger that panted throughout the kasbah, along the corridors — but mostly the danger to her heart was what she wanted to flee from.

The sleepy Arab boy, his hood drawn over his head, had looked astonished when she slipped into the stable. She had shown him the mount she wished to ride; by sign language she had communicated with him. The astonished and slightly frightened expression returned instantly to his dark face and he had turned his head from side to side while making a helpless gesture in the air.

"Shareef will be angry." He spoke in Arabic. "There will be foam on his lips when he learns of this!"

She looked into the long eyes that were full of mystery, then moved determinedly toward the black horse she chose. She had seen the prancing black in the courtyard before, but just when she found she could not recall now.

She had said to the Arab boy, "I don't understand a word of that gibberish." She had smiled, actually felt herself smile, feeling as if she were playing a game and there were two of her instead of one. "But thank you for not raising an alarm."

The boy blinked. Reluctantly he led the horse across the gardens after she had nudged him insistently. Beyond the gardens was a stretch of sand and low dunes that were golden and mysterious beneath the moon. Platinum mists rode the waves of dunes and rose above in breakers of coiling, curling wisps that spilled finally into flat tongues.

The boy looked on with a still solemnity, clutching the bridle in his strong little boy's hands as she sprang expertly into the tooled orange saddle and pressed her legs against the black's flanks. Rearing up, the horse was black as a midnight without moonlight. The moment the horse came down, she whirled with him and cantered away from the hidden gate Beni had reluctantly brought her to. Away she flew, like a horseless rider into the moonlight.

Spinning about, Beni ran to the kasbah at full speed. The young woman must be stopped. *"Sayyid!"* he shouted.

Rosette still stared at the moon. The desert spaces stretched lonely around her. Beneath the black's hoofs lay the sparkling crystals on the sun-dried earth. Large dunes spread before her, some straight and high, some like reptilian shapes, others yet undulating like the sea.

She pressed her finger tips to her throbbing temple. What is it that I am running away from? Who am I really? And where can I run to in this alien vastness?

At first there was merely a moving spot behind her. It was formless, but as it drew nearer she saw that it was a horseman. He rode steadily across the sands, as if he knew each grain by number.

Was that him calling to her? She set her black off again, the hoofs padding over the sand softly. As she turned again to watch the rider she saw his robes flying out behind. A white blur—they were coming fast, horse and rider.

"Stay where you are!"

She heard the command and the soft sound of the other mount, saw the magnificent white stallion. He was like a moving marble monument, unearthly. The snort from flaring nostrils and the toss of a flowing mane made him seem to instantly come alive.

"Where have I seen a horse such as this one? Not here, not in the Sahara, but somewhere else." Rosette's lips moved mutely as she questioned her remembrances of the past.

With the moon behind her, she couldn't know that her hair took on a coppery glow to the dark eyes watching her. She was looking at the glowing white figure with dark countenance and she did not know whether to feel secure in his coming or fear of him. Rosette decided it was certainly fear, for she felt a faint horror steal over her.

Closer now, his face was cast luminous beneath the moon, his eyes fiery coals. If there had been fire and steam, she would have thought him and his horse to be a two-headed dragon come to devour her.

"It is not safe for a woman to ride out alone." He stated this as a fact.

Her palms were suddenly slippery on the reins. Lifting her head, she could see other shadows not far behind him. "Bodyguards," he informed her. "They are always close by. You have good eyes."

"I — I . . ." she bit off.

His eyebrows, cast golden, rose as he coolly

asked, "Don't you remember anything? Nothing of the past?"

"No, I mean, not all."

"Come along, Rozelle, you must be ill and I insist you rest."

Rozelle? The frown deepened on her fine brow but she said nothing to that. "Bodyguards," she echoed him, trailing beside him meekly.

"Yes, you will never be in danger while in my company."

The sighing of the wind carved its mark on the sands, and she shuddered both inside and out. Her body felt like ripples in a pool after a stone had been tossed. Why hadn't she kept going? Was there no fight in her, or did she merely see the futility of trying to escape from such power?

What was happening to her? She barely knew this man who rode so commandingly a little ahead of her. Had she been foolish enough to believe herself in love with him? Somehow, it seemed she had.

She would have to take special care with her movements, Rosette decided urgently. This man was angered by her defiance, and he had called her Rozelle. Who was this other woman she was supposed to remember? Foggily, the picture in her mind showed a woman searching frantically for her whereabouts. Who?

The screens were removed from that remote part of her brain, and another woman had stepped in. Rozelle Modestia?

"Do you remember anything now?"

"Yes, you are Shareef here." That much she did know about this man beside her looking anything but concerned over her welfare. What had they been giving her to cloud her brain?

In the Riad Hadji stood waiting with Zarifa. Rosette felt much like a naughty child being returned home after having run away. Hadji stared straight through her it seemed.

"See to the matter," Shareef clipped to Hadji.

As if mesmerized by not Hadji but Shareef, Rosette stared at his fierce-looking apparel. He wore the white robe, and strapped to his left side hung the curved blade of the dagger of the Moors in its silver sheath. Her eyes leapt to the saddle where yet another fierce weapon hung, a firepiece, with silver weaving its fantastic patterns along the butt, the trigger guard, and wherever space afforded. She gulped. Just how angry had he been when he had been forced to go looking for her?

"Come with us, Rozelle," Hadji was saying. "We will take care of you now."

Hadji was solicitous. But Shareef turned on his booted heel, as if he washed his hands of anything further to do with her. He strode from them, leaving the young woman staring after him in shivering admiration and bemusement.

He surprised her by turning back, speaking

loud across the way. "We will not be parted again. Hear this well, you shall answer only to me. I am sheik here. I am your brother, your only living relative, your guardian. Heed my commands well, *sister!*"

"I am not," she hissed across to him, "not your bloody sister!"

Dark eyes clashed like thunderheads. "So," he drawled, "I am beginning to believe this — indeed now more than ever. I take back what I said earlier. No sister of mine would have acted so foolish and impertinent!"

With that, he disappeared inside.

Chapter Sixteen

After drinking the herbal tea Zarifa brought, Rosette found it impossible to make her body react to the signals her brain sent out.

Now Zarifa was bent over Rosette, who lay face down on the padded bench. She was not even surprised when Zarifa began to massage her, gently and soothingly. But Zarifa, having forgotten the henna, foolishly laid aside her task for another time.

Besides being moonstricken, Rosette was drained, emotionally and physically, and she welcomed the darkness that finally enveloped her. But she kept envisioning Hasan in the moonlight, compelling and manly. She slept soundly through the wee hours.

Dawn brought Rosette slowly awake. She stretched languidly, easing her aching muscles. Then she ceased all movement. As she recalled the night before, her abandoned behavior washing over her with embarrassment, her whole body trembled.

Had it all merely been a fanciful dream? Had she really raced away to try freedom across the moonlit sands? Oh! Even had it been a dream, why would she be trying to escape?

Rosette, her head rolling on the pillow, looked around her lavishly draped and appointed apartment, at its exotic coziness. But why would I want to escape from all this? I love it here, here at El Taj — with Hasan. Why had he appeared to be a stranger in her dream then?

Softly she gasped. If the night had been real, she could have been carried off by wandering nomads or desert bandits. That made her think of Hadji and his terse warnings. A profound curiosity was roused in her again. But she mentally cursed her memory. She might possibly have been mistaken, even as she tried to think hard on it now. The Frenchman. He had perhaps never met Hadji before, and his strange manner certainly might be due to some inexplicable cause. It seemed to her, though, that Monsieur Maudet must have met Hadji before, in some other setting, and that Hadji knew it. Maudet, somehow, seemed connected with Hadji.

But how could that be? she asked herself next. This must merely be her crazy imagination working overtime again.

Rosette scrambled to sit with her legs tucked beneath her. Her thoughts persisted. Maudet had lost his strange uneasiness while in the presence of Hadji, and Hadji met the Frenchman more than halfway to be friendly. What was there between the two of them? Had Hasan noticed this also? In what setting had she seen Hadji before? And the Frenchman?

Something treacherous was afoot. But what? *What?* Oh, she wished her mind would clear and be swept of the cobwebs so that she could think clearly.

"There is deception here," she said to herself. In what form and face she couldn't be sure.

At that moment Rosette felt that the words were true, horribly true. How much, she wondered, did this deception involve her? She was beginning to think very much.

That same day, to the utter surprise of Rosette, the party left El Taj, the Frenchman and the others with him. Before their departure, however, Maudet came to her apartment. He looked refreshed and recovered from his travel-weariness, ready to challenge the desert once again.

"Goodbye, mademoiselle."

She held out her hand. He took it with a gallant gesture, making her feel feminine and warm.

"Goodbye, Monsieur Maudet. It has been a pleasure," she said softly in return. Why was he leaving so soon? She wanted to ask, but something told her she need tread carefully where Maudet was concerned.

His pale green eyes watched her, as if in intense search. "I am so sorry that I've made such a foolish mistake."

She blinked fast, confused. "Mistake?"

"In thinking you — " he paused — "I made a mistake to think you would come away with me," he said, so softly, while she frowned. "Goodbye, and I shall return someday."

"Oh, will you?" she said, wondering why she did so.

"Yes, and thank you, and the Shareef — for the hospitality."

"You may thank me, monsieur, yourself."

It seemed to Rosette that the desert wind had brought Hasan al-Shareef into the chamber. Why did she suddenly feel faint? All clammy?

Below the turban, an eyebrow rose stiffly. "What is it, dear sister? You put your hand to your head. Is there an ache there?"

He surely did not sound concerned, but rather angry and clipped. "I — why, yes, suddenly I seem to have — to have developed a headache."

A long, uncomfortable moment passed finally.

Then Maudet, as if moved by an irresistible impulse, bent over Rosette's hand to place a warm kiss in her palm. He straightened, his hand dropped down against his side and, without another word or look, Pierre Maudet strode from the chamber.

"Roselle." Hasan's voice cut through her already taut nerves. "Do you know what that scene made come to mind?"

She faced Shareef with a terrible feeling that had begun to ravage her while he stood glaring at Pierre Maudet. The Shareef was jealous! Whether to be happy or sad over this revelation, she could not decide. And why, why was he staring at her so darkly now?

"What?" she innocently asked.

"That Monsieur Maudet hopes to see more of you—even plans and pines to."

"Perhaps," she returned airily. "It may be so. In fact, he did say he would return."

"He may even be in love with you. The look was in his eyes."

She faced him squarely now. "What look is that, Shareef?" For some reason she couldn't explain to herself, she felt odd saying his name this morning, and she used only the one, the other was too personal.

He looked at her. In his eyes loomed a piercing

wistfulness. He opened his mouth, but the words did not emerge. At that point Rosette felt he was on the point of telling her all that she longed to know.

But the look faded. His lips closed and he strode brusquely from the chamber. Suddenly scalding tears rushed to her eyes. Hasan, oh, Hasan . . .

But he had already gone out.

"I shall never drink that stuff of Hadji's again," she sniffed resolutely. "I want to know who I really am—and just what is going on around this . . . this bloody place!"

The next day was the same, the next, and still the next. A grimace crossed her lovely features, but she felt at the same time a certain form of pity when Hadji came in to beg.

Now he was turning angry. "Drink, Rozelle. The medicine is good for you. Drink!"

"I will do no such thing. Take it away!"

He gathered her wrists in one hand and started to pull her up from the cushions she had been reclining on when Hadji entered. "You are in no condition to argue with me, Rozelle Modestia!" he ground out.

Even though Hadji was inflicting some pain, she tossed her head in defiance, her cat's eyes glowing. "If it's an argument you want, you have it, Hadji-ben-Haroun!"

Two servants appeared just then, one bearing a meal on a tray, the other bearing a water jug. Hadji at once pressed her hand gently, after releasing her wrists. But she did not care if the others were present or not. She continued to glare at the much-perplexed man.

With the servants finally gone, Hadji pressed the offending glass into her hand and whined. "Drink it?"

"Oh, damn you!" she shouted, and stalked from her apartments.

Rosette discovered slowly, regaining her own will, that indeed she was being deceived. She began to wonder in this intrigue if Shareef was in on it too. In fact, he may very well be their leader in this. But soaring joy washed over Rosette as truth dawned.

"Shareef is not my brother!" She twirled in the filmy drapery she wore today, one that revealed, if one looked closely enough, her long, shapely legs and the dark shadow between.

"I knew it! Oh God, I just knew Hasan al-Shareef was not related to me!"

Now he would let her go, go back to whatever she'd been doing in her life before all this.

Rosette halted. But first, she told herself, first I must discover for myself why the deception.

Her drapery fluttering like gossamer wings, she raced from the chamber.

"I already know, Hadji. Enough time has passed for me to realize, without that medicinal brew, *who I really am*. My name is—" She faltered, pressing tapered fingers to her throbbing temples, as Hadji leaned forward expectantly. "I am Rosette—Rosette Forrest. My home is in England—and, oh, what have you done with L-Lucie?"

"Ah, I see you are angry. Please forgive me for upsetting you."

"Tell me why, Hadji? Why have you done this to me, this deception! And where is Lucie H-Higgins?"

"Ah, you remember well." He sighed. "I will explain."

The pain in Hadji's face made Rosette suddenly sorry for him, and her voice softened. "Please—go on, Hadji." Her almond eyes stared into his black ones.

"She, Rozelle Modestia, it is true, she died of a fever. She was under my care, as you are now. We were in Morocco, at Shareef's house there. She had been with her friends, some French, some English. She always liked to carry on, you see." He shrugged, and simply added, "The next day she was ill, burning like the desert sands." He would not say that she had been with Monsieur Maudet. For some reason, he was loathe to reveal what he did know of the man. This would be too dangerous to himself.

"And what did you do, Hadji?"

"Before I could send word to Shareef, Rozelle Modestia became unconscious — and withered right before my eyes, like a rose, consumed by heat." He sobbed raggedly then. "She died, my beautiful, spirited Rozelle."

"You loved her, too." Why should this cause a pain in the region of her own heart?

He nodded. "Everyone loved Rozelle — she was so full of life." He would not add "wild," either, though she had been.

Rosette stared but saw nothing. She tried picturing this young woman, so like herself in countenance. But all she could imagine was a lovely rose relentlessly snuffed out by flames.

"In her chamber of death there had been no flowers," Hadji was muttering, "no flowers, no lighted candles, no lips that moved in prayer. She could not pray —" And so the Frenchman did not pray, but only guarded her fiercely until he himself brought her away, to be buried, whatever, Hadji had no idea.

"Dead people do not pray," Rosette murmured, feeling sad for Shareef's sister. "The living pray for them," she added, with head bowed.

"This one time I could not pray," Hadji said

with solemn truth. He suddenly looked old and bowed. The two lines near his mouth were deep in grief.

Rosette did not know what to say or do next. In his eyes there remained a fixed expression of ferocious grief, as if he suffered from some dreadful misery and cursed himself for that suffering. He peeked up at her, slyly, then looked down.

"Hadji? What will you do now?" She could ask the same for herself, she thought.

The guilty look that had mingled with grief, that had been stamped upon all his features, vanished.

"You will not tell Shareef? Perhaps you will go away? Back to England? I will help you with the journey myself," he rushed on. "When Shareef goes to Morocco. I will see you gain your freedom. Is this not what you wish, Rosette Forrest?"

"When is my—when is Shareef going to Morocco?"

"Next week, on this day."

"He will still be angry and punish you, Hadji. When he returns and discovers I am gone. How will you manage to escape from his wrath unscathed?"

He moaned. "I do not know this." His legs unfolded and he came to his feet like an aged man. "I will go and think on it now."

As she moved restlessly about the apartment, she thought: I really want to remain right here at El Taj. But now that her mind had cleared even more she wondered how she could cherish and want to be with a man she did not know very well. Then, an idea formed in her mind, giving her brand new hope.

Here it was, a plan.

She found Hadji sitting cross-legged on his cushions in the Horm, meditating deeply. Only his black eyes moved to open as she quietly entered the place of asylum.

"Hadji, I have discovered the solution. For you at least."

"Yes?" He stirred only slightly.

"For now, I mean for a time, I wish to remain Rozelle Modestia." She grinned sheepishly. "What do you think?"

"For a time—and then?"

This was something Hadji himself had not considered. It had taken this bright young woman to bring it to light. The deception would have had to end one time or another, and soon.

She shrugged, saying, "Whatever is willed. *Incha'Allah.*"

"*Incha'Allah,*" Hadji repeated. "God willing, you will not be found out." But Hadji thought it already too late.

When she was gone, Hadji sped along the corridor, going in the opposite direction Rosette

Forrest had taken. He made his way to his apartment and hurriedly gathered all his possessions, concerned only with reaching his brother's before night fell in earnest.

What about Lucie? Rosette wondered sadly later that day. She went in search of Hadji once again. But he wasn't to be found in his chamber nor was he to be found in the Horm or in the garden when she searched these places next.

She was rushing about so madly that she bumped right into the one person she had no desire to see at the moment. Shareef was just returning from maneuvers in the desert. He held her at arm's length, studying intensely the excited flush of her dewy cheeks.

"What is my little flower up to?"

Rosette, who suddenly shied, trembled, and moved her lips nervously, saw that Shareef could not help himself as he stared hard at her.

There was a new womanliness awake in her, so intense with life, as if she had suddenly become aware of herself as a beautiful woman, he was noticing. She had been this before, he realized. But now there was a marked difference. His brow darkened as he thought of what had caused it. Pierre Maudet came to mind, like the rush of dark wings he wouldn't mind clipping with his trusty blade. Could the Frenchman have brought about this glowing, vibrant change in her?

Rosette saw his lean, handsome face distort

before her eyes. He looks feral, like a savage, she thought with some trepidation in her breast. Whatever the cause of his sudden anger, she decided it best to humor him in this.

"Hasan! Hadji has gotten me all excited!" Her eyes sparkled like a cat's in the dark. "He has been saying you are going to Morocco." She found his hand and tugged. "Please, oh please, take me with you?" Aha, her chance to be away from here, before it was too late and she lost her heart.

Shareef pulled his hand from her gentle grip. "Take you?" He shook his turbaned head. "That is out of the question."

"Why?" She bit her lip as her eyes beseeched him.

"Because I am going on business and will have no time to look after you. Besides, you have, ah, you have not been yourself since your last visit there. That may lie at the root of your illness. I think you will remain here, for a long time to come."

Oh, Lord, no! He couldn't mean that? Petulantly she whirled away. "I can take care of myself, Hasan, and I am not all that ill, as you think." She smiled to herself. "It was just that time of month, b-but it has passed now." With a different smile, she faced him again. "I have never felt better!"

"No." He stared away from her lovely face that

was flushed with excitement, and something else he didn't care for the looks of. "You will have to remain put this time, I'm afraid. Uh!" He reached out to silence her with a finger pressed to her lips. "I am firm in this, Rozelle. Do not question me again in this. Now, I must go and meet Tarek in my apartment. We have matters to discuss before my departure."

"When?" she asked without looking at him.

"A week from today." He took in the crestfallen look. Then a notion struck a sour note in him. "Is there someone special you wish to see in Morocco? Perhaps Monsieur Maudet is on his way there?"

How close he had come to the truth, he was to think later, much later.

She flushed wildly as she met his eyes. "What do you mean?"

The velvet green in his eyes narrowed; they traveled the length of her slender body wound in ash-rose drapery. He flushed at the dark shadow of femininity between her legs. He broke out in beads of sweat that immediately dotted his high forehead.

Rosette felt as if his hard fingers actually touched her body, though it was only his eyes that raked her as if of a will of their own while he fought with them to behave. Time hung suspended, quivering between them, gazes locked in a man-woman spell and struggle as old as time itself.

"I mean," he said, finally, with a guttural growl, "you wish to see him again. Don't you?" His eyes stared beyond her, it seemed to her.

She smiled secretly, and nodded, saying, "I wouldn't mind seeing Monsieur Maudet again. Does this bother you, Hasan?"

He laughed, but the sound was mirthless. "You may see whoever you wish, dear *sister*. As long as it is just a pleasant diversion, Rozelle, and nothing more serious than that."

Her eyes blinked wide. "You cannot protect me forever, Hasan!"

"No. But I can *love* you forever," he answered in a strange tone.

"I realize you love me, Hasan." She cleared her throat and smiled. "As a sister."

"Oh, that is just what you are, precious flower." He smiled tenderly. "A woman that I love very much."

She returned the smile, but she found the need to force it this time. If only you knew, Hasan, if only . . .

"Are you saying that you will choose my husband also?" she asked, wondering if they'd been over this all once before.

He stared off in the direction of his apartments. "Will I? Yes, and I shall choose the time, and the man."

He started to move away from her and she stepped up close to his back, staring at the long length that rippled with muscle beneath the thin shirt he wore. She shivered with the desire to touch him, but hadn't the nerve to do this.

"When is the time?" she asked Hasan.

"When that time comes we will both know it."

With that he continued to walk, with long strides along the garden path, heading toward the door leading to his apartments. Tarek, with his long, dark, somber face, stood there waiting impatiently.

Another stood above on the balcony, one that neither the Shareef nor Rosette had noticed. With a smile born of evil motive the eavesdropper moved back into the heavy folds of drapery.

Chapter Seventeen

The deliciously exotic fragrance was jasmine. Smelling the delectable scent on her glistening, clean skin, Rosette stepped up from the deep tub while Zarifa handed her a soft linen.

Rosette hugged herself. Her body tingled and glowed; she felt utterly feminine, sweet-smelling, her luxurious hair sparkling like liquid fire about her slim shoulders and arms. To dry her hair, another linen, orange and gold striped, was wrapped turban-style about her dark copper curls. Her eyes shone, the tawny depths like burnished gold.

"Here, Rozelle." Zarifa slipped a deep indigo

robe over Rosette's bareness, searching as she did this the lower curve of Rosette's bottom. She had to be sure to put the rose on the right cheek.

Zarifa hesitated a moment. A serious thing plagued her. Hadji did say right cheek, did he not? She shrugged, pretty certain she had heard right cheek.

Quietly and content, for now, Rosette climbed onto the cushioned table. Zarifa was going to give her a body rub with the musky oils. She remembered Zarifa doing this once before, when she had returned from the midnight ride in the desert. How foolish she had been, to think of it now.

"Mmm, that feels good . . . so wonderful, Zarifa."

The body massage was a replenisher to her spirits. Now Zarifa worked at her posterior, and Rosette murmured in sensual delight. Suddenly the woman stopped and boggled, with a gasp of surprise following.

"The rose!"

"Zarifa, why did you quit just when it was feeling so good? Rosette tried to see over her shoulder.

"You . . . are . . . *her!*"

"What?"

"You *are* Rozelle Modestia!"

"Oh that." Rosette rolled to her gentle hip, one full breast peeking with a dark-rose nipple from the crack in the robe. How could she even begin to explain to simple Zarifa? "No, Zarifa," she sighed and spoke, "I am *not* Rozelle Modestia. That is all a bad mistake. Nothing—"

"Ah! Ah!" Zarifa shook her turbaned head in vigorous actions. "Hadji has made a mistake!" She pointed to the perfect rose just beneath one cheek.

"I can't see what you are talking about. What is it?"

Rosette twisted this way and that, to no avail, for she could see nothing behind her on her person. Zarifa began to back away from the table, so distracted that she failed to hear the young woman try to explain.

"Hadji-ben-Haroun has made bad mistake," Zarifa persisted, her French twisted with Arabic. "You are not dead . . . a *ghost?*"

"Zarifa, I cannot understand what you are mumbling over. Just speak French, will you please?"

"I will go now," Zarifa did mutter in French.

"But you cannot! You are not finished with . . ."

"Hadji has brought back a *djinn!*"

"No, no, Zarifa!" Rosette then reverted to French. *"Non, non,* Zarifa, I am not a spirit, or—or a witch!"

Rosette turned to moaning in frustration. Oh, bloody damn! What now?

But Zarifa fled the chamber. Shamara, just behind a scarlet curtain near the door, tossed back her dark head and mocked with silent laughter. While Rosette rose from the table, disappointed and troubled to say the least, Shamara saw her chance and slipped from the chamber. Gleefully she spoke to her clever self:

"My Hasan Mark. He will never marry the Englishwoman now, and never know how he truly loves this witch. He will always believe her to be Rozelle Modestia. But I know better." Her voice pitched lower than the hiss of a snake. "I know who she really is. It is no wonder they were both named after the rose: one on the left, one on the right."

Standing in the same place, the robe gaping, Rosette blinked and frowned after Zaifa's hasty exit. Her gaze then fell to the henna paste on the floor and her puzzlement continued to grow. She drew close to the table. Had Zarifa meant to use it on her? But where? She bent to retrieve it, staring down bemusedly at the auburn stuff.

"Egyptian women used this long ago to color their hands and feet. Surely Zarifa hadn't meant to—" Rosette shook her head, unmindful that her robe had slipped even further to bare the tip of a peaked nipple.

This was how the sheik found her. He swept in and halted, his robe fluttering, his velvet dark eyes riveted to one thing, and only one. He cleared his throat to announce his presence and Rosette at once caught where his hot gaze rested. She swiftly concealed the bare breast and flushed from head to foot.

Now Shareef continued as he had intended, to search for the cause of Zarifa's strange behavior. He came to tower over Rosette. Manfully compelling, his eyes darkened until the obscure green was almost black.

"Did you beat the servant?"

"M-Me?" Rosette blinked up at the grimly set visage in confusion. Then she realized what he had said. She made a disastrous mistake then. "I would never strike a servant. Never," she said in perfect, musical French.

"Say that again," he slowly rapped out, staring at her hard.

"I would never—" Rosette realized her brash mistake too late and gulped hard.

"You speak French."

"I—I . . ." She hung her head. *"Oui."*

He fixed his eyes on her mouth, as if daring her to do so again.

Rosette could not for the life of her think of one single word to assert as fact that she was indeed his kin. Besides, she disliked even the thought of becoming a bald-faced liar. Yet, under the circumstances she had to do something, say something. It was too soon to reveal her true identity. She needed more time to get to know him better for her plan of escape to succeed. To get to know the real person, without the drugging potion in her. She had to get to know the *man,* not the *sheik.*

Dear God, help me, Rosette cried inwardly in prayer.

The strength to stand up beneath Shareef's steady gaze without wavering an inch was swiftly washing away. "I—I don't know too much French. J-just a little. I learned it while—"

"While you were with Pierre Maudet, no doubt." A smirk twisted his lips momentarily, then vanished.

She breathed easier, with an inner sigh of relief. "Why yes! How did you know?"

He avoided that question and posed one of his own. "What do you have there in your hand?" He watched her display the henna in her smooth palm.

"Get rid of it. Your fair complexion looks best without it." He reached out to brush her hand.

"Of course. I remember. Zarifa must have dropped it in her haste. I could not begin to tell you what was troubling that woman," she said truthfully.

Her hand shook as it left his outstretched one to place the jar on the cushion. His arm fell back to his side and she stared down to avoid his eyes that kept studying her in close proximity.

"Come, Rozelle." He gestured with a sweeping

hand toward the sofa upholstered in blue velvet, strewn with myriad colored pillows. "Rub your hair with the towel and I shall then brush it for you." He smiled mysteriously, adding, "Like I used to. Remember?"

"Yes-Yes, I — I do." she gulped.

Rosette could scarcely credit a scene with him brushing her hair. She turned her back on his eyes which, as she rubbed her hair the rest of the way dry, bored into her with a heat she could almost feel. Then, in her robe, she sat as he had asked and he came up silently from behind, a brush from the table in his hand.

"Am I hurting you?" he inquired after several strokes tugged down through the auburn length of the coppery, up-curling ends.

"No-No. It feels good, Hasan."

Rosette stared down at her hands, meaning every word she had said.

"Just like it used to?"

A short silence ensued before she finally answered yes. Anxiously she began to stare down at the exotic swirls in the carpet. Her heart hammered hard as she wondered what he would do next. She strove to ignore the desire which, throbbing through her veins along with a delicious lassitude, spread through her blood and limbs. Rosette's mind cried out: I do not want this feeling! It will only hurt me!

Green flames flickered and gleamed between

Shareef's thick lashes. He paused and frowned, where she couldn't see him. "Rozelle Modestia," the name was a savage hiss from his sensuous lips.

"Yes?"

Rosette felt herself tensing at the derisive tone in his voice. She twisted about to see his dark face, curious over what he was thinking. But his eyes were fathomless now and — was it danger she saw lurking there? A threat? Quickly she looked away.

"Little sister."

Long, cool fingers touched her nape and then executed a fiery trail along the slope of her shoulder, drawing the length of her hair aside with the other hand. Rosette's gaze skittered across the carpet and, her eyes darting to the huge, pillow-strewn bed in the corner, widened in shock. Eyes returning, they then fell to his dark hand resting firmly on her shoulder, and she realized the desperate need in her to touch him. Not yet, she told herself, you need more time. What am I saying? Why is he acting so strange? Why is he touching me like this?

"I had wanted no repetition of similar circumstances," he began deeply, "of that night I came close to making love to you. Recall, dear sister?"

Her eyes flew wide. *Had* wanted? Didn't he *still* want no repetition? He was beginning to excite and frighten her both at the same time. His touch, so tender yet savage, made her think of warm sand beneath the desert sun and now, now the pressure of his hands on her changed subtly. There did not seem to be an inch of her that was not on fire. A gasp tore from her when the fingers and his right hand slipped briskly beneath her robe.

"This is what you want, what you desire, is it not?" he rasped in her ear.

"It — it is wrong," she stammered out.

"Ah, but you did not think so before. In fact, you did not even care whether we were related — or not," he said the latter with emphasis.

"Or — " she swallowed hard — "or not?"

"That is precisely what I just said, *Rozelle*. Or not."

He alarmed her further by sliding over to cup a swollen breast. "Shareef, don't do that!"

It was a plea for mercy, but he held fast. When she began to struggle, his fingers grew bolder by squeezing a taut peak. Her head rolled back and met with his hard chest, and he captured her there, his other hand cupped beneath her chin. There was nothing she could do; he held her captive like a spider does an unsuspecting fly.

"Please," she whimpered, "don't do this to me. I — I was wrong, Shareef. You were right, we should not have become so . . . so . . ."

"Intimate," he sneered into her small, shell-like ear. He stared down as she looked up at him pleadingly. "What is it you beg me for, *my sister?* To make love to you? To leave you be?"

His fingers grew much bolder, and Rosette made a sound that was half whimper and half gasp. He held her prisoner by one globe of her heated flesh. "Let me go, please, Shareef!"

"Do you not still desire me, Rozelle? What has happened to change all that?"

"N-Nothing, Shareef—I mean—"

"So it is Shareef now?"

Her heart beat so furiously in her chest that her hands clasped a fold of her robe as if it could slow her heartbeat and offer her the protection she so sorely needed. What was wrong with her? Is this not what she wanted, to be kissed and fondled by Shareef? No, she told herself vehemently, not like this.

They gazed into each other's eyes as intently as on the day when the sheik had entered the tent following the sandstorm.

"Was it so foolish of me to believe that it was your heart which spoke when you said the words 'I love you'?" Swiftly he swept aside her robe.

His breath caught raggedly, seeing her for the first time in all her unbridled beauty and charm. Then, eye looked into eye, questing, with passion unleashed. But she jerked the robe over her nakedness, closing herself from his leering face.

"Oh," she breathed, "you are wicked indeed!"

"So, you did not judge me thus because of the

hunger I have concealed in my heart before! Is it not better to display my passion openly? But, no, you seem to think otherwise, my precious!"

Dark amber lashes slowly closed over her eyes, but only for a moment to shut out this sheik of sultry moods. She could not find a suitable answer, for her confusion reigned. What is he up to? What is this dangerous game he plays? And why?

"Yes," he murmured, "words are so very often of little use." His tone was little above a whisper. "My precious desert flower. It is time we became more intimate. I have watched you and wanted you for a long time." He swooped her unceremoniously up into his brawny arms, ready to bear her to the downy bed. "Have you any fear of the consequences now? As you did not before?"

But you are *not* my brother, don't you see? she wanted to scream at his head. She held her tongue on that and answered, "Such as?"

"Well," he chuckled derisively. "You are my flesh and blood. . . ." He let it hang.

"I am your sister," she lied, frightened of him now more than ever. Danger hovered, coming even closer. She dared not let on she was other than his sister. She had to play this game out, no matter who the winner might be. He had altered his countenance so alarmingly and she didn't like the man he was now. He must not learn they truly were not related.

"Do you love me?" Shareef asked her suddenly.

"Yes, of course." She bit her lip as soon as the words emerged.

"Then there must be no delay. We must make love at once. It is as I wish also."

She kicked out and, connecting with his shin, struck backwards and put an obstacle in his way. He stopped to growl low in pain. With a courage she was far from feeling, she shouted at him, "I do *not* wish this scene! You bloody devil of a sheik!"

"By God, woman!" he cried angrily. "You will be taught a lesson and must know that the flouting of my wishes is a dangerous pastime!"

The hot blaze of anger in his words did not seem to disturb her too seriously, for she watched everything he did with her misty cat eyes. Watched his arms ripple as he laid her on the pillow-strewn bed; watched him leave to remove his robe, leaving only his thin *serrouelles* encasing his long legs; watched him begin to unwind his blue turban and then think better of it.

"Your skin is—" She halted, staring up at him in puzzlement.

"Not dark all over," he finished, with a white grin.

Her riveting gaze went down his chest, over the smooth mounds of muscle and golden hair thick and crisp. Here and there white scars stood out, some deep and some long, but mostly they appeared to be stab wounds. Her breath caught. He was like some fierce, battle-scarred viking lord of old. His skin was as fair as her own! Then, lower, the golden fleece trailing down, down, and once she caught a glimpse of his protruding strength, the beauty of his maleness standing out in readiness, she gulped. However, Rosette caught no more than a fleeting glimpse, for she leapt from the bed in a rush with a look of complete terror riding her heart-shaped face, holding up her hands to keep him at bay.

"No, Hasan! You must not touch me—remember you said this yourself not long ago! It is wickedly wrong!"

She quickly tossed on the robe she had dragged with her. He chuckled and was after her in a flash. Rosette pummeled him on the muscled caps of his shoulders until he hastily tossed her back onto the bed, as if she were no more than a sack of flour. He fell to the already mussed bed to straddle her at once, beginning once again to peel the robe from her. He looked at her with unconcealed passion in his eyes, a green as soft velvet now. The verdant color stunned her and she caught her panting breath in her throat.

"You will never catch yourself a husband, my precious. Not as you are now, as cold as winter."

He grinned down at her gaping mouth. He nodded.

"B-But . . ."

"No buts. Just be still!" he growled with a guttural sound.

She thought fast then. "It is little you know, Hasan al-Shareef! For I can have my pick of men, and I've been asked plenty of times!" Thank God she remembered some of what Hadji had informed her of concerning Rozelle Modestia.

"Ah, you strive to bring my anger to the fore, thinking I shall give you a pat on your pretty behind and release you?" He chuckled deeply, a rich timbre to his laugh.

She stared, sinking, her almond eyes darkening to burnished gold. He was wearing that smirk, the one in which it was easy to read both malice and triumph. What did he have in store for her? How much did he actually know? Was he merely playing cat and mouse with her?

"B-but you *will* release me?" she asked.

"It is a matter of which—" he smiled, shrugging—"hmmm, to which I must give some very serious thought."

"Seriously?"

"Indeed." He lowered his head, a frown falling over his brow. "And now, my precious rose, a kiss."

His lips merely brushed hers in the whisper of a kiss. "Sweet, my love. We have plenty of time, as there's no rush."

Silently she hated him for his mocking smile and manner. Oh! Shock went racing through her then. Why hadn't it occurred to her until this very moment as they lay half naked, his body pressed boldly against her hip.

"Oh . . . you know!"

"Know what?" Shareef pretended ignorance. Then he stared narrowly at the stark white and very frightened face below him. "Would this matter all that much if I did? Do you think the truth would hold me back? Wild horses couldn't — "

"B-but there would not be much point in ravishing me, w-would there? I mean, Shareef, Hasan, I shall not give in to you," she ended with steely determination.

"Rape?" He snorted as if he found this incredible and incongruous. "You can calm yourself, my precious. You jump to all the wrong conclusions. I've no intention of going to such, uhmm, drastic measures. I never have." He caught himself then, recalling the captives he'd taken as a lad. He went on, "Ahh, you must learn to not take everything I do or say so seriously."

He smiled wickedly at her puzzlement.

"B-but you *have* undressed me!"

Rosette shivered from the ruthless hardness of his body so taut with urgency against her own softer frame. Her own desire frightened her more than she admitted to herself, for she didn't know how long she could hold out. She had never felt quite this way before. Nothing in her life had prepared her for the dangerous position she found herself in now. The game of love was suddenly not so . . . *love?* She caught herself. I have played this game before, been this way with another. Yes, and she was not having any more of the suffering! Perry Marland, he had hurt her. She had vowed to never fall in love again! But had she truly been in love back then with Perry? No, she did not think so now. Compared with this man, this sheik, Perry could be called a callow youth!

Shareef shook Rosette, grasping her back from her reverie as he drawled cruelly, "I repeat, *Rozelle,* it is time we became better acquainted."

He called her Rozelle again. Then he did not know? she wondered. He must be very base to continue this, this—otherwise he would have quit this game long ago. Was he still toying with her? Or was he merely angry with his "sister" for some reason, perhaps because she hadn't relented to having him choose her a husband?

Her nails bit into his shoulders, then. "Hasan! I've had enough of this silly game. I wish for you to let me go now. I am not sure that I love you anymore, for you have become horribly wicked!"

He swore nastily, rising from the bed and taking a satin pillow with him in the shape of a leaf.

She gaped. When had he removed his trousers! Rosette began to giggle and could not stop for the life of her. She pointed to the green pillow, holding her belly to keep it from aching. "You look just like Adam in the Garden of Eden!"

Shareef peered down at himself, frowning darkly. Glowering, he gazed into her laughing eyes alight with sparkles of gold. "So, you were there with him I take it?"

"Adam?" She tossed her head impishly. "Of course, all us women were there, silly!" She giggled behind her hand.

Alarm shot through her next for, laughter abruptly discarded, he came upon her in a rush, bending a knee upon the bed and taking her roughly by the shoulders.

"Where is my sister? Tell me or I shall have the living daylights beat out of you!"

"She is d-dead!" Rosette cried out as he bit cruelly into her flesh with steely fingers.

"You lie!" He shook her until her teeth rattled. "Who is in on it? Hadji? Perhaps his son, Tarek, also?"

"T-Tarek?" She blinked into his furious face.

"Tarek, I'm sure you realize by now, is one of my deputies, one of the less trusted I've lately discovered. He is qualified to take over as chieftain."

"H-he is more qualified than *you?*"

"Of course, you silly nit. Arab blood runs in

230

his veins. He is next in line should I come to, uhmm, a fatal accident. It is Hadji who would love to see his son as chieftain here. I knew, really, I should never have trusted the man!" He turned on her again after looking aside in a vacant stare. "Who are you? Answer me!" He shook her again and stared, hypnotized, as the auburn curls, so like Rozelle's, tumbled about her shoulders and breasts. "Have they done away with Rozelle? Am I next in line in this deception?" He groaned painfully then. "Is she, my only flesh and blood, really dead?"

"I—I am not so sure now. Hadji had drugged me. Oh," she sobbed, "I am so confused. I just want to go home to England!"

She gaped at him then.

"England?" both said at the same time in surprise.

Now it was Shareef's turn to be confused.

Rozelle had always said this, that she wanted to return to England where Oakhill Manor awaited the Rawens should they ever want to return there. The lands were still in the Rawen name, of course.

His voice gentled now. "When were you drugged? Do you remember?"

"First?" She waited for his nod before going on. "I—I think it was in Tangier." She shrugged helplessly.

"But that is where Rozelle went for a visit." His

231

gaze traveled the length of her then, coming to rest on the quivering white hips. "Turn over," he ordered.

"What?"

"I want to see if it is there." He began to roll her onto her stomach, but she gave him token resistance. "The rose."

"Zarifa said this also. What is there to see?"

Unceremoniously he flipped her onto her belly. He groaned then. "My lord, you *have* been drugged. The rose is indeed here." He gathered her up into his arms. "I am sorry, Rozelle, so sorry, little sister for mistrusting you!" He stroked her head gently. "Thinking you another, I wanted nothing but to hurt you, frightened you into confession."

Wide-eyed with wonder and fright, Rosette clung to him fiercely, needing something to hold onto at the moment. Dear God, *I have a rose!* What am I to do now? Who would ever believe her to be Rosette Forrest now? Worse yet, who had given her the rose? Or had she always had one?

She suddenly owned no illusions as to her own fate. She was to be held in bondage, bittersweet, maybe forever, with the man she had loved when first she laid eyes on him, despite her stupor. But now that she had experienced his cruel nature, had been the object of his devastating hatred, could she continue to love this man, this terrible sheik of El Taj? She shivered inside. *I do not want to love any man!*

If Rozelle Modestia had been murdered, then who was next in line? There must be a dangerous conspiracy going on here, and her only course of action was to escape. Love again had become her own worst enemy.

"I will never love again," she vowed mutely, vowed as she had what seemed an eternity ago. *"Never!"*

Chapter Eighteen

Morning dawned in a shower of desert radiance. The platinum glow seemed to invade every crevice and corner of the kasbah. But Rosette put it down to a feeling that was inside herself. A dangerous feeling she acknowledged, that needed to be escaped from.

Rosette could not long endure much more of the menacing intrigue here at the kasbah. She had to escape.

Rosette walked the length of the chamber, up and down the many carpets that decorated the marble floors. Would Shareef allow her to go without an argument? Seriously she doubted this. How could she steal away then without him noticing? He had the eyes of many watching and patrolling at every hour of the day.

Rosette gave this difficulty some very serious consideration. That part of her mind which made important decisions in life was yet misty and dim.

With pert chin in hand she mulled this over. At last the solution arrived! Disguise! To ride out in disguise, garbed as one of the young boys who every day rode out with supplies intended for Shareef's tents.

Rosette stood to ready herself for the day. Who could she confide in, to help her escape? Who wanted her away from El Taj and wouldn't balk at any obstacles? Her answer came almost too quickly. Shamara. All Rosette needed now was to overcome the language barrier that stood between them.

Zarifa stood wringing her hands, peering this way and that along the corridors as the two young women stealthily hastened into the apartment Shamara shared with three other concubines. With the door closed securely, Shamara whirled to face Zarifa in a colorful flurry of sensuous drapery.

"Tell her she must wait here. The other girls will stay away, and she will be alone," Shamara addressed Zarifa, but studied the fair one's face for signs of treachery. Shamara saw none, only the lovely face alive with the desperate need to escape.

"I will bring the boy costume to her," Zarifa added.

Employing French, Zarifa translated. Who Zarifa feared more, Shamara or Hadji, she couldn't say. But Hadji had vanished not too long ago, and this young concubine and her new lover, Tarek, seemed to be slowly taking over El Taj. Zarifa was much too afraid to bring this news to Shareef. His mood had been ominously dark the past few days; he sat now in his apartment imbibing rich, potent wine. What was El Taj coming to? Zarifa worried.

Rosette nodded vigorously to each softly spoken order that Shamara issued. There was a savage gleam in the young Berber's dark eyes and Rosette put it down to Shamara's joy in being able at last to have Hasan all to herself, without the hindrance of another young woman who took up any spare time the Shareef might have.

Much to Rosette's surprise, Shamara leaned forward to give her a brief, sisterly hug and then was gone.

Night shadows deepened and footfalls slowed in the corridors until they ceased altogether. Rosette had munched on nothing but fruit for hours and lazed about on colorful silk cushions and jasmine-scented pillows. A sensuous air, exotic in flavor, hovered all about, even to invade Rosette's senses. She rolled onto her belly and laughed softly. There was nothing to become excited about, not at a time like this!

With all the fruit and mint tea she had consumed laying heavy in her stomach, Rosette soon grew drowsy. Her eyelids fluttered and then closed against the warm, exotic setting.

Was she dreaming?

Lips were moving over her face, warm hands exploring her waist and caressing her back. Then it hit her. Liquor fumes wafted in the warm night air.

"Ah, you are lovely . . . so lovely. Where've you been hiding?"

Before Rosette realized his intent, Hasan seized her by the shoulders and pulled her passionately against him. Her lips were smothered by the descent of his, hard, bruising, and possessing without tenderness or mercy. As Hasan's arms crushed her to him, Rosette's heart began to thud. He thought she was Shamara! He greedily kissed her lips, and instinctively her hands went up, but he only brought her breasts closer to curve her body taut against his own muscular length.

Rosette was about to protest, but to speak might give herself away. When Hasan's kiss lowered again and deepened this time, she yielded and melted as though it was his right to devour them to the fullest measure.

"Ah," he moaned gutturally, his voice thick with wine, "you are lovely to kiss — whoever you are?" He tried to see her in the dark. "Shamara? Is it you?"

He did not give her a chance to answer. One female was as good as another, she guessed. Rosette felt as though she were drowning in the sheer male power of his passionate kisses as they continued. Melting, she was conscious of the hardness of his cheekbones. He sensed the yielding, and his hands moved more caressingly, one raking through her heavy, rich weight of hair, the other moving to stroke the bare shoulder beneath her robe. He seemed to be drawing her very self into him, deepening the kiss he gave until her entire being was dissolving in a molten heat of desire. Whirling in a fiery tumult, she slowly began to submit to his increasing physical domination of her body. Beneath these primitive forces, his gently forceful kisses soon had her gasping for one tiny breath, but still he didn't cease. He seemed to be caught up in something beyond his own man's desire as his hands found the circle of her breast, with only the short bodice covering them, and he molded, stroked, exciting her senses beyond endurance.

"No!"

Rosette gasped, shocked awake at the pulsating contact of Hasan's hard fingers. She had been so sure he would have passed out by now after the great amount of wine he had drunk. He *should* have. But no, his ardor only grew apace, while she became increasingly aware of her innocence. She panicked, but her muffled protest was lost yet again beneath the firm pressure of his crisp lips and the strange power he wielded over her, even in his state of inebriation. She feared that if she yanked away from his tormenting fingers he would become further excited, and decided instead to let him have his way. Soon he must surely pass out, she thought naively.

The preliminary act continued to plunder and rape her senses, and Rosette was not so confident any longer. He began to arouse her now with a deliberate, inexorable slowness. This could not be happening, not yet, but her ragged breathing attested to this intense pleasure with a betraying sigh from her lips. She writhed helplessly, but his arms only encircled her waist, and he bent his legs slightly to fit their bodies closer together. His guttural groan as a mingling of conquest and yearning.

"How I want . . . want you," he mumbled brokenly.

Rosette stirred against him. "Not now," she begged, "not yet — please."

"Not now?" He chuckled low. "Even if I wanted to, I could not halt this now. I must have you."

"I — I am not ready!"

As soon as the words were out, she was forced backward onto the cushions of the sofa. He meant to make her ready. Through the flimsy fabric of her outfit she felt his muscled ribs against her breasts and the hard muscle between his legs pressing into her bare thighs. She continued to struggle with a desire to wind her arms about his neck, to cling to him. Again his lips moved to capture hers, but this time he parted them wide. Their sweat-slicked bodies were one, it seemed, and she experienced a deep, pulsing start inside. It was a hot sweetness and, like a blade, it pierced.

"No . . ." Rosette cried against his invading mouth, even though this primitive need ached through her. "Let me go for a time — please."

He seemed not to hear her begging him in his befuddled state, and exerted a pressure over her will that she could not fight. A shudder of pleasure-pain left her throat as his encroaching hand found and caressed a round globe that now swelled, the nipple rising beneath his finger tips. His kisses continued to possess, his tongue to plunder her soft mouth, stabbing deeply. Next he explored her hips and thighs, his burning touch bringing a gasp that tore shudderingly from her parted lips.

"Perfect," he rasped, "you are perfect — a goddess born to love."

His mouth curved against her lips as he spoke the words.

A sweet, sweet ecstasy claimed her at his increasingly intimate caresses, and she was foggily aware of how much she wanted Hasan to totally possess her. It is too soon, her mind raged while her traitorous body wanted to continue and furthermore have him complete this act. His strength was too great for her to ward off the inevitable. If he didn't pass out soon, Rosette knew he would certainly have his way. Then, she remembered earlier words, from him, a promise as to his actions. Somehow, she wrenched her mouth from his long enough to say what she needed to.

"You would not rape me?" she boldly asked, unconsciously making it sound something close to a challenge.

"Why should I?" he murmured thickly, pursuing her lips. "Why, when you already open your sweet thighs to me?"

Rosette snatched her face aside. The blood

thundered like a powerful waterfall in her ears when she realized he was correct. Her thighs were indeed yielding and shockingly eager. She tensed them now, determined to permit no entry.

"There is a first time for everything in a man's life," he threatened. "Say your name now so that I might speak it as I love you. Shamara? No, I think . . . not." He sighed deeply before rambling on. "Akila? Zanaide? Jamila?"

"No, no," she said, stung by jealousy. "None of . . . ah, yes, I am —" she bit her lip thinking of which one to choose — "Jamila, I am she."

"Ah." He chuckled. "I thought so. I dare say, Jamila, your body is lovelier, far, far more exquisite than I remembered it to be."

Oh, blast him! Rosette could just imagine him grinning stupidly from ear to ear. Well, *you besotted fool,* she pursed her lips in the dark, her mind steaming. She would show this sheik that Jamila had never been so good. Jamila had never been like this before! Before he passed out, Rosette planned to give him a taste of what a real woman was like. Poor Jamila! After I have gone from this place, Hasan shall forever be in hot pursuit of that concubine — for that is what Jamila surely must be.

"Hasan, my lord," Rosette began sweetly, throatily. "Do not be so hasty, my love, *kiss* me and *caress* me longer, hmmm, and then you may have your way with me."

I shall outfox the fox, Rosette smiled to herself in the dark. .

Convulsed with low chuckles, Hasan drew his head far back. "May have you? May? I shall, Jamila, before this hour is past. But first, it will be as you shay . . . say. I have already waited out the pain — " he sighed — "and a while longer shall not torment me overmuch. Come then, Jamila, and kiss me in your turn, as only you know — " hiccup — "how."

Of their own accord, on demand, Rosette's tender lips searched with a true yearning for his that shocked her. His laughter died, leaving only a trace of a rumble in his heaving chest. The familiar hunger rose in her again, to swamp her common sense. She was playing with passion's fire, she knew. He no longer needed to hold her tightly, and had shifted to place her on top. Now she was pressed all the way to him, her hands of their own accord moving to restlessly clasp about his neck. The hair was crisp and thick there, but she never stopped to realize he had removed his turban long ago. His mouth opened, returning her kiss passionately, Hasan tutoring, Rosette learning to give and give. Instinctively she rolled her hips in sensuous movements, and the upsurge of his own ground into hers.

"This is — is certainly a surprise," he growled,

cupping the side of he neck where moist tendrils coiled about his finger tips. He could feel the pulse that throbbed madly there, but his mind was on more pressing matters.

His warm, hard muscle lifted intimately against her, straining to get closer to the softest, tenderest part of her thighs. Now his hands came up to seek out her hips, her waist, up, up to her petal-soft breasts. His knee forced entry between her legs, the strength of his abundant manhood a fiery heat against her softest female flesh. Suddenly Rosette was not so confident of outfoxing Hasan. He had proved to be bold and demanding, even though she thought to have the upper hand and satiate him, enough to send him into a stupor. Then she planned to leave him quietly to sleep the night off in Shamara's room. But now . . . now I must hurry, she told herself, soon they will come for me to escape. Go to sleep, damn you! she wanted to scream at his besotted head.

"You are intoxicating," he mumbled against her silken throat.

As if he were not drunk enough! her mind flared and she gasped as he searched with the blunt staff where she was softest. The circles of her round breasts were crushed achingly against his steely hardness. But only for a moment before he impatiently lifted her to remove the gossamer bits of clothing, yanking the whole with one hand. He twisted aside to begin shrugging out of his own, but his baggy trousers gave resistance.

"Jamila . . . I am so hot for you . . . could you—damnation!"

"No!"

She'd had enough of this game. In the next moment she could tell she'd made a fateful mistake; he was angered further as he ground out the words between his clenched teeth.

"No! Hah! We shall see about that! Your teasing slut game is over, Jamila, and I will have you now!"

As both garments, hers rent in two, were cast to the floor, she saw her chance to escape. He could never catch her as befuddled as he was. It was now or never! She attempted to roll away.

"Hasan, I—I was only playing a g-game. L-let me go!" A tiny sob swelled from her throat.

"Game!" he choked and thundered as he flipped her once again, unceremoniously, onto her back. "Bitch! We'll play the game, but my way, now."

She held back, protecting and shielding her secret place with both splayed hands, but he mounted he expertly, unsheathing his rigid muscle.

"I—cannot, Hasan!" she cried softly, then louder, "I cannot go through with it! You see I am not who you think, and besides, I am a . . ."

But she never finished. The pressing weight of his strong man's body fully pinned her down; that scorching boldness probed, gently at first, and then he started to enter her tightness slowly.

"What?" he said, puzzled as the resisting flesh.

"Hasan!"

Now a searing, bittersweet pain exploded in her as he plunged deep within, breaking all barriers. His lips muffled the cry that whimpered from her. But it was not from pain, but a shocking pleasure she could never have imagined. He changed his pace, and began to move slowly once again, inside her fully this time. Her pleasure rose, and he kissed her delicately until the burning flame of fullness didn't ache anymore. He quickened his pace and she began to respond, each thrust bringing her higher until she experienced a level of pleasure she never knew existed. Now she not only squirmed but arched as she climbed the ecstatic mount higher and higher yet. Her eyes flew open and, lost in the abandonment of passion's joys, she cried out his name, again and yet again. His movements increased in speed and in intensity of thrust, and hers also increased, naturally, womanly, her whole body attempting with every move to heighten the exquisite sensations she was experiencing within. All sensation rose further as her pelvis tipped upward to obtain as much penetration from the driving shaft as possible. Before, her body had possessed a great longing she could put no name to. Now she knew what it was as it struck, and together they soared to that effusion of mind, soul and body. Her whole body suddenly plunged into a series of muscular spasms, shaking her with waves of the greatest excruciating pleasure. She tossed back her head as the fiery storm released and thrilled her deepest hidden recesses. Gentle, soft, and delicate as down, they returned from heaven to earth.

Silently Hasan took back what he had called her. Not a bitch was she but an angel—Jamila—he now loved the mere sound of her name in his head, befuddled as it was.

The sensuous storm was followed by a state of utter calm, her body feeling absolutely quiescent. She held him close, breathing in the clean, manly scent of his hair, lingering tenderly in the now-subdued glow of their passion.

Rolling with a deep, satisfied groan to his side, Hasan murmured his exhaustion and fell at once into a deep, blissful slumber, his big arm wrapped possessively about Rosette's slim waist.

After he left her, rolling to his side, Rosette cautiously slipped from the pillow-mussed couch. She moved so as not to awaken him. Hah, the man was already in another world, dreamless and deep.

"Ah, so you have finally left me, Hasan, my

sheik." Hands cocked on her hips after snatching up her robe, she added softly, "If you remember this night — " she retrieved too the slippery outfit she'd worn — "it will be a miracle, my sheik."

She turned swiftly toward sounds waking in the corridor. "But now I must leave you," she said and moved like a lovely wraith in the night.

Chapter Nineteen

Hasan al-Shareef was in a flying rage. He was worn to a thread, his mouth tasted as if a whole Arab army had camped within, and an excruciating headache had split his handsome skull asunder.

The older man just stood back shaking his head with pity for the young sheik who held his head as if it were fashioned of delicate dove eggs soon ready for the hatching.

Hasan shot quickly to his feet, as if he'd just remembered something. "Well, did you find Jamila for me, Samein?"

"She is nowhere to be found, my lord." Samein

shrugged his wiry frame. "The females I have questioned say Jamila left here months ago, to go live with another tribe where she was to have become the wife of Ibn Alasid."

"By whose orders was Jamila free to leave?" Hasan asked tersely.

"First she was captured by Ibn Alasid. Then when she discovered she loved him after escaping and returning here, she ran away to him." He nodded and shook his head. "Jamila was a strange girl."

"Yes, most females are," Hasan said ruminatively. Then he tossed his hands high in the air. "If you knew all this, then why did you go in search of Jamila for me?"

"The girl could have returned again, my lord, for all I had knowledge of. You said yourself the one you sought went by the name Jamila. There are many females here, and it is hard to keep track of all their comings and goings. You yourself have sent many away, as many as you have brought here." Samein grinned. "Jamila was a very restless concubine. At first she did not know her own heart; not many of them do."

Hasan cursed and grimaced over many things, besides his sore head. "Now it seems that Jamila does know." He sat thoughtful for a minute, then said, "Bring Shamara to me." He frowned at what he'd said. "On second thought, forget it.

Bring instead all my concubines and line them up here before me."

A half an hour later the women were there, all shy smiles and prettily flushed faces. The years had passed, but many of them had waited and pined away in hope that they would be chosen by the handsome sheik for a night or two. They postured and flirted with the sheik, each one trying to outdo the others. He strode up and down the line, lifted a chin here and there, and sometimes gazed deeply into warm brown or black eyes as he searched for some sign of recognition in not only his mind's eye but from one woman in particular. Frustration reigned, for each and every one seemed to be remembering nights of passion shared.

"Jamila," he said, his eyes scanning the line of pretty faces for a reaction, any reaction at all. All he received for his effort was pouts, all disappointed when he said the name of the absent one.

"Take them away," he ordered, waving his robe-draped arm as he sank into deep, black cushions. With his chin resting upon one wrist, he frowned. "Jamila . . . damn!" Who had been the passionate female that had deceived him? "Samein!" he thundered.

"Yes, I have returned, my lord. What is your wish now?" he wondered out loud, with something close to disappointment. He would rather that the sheik spoke to him of affairs other than searching out a woman. Like asking his advice on the constant thievery of their supplies, or which English or French had destroyed their waterholes, by being careless. But Hasan al-Shareef had never killed any of these, only frightened them off with a scare that would curdle any English or French blood.

Hasan rose again. Physically he was feeling much better, though his frustration boiled over. He looked no worse for wear. He had changed into buff trousers and a cream-colored, long-sleeved tunic in the last few minutes. Amid his frustration, there loomed the misty image of a lovely, sensuous woman, one who remained faceless, a mystery to him. What was he to do next? he wondered peevishly. He should have left for Morocco hours ago, but was determined to resolve this problem before his departure.

"What she gave was worth a king's ransom," Samein suddenly blurted, then wished he had remained silent about what Zarifa had disclosed to him.

Hasan spun about. "What she gave? What do you mean?" he said low.

"Your mystery girl was intact, my lord, a virgin. Zarifa was very nervous and shy in the telling of this, but I finally got her to speak of it. She had gone looking for Rozelle when the—I mean, when your sister was not in her rooms this morning. The woman, or girl, you had on the couch in

Shamara's room was a virgin."

"Why in hell did you not tell me before this?" Hasan thundered.

"I only just learned this myself." Samein dipped his turbaned head as his sheik flushed.

"Where is Shamara?"

"She has a new lover, my lord."

"That tells me where she is?" Hasan frowned. He couldn't very well punish Shamara for her insolence. It was he himself who ordered her to leave his apartments. "Who is this lover?"

"Tarek. She goes to his tent every night."

"No wonder," Hasan murmured.

"My Lord?"

Hasan waved a negligent hand. "Never mind." He then cleared his dry throat. He took a sip of water. "Send my sister to me. I will visit with her for a time before my departure."

"She is not about. Zarifa says she has not seen Rozelle Modestia the entire morning."

Samein was seriously beginning to fear for the sheik's sanity. Indeed he was fearing for his own.

I was only playing a game . . . let me go!

Hasan spun about on the couch. "What did you say?" he asked Samein.

Samein shook his head. "I said Zarifa has not—"

"No, what you said following that."

"I—" Samein stuck a finger beneath his turban. He shrugged after a moment of rubbing his

253

temple. "Nothing, my lord. Not a word after that."

I cannot, Hasan . . . I cannot go through with it!

Hasan stood in one brisk motion, rasping, "I hear this elusive image speak English. Now I know I am going a little crazy!" His scar stood out against the pressure in his face.

"A little, my lord?" Samein smiled feebly.

"Well then — to the limit!"

Hasan al-Shareef was fit to be tied. The kasbah had been searched high and low, scoured stone by stone, inch by inch, but still no sign of Rozelle Modestia. She had vanished, it seemed, into thin air.

"In fact," Hasan was saying, "two women have disappeared. All in a day's time." His eyes narrowed in a sneaking, dreadful suspicion.

"So true," said Tarek, his arrogant face hiding all feeling on the matter. "Have you checked the stables then? To see if she has ridden out alone? I have knowledge that your sister has done this since her latest return, and late at night."

Hasan snorted irritably. "Who can tell with so many disappearing from El Taj. Jamila, Hadji-ben-Haroun, now the two women." He frowned again. "There are six horses gone, four camels, and two asses! Beni says he cannot account for three of them, but thinks to his best knowledge that they were taken early this morning."

"Before the sun was up?" Tarek inquired with a casual air.

Ignoring that, Hasan said, "Tarek, have you any knowledge of where your father has gone off to?"

"Not the least, lord Hasan. Along with him has gone Asad. My father's comings and goings are none of my affair. He does as he wishes." He is a coward, Tarek kept to himself.

"So true."

Hasan rose to make ready for his departure, then noticed that Tarek had not asked to be excused. "You will be going to Morocco with me then?"

"I was about to . . . ask that I might stay behind. I have a feeling as to which tribe has stolen the guns that disappeared two weeks back. Our enemies waste little time in trying the new weapons out. We are being blamed for many raids of caravans going to the south."

"Well then, Allah go with you, Tarek Ibn-Haroun."

Tarek peered out of the corner of his black eyes, "And with you, Hasan al-Shareef." You white English *Roumi,* he added to himself.

With that, the handsome Arab strode from the sheik's apartment, and his chieftain watched him go, having a strong feeling he would never see

Tarek again. Guns disappear, men disappear, and one woman in particular has vanished.

Hasan gnawed his lower lip, perplexed and miserable. One and one makes two, doesn't it? he asked himself. Or in this case, did one and one make one?

"Ahhh!"

Hasan tore his turban from his head, mostly to relieve the headache that had returned. But then he stared down at the yards of *cheche* and shook his tawny head, allowing burnished waves to spill over his high forehead. "I'll be bloody damned if I know."

He tossed the turban aside.

Part Four

Pretty Pauper

'Mid pleasures and palaces though we
* may roam,*
Be it ever so humble, there's no
* place like home.*
    — *John Howard Payne,* Home Sweet Home

Chapter Twenty

The wheels of the smart carriage sang up the long, curving drive to Southend Manor. The woman leaning out the window was deeply tanned, her cheeks dusky rose with youth, and some anticipation.

Home. Rosette Forrest was home.

"It does indeed feel good after being away for almost a year." Only one thing was missing in this homecoming. Lucie Higgins was not with her. She had hoped that when she arrived in Tangier Lucie would be waiting for her. But no such luck. The staff at the hotel she'd been kidnapped from hadn't seen hide nor hair of the maid. They'd not remembered Rosette either. She hadn't stayed there long enough for them to call up her countenance or Lucie's.

"Rosette."

She turned to her companion, Pierre Maudet, when he spoke her name. "Yes, Pierre," she said with affection.

"You seem happy to be home. Are you really?"

"Why of course, Pierre. Why should I not be?"

Unable to help herself, Rosette turned from him to face the sprawling mansion looming at the end of the drive. Moss and ivy climbed up the corners and red and white late-summer roses were yet in bloom. How beautiful is England! Rosette mused to herself.

"I don't know," Pierre said with a shrug. "You seemed very joyless on the journey home." He stared along the pebbled curve that swung toward the stables. "At least up until now."

"I had matters on my mind back then, Pierre." Her face lit up when Allan stuck his head out from the tall stable doors. "Driver! Pull right up over there, will you?"

"Rosette," Pierre went on urgently, "I must speak to you."

"Pierre, I am right here, have been for hours upon hours. What is so urgent? Pierre, go ahead."

What was wrong with Pierre? Why was he suddenly so blasted nervous?

"Not here, Rosette, not now."

She smiled indulgently, but concealed a frown. "Well then, when?" she asked, wondering if he would ever speak of what bothered him.

Pierre hadn't a chance to answer before the carriage was halting in front of the stable doors. Without waiting for her companion to alight as was proper, Rosette stepped down after flinging wide the carriage door. She flew across the ground and into Allan's shyly outstretched arms, a flurry of pink muslin and flying auburn curls.

"Miss Rosette, you're b-back," Allan Hastings choked and stood back bashfully. "Aren't you going up to the house? Jayne will be all in a dither if you don't go and see her first before coming out here."

Allan appeared worried over something, Rosette noted at once. But she said, "I know your wife, Allan, and she knows I couldn't resist coming out here to visit first with Moondust."

Rosette, popping into the sweet-smelling cavern, instinctively felt something amiss. Something was very wrong here. There stood open a vacant stall. "Allan, where is? . . ."

She whirled and took in the pain written there on the man's sunburned, lined face. Allan lowered his head.

"Your favorite mare done ran away, Miss Rosette, milady. I tried to catch her. I guess she couldn't take the lonesomeness, without her master here. She's gone and become wild."

"Wild?"

"Yes, Miss Rosette. So says some of the neighbors who saw her flying like the wind to get away from them so's they couldn't catch her. She hid herself in the forest, and folks say she only comes out when the moon is full."

"Moondust," Rosette uttered and looked out across the moors in a vacant stare.

"Guess Moondust is living up to her name, huh?"

A tear squeezed from Allan's eyes as he gazed in the direction the mare had fled when after six months her master failed to return. "I sure do hope she'll be coming back, now that you've, ah, returned Miss Rosette." He shook his head with the greasy tufts of hair sticking out every which way from his cap. He finally remembered to remove the hat, and stood with it twirling in his hands. "I am real sorry, and I guess it's all my fault 'cause she run away. But, Miss Rosette, she just wouldn't stop."

"I know, Allan, I understand." Rosette sighed unhappily. "Maybe she will come back, as you say."

She stared out across the moors once more, then stared down at the ground, at nothing in particular.

"Is there something amiss, my darling?" Pierre

came into the stable after paying the coin to the driver.

Rosette turned with her eyes downcast, her misery plain to see. "Nothing, Pierre, that I wish to speak of now. We shall go into the house and have that talk, if you don't mind."

Pierre frowned in bemusement, then addressed the groom. "Has something happened here? Why did Rosette appear so miserable?"

"She'll tell you." Allan scratched his head thoughtfully. "Say, aren't you, uh, Paul Moreland? I thought I heard Rosette—I mean Miss Rosette—call you Pierre."

"How did you know that?"

"I have a good mind for names and faces," Allan said proudly.

"Keep that a secret, will you, ah, Allan?" He flipped the groom a few coins. "Is that enough?"

"Well . . . I—I don't rightly know what this is all about."

Worry lines deepened in Allan's face.

"Good. Just forget you ever heard the name." Paul Moreland left the man staring after him with a puzzled grimace.

After stuffing the coins he really didn't want in his breeches pocket, Allan turned sadly back to cleaning out Moondust's stall. For good luck, just in case, the little man forked fresh hay into the bin and stood staring into the emptiness, praying for Moondust's return. But, really, he couldn't see what good it would do even if the horse returned. The house and everything that went along with it belonged to another now. How was Miss Rosette going to take the bad news? Where were they all going to end up? Especially the poor lady — she was penniless now.

Inside the manor, Rosette was being greeted by half the Southend staff. These few remaining appeared strangely nervous over something, but Rosette put it down to her having been absent so long this time. She failed to notice how few of them greeted her. All she really wanted was to take a nice, warm bath and crawl between silky sheets and go to sleep. Soon she could escape the servants, but not so the memories. They were already beginning to crowd in on her, the moment she had stepped over the threshold. Why did memories have to be such enemies, she wearily wondered.

But first things first, and Pierre Maudet was coming to have that talk with her. What could be so pressing that it couldn't wait a few days?

Rosette dragged herself upstairs after informing Mrs. Hastings she would meet Pierre in the drawing room in half an hour. It looked like her bath would have to wait too. But why had Mrs. Hastings hesitated to do her bidding? Rosette shrugged it off again, too tired to pursue the reason for the strangeness of the servants since she'd arrived.

As she splashed cool water onto her face and rearranged her hair, Rosette reflected back over the past several weeks. Come to think of it, almost a month had passed since Pierre had found her wandering about Tangier in search of Lucie. Lucky for her she'd had some money put away in her retained reticule otherwise she would have been out begging when she met up the Frenchman. He had been a godsend, without which she would not have been able to make it home as quickly as she had. But it was odd in itself that Pierre had popped up when he had. Even odder was the fact that Pierre had a house — not from Southend, he'd said.

Rosette searched her closet for comfortable slippers to wear. When they couldn't be found, she decided to just wear the shoes she had on. Staring into the closet, Rosette noticed the disappearance of her most expensive evening gowns. She'd had a fortune tied up in clothes here — the upstairs maid must have taken them down for cleaning and pressing. A frown appeared on her forehead. They hadn't known she was arriving today, though, so how could — again she let it go. There would be time enough for questions later.

When Rosette straightened from her bent position, the dizziness assailed her again. It couldn't be hunger. They had stopped off at the inn at the crossroads and she had again eaten like a horse. She devoured everything in sight, and had been ravenous like that for two weeks now. What can it be? Rosette wondered, and searched for a good reason why she wasn't feeling at all well lately. Her appetite was good, but still she felt nauseated afterward. Was it because she truly missed *him?* Absurd! But throughout the long, hot ride from London, when she ought to have been enjoying the English countryside, she had found herself seeing instead a pair of velvet green eyes.

I have vowed to never love again, and so be it. The only reason I fell in love—or thought I had—was because of that horrible concoction Hadji forced me to drink. Ugh! It made her nauseated just thinking about the awful taste it left in her mouth. And now, yes, this could be the reason for the nausea.

That I ever got to Morocco in one piece is truly a miracle. She had sweltering during the day, and froze at night. She had almost wished for the borbor that Hadji had plied her with the first time through the desert to make her forgetful.

She could thank God for keeping her safe in the desert while traveling with those two burly Arabs who couldn't move fast enough to get her away from El Taj. They had joined up with another pair that seemed to have not been far behind and finally caught up. Shamara couldn't wait to see her gone, no doubt.

Pierre was waiting for her in the drawing room when she went downstairs. He was standing in the middle of the half-empty room, staring about as if he'd lost something. He noticed Rosette standing in the doorway, looking just as confused as he was.

"Where is all your furniture?" he asked, watching her walk slowly into the room, staring around at the emptiness.

"I—I am just as surprised as you are, Pierre." She turned to go back into the hall. "I'll summon Mrs. Hastings to get this cleared up. There must be a reason." She halted where she was, thinking: First the clothes are gone, and now this.

"Rosette . . . I am not . . . don't you remember me?"

Pierre had come up behind her so quickly that she was startled for a moment. "What is it, Pierre?" She faced him, looking drained in her confusion. A hand went to her head that suddenly ached unbearably.

He took the hand down and pressed the softness in his own palm. "I have something very important to dis—"

At that moment Jayne appeared before the threshold, and behind her stood a tall man, neatly dressed, with red beard and mustache. Rosette turned toward them and, seeing the stranger there, felt at once cold and uneasy. Something was going on here at Southend, and this man has a part in it, a feeling deep within told her.

Jayne was about to speak when the man interrupted. "Let me introduce myself, Miss Forrest," he began importantly.

Rosette kept herself from flinching. This stranger addressed her not as *Lady* Forrest, but as *Miss*. Holding her breath, Rosette waited for him to go on.

"Miss Forrest," he repeated, to gain her full attention, "My name is Wayne Rutland, estate manager of young Baron Rawen."

Rosette had stopped listening to the stranger. Instead she was staring beyond the tall, businesslike man. The hall had once been furnished with lovely French appointments; now it was almost bare. Why had she not noticed this before?

Words filtered through her brain while the man continued to explain something that should be of great import to her: Liquidate; satisfy; confiscation. "So as I am his advisor . . . as the master of Oakhill is always away."

Rosette didn't allow him to go on, blurting out, "How can you be advisor to someone who is never present? How can you solve matters this way?"

"No matter, Lady Forrest." He coughed nervously over the title and lifted his brow with an exasperated sigh. "Do you mind if I go on?"

"Yes, I do mind, in fact!"

She took a step forward, leaving Pierre dumbfounded directly behind her. "You are telling me that Southend has gone to another during my absence? There must be a horrible blunder somewhere!"

He held out an important-looking paper for her to see. "There has been a mistake, Miss Forrest, but you see, it was your father's own mistake. Here, you see his signature. He did not leave you a wealthy woman as you thought, but owed Baron Rawen a considerable amount of money. As you know Oakhill borders your—ah, Southend, and in order to settle the debt owed I have taken matters into my own hands and have, as you see—" he waved a hand about the hall—"I have begun to liquidate."

Tears of rage and fear began welling up in Rosette's soft, sun-brown eyes. "In other words, Mister Rutland, you are telling me that I am penniless and without a roof over my head? That I must leave the only home I have ever known to—to someone I don't even know?"

"But you do know him, Miss Forrest, he is your neighbor. Lord Forrest and the young baron's father were great friends, even though yours borrowed a huge sum just to keep Southend alive. I am sorry again, but the debt must be paid. We have bills, too, Miss Forrest, and I am sure you understand."

Paul Moreland, alias Pierre Maudet, stepped forward gallantly to enter the conversation. "Excuse me, but I think you have made a mistake, Mr. Rutland. Lady Rosette Forrest owes no debt to young Baron Rawen. It is I who owes the debt, and shall pay it—" he coughed behind his hand—"I shall pay it soon."

"Of course."

"You doubt me?" Moreland challenged.

"Your name, sir?" Wayne Rutland inquired.

Paul turned to Rosette with an expression of deep regret. "My name is—" he sighed deeply—"Paul Moreland." He saw Rosette's mouth gaping. "Rosette, I tried to tell you before. But now you know."

"But why, Pier—Paul? Why did you assume an alias?"

She shook her head to clear it. This day was indeed becoming too much for one woman to bear.

"Could you please tell me, Mr. Moreland, how it is that you owe the debt instead of Miss Forrest here, as it states on these old documents I've discovered in the Rawen coffers?"

"My estate flanks Southend. You must have gotten your places mixed up, Mr. Rutland. It is I who owes the debt instead of Rosette's father. But I shall pay up."

"Mr. Moreland, the paper here says it is Lord

Alfred Forrest who must pay, or his legal heir, who in this case happens to be Rosette, of course. It's all here, in black and white."

Rosette clamped a hand to her forehead. "Excuse me, but I have to sit down! Mrs. Hastings, water please."

Rosette stared at the luxurious, blue-and-cream carpet that luckily still covered the floor. "Do I still have the right to order my own servants about?" she wondered out loud.

Jayne smiled kindly. "Yes, *Lady* Forrest, I'll get that water for you right away!"

Jayne stuck her pert nose high in the air as she strutted importantly past Wayne Rutland, estate manager to Oakhill Manor. What a mess, Rosette thought silently. Poor Mrs. Hastings, she must have had a time of it with Mister Rutland while I was away.

"He must have mismanaged, or—or something like that," Rosette mumbled to herself. She looked up then, when there was a lull in the heated conversation between the two men. "Pierre . . . oh, I can't get used to calling you Paul. But I shall try." She groaned then. "How is it that you are not Pierre Maudet but Paul Moreland? Please tell me, Paul, before I go insane right here and now."

Paul Moreland cleared his throat. "Haven't you ever thought me to be familiar? Rosette, look at me, who do I look like?"

"I have looked at you, P-Paul. But I can't say that I remember you as being a neighbor. All I know is that the Marlands . . . are . . . down the road. You do seem to be a familiar face from the past. But—"

"Don't you remember, the ball at Marland's?"

"I—I danced with so many at that last ball, but back then I had eyes only for the man who was to marry me."

"Perry Marland."

"Yes." She could hold her head up now, for Perry was completely out of her mind. "But you didn't answer me, Paul."

"Why the alias? I'll tell you, ah, if you will excuse us, Mr. Rutland?"

"I was just on my way out, anyway. But I will return in the morning to speak with you both. See that you are here, Mr. Moreland." He shook his head as he went to the front door to show himself out.

Paul took Rosette's cold hand to lead her to the sofa, then sat down beside her. He cleared his throat. "I had to use the alias, Rosette. I followed you to Tangier, and employed the alias after your maid, ah, Lucie, informed me that you wouldn't see me. She said you wanted nothing to do with the Marlands, and seeing that I was Perry's cousin, well, I knew you wouldn't even speak to me. So—" he sighed—"I employed the name Pierre Maudet. I even went so far as to speak with a French accent. When I discovered you had been abducted, I did some fast detective work. Lucie could tell me nothing, she was in such an agonized state after your disappearance. Your next question must be: Where is Lucie? I wouldn't know, because I joined up with two other Frenchies, true legionnaires, going into the Sahara, and the next time I saw you was at the kasbah. Believe me, I almost thought I had the wrong girl, because you looked so different. Besides that, all the French-speaking Arabs there were saying you were the sheik's sister."

"Did you really plan to return?"

"Oh yes, but first there was business in Morocco. . . ." He let it hang.

"Paul, why did you follow me in the first place?"

"Because I adored you when I really got a good look at you in Morocco."

"And now?"

"Now I love you."

Chapter Twenty-one

Morning sunlight streamed through the dining-room window. Breakfast had been laid out earlier; coffee cups sat half-full, each plate of food barely touched.

Rosette, in an old russet, brocade dress, moved from the ceiling-to-floor window she had been gazing out of, and turned to face the man with a concerned light in his soft, green eyes.

"Paul, I cannot allow you to lie for me and pay the debt. If my father owed Rawen this money, as indeed it seems, then it is I who should let Mister Rutland continue to liquidate. I have no choice in the matter. A debt is a debt and must be paid!"

Paul stared adoringly into the woman's eyes, eyes like burnished gold. "But, darling, Mr. Rutland means to take Southend, the total estate, lands and all." He shoved the now-cold coffee aside. "I plan to see Deerhurst after I leave here."

"Deerhurst? Who is he?"

"My estate manager and advisor."

"What can he do, Paul?" She still felt odd saying Paul, when she had known him only as Pierre before yesterday.

"Seeing as you are without an advisor, you can appoint Deerhurst for Southend's also. Do you agree?"

"Oh, Paul, I am plumb tuckered out from all this awful business! I—I was even ill this morning before Mister Rutland arrived."

Paul really looked concerned now. "Ill? You mean you—" He could not go on.

"Yes, I—I did."

"You threw up." He said it for her.

She nodded.

He took hold of her camellia-pale hand, not wanting to say out loud what was really troubling him. He let the subject drop then, believing that Rosette would have told him if the sheik had ravished her in any way. Certainly she was not "that kind" of woman, one who would have "let" him.

"It is too much for you, darling, that's all. It'll all be fine soon, you'll see. Come away with me for the remainder of the summer. Deerhurst will handle the sticky matter here himself. We can go to London and stay with some friends I have there. I, uh, don't have my own town house there yet, but I really plan to soon."

"I have already told you, Paul, I can't go away, not yet. Not when the servants and Southend need me."

"Hell with servants!" Paul swore angrily, his face a mottled red. His green eyes darkened, but not as dark as another pair Rosette tried hard not to remember.

"Paul!" She pulled her hand free, looking at him with utter disbelief written on her face. "How could you even say that? These people here have been with our family as long as I can remember, and, besides, there aren't many of them left. Only the faithful ones have stayed on, despite . . . oh, how could you, Paul?"

"How?" he almost snickered. "Southend never meant a thing to you before. How come all of a sudden?"

"Southend does mean something to me! And, Paul, you said yourself that Rutland means to take Southend."

"So, so I did! But, Rosette, you'll need for

nothing at Heathcliff. I can make up for all you might, I say *might,* lose here."

"What is that supposed to mean?"

"You can come and live with me, as my bride or not. Although I prefer we be married. But if not, you can just stay on at Heathcliff, and even if you don't ever, I mean you don't wish to become my bride right away, I can wait. I'll wait forever for you, your wish is my command, darling Rosette. I'll always worship the ground you walk on."

If only another man would have said that to her and meant it, she would have followed him to the ends of the earth. But he had frightened her and his world was not hers. His was a mystical, confounding place to live, even though beautiful at times.

She was brought back to the present and stared at Paul sternly. "Paul, you lied when you said you owed that mountainous debt. I cannot live with lies of any kind! I am sorry!"

Seeing the tawny depths of her eyes turn to gold fires, Paul shook his head with sore regret. Only he knew that there were qualms over what he was about to say.

"I'll never lie again, Rosette, cross my heart." He did just that. "Believe me. But will you come live at Heathcliff?"

"Oh, Paul, I just do not know." She ended with a groan.

Rosette stood and walked, looking with longing about her rooms. They had been stripped of furniture, but one or two pieces here and there remained standing. Mister Rutland had wasted no time taking all the finest chairs, sofas, love seats and tables! She had just come to realize how very much she loved it here at Southend, where she had been born and raised. If only she could go back . . . back to what? she caught herself wondering next. Her entire childhood right into teens had been lonely and depressing. Why was it that every time she loved something, started to, it was snatched from her? Was she never to feel secure at all in anything? What a sad way to walk through one's life!

"Rosette?"

"I would like to be alone for a time to think over some things," she murmured to Paul who had been trailing after her like a puppy.

"You will give me your decision tonight?" Paul said hopefully. "May I pick you up for dinner at Heathcliff?" Even as he said this, Paul worried over something, but he hid it well from her.

She looked down over her pink afternoon dress. "But, Paul, I've no pretty gowns to wear. I would be embarrassed to show up at Healthcliff in an old gown."

"There's only the servants and myself there, Rosette. Besides, don't you remember that I bought you several gowns that you haven't even worn yet?"

Yes, she did remember now. But they were all travelling clothes, hardly suitable for wearing to dinner. But one of them would have to suffice. It suddenly struck her strange that Paul didn't know the difference between a lovely evening gown and a travelling dress. It wasn't important really, she finally concluded to herself. Only Paul would be there.

"Yes, Paul," she finally relented with a sigh. "Pick me up at seven."

Rosette had been wrong in thinking that Paul would be her only dinner companion at Heathcliff. As it turned out, Mr. Wayne Rutland arrived unexpectedly, just as they were beginning the meal, and another place had to be set at the long dinner table.

"I won't be staying long," Rutland said, seating himself and forming a church steeple with his long fingers. "No food, just coffee," he said to the servant standing there with a plate in one hand and her arm cocked at her left hip. "You can take that back to the kitchen, thank you, I've already eaten."

"Just put that down over here, Milly. Perhaps Lady Forrest would like another portion of your delicious chicken."

Milly peered down at the auburn head fashioned upswept in a bunch of riotous curls.

"This is all there is, there ain't no more where it come from," she said churlishly.

"That's fine, Milly." Paul gritted his teeth. "Just set it down, please, and just bring up some more coffee and tea, then that will be all," Paul told his rude servant. He would have to speak to her later, he could see.

Ignoring Rutland, Paul attacked the chicken as if he hadn't eaten in two whole days. Rosette had tasted the chicken and, finding the fowl not only tasteless but undercooked, she picked at the peas and carrots which were mushy. Not only was the food surprisingly poor, but Rosette began to wonder where Paul's other servants were hiding themselves. Her answer was soon to come.

"We've been over all this before, Mr. Rutland," Paul was saying after the estate manager finished what he was explaining. "Lady Forrest doesn't owe Rawen a thing. Can't you get that through your head?"

"Paul!"

Paul's hand had risen to his mouth when Rosette voiced her astonishment at his behavior that was again uncalled for. He thrust his hand from his mouth in a childlike gesture, saying, "Shall we take a walk outside? Rosette, have you finished?"

"Yes—" she cast a jaundiced eye to the poor fare—"I think that would be a good idea."

His eyes jumped to her face, but he seemed to be looking clear through her to the other side. "What would?"

"Paul . . . to take a walk outside. What else?"

"Oh, yes, yes, the walk."

Rosette shook her head as Paul led them from the dining room out onto the terrace overgrown with climbing ivy, and flagstone not yet swept clean of last year's leaves.

"Here are the gardens, Rosette. Look at the roses, aren't they lovely?"

"L-lovely, Paul."

Rutland smirked off to one side. But Rosette could hardly credit what she was seeing. The house—like the stable she could see through the trees—was in poor repair. Even the gardens here had been sadly neglected. The servants—why, there were hardly any to speak of. In fact, she had only seen the one. Molly? Milly? Rosette mentally shrugged it off.

Rutland moved to stand off to the side of Rosette, remarking, "Looks like you're going under, too, Moreland."

Lowering her brow, Rosette glowered at the man who was all business.

"Well, I have been away for almost a year, you know," Paul said peevishly.

"Are your servants also gone away?" Rutland asked, lazily hiding a smirk.

"They are. But soon they will return."

Rosette decided that Paul appeared, standing there as he was on the terrace, as gaunt as his surroundings. Poor Paul, was he as beggared as a church mouse, too? It suddenly began to appear he was.

"Oh," was all Rutland murmured, his nose uplifted. "I must be going," he said suddenly, nodding politely to Rosette. To Paul he said, "The young Baron Rawen is on his way home."

"What?" Paul swung about to face Rutland's back just moving toward the path leading to the front of the house. "Did I hear you correctly?"

"Didn't I tell you? Sorry about that, Moreland. Yes, I received a message just this morning." Rutland continued to walk, tossing back, "He will arrive in a week's time. I've already notified those at Oakhill."

"Oakhill, Oakhill," Paul was muttering over and over.

Paul moved away from Rosette, to run his fingers through his tousled blond hair. "Damn," he swore. Paul knew he would have to work fast now. Mr. Rutland was going to have an accident, sooner than he himself had anticipated.

"Paul."

Rosette placed a cool hand on his arm. When he faced her, Rosette caught her breath at the wild gleam in his eyes. She had been about to tell him she couldn't possibly move into Heathcliff, for it was plain to see that Paul couldn't help her in any way; he hadn't the funds. But she herself could help Paul out, by taking a job as a governess near Heathcliff. He still hadn't changed his expression, so she went on, "Paul, is there something else you have been keeping from me? Is there a reason why you—you have been losing money?"

He snatched up her hand and squeezed almost painfully. "Yes, Rosette! Oh God, I have been keeping something else from you. You see, I—oh," he moaned, "how can I tell you!"

Paul wrenched away from her, pounding a fist into a palm. This smarted and he shook the hurt from his hand.

Rosette walked over and laid a hand gently upon his shoulder, feeling the rough texture of his jacket. Funny she had not noticed before the poor quality of Paul's clothing. It seemed to her, now that she thought of it, that Paul owned only one or two fine suits of clothes. She dragged her eyes from the jacket to stare at his handsome profile. Why hadn't she ever noticed either what a handsome man Paul is. Had her musings been too wrapped up in another? One who was handsome, yes, but in a rugged, lean-jawed, dark and mysterious sort of way. Her cat's eyes glowed for a moment or two, then turned normal once again.

"Just tell me, Paul." She laughed lightly then. "I'll consider one more lie, I suppose, if there is one. But that will be it," she said mock-sternly, "no more after that!"

Paul groaned. "I have lied to you so much, Rosette, I don't know how you can ever find it in your heart to forgive."

"I've a big heart, Paul!" She grinned charmingly, but now she turned serious. "Please, just tell, for I've already said I shall forgive you this one last time."

"I — I am the Baron, R-Rosette."

"You — you are? Truly?" Rosette suppressed the urge to laugh out loud. "Which baron, Paul?"

"Baron Paul M. Rawen." He hoisted his chin as if proud of the name.

"Baron . . . Rawen?" Rosette wanted to choke suddenly, her throat was so clogged with hysterical emotion. "What does the M stand for?"

"Moreland, of course," he said haughtily, "my middle name."

Baron, my eye! Turning, Rosette looked deeply into the trees beyond the unkept gardens, watching the early mists lying low on the carpet of leaves and moss. *Baron!* She suddenly knew an urge to run, run fast into the forest and lose herself, to live like a hermit and be free of life's complications. A gypsy, that's what she would become.

"I might do just that, the way things are

284

going," she said, unmindful she said this out loud.

Paul tracked her line of vision, reading Rosette's thoughts, for Paul had known this very same feeling more often than not. "It's not all that bad, Rose," he said using his pet name for her, knowing this made her smile. But she wasn't smiling this time, so he took her hand reassuringly. "I'll get what's coming to me, Rose. All I've to do is to prove I'm the rightful heir to the estate. The place is rich, Rose, love, and all will be ours someday."

"Ours, Paul? What are you talking about?" She faced away from him as she asked this.

"Of course, don't you see? You won't owe me a thing, because I would never hold you to that debt."

"What? Who is this imposter who is to arrive at Oakhill in a week's time, then, Paul?" She looked into his face that betrayed great worry.

He looked aside, so she couldn't catch the hatred that had leapt into his eyes. "He is the real bastard that my father sired, not I. *This* house should be his, and I should be living at Heathcliff!"

"Oh, but *this* is Heathcliff." She peered at Paul with suspicion reigning. "This is, isn't it?" She waved her arm slowly in the air, indicating house and lands, then let it fall even slower. "I have a feeling . . ."

"You are right, Rosette, about that feeling. This is Oakhill."

"Oh, dear God!"

He went on as if she hadn't exclaimed. "The names were changed years ago. It doesn't matter, the names aren't important. What is is that I belong at Heathcliff, and not here." He snorted in derision, as if just realizing the poverty of his surroundings.

Rosette, having collected herself from mild shock, pressed finger tips to her pounding temples. "This—is all very, *very* confusing! Tell me, Paul, why does Mister Rutland name Oakhill as such and not Heathcliff, as you say it really is?"

"Heathcliff is the newer, enlarged version of Oakhill, that's all."

Rosette shook her head, saying weakly, "Oh, yes, that's all."

"You don't understand, Rose," Paul said helplessly.

"You bet your booties I don't. Go on, Paul, *please.*"

"As I was saying, listen well, Heathcliff—"

"I know, the newer version of Oakhill. Heathcliff is the newer version of Oakhill."

"Rosette, please! Settle down."

"I shall try . . . believe me." She crossed her slim arms over her pert bosom. "Go on."

"Rutland doesn't realize the change, you see!"

286

"Humph, how could that be?" she snorted through a fine nose.

"He, you see, he was appointed only several years ago as estate manager, don't you see?"

Rosette tipped her russet head. "But *who* appointed him, when it was your place to do this?"

"The imposter! Don't you see? He, this phony baron, has stolen the real Heathcliff from me."

"You make Heathcliff sound like a dog. Paul?"

"Don't ask." He held up a finger. "Don't ask me how he did this!"

"I am in no mood to ask you any questions, believe me!"

Rosette had to sit down, and she chose a white wicker chair, not caring for now if she trusted the piece to support her weight or not. "I believe I am more confused than ever, Paul. Tell me, won't this phony baron return here instead of Heathcliff?"

Paul bounced from one foot to the other, so excited was he. "Aha! Aha! Now you are catching on! That is exactly what I hope to accomplish! When Rawen returns—so the sly boots calls himself—he will ask to see the deed to Oakhill and—"

Rosette interrupted. "And this rundown estate *is* Oakhill!" She pursed her lips tightly then, before asking, "Do you have the deed to

Heathcliff, the newer estate, in your possession? You had better, Paul."

"No," he said sheepishly, "but I know who does have it."

"Who is that, pray tell, Paul?" Breathless from all the tension she'd been undergoing, she waited with anticipation to hear whose name it might be.

"My half-sister!"

He watched her face for its reaction.

"Who . . . is . . . she?" Rosette sat on the edge of the wicker, not trusting her legs to unbend and support her.

Paul patted her hand as one would a child. "Not now, Rose darling. Later—" he smiled shrewdly—"later, you will learn all there is to know pertaining to the Rawen mystery."

"Oh, dear God." Rosette plopped back to sigh deeply. Where did she fit into this web of deceit and cunning? Right in the middle, she deduced. That's where Southend along with this very frustrated owner sat!

Chapter Twenty-two

"Hmff!" Rosette paced the priceless, blue-and-gold carpet in her sunlit bedroom. "I'm fortunate to yet have a bed and a pillow to lay my head down on at night!"

She wore her pink silk wrapper, hugging the draping Chinese sleeves about her slim arms. "See him just try and take this from me! Whatever I happen to be wearing at the moment, that pestiferous Rutland cannot have the clothes that are on my back!" she fumed and raged about the room.

He wouldn't dare take all the rest of her clothes — would he? She faced the mirror and her reflection nodded, "Absolutely."

Soon she wouldn't have a roof over her head. As it was, few of her finest gowns and shoes remained in her wardrobe. "Why must he take my clothes, too? Is he some kind of a pervert? Ah! That Rutland is a blood-sucking vulture, to be sure!"

Another week had already gone by, and Rosette could hear her own voice echoing softly through the emptied halls and rooms. She clenched her hands into tight fists of frustration. "How very generous of the man, he has told me I can stay on at Southend even if it takes me a year to secure a position somewhere, and find a place to live."

"If you ask me, I'd say you was talking to yerself, Rosie, and so what were you doing that for?"

"Oh, I didn't hear you come in, Jayne." It was the housekeeper, Mrs. Hastings, who also served as her personal maid now that Lucie was absent. Jayne was a plain and pale, mousy little woman, with a heart made of pure gold, and Rosette adored her.

"I was just thinking out loud," Rosette added with a smile for Jayne, who'd been with the family even before Rosette was born, just like Lucie.

"And cussing out loud you were too. Your

poor father'd turn in his grave if he heard you, my lady."

"Thank you, Jayne."

"For what, then?"

"For calling me 'my lady,' that's what. You're a dear, it was very sweet of you to think of me as such." She sighed. "After all."

"After all! Now just listen to you. Is this my little Rosie talking?"

Jayne pointed at the mirror, gold-framed, and lucky was Rosette to still have it hanging in the house. "Look there, girl, you're made of much tougher stuff than that what you're sniffing and ranting over. And you're still a lady, every glorious inch of you. You'll be pulling us through, too, I just know it." She wouldn't say just how she knew. "I'll never leave your side, my lady, always remember that."

"Thank you, Jayne."

The maid went about collecting items to be washed, and then left Rosette alone with her thoughts once again. *She just knows I'll pull us through, huh?* She had already scanned the local ads, and there wasn't one position available at the time for governess. *And Jayne, bless her heart, how could she tag along even if I do secure a position?*

Rosette walked to the window to stare outside, down there where she used to romp and play in the garden. How lonely she had been as a child, a sad-faced doll dressed up prettily with no place to go, no one to play with. But for the maids, at times — she used to even play with them when they weren't too busy with their many tasks, which wasn't all that often. *I can always be a maid? Oh no, not I. I shall not sweep and scrub somebody else's dirty floors or do a lady's bidding.* She just couldn't picture herself wielding a mop or carrying trays upstairs.

Rosette laughed, with a touch of irony in her tone. She had been doing that very same thing all week, but for herself, not others. Only two maids remained at Southend, and they were plumb tuckered out from doing the cooking and seeing to other household duties. One thing was certain: There was little furniture to dust and polish!

And now, of all the gall, Mister Rutland had the very nerve to invite her to a ball! The homecoming ball being thrown for none other than the baron, His Phoniness. "Oh, the shammer!" Rosette cried indignantly.

What does Rutland hope to accomplish by making a complete fool out of me? He has already managed to disrobe and put me out of countenance. How can I ever hold my head up around here? Who will have me as governess knowing I have fallen into poverty? First the scandal of Louise and her Frenchman, and now Papa and his mountainous gambling debt! Noses had turned up at her, and would even more so. People could be cruel, she knew.

"But don't you see?" Rutland had said to her just yesterday. "By attending the ball you will meet those in need of a cultured and refined governess or what have you."

What have you—indeed! Rosette sniffed now even as she had then. Meaning no more than a maid—a scullery maid was what the long-nosed Rutland had in mind for her! That man has no heart at all. If she had it in her, she'd wring the devil's neck!

Rosette tore down from her wardrobe the one remaining gown she had been concealing for a time like this, when she would have to retain some of her dignity. She would need to do some alterations on it, for the bodice was now too tight for her fuller bosom. She eyed the yellow satin gown adorned with bewitching black lace at the dipping bodice and sleeves, the skirt sprinkled with the tiniest sewn-on yellow roses; and there in the wardrobe, yes, her yellow satin, high-heel slippers were still there.

"Oh yes," Rosette purred, "I shall go to this blasted ball." She faced the mirror as she held the gown pressed to her front. "And I shall meet this wicked, conniving baron who has wiped me into poverty. I shall have the homely, grubbing jackanapes drooling at my shoulder before the night has seen the witching hour. Just see if I don't!"

Down the road, several miles from Southend, the young Baron Rawen tooled his carriage with expert hands. The high-stepping horses, purchased in a crowded section of London by the highest bidder, expressed their delight to their new master by whinnying back to him and tossing their huge heads.

Baron Mark Brandon Rawen smiled over this. The beauties loved the fresh air, away from confines of city life, and the freedom to trot down the dusty, country road. The baron breathed deeply of the sweet air. He loved it too, he was discovering, and he could hardly credit his senses. But here he was, far from the Sahara, with its relentless sun pouring down, and Morocco, the busy tourist hive.

"I've found something out for you," Wayne Rutland, seated beside Mark, brought up now. "It seems that your neighbor—a very lovely one I might add—owes you."

"Owes me?" Mark Rawen lifted a tawny eyebrow that matched his wind-ruffled hair. "How is that?"

"Your father won at cards, at Fife's, while playing with a certain Lord Alfred Forrest—"

"Wait a minute. Forrest?" Did the name ring a

bell just then? "Go on. This is becoming very interesting. A lovely lady involved, and you say my father won?"

"He did, and big! All I can say about Lord Forrest is that if a man gambles when he's too drunk to know what he's doing, then he deserves all he gets."

"You mean all he loses."

"Yes. He lost."

"So, Rutland, I mean Wayne—where is this Lord Forrest? And who is the beautiful neighbor you mentioned?" As he said this, though, his eyes remained unlighted, emotionless.

"She's Lord Forrest's daughter. But you won't be meeting up with Lord Forrest himself, that's highly impossible."

"Well let's have it. Why not?"

"He's deceased."

"Sorry to hear that. I hope the game of high stakes wasn't the cause?"

"Oh no! He climbed into his deathbed after his wife Louise ran off with some Frenchman."

"Too bad, I really mean that. So, has the lovely lady paid up? I would like to get what's coming to the Rawen estate, and a game is a game. But I am not so cruel as to see the little lady completely penniless."

Rutland sat back smugly. "I've already begun

to liquidate her possessions. The house comes next."

"The house, too?" Out of the corner of his eye he saw Rutland nod. "Some stakes!" Mark whistled.

Mark Rawen, his high forehead lowered broodingly now, tooled off into a bumpy, dusty lane leading up to a mist-shrouded house in the distance that stood in poor repair. Mark shook his head, realizing how much time had really passed since he last gazed upon his childhood home. Run-down the house was indeed, as were the grounds and outbuildings. He could see already that he would have to roll up his sleeves and get to work. Besides, he needed the diversion to keep himself from dwelling on futile mind-wandering and worries that nagged.

"I'm sorry, Baron Rawen, to intrude on your private thoughts and observations after being away so long, but — "

"Please, Rutland, I'd prefer you call me Mark. We are well enough acquainted by now. I'll have to become used to the name again anyway. As long as we're on a first name basis now, Wayne," he laughed at himself, "what were you about to say?"

"You are on the wrong road. This goes to the residence of a man by the name of Paul Moreland."

"I've never met the man, but it seems to me

he's a shirt-tail cousin of mine — " he rubbed his chin in thought — "or was it the Marlands he's related to. However," he said and shrugged. He swung about on the high seat as the news sunk in belatedly. "What do you mean this is Moreland's residence? This is Oakhill. Of course not as I remembered it being — it used to be a lovely, cared-for place — but Oakhill just the same now. This land has belonged to the Rawens for centuries. Look over there, those huge yews, why, they're as old as the house, hundreds of years, planted long ago by my ancestors. Hell, man, I grew up here!" Mark tossed a muscular arm clad in new, dandy duds in a wide arc in the air.

"But th-this place is called Heathcliff," Rutland stammered.

"Be damned if I ever heard of the place." His brown hand came up to stroke the new beard he sported, which gave him the look of a ship's captain. "Wait a minute." He drew the leather up to take in the slack and halt the magnificent chestnut horses. "I do recall my mother mentioning something . . . a thing about a place named Heathcliff. Either that, or I dreamed it." He shrugged wide shoulders in his new suit of gray, and a creamy white shirt with matching vest. "I have been away for almost fifteen years, give or take a short visit or two, like the time I met you in London— What the devil!"

The team of frightened horses screamed their surprise and danced off the edge of the road as the shot rang out and met its target. Rutland was slumped over in his seat, the red stain spreading over his shirt near his throat. His hand slid away from his vest, where he had been in the process of digging something from out of there. "They . . . are . . . not . . . here." He coughed and blood gurgled from his mouth, foaming over his chin and staining his lapel. "The papers . . . gone . . ."

Baron Mark Rawen wasted no time inquiring about what papers. Letting Wayne Rutland slump against his shoulder, Mark snapped the buggy whip high above the horses' heads, and they, responding like the blooded breed they were, took off in a bound, flying up the lane now headed to the house.

Mark tossed a quick look over his shoulder to see if anyone pursued from the bushes where the shot had come from. At least, he thought that direction was where it must of come from, as there was no other cover for an ambush back there.

Enraged because he couldn't go after Rutland's assailant, Mark brought the carriage to a skidding, dust-raising halt in front of the manor, keeping one arm outstretched to make sure Rutland did not fly forward. Milly and her husband Ben, the only servants in the household, came running out to give aid to the stranger.

"Aay, ain't that the man who come here the other night with that fancy face lady?" she asked her husband, but he shot her a dumb look before helping to carry the fatally wounded man inside.

"Fetch a doctor, and be quick about it!" Mark Rawen shouted at the gaping man standing at the foot of the worn sofa.

"Huh!" Ben pointed at his own burly self, his puffing chest. "I ain't got no horse, mister."

Mark stared the man up and down, rapping out. "Where the devil did you come from?"

"I been here ever since—"

"Shut yer mouth, Ben, we ain't suppose to say nothin'!" Milly ordered, her greasy face grinning at the handsomely attired gentleman. "My, ain't you a pretty toff, where'd you come from yerself?"

"Damn." Mark shot up from where he'd been kneeling over the man, stuffing his handkerchief into the deep wound. "Watch him, it is the least you can do. I shall fetch the doctor myself. Where does he live, can you at least tell me that?"

"Down the road apiece."

"I know, why don't you just come along and show me, mate. You," he said to the dishevelled woman, "watch him, and don't let him remove the handkerchief. You could fetch some clean linens while you are just standing there doing nothing." And looking stupid, he caught himself before adding.

"Humphh!" Milly snorted after the dapper-garbed back of the gentleman. "Them high folks and their uppity ways. Hope he ain't staying in these parts. He might be good to look at, kind of hard and handsome, but he sure gots a bad temper." She headed toward her messy kitchen. "Besides," she said selfishly, "we ain't got much grub to be handing out to every stranger comes along. Sure and he won't be getting nothing from me own garden!"

While Baron Rawen fetched the doctor posthaste, a ruddy-faced individual disappeared with his American-made rifle further into the bushes and forest where his horse stood waiting. The horse waited because she could do nothing else. She had once flown free like the wind through forest and dale, but old Jessie had caught her, yessir! Now that she had been beaten a little, she came around to do Jessie's bidding. Jessie spat on the ground, a dark brown stream of spittle. But still Moondust shied away and rolled her gold-flecked eyes when the paunchy man neared. She tried to nip at him but he gave her a good pike in the ribs with the butt of his Colt rifle, his proudest possession. Yessir, this old Colt had brought Jessie good fortune. His voice held a nasty ring to it when he laughed now. Won't be long before that new boss, that yellow-haired toff, would pay up, and pay up good he better to old Jessie. "Come on, Goldie, let's get the hay outa here!" He hauled himself onto the mare's golden back.

Mark Rawen returned to find Wayne Rutland's name would have to be added to the death register. What papers had Rutland been trying to tell him about? he asked himself. And who would want to murder his estate agent in the first place? Someone who didn't want Baron Rawen finding out about some papers that no doubt belonged to him, that's what.

"Get this room cleaned up," Mark ordered Milly, and to Ben he barked, "Help me get this gentleman into the carriage. It's going to be his last ride — home."

"Say, who do you think you are ordering us about like that?" Milly said with an ugly smirk on her greasy face.

"Baron Mark Brandon Rawen, that is who. Oakhill is mine, and if you do not want to find yourself out on your backsides, you will heed my orders."

The doctor blinked along with the others, in awe and something else as the baron walked away with the body of Rutland between him and gaping Ben while Milly stood now scratching beneath her greasy mop of hair. She

shrugged, talking to herself, "Who cares who's
the owner of Oakhill, as long as Ben and me get
. . . say, maybe we'll be gettin' somes wages
now seeing as this here gent come along. That
there Moreland fellow never give us much more
than a penny or two to keeps us going." Milly
set about at once putting the room in order,
humming as she went to fetch her mop and
pail. There were some toffy clothes upstairs to
be getting rid of too!

Chapter Twenty-three

The carriage jerked to a halt. Up the sloping velvet-green lawn stood Heathcliff. Paul Moreland, viewing the impressive facade from a distance, felt perspiration trickle beneath the sleeves of his brand new suit of clothes. He set his carriage into motion once again, telling himself it was now or never.

He straightened his posture and put on a commanding expression as he brought the one-horse carriage to a halt in front of the house. A weathered old man had come to the door, and now he stepped down to greet the stranger, his rusty legs moving laboriously slow.

" 'Tis a fine day," Pickworth said creakily, smiling jovially. "What can I be doing for you, sir?"

"You can show me to my room, ah? . . ."

The ruddy-faced servant eyed this stranger with suspicion. "Uh, who might ye be, sir, that I'd be showing ye to a room at Heathcliff?"

"I am—" Paul squared his shoulders—"I am Baron Rawen, and what is your name?"

Pickworth's jaw dropped several inches, causing a second jowl to appear at his throat. He twisted about, shouting two names, knowing beforehand that Harriet and Barbara were peering covertly from the side window to see who this new arrival might be.

Two women appeared shyly at the door, one thin and tall, the other chubby and short. Barbara, the latter, stepped down to join Pickworth at the bottom of the wide, stone steps. Her voice creaked as she greeted the man just stepping down from his high seat. Harriet chimed in, her voice deeper, though she was the frailer of the two elderly women.

At the same time: "Good morning to ye, sir." Both looking to Pickworth for explanation of this early arrival.

"This is the baron, ladies. 'Tis been a long time, sirrr," Pickworth said, rather disappointedly, in his highland brogue. He stuck out a pawlike hand, and Paul took it. As he pumped the hand, Pickworth went on, "You be just in time for the party—your own ball, sirrr."

"So I heard. Ah, I met Rutland down the road apiece." Paul tossed a glance over his shoulder as if expecting the man at any moment. "He'll be showing up later. So, if you don't mind, I'd like to be shown to my room to rest and freshen up."

After Paul—the Baron Rawen—had been shown to his room at the top of the stairs, the three elderly servants held a meeting in the kitchen. It was the table at the back of the kitchen, where they usually took their meals together, having priority over the others, and now they wished for some privacy to gossip.

"Well," Harriet began, "it has been a long time, almost fifteen years since we saw the young baron last. People do change, ye know." Still, she shook her head over something and frowned.

"There's something different about the eyes, but I can't put me finger on it. Did you notice anything strange, Harriet?"

Pickworth put I, "I know what 'tis that be different." He chuckled deeply. " 'Tis our own eyes that can't see so well anymore!"

"Yer right there," Harriet said, chuckling. "Us three been with the Rawens forever it seems. The younger maids and laddies here wouldn't be remembering the new baron, they come here to us only five years ago to help keep the house up." She sighed as if this were a monumental task.

"The gardeners, too, they all be young'uns," Barbara remarked in her aging tone.

Pickworth scratched his balding pate. "Just wish I could remember what 'tis I should not've forgot. Can you remember, Harriet? Barbara?"

"No, Pickworth, you never told us what you wanted help with remembering."

"I remember something important," Barbara suddenly said.

"What's that?" Pickworth and Harriet said together.

"There's going to be a ball tonight and we better be getting our arses moving."

"Sure now. Ah, what's the name of that fella we didn't like snooping around here? The baron mentioned his name."

"Rutland. He be the one moving the furniture in here like he owned the place." She slapped her knee and laughed boisterously. "The estate agent, Rutland! The man who told us to be setting up the party, that's who. Don't ye remember?"

Harriet cackled. "Nah, it was *Ratland!*"

"Sure hope he don't show up again today," Pickworth said with visible disdain. He hoisted himself up from the table and walked with the ladies to the hall. " 'Tis sure crowded with all this fine-looking furniture from Southend sitting here and there. Ah, the poor Lady Forrest, wasn't that her name? Do you think she'll be showing up here tonight?"

"And why not? Everybody from far and near'll be coming to the ball. I'll not be seeing the fun, though, no sir, I'll be tucked in me bed by then!" Harriet said with the imperiousness of a long-standing servant of the Rawens.

Watery eyes belonging to Pickworth lit up. "You ladies can be going to bed if you choose. 'Tis the first party since the moon was blue, and this old body'll not be missing the fun. Not on your life!"

Harriet and Barbara hid smiles, knowing Pickworth would be abed himself before long, unable to stay awake for the merriment.

"I got goosebumps over all this," Barbara said to Harriet as they made their way to their quarters by the back stairs.

"Sure and it's spooky, after all these years," Harriet said with a shiver. "I'm glad I'll be abed."

Several miles down the road and up the lane, Rosette awoke from her afternoon nap. A premonition that something was amiss would not leave her as she made preparations to dress for the ball. It had all begun when she had taken one of the mares for a ride over to Oakhill. A carriage she had never seen before had been standing outside, the team lathered, two strange men just alighting from it. Then her eyes had picked out the countenance of Ben, the only male servant at

Oakhill. But the other man was young and tall, with tawny hair burnished in the sunlight. Even from that distance there had been something disturbingly familiar about the way the young man walked. She had studied his long, lean back as it moved to enter the house. It had been obvious to her that he was someone of importance, because he had preceded Ben inside, and because he moved like a man of the world, as if he owned everything in it—including Oakhill.

"But of course that is impossible," Rosette said to herself now. "Paul owns Oakhill." She frowned, wondering out loud. "Or does he? Come to think of it, I don't know all that much about Paul Moreland, other than what he has told me." She walked over to her wardrobe and stopped. Then again, she couldn't set much store by what Paul told her. He was always telling little white lies, and some not so little, if the truth be known.

"Jayne," Rosette called from the door, having heard the maid passing by a moment ago humming as she went about her chores.

"Here I am," Jayne called from the next room. A moment later she poked her head around the door. "Would you like me to be helping you to dress for the party now, my lady?"

Rosette smiled sweetly, "Yes, Jayne, Paul will be picking me up soon." She twirled, flutters of excitement running through her. "I am on my way to Heathcliff!"

But Paul didn't arrive to pick her up. Instead, it was a young man sporting a handsome suit of livery, his robust frame ramrod straight at the driver's seat. A pair of perfectly matched chestnuts pulled a well-sprung carriage, one that was not new but obviously had been lovingly cared for. A coat of arms emblazoned the door, one she didn't know, or had she seen it long ago passing by Southend, when she was just a child?

After exchanging a few words with the driver, Rosette was helped into the carriage gallantly and then they were off. Rosette sat back against the velvet seats that smelled a bit musty, and gazed at the countryside. From where it had been hiding, the moon came up and cleared the trees, now shining atop the dark, leafy silhouettes. Sounds seemed to be magnified all around, like the chorus of tree frogs and crickets. It was a magical night already.

Her yellow dress had a heart-shaped neckline and the snug bodice pushed her full, young breasts up into white, shapely mounds, and nestled in the crevice was a yellow rosette. She had brushed her squeaky-clean hair until it shone like red-brown silk, then pulled the hank back into thick curls that coiled atop her head, and Jayne had fastened the curls with gold pins. She sparkled like a fairy princess. She just prayed the nausea wouldn't return to ruin everything. She was bound and determined not to let anything, not ever her troubles, spoil her night out.

The sloping lawn was cast into a fairyland, and the facade of the manor glowed like a castle all lit up by myriad candles, with a festive air.

Paul stood fidgeting nervously where he met her at the entrance after she had alighted from the carriage. He lowered his head to whisper in her ear, and her eyes lit up, her mouth opening in surprise.

"Paul, how did you do it?" she asked as he tucked her arm into his possessively.

"Not now," he shushed her, adding, "Later."

She frowned amusedly, letting him lead her into the foyer where marble floors and heavy statues graced the hall. At the back of the entrance hall a circular staircase wound upward to the second floor. The furniture here was masculine, heavily carved and ornate, and she saw several of her own pieces from Southend, drawing a frown from her unlined forehead. That phony baron and Rutland, the very gall! She caught herself in time—she was going to be diligent tonight about having a good time.

"It is beautiful, Paul," she said in truth. "I can't remember ever having visited Heathcliff before." As they moved along through the crowd, some faces vaguely familiar, Paul stopped to introduce her to those he had already become acquainted with. "Do you know all these people?" she asked Paul in a soft voice, looking around the well-dressed crowd.

"No." He chuckled. "But they seem to know me, at least they pretend they do. Right before you arrived, a sweet lady came up and said it was nice to see me again, hoping I was home to stay." He shrugged with a low laugh. "Don't you see? My plan, everything is working out perfectly."

"What do you mean, Paul?" She continued to study the crowd, wondering out loud, "Where is Mr. Rutland? I thought surely the pest would be immediately hovering near like a bloodhound."

"He, ah, he'll be around shortly, no doubt."

Paul swept her into his arms on the dance floor as the musicians started up the first waltz tune. She was growing vexed with Paul's mysterious behavior. With Paul pressed close, the material of her gown felt sensuous and sheer, prompting her to remember what it was like to be against a man's hard body. It was obvious that Paul was disturbed by her nearness, but instead of her being bothered by this, she was painfully reminded of another male form. Paul could never compare with that one she tried so hard to put from her mind. He, Hasan, was always tucked into the deepest recess of her heart and soul. His countenance was already growing dim, and she was glad that she had willed it thus. She'd had enough problems without dwelling on Hasan, too.

Above the marble mantel over the fireplace, Rosette could see herself and Paul in the gilt-framed mirror, whirling around with the others on the dance floor. He still hadn't answered her concerning Rutland, and he seemed worried over something. She was about to question him again when, looking into the mirror, her eyes were caught and held by a pair of dark ones. It was as if she had been dealt a staggering blow, and she couldn't understand why she suddenly felt this powerful, unnamed emotion wash over her. She had never seen this man before, and they hadn't been introduced, giving her to believe he'd just arrived. At least she couldn't rightly recall Paul having introduced her to him. She had met so many since her arrival that her mind was spinning with the sea of faces and names she tried hard to remember. She twisted in Paul's arms in order to see the man standing at the fringe of the crowd.

"What are you looking at?" Paul asked her curiously.

"I was wondering—" she began, then stopped. Where had the stranger gone off to so suddenly? She continued to look this way and that, but there was no sign of him. Had she only imagined the stranger? No, she didn't think so. He had stood out, even in the mirror, not only as a good-looking man, but also as a personality—one that would be impossible to ignore. With a little twist of her head, this time she sensed the dark, compelling eyes trained on her. Her curiosity had earned a shock now that threatened to make her swoon.

"Who is he?" she managed, her body stiffening.

Paul froze. He finally saw who Rosette had been visibly searching for, and his face drained to a total lack of color as he stared over her shoulder to where the man with the lean jaw stood.

"Damn," Paul hissed and broke off, seeing Rawen come striding their way.

Rosette hardly heard Paul's sibilation. She was completely mesmerized by the huge man moving through the crowd milling about now that the music had stopped. He was at least a head taller than most men in the room. Feeling faint, Rosette's eyes strayed to the right to keep from staring at him. Someone was stepping before the band to request a new number be played.

Within seconds he was standing there, long strides having eaten up the distance that separated them, staring down at Rosette in astonishment. A tawny lock of hair waved across his wide forehead; his dark eyes below registered recognition; the nostrils of the retroussé nose were flaring.

Rosette shivered, her limbs a jumble of nerves. Was she supposed to know this man? He certainly seemed to know her, or something about her, but he maintained silence, as if waiting for one of them to speak first to make the introductions. They were all spared the moment then as a woman Rosette had met earlier broke the tension.

"Baron Rawen," Lady Meredith York clucked. "Shame on you for not introducing me to this handsome man." She turned chiding eyes upon the younger woman. "And you too, Lady Forrest. Do I have to introduce myself then?" She batted long, red lashes at the tall stranger she had feasted her eyes on from across the room. Looking at him, Lady York seemed to melt right before their eyes.

The genuine Baron stiffened, then said in a smooth tone of voice pitched low, "Mark Rawen, Esquire, at your service, madam."

"Oooh . . ." Lady York crooned. "Such a deep voice. A relative here, and a knight, no less!" She sidled closer to this late-comer to the party, releasing the pinching grip she'd had on Paul's arm.

"Not quite, madam. . . ." He let it hang, and Lady York couldn't decide which he'd discounted as fact.

"Well, anyway, if the moonstruck baron will not introduce us, I shall," she tittered.

"Never mind," Paul broke in with a low growl. "Ah, Sir Mark Rawen, Lady Meredith York." He turned to catch Rosette's pale look. "And this is my companion, eh, I hope someday my bride, Rosette Forrest, Lady Southend." He said it all wrong, but no one seemed to notice.

Lady York swished her painted fan. "My, my," she gushed, "the tension in this room is so thick you could slice it with a knife. What — ?"

Before she could go on, the musicians struck a chord, this time launching into a hauntingly romantic waltz tune. "Lady Forrest," this Mark Rawen began. "May I have the honor?" He crooked an arm clad in finest gray velvet.

Paul gaped, watching her go to him as if she were caught in a spell. Trembling, Rosette gazed up into the fathomless, dark eyes she swam in. His dusty, brown lashes swooped low, viridescent eyes taking all of her in from head to quivering hem line.

"Yoo-hoo, gorgeous, save a dance for me," Lady York called after the couple already melting into the others dancing. Looping her arm into Paul's she chuckled. "Now's your chance, darling," she giggled vacuously then.

With hatred aglow in his pale green eyes, Paul watched Baron Rawen gallantly sweep Rosette into the lilting waltz. What was the bastard up to, Paul wondered, trying to beat Paul at his own game? Perhaps not, not if Jessie had done his job as planned.

A cynical smile played across Baron Rawen's lean face, but the new beard he sported concealed most of it; even his thin scar was shadowed beneath the dark chin hair. It was all very puzzling what he'd just learned, but he needed more answers.

Caught up in a web of pleasure, Rosette allowed Sir Mark Rawen to pull her closer. Again, as when she had found his eyes in the mirror, she felt there was something vaguely familiar about this man. Somehow she found herself comparing him with Hasan al-Shareef, and discovered troublingly he not only resembled Hasan in countenance but made her experience the same strong emotions. Was it only because Hasan was still such a part of her? More than she realized? Or was she to begin finding Hasan in every tall, handsome stranger she met up with? At last, maybe Sir Mark could help her to forget Hasan.

The constant scrutiny of his dark eyes brought her usually protected shyness to surface; yet it was she who broke the scintillating silence between them.

"You are staring, Sir Mark. Do you always stare so at young women you dance with?"

"Only when they are as lovely as you are, Lady Forrest," he returned quickly. His legs brushing hers slowed. "Would you like a bit of fresh air, out on the terrace?" He nodded in that direction, his lean jaw profiled for her.

"I suppose that would be the likely place to go for some fresh air, wouldn't it," she stated, giving consent for him to escort her there.

As soon as they had stepped off the terrace into the garden path, the inevitable happened. Sir Mark pulled her into his arms. He kissed her lightly on her moist, upturned lips. "I have known a great desire to kiss you, my lady, ever since our eyes met in the mirror."

Rosette shrugged out of his masculine embrace and, turning away from him, she said, "I have not, Sir Mark. You remind me of someone I am trying hard to forget." Her lips burned still where he had softly, gently kissed her. Again, that familiarity.

Behind her back, the baron smiled knowingly. Staring at her glorious head of hair sprinkled with moondust, he experienced the greatest surge of joy he had ever known. There had been only one other time to match this, when his eyes had met with another's after a sandstorm. He wanted to take her up into his arms now and whirl her about, kiss her and love her forever and ever.

"Your lips also tasted familiar to me, my lady," he said in a bold, breathless voice. He reached out to run a long finger along the lovely curve of her neck. "You tremble at my touch."

"Y-yes," she said gently, "just like it was with — him."

"Does this old lover of yours have a name?" He slowly walked around to face her.

"I—I would rather not speak it now, please.

It—it bothers me too much to be reminded of him just now."

"Why?"

Eyes, like obsidian, had the moonlight reflected in them. Sighing, Rosette said, "Because I—I think I loved him very much. But he is far away now, and it's better this way."

"You *think* you loved him, or you know?" he said deeply, softly, with a little urgency.

"Oh, please, Sir Mark, no more about him." She dropped her chin, her moist eyes staring into the rose bed. "It just makes me sad."

"But one as lovely as you should be happy and enjoying life. Are you ever happy, Rosette?"

The first time he said her name sent little thrilling shocks through her. Yes, perhaps this compelling stranger could help her forget. "In a way, I g-guess I'm happy. But at the moment I have—" she sighed—"I have great problems plaguing me."

"Perhaps I can be of help some way."

"I—I really don't see how."

"I am very wealthy, you know. Tell me what it could be that troubles you so very much?"

"I—I am losing my home, Southend." She choked on a tiny sob. "What started out as my father's debt is now mine. He left this life owing our distant neighbor a great sum of money. It fell on my shoulders."

He ran a tanned finger along the mentioned

part of her body. "And this should not be, not on these lovely shoulders."

Finding her trembling once again, he acted the gentleman and dropped his hand back to his side, but reluctantly. Actually, Baron Mark Rawen could go on fondling her all through the night had he his way with Rosette Forrest. He could see, though, this would take more time, to go easy on her.

Mark Rawen grinned, showing half of his neat rows of teeth. "I would love to kiss away your troubles, but that is not the answer. Besides, my lady, I am known to be a gentleman." *So far—* he kept this to himself.

The pleasure of his deep male voice whirled inside and plunged clear down to her toes. "I — I must help myself in this, Sir Mark. But I do thank you for your offer." Her heart skipped a mad beat as he sighed deeply. Suddenly her hand slipped to her belly. Oh no, not now, she prayed.

"What is it?" he asked, seeing where her hand rested.

"Nothing, I — I just feel a bit dizzy."

He smiled warmly. "Down there?" He inclined his head.

Lightly she laughed, her hand falling away. "I think I have a bellyache too."

"Shall we go back inside?" He stared up at the huge, orange moon and then back down into her alarmingly pale face. "Or not such a good idea just yet?"

She flushed with embarrassment. "I'll be fine, really."

Such a gentleman, Rosette thought with a soft smile as Sir Mark ushered her back inside, his fingers warm and secure over her arm, sending tingles throughout her shoulders and breasts.

Before they could enter the fringe of the now-gay crowd, he turned to her. "I have gently enjoyed your company, my lady. But I have to get back home posthaste. I also have pressing matters awaiting me."

Where is home, Rosette wanted to ask. But that would be too impertinent, so she merely nodded graciously. She really wished he wouldn't leave her just yet. He had been such a balm, soothing all her troubles away in the short time she had had with him. Just when she was working up the courage to ask if she would see him again, he spoke up.

"May I call on you at Southend?" His dark eyes delved deeply into hers.

Rosette lifted her gaze from the white cravat that contrasted with his tanned throat. Southend had come easily to his lips, she noticed. He must have a good memory, that's all, she decided. "Yes, please do."

He took up her hand to squeeze it gently, and then he was disappearing into the crowd. Paul's dark face loomed up before her and she was suddenly very sorry. She had wanted to call Sir Mark Rawen back and tell him how to get to Southend. He was no fool, though, that was certain. He would find her place.

"Rosette?" Paul tried to gain her attention.

"Not now, Paul, I'm thinking . . ."

Then her eyes flew wide. The baron! He hadn't showed, and the hour was too late for anyone to arrive now. Who cared, she thought, up in the clouds, unable to wait for tomorrow to come.

Chapter Twenty-four

Morning sun penetrated the waking haze of Rosette's lingering dream. In it she had been waltzing with Sir Mark Rawen, his compelling masculinity and dark gaze staying with her like a tangible thing, bringing her groggy brain much unrest and confusion.

Now it all dimmed and she was wide awake, bounding from her bed to relieve her sudden nausea in the basin. Dry heaves racked her stomach, reminding her she had not eaten much the evening before. There had been too much excitement over the party to more than nibble, even though tables had overflowed with delectable food, meat and drink.

It hit her like an explosion then, where she sat hunched on the carpet. Sir Mark Rawen had been the stranger, the compelling man she had seen with Ben entering Oakhill Manor. What had Sir Mark been doing there?

Again dismissing her morning sickness as part of the unusual circumstances that surrounded her of late, Rosette gingerly rose to her feet. Looking into the mirror, she was greatly shocked by her pitiful appearance. If this kept up, she told herself, she would have to pay a visit to the doctor. If he could only give her something to ease this temporary malady, at least until things settled down a bit, she would be greatly relieved. But try though she might to assure herself it was nothing, there remained the niggling suspicion that she could be with child.

Then she laughed softly. "One time? Surely not."

Dressing herself in an old, ribbon-trimmed dress, and fastening her hair in back with a ribbon of the same color russet, Rosette went down to the kitchen to make herself some toast. That always helped calm down the nausea. After the toast and a cup of coffee weakened with cream, she left by the back door and strolled the garden.

Refreshed and rivaling the late summer

blooms in loveliness, Rosette stood gazing up at the mild, blue sky above the trees. Contentment was hard to come by, though, for her future was troubled and uncertain. So much had happened to her in the past year. She cocked her head, watching a little bird flit from branch to branch serenading her.

Now, looking back, Rosette wondered if she had been wise to visit Africa. Times had indeed been in a sorry state before her departure. But had she only leapt from the frying pan to the fire?

Her focus shifted suddenly, and her gaze made contact with something, something white-gold weaving slowly among the copse of trees that bordered the garden. Her heartbeat picked up. She was powerless to move for several moments, wondering just what she had seen. When the horse nickered and blew, Rosette recognized the sound and hoped to God Moondust had returned to her.

With a well-turned ankle peeping from beneath her hem, she stepped along the path, her skirts held high. "Moondust," she called. "Come girl, is that you?" and walked faster. Oh please, let it be Moondust, she prayed. She heard a low curse and command, and then the pounding of hoofbeats.

She was on the lawn now and running toward

the first trees. But all she could hear were the beats growing faint, and, as she waited, nothing more. Silence, but for her labored breath. Even the birds had stopped singing.

That night when Rosette entered the living room where Sir Mark awaited her, she found him staring about the room, contemplating the bareness. Hearing her enter, Sir Mark watched her approach him, reading much of her troubles from the emotions reflected in her lovely, tan eyes, alive with yellow flecks.

"You were not fooling one bit when you said last night you were losing your home. This is serious," he said gently. He contemplated her melancholy. "Is there somewhere we can sit?"

"Of course," she said, near to a laugh.

On the terrace, Jayne served them iced lemonade. "I'm afraid there's nothing stronger in the house." Jayne smiled at the picture of male exclusiveness. He was indeed a man apart, no pigeon-hearted chap here, she determined.

Sir Mark hoisted the tall glass in the air. "This will do very well." He felt Rosette staring, and he went on without looking at her. "I am not a great drinker. Hardly ever imbibe strong liquids, in fact."

He could still feel her staring, and he began to wonder how much she recognized in him as Hasan al-Shareef. The scar lay beneath his short, dark beard, well hidden. Perhaps it had merely been the tone of his voice suddenly familiar to her. Before she found him out, though, he needed some answers. Like why she had been drugged, with him believing her to be Rozelle Modestia. How deeply was she involved in the conspiracy, if that's what it had truly been. But first things first, like the reason Pierre Maudet was posing as Baron Rawen—himself!

"Rosette," he said, turning and surprising her. He laughed, a deep sound in his chest. "How well do you know Baron Rawen?"

"H-he has only just returned to England," she said cautiously, "as I have myself."

That being not the answer he sought, he went on with another frame of questioning. "Did he travel with you?" His dark eyes stared forcefully into hers, delving for the truth.

"Yes, I—Paul and I met in Morocco," she said, even more carefully. She looked aside to conceal a frown. What was he getting at, prying as he was?

"Paul?" he asked suddenly, unwavering from his course.

"Paul M. Rawen, the baron." She blinked at him as if he should have known this himself.

"Ah," Mark murmured with an impeccable smile. "Of course, he did say something to that nature, ah, last night, didn't he." He stroked the dark, manly beard. "Tell me more, Rosette, I am interested in knowing possibly could we be related somehow. That is, Paul and myself."

Rosette had reason to be wary of Sir Mark Rawen now. He puzzled her continually. He had arrived in a smart, new phaeton, pulled by magnificent chestnuts. He was a stranger to these parts, so she believed, which led her to a question of her own.

"Tell me something first, Sir Mark."

He dipped his head gallantly as she paused. "Just ask, my lady."

She endeavored to avoid the passionate, velvet depths of his warm eyes. Why, they had green in them, just like . . . oh, she would not allow Hasan to enter her thoughts just now, they were befuddled enough as it is.

"I—I hope I am not overly bold in asking where you are staying, Sir Mark?" She blushed fiercely when his gaze dropped to study her lips. "C-could you tell me?"

He smiled over her nervousness. "Oakhill. I own the estate."

"Y-you?" She gripped a fold of her russet afternoon dress, and he caught the high-strung movement.

With large, lean hands, Mark moved to press the strain from her fingers. She flinched at his touch, and he smiled this time gently. "Why does this seem strange to you? I have always owned Oakhill, and have been away from it for, ah, for several years," he ended brusquely.

"Oh," she merely murmured. So, she thought, here sat the phony baron right beside her! He had been covering himself, but why? For what reason? Quickly she recovered to ask, "Do you perhaps know a man by the name of Rutland?"

"He is, or was, my estate manager." Mark heaved a deep sigh. "He was shot and killed just yesterday upon my arrival."

Trembling like a leaf, Rosette's hand shot to her forehead. "You will have to forgive me, Sir Mark, as I am not feeling well again and must go lie down. Do you mind?"

Mark stiffened. She was brushing him off, telling him to make a hasty exit. He wouldn't have this, not now when he was getting close to answers sorely needed.

Gasping, Rosette felt him grip her wrist. The movement had been quick as a viper; she hadn't seen it coming. "Sir Mark, you are hurting me. Please let go of my arm."

"Ah, my lady, not yet." His eyes bored into hers mercilessly. "You are in debt, remember, and are held liable for payment. You owe me, my lady."

Moist lips parted incredulously. "You are a

fake, sir, and if you do not unhand me, I shall call—call—"

"Call all you want, Rosette," he challenged. "But who will heed your call? A simple housemaid?" He laughed with an implacable sound. "Or perhaps you have a stout butler awaiting your distress signal?"

"No, none of those!" She rubbed her sore wrist that was released finally. "Just what do you want from me, sir, you already have all that I own. Would you throw me out the door now?" Gulping, Rosette was near tears.

"I shall bargain with you, dear Rosette," he said, and let it lie.

"B-bargain?" She laughed ironically. "What do I have left to bargain with, pray tell?" She waved an arm toward her empty house, then showed him the grounds with a sweep of her slim arm. "They are yours also." Her fingers at last plucked at the bodice of her old but still lovely dress. "And you have most of my clothes, too. Tell me, sir, where the bargain lies?"

Boldly his eyes traveled down the front of her russet dress, lingered at her waist, and then swept up to meet her unblinking gaze. "You have more to bargain with than you realize, my lady, worth far more than a hundred holdings put together—and more."

"Oh no!" Rosette's voice quivered angrily. "I shall not become your h-harlot! Never!" She made to stand, but he jerked her back firmly down, in the garden chair. Her eyes narrowed up at his stern features. "And I thought you were a gentleman!" She let out a feminine snort from her fine nose.

"A gentleman I am not when someone owes me and refuses to pay up." He laughed resolutely. "But pay in full you shall, Rosette Forrest, or else face a jail sentence for murder."

"Why," she nearly choked, "whatever do you mean?"

"Rutland was murdered, true?"

Though giving him a perfunctory toss of her head, her voice shook when it emerged. "I would not know that for sure."

"You own a horse, Moondust, missing since you left Southend?"

"Y-yes." Her frightened gaze raked the woods bordering the garden and then swept back to his forcible gaze. "But what?"

"I have been to see our neighbors, not too far from here." He took in her confusion, and proceeded to add to it. "Your Moondust has been sighted by a bloke of questionable character, the perpetrator of these crimes, perhaps?"

He was asking her? "G-go on," she stammered, already fearing the worst.

"I personally believe Rutland's murderer was riding your horse."

He watched her go deathly pale.

"No . . . oh no!"

Before she passed out, Rosette saw him antici-
pating her weakness and reaching out to break
her swoon. Then she spun off into a nightmare of
confusion where white horses turned into black,
dragonlike beasts.

Chapter Twenty-five

When Rosette regained consciousness she found herself lying in her bedroom, with the vague impression that strong arms had lifted her carefully. A cool cloth had been placed on her forehead, and Jayne hovered near.

After Rosette's eyes made a thorough search of the bedroom, she sighed with relief.

"He carried you up here," Jayne said softly. "When he saw you were going to revive, he took his leave. Are you feeling better now, my lady? You sure gave us a fright for a time there."

"Us?" Rosette asked, just returning fully to her senses. "Why would Sir Mark care? He is a cold, unfeeling beast who thinks only after his own welfare." And, of course, pleasure, she wouldn't add out loud.

"No, no, Rosie. I think you're wrong there. He was very concerned, and you were very cold and pale at first." Jayne looked down at the clenched hands, like closed camellia petals, over Rosette's stomach. "I know you haven't been all that well since you arrived home. Could you tell me what is ailing you?"

Fear that her condition was indeed pregnancy and was being found out lent a trembling note to Rosette's normally even voice. "It is true, Jayne, I—I have been feeling poorly." Snatching the now-warm wet cloth from her forehead, Rosette eased herself up to perch on the edge of the bed. Forlornly she scanned her bedroom as memories crowded into her mind.

Her parents had never doted on her, and their indifference toward their only child had always been felt. A loveless childhood she'd known, and had been an even lonelier teen, always in search of someone with a kind word. One thing was certain now: Perry Marland was a person of the past. She was grateful he was away in Europe, as she'd overheard during the ball. I'm positive I would be able to face Perry now and hold my head up high without a quiver or a qualm over Mama's scandal. Despite the distressing circumstances surrounding her even today, she felt quite strong and able in body and mind to face another day—and Sir Mark Rawen!

"You should try and eat something now," Jayne broke into Rosette's reflections.

"I really don't think that I can. Besides, I'm not very hungry." Rosette pinched a fold of her dress thoughtfully, not looking up at the maid. "D-did Sir Mark leave a message?"

In that, Jayne took heart. But she wouldn't let Rosette catch her smiling over this. "Oh yes. He said he'll be picking you up at seven to take you to Oakhill."

Bounding from the edge of the bed, Rosette bristled at the gall of Sir Mark. "He . . . what?" Her eyes, like fiery topazes, snapped and spoke volumes along with her voice. "I shall go nowhere with that man—that . . . that ooooh!"

"But you must! He holds your future welfare in his hands," Jayne said beseechingly.

"No! I despise Sir Mark—and everything he stands for. He is an evil, l-lecherous m-man," Rosette stammered out her fury.

Jayne put on a serious mask. "He said you would not like going to prison, my lady."

Rosette whirled on the maid. "H-how do you know that?"

Jayne heaved a tiny sigh. "He said as much."

"He cannot do anything to me, Jayne. He is a fake, a . . . a phony baron!"

"Forgive me for saying, but I don't think so.

There's more to that man than meets the eye."
She took in the young lady's scowl. "I'll be helping you get ready soon, after I draw your bath,
my lady."

"I shall not go to Oakhill. A hundred horses
could not drag me away, not with Sir Mark!" Rosette bit her lip, tasting blood. Oh, that man
wreaks havoc with my emotions, she wouldn't
say out loud.

Not in the usual pleasant anticipation of a
young lady readying for an outing, Rosette reluctantly had donned a simple gown, toffee and
cream in coloring, devoid of any fancy trim-
mings. Under lock and key, she hid her inner-
most feelings from Jayne, but she wondered if
she would be so lucky with Sir Mark. Those dark
eyes seemed to peer and see into her very soul.
She would have to come to grips with her emotions, for it was plain that Sir Mark was through
toying with her.

Not so mysteriously, one of her bags had been
returned, delivered just that afternoon. Believing
this to be Paul's doing, she could relax further,
knowing that her friend was near. But where was
Paul? Why hadn't she heard from him lately?

Finally but reluctantly, she had given in to
Jayne's pleading. She sighed now, piling her
waist-length, russet hair atop her head. Sooner

or later I am going to have to deal with Sir Mark
Rawen anyway. She would go to Oakhill, but
only for a visit, she told herself, and nothing
more. To discover exactly what Sir Mark had in
mind for her, and exactly to what measure. With
daring abandon, Rosette allowed a few shining
tendrils to escape and hug her cheeks enchant-
ingly.

The phaeton arrived promptly at seven. Settled in the plush velvet seat while the obsequious
driver pulled away from Southend, Rosette studied the gown she had chosen. Rather, she
smirked, the gown Jayne chose. Now that she
viewed the bodice from above instead of her mirror, noticing how décolleté the gown was, she
knew a sudden urge to stop the driver so that she
could return to tear it off. But she suppressed the
urge, assuring herself that Sir Mark had business
in mind. He wouldn't dare press the same issue.
But try though she might, she had trouble convincing herself that Sir Mark would revert back
to the perfect gentleman he'd been at first.

Rosette was mildly surprised when she stepped
down into the yard and took a better look at her
driver. Gingerly she left Ben standing there looking after her as she walked to the door. Before
she reached it, though, the door was swept wide.
Milly greeted her with a warm smile. Rosette noticed at once the transformation in the housemaid, who had the last time she'd visited here

reminded Rosette of a fishwife. Even the uniform Milly wore was clean and crisp, her white apron without spot.

"Welcome, Lady Forrest." Milly bobbed a practiced curtsy. "Lord Rawen, he ain't — uh, he's not yet returned from his outing, and he said for you to make yourself at home in the parlor."

That sure of himself, was he? Rosette snorted softly to herself as she followed sashaying Milly into the equally transformed parlor. Sheepishly Milly grinned at the young lady's surprise.

"Cleaned up the place a bit and had some pretty furnishin's brought in from London. He works fast does Lord Rawen."

Indeed he does, Rosette kept to herself. The bold cock is pruning his feathers and his nest, but for just what she tried not to dwell on for now. The room itself bore evidence of Sir Mark's masculinity and self-reliant hand at decorating to his liking. Dark sofas of carnelian sprang up, flanked by tables of Italian decor; a presence seemed to lurk there. Rosette glanced around slightly nervously, as if expecting Sir Mark at any moment. She shivered, for some strange, inexplicable reason reminded of Hasan al-Shareef.

Milly smoothed work-calloused hands over her clean, new apron. Shyly she peered into the lovely, young face flushed with some unnamed emotion. "He'll be picking up some more brand new items for the house." Milly shifted on her feet shod in the pinch of new shoes.

Curiously Rosette eyed the housemaid as she lifted the hem of her spotless apron to wipe a corner of the table free of a speck of imaginary dust. The maid lingered. Rosette sighed and wondered if she should sit or stand.

"Do you know who Sir Rawen's been out to meet with today?" Milly put her nervousness into conversation. It wouldn't do for the lady to be leaving so soon because of becoming bored.

"No, I couldn't possibly know," Rosette ended with a sigh laced with boredom, just as the maid suspected.

"He's an old friend to the family of Sir Rawen's."

"Oh." Rosette didn't really feel all that curious over Sir Rawen's acquaintances. "Who is that?" she asked, just to be kind to the worrying maid.

"Disraeli, that's who!"

"Disraeli," Rosette echoed, her focus shifting from the maid to the velvet lawn outside the window. To walk there, barefoot, enjoying the afternoon, free, happy, without care. With someone beside her? But who? Was there no one in this world she cared to share her life with? She might despise Sir Mark, but she still responded to him. Why? She could look up at him and her breath would catch and she could feel the color sweep up into her cheeks. She had to admit that he bothered her, just as Hasan al-Shareef had. Her body ached with desire, but that was because Hasan had been her initiator. And now the constant scrutiny of Sir Mark was reaching that hidden sweetness in her woman's inner core. She would have to play the game cautiously, see what he had in mind, or else she would fall prey to his advances, ones she knew would surely come sooner or later. Later she could cope with. Now was too soon.

"Gladstone and Disraeli," Milly was saying, "they're in the middle of every political storm inside and outside parliament. But Disraeli, he's always been interested in the condition of England, and he's the one Sir Rawen met with today over lunch."

"I see." Indeed Rosette recalled the name Disraeli. His ministry carried through an impressive program of social reform and marked an important stage in the building up of the British empire. But she wasn't interested in the two bitter rivals and their politics. "Will Sir Mark return soon?" Otherwise she might as well return to Southend, she thought as she inquired.

Every object and each piece of furniture spoke of vast wealth, and Milly gestured now with an apology to a settee upholstered in plum cloth embroidered with shiny golden threads.

"Thank you." Rosette sat, gingerly and with posture stiff on the edge of the settee. To await the esquire who held fate in his deeply tanned hands. Where had he acquired such a bronze color? she wondered. Couldn't be natural, for she had spied his paler skin beneath the immaculate collar of his shirt.

"I'll be going about my tasks now," Milly said. "Would you be wanting something to drink?"

"No, I'm fine. I'll just wait." But not too long, Rosette told herself. The rudeness of the man keeping her waiting, it was almost unheard of!

After only a couple of minutes' passing, the realization of what she was doing took hold. She should flee from here. But where could she go? Jayne was right. Sir Mark Rawen held her fate in his hands. There wasn't a single place for her to hide. But she'd made a stupid mistake in coming here, thinking Sir Mark would be lenient with her. But just who did he think he was? Jayne seemed to think he was indeed someone important, that his actions spoke louder than words. He was well used to being in command, she had said.

"I see that you have made yourself at least halfway comfortable."

Rosette felt her nerves jerk as though in contact with fire. His deep, male voice broke into her reflections. She had been sitting with her profile to him, but now Mark saw she faced him with a proud, undaunted tilt to her fine chin. He understood at once that the last thing she wanted was to appear vulnerable in his presence.

"Under the circumstances of late, and especially today, I find total relaxation hard to come by." Her posture and pose bore evidence of the statement. But she was also contemplating the elegant dove-gray coat he wore, with trousers to match. With a jolt she caught herself blinking over the ample display of manhood. When his low chuckle sounded, her focus shifted and met green eyes that impaled her mercilessly. Again she asked herself, where had she seen eyes like this. Like quick autumn birds, the orbs of her eyes skittered off and came to rest on a chair covered with plum, fine-cut velvet.

"My, don't we sound brittle and cold this evening," Sir Mark drawled. He cleared his throat, adding, "You would do better to be more gracious, as you shall soon learn, my dear."

With a little twist of her lips, she asked, "Just what are you insinuating, my lord?"

His own lips, sculpted and sensuous, curled up at the corners. She experienced a second jolt, this one not unlike the piercing of desire. Though she told herself not to be affected by his manliness, it was hard to accomplish. He struck a chord of sensual awakening in her, one known to her before, but short-lived after Hadji's drug had worn off. While under the drug, she believed she had known a false sense of desire and thought herself to be in love with Hasan. She now felt as if caught between the acts of a play, one becoming increasingly dangerous.

"I am saying . . ." He didn't finish, just frowned thoughtfully above her.

When had he come to stand there? she wondered. Courage, she prayed, don't leave me now. His eyes had hardened as she gazed up at him, and she noticed with a stab of pure terror that he indulged in studying her at his leisure. From above he could see right down into her bodice!

"Sir, you are too bold!" Rosette shifted, snatching her shoulders back to make her bodice taut and no access given to her naked bosom.

But still he continued to survey the alabaster perfection of her skin left bare above her bodice. He came around to face her head-on. Rugged features very similar to Hasan's confronted her, but Rosette forced herself to take firm hold of her courage, even though her emotions raged fitfully.

"It is obvious you wish to avoid my eyes," he murmured, "also my touch." Mark ran a finger lightly over her kneecap. "You are lovely, beautiful as summer's first blushing rose. Rose, bleeding rose . . ."

So taken was she by the depth of raw emotion in his reverberating tone that Rosette stared mesmerized up into piercing eyes owning fathomless color, unable to rip herself away to keep from drowning in them. She had, yes, she had experienced this same moment, but when? Where? When would she hear the inward voice reveal to her the stunning mystery she found herself enmeshed in?

"I—I am not b-bleeding," she said shyly, softly. "What do you mean, Sir Mark?"

"Your heart bleeds for attention, someone to care, to love you." Two fingers pressed upon her knee. "Am I correct, sweet Rose?"

Rosette thought anew that in a short time she would be safely back to Southend. Yet in the fore of her mind she was becoming alarmingly aware that the false security her childhood home afforded her at the moment could not last. Vainly she sought a haven for her heart.

"Compliments or pity, my lord? Which shall it be?" Rosette allowed a husky purr in her voice.

"Compliments would be more to my liking, dear Rose, to lavish upon your head. But tell me, which of your parents cast you aside?" When she would not look at him, he went one further. "Well then, was it both?" The whole palm of his hand cupped her knee now, but still she didn't seem to be affected by the warmth.

Rosette stiffened, and, noticing the familiarity of his touch, brushed the heated palm from her leg. "Again you go too far, now with both words and deeds."

"Deeds?" He chuckled, his face altered to boyish handsomeness.

Casually he left her to go and pour wine from a decanter that stood ready upon a marble-topped side table. From a sidelong gaze he watched her every skittish move, the restless twitching of her legs, and the busy fingers creasing folds in her gown. He smiled to himself.

He soon returned, offering a dainty goblet to her nerveless fingers. She had ceased all motion. "Not thirsty?"

"I would much rather you speak of the matter which brought me here in the first place." She finally took the proffered goblet and twirled it, giving no indication of tasting the amber liquid.

He chose an armchair in the style of Louis XVI, letting his tall frame down easily, stretching long legs out beside the hem of her gown. Laconically he said, "Your future is shaky, to say the least, sweet Rose." He sipped the wine, then placed the goblet aside. "As my wife you shall have no such worries. I would like an heir, and you need a way out of your frightful dilemma."

"No!"

Bounding to her feet, Rosette made a dash for the door, leaving her drink spilled and seeping into the fine carpet. Swiftly he was on his way, overtaking her before she could step into the hall. She stood stunned, speechless, as he gripped her wrist after spinning her about to face his impending glower.

"I don't understand any of this," Rosette stammered.

He shook his tawny head, releasing a lock of hair that at once mesmerized her. Words of further confusion sprang to her lips, but she could not utter them, not with his virile form so close to her quaking thighs. The moment hung suspended. The firm quickness he had come to terrified her, as no man had made her feel such sweet desire before. No one, but . . .

"I have asked you to become my wife," he said quickly and firmly.

"No, you have told me, Sir Mark. So, it has come to blackmail?"

"Oh, lord, is that what you think?" He found her other arm and squeezed it gently, but masterfully. Her chin sagged and he lifted it between thumb and forefinger. "I want you," he whispered softly, as if others listened.

"You want an heir!" she breathed the words out hard.

"Also a wife, and I cannot think of another in all of England as lovely as the rose that stands before me here that I would wish to wed." Mark drew her closer. "Look at me, Rose. Look hard."

Shyly she gazed into eyes that indeed produced a powerful effect in her breast, not unlike breathlessness; and her heart began to flutter with the fear that he was going to kiss her as she had never been kissed before.

SONYA T. PELTON

"Ohh," she cried when the crisp lips brushed hers. "Mark, please . . . don't!" She shoved at his chest in a futile attempt to ward him off.

His tongue flicked over the part of her lips that was heart-shaped, titillating the nub in the pink bow, then going shockingly underneath. At the same time she licked her nervous lips and tongue met tongue tip.

"Oh, Mark, Mark, don't do this to me. I have had enough. I am so afraid to—to feel, b-because . . ." She couldn't finish. "You could never know." She choked on a sob.

"Try me, please. I am not a thorn to prick the rose and leave it lie bleeding. Rose, I shall not hurt you, I promise. Just marry me, and you will never know fear of rejection ever again."

"Why?"

His brow rose in a furrow. "Why do I want to wed you?"

She nodded yes and he pulled her forehead to rest on his chin.

"Ultimately to have children and . . ." He brushed his lips over the shining auburn crown. "Believe this or not, Rose, but I love you," he said soft as a summer current of warm air.

"B-but you hardly know me. We have only just met, and I—I thought you . . ."

He wouldn't allow her to finish. "Whatever I thought before does not matter. I only know that I must have you—forever."

346

"Even if Moondust was ridden by a b-bloke you thought to be Rutland's murderer?"

He stiffened, then just as quickly relaxed. "He still may very well be. The dark rider, so he had turned out to be, has avoided myself and my men at every turn."

"Men? You have men out looking for him?"

"Yes. The sheriff and I have several posses out. But that stolen horse of yours rides the wind and gallops like an invisible wraith in the night."

"I would like to catch up with this fellow who has gotten Moondust away from Southend! Now I know why Moondust has never returned." Rosette leaned sad and heavily against his chest. "I loved that horse, and she me. We were inseparable." Her eyes suddenly narrowed with a light entering to create a golden glow.

He tenderly bussed her forehead. "Now that we have that out of the way. Rose, my sweet Rose, say you will become my bride by the fortnight?"

As if hypnotized and devoid of emotion, Rosette stared unseeingly at some distant spot, muttering, "Yes, Mark —"

That night back in her bed at Southend, Rosette woke from a dream in which Sir Mark turned into a two-headed beast. Curled up on her knees upon her bed, Rosette worried her lower lip as the realization of what she had committed herself to came flooding back. How could she have yielded, when all along she wished to avoid matrimony, and especially to Sir Mark Rawen? What had possessed her? The pressure of his hands and strong frame against her had left her without a will of her own. How could she come to know the joys of life when Mark Rawen terrified her and was a total mystery? How could she become his bride not knowing his true nature? She squirmed under the sheets. Even the thought of Sir Mark bedding her was almost beyond her. What would he do when he discovered she carried another man's child? For now she knew indeed she was in the family way, with the qualms returning twofold, her time two months since last flux.

Sighing, she lay back down to fight the nausea. I cannot marry Sir Mark. I shall tell him tomorrow, yes, and then leave Southend. Jayne was right. Sir Mark is not who he says he is. He is truly the Baron Rawen. Then who is Paul M. Rawen?

Amid her mind's tumult, incredibly Rosette found sleep.

Part Five

Dark Rider

*Promises by night be not binding
in the daytime*

— *Arab Proverb*

Chapter Twenty-six

The lands marched side by side, with Oakhill on one end and Heathcliff on the other, Southend in the middle. Brother and sister, dissimilar as night and day in countenance, stood together secreted in a back room at Heathcliff poring over the acreage on the map Paul had just sketched for their evil scheme.

"Why, it would take close to an hour to return to Heathcliff after the nasty job is done!"

Gold-flecked eyes glittering with a fiery heat, Rozelle Modestia turned to face her brother. "How in the world could we ever pull it off and not get caught?"

Frustrated, Paul studied his sister, stunningly beautiful in a Worth gown, one that seemed to float around her even as she stood still. At times there was the need to check himself in the presence of his sister. In countenance she was so like Rosette Forrest that he couldn't believe his own eyes. But that was where the similarity ended, in face and form. Otherwise their personalities were of a total opposite. Whereas Rosette was sweet and charming, Rozelle Modestia on the other could be truly coldhearted. His own sister—conniving, deceitful, and even willing to murder her own flesh and blood, her half-brother that is to say—was very much like Paul himself.

Rozelle faced the mirror, admiring the carved and lacquered frame as much as her own gorgeous face and figure. They, herself and Paul, had been to the London shops that day. She had overspent, purchasing some gowns in satin, muslin, all with a Paris look about them, some with layers of white lace at the bodice. She stared haughtily at Paul in the mirror behind her.

"You should have done the deed while at El Taj." She shivered, just the reminder of the kasbah making her ill. "They were together then, you had the chance, then all would have been ours. Why have you waited so long to get rid of them?"

"I've already told you, dear sister. I'm in love

with Rosette Forrest and I mean to make her my own."

"But we wanted them together, don't you see, so we could destroy them both, not just Mark. I wanted Rosette Forrest out of the way, too, in order to gain Southend. You know the estate sits right in the midst of the lands we want to join. We would be famously rich, and now you want to go and spoil all, for the love of that woman you call my twin." Rozelle Modestia peered at her beautiful face once again. "Is she really that much like me?" She caressed her magnolia-complexioned cheeks. "Is she really as fair, and do her eyes sparkle like warm topaz?"

"I'd be lying if I said she's just like you, dear sister, because Rosette's countenance defies description."

"Oh, faugh! You simpleton, you said she's just like me, you told me so earlier."

"Alright, she's your exact image, if it'll make you happy then." Paul complied with her silly willful notion.

"But I want to be the most beautiful in all of England, and do not want a twin." Rozelle studied her body's profile in the mirror while Paul groaned in exasperation. "Is she thinner than I? Tell me Paul, I want to know."

Paul gritted his teeth. "Yes! She's thinner, and she's ah, a bit larger on the top."

"Ohh," Rozelle moaned and glared at her

brother. "You'd better get rid of her too, Paul. I want her dead, just like my mother died because of Baron Tremayne Rawen."

Here we go again, Paul groaned inwardly. With a long drink in hand he settled down into a deep, leather chair. They might as well get this over with, he had a long ride back to Rozelle's town house. He waved his hand in the air. "Go on, I'm listening."

"The baron never gave Mama a second look after he kept her in that shabby London rooming house and sired two bastards on her. You remember yourself, Paul, you watched Margaret turn into a harlot just to feed and clothe us and put a roof over our heads."

Paul bristled. "How would you know what it was like, you were only a babe. You were the one the baron took in, and he even went so far as to create the impression you were Mark's sister, and not half that blood as you really are."

With slim arms cocked at her hips, Rozelle Modestia went on with her tirade. "Oh, faugh! Mark Brandon was always Papa's pet, and in his eyes Mark could do not one wrong. You and I both, his bastards. I can't even remember Mark's Spanish mother, and a lot she cared for me, sending me away only a babe on that horrible journey into the desert! The bitch never could compare with Margaret, even though neither do I remember her. I just know Mama was a gentle person, not some high-born aristocrat. And the baron, ha, a dissolute character him. I'm only too happy that he perished under the hands of thieves in the Sahara!"

"You were there too, but your life was spared by those so-called desert thieves who took you and Mark in."

"I hated them, and the sheik who adopted Mark — Hasan al-Shareef — faugh! I couldn't wait to get away from the arrogant bastard and stay in Morocco with my friends."

"He loved you as a true sister, Rozelle, not that I give a damn, but it is you who was given your father's name, not I. I had to live with the name Moreland, Mama's wretched name."

"Related to the Marlands, who are also very wealthy. How is it that Mama herself never married into wealth like her cousins?" Rozelle pulled a long, bitter face.

"Because, dear sister, she fell in love with a rogue, the Baron Tremayne, our father, no less. It was I who watched Mama die after she contracted a social disease from a filthy, drunken sailor. I'd have killed him had I found where the bastard had gone off to."

"Who knows," Rozelle taunted, "maybe that filthy sailor was our real father. Tell me, who resembles the Baron Tremayne? You? I?"

"I wouldn't know, I don't remember." Paul clenched and unclenched his fingers. He stared back in time, to the marketplace in Morocco where he had met up with his sister again several years ago. He had been wandering, taking jobs here and there where he could. He had left Oakhill, the run-down estate his father, the baron, had housed his mistress in for a time. But that was all Milly had remembered of Margaret, that she'd been Tremayne's whore. She'd been a beauty in her time, Milly had said. Margaret — Paul wondered how many lovers she had really known while at Oakhill. Had she been true to the baron then? What if she'd been lonesome and taken in a lover herself? Why had his father kicked her out, sending her to that rat-infested hole in London?

What if — Paul gulped hard. If Lord Alfred Forrest himself had taken a mistress. While sleeping fitfully on the voyage back to England, Rosette Forrest had murmured of sad memories in her sleep — of her father, Louise's scandal. Paul swung about to stare hard at his sister's back as she yet admired her beauty in the mirror. Could she be — could Rozelle Modestia in fact be Rosette's sister? Perhaps it was only he, Paul Moreland, who was Mark's half-brother? He sighed. No matter, they were still bastards to the bone, he and Rozelle Modestia. All that really mattered was that they do away with one man, and then all would be theirs. He narrowed his gaze at Rozelle with malice aforethought. Ah yes, theirs, his and Rosette Forrest's. Later he wouldn't need his sister—if that's what she truly was—but for the time being he could use her in his plan. Just as he'd used Hadji, only a pawn. He had seen Rosette and used her too at first. But love had struck him upon seeing her in the exotic setting of El Taj. He planned to dress her thus after he made her his wife, in filmy draperies. If Hasan had taken her maidenhood he would have even more reason to slay the man.

Yes, he'd had ample chance to do away with Mark Rawen while at El Taj. But his first plan to have Rosette blamed for Mark's murder failed miserably. Ah, how he would love to see Mark Rawen's face if the two, Rosette and Rozelle, stood side by side. But this wasn't to be. Mark thought his sister dead. Ha! She was probably no more his sister than Rosette Forrest herself.

Rozelle whirled from the mirror, her soft, round breasts holding Paul mesmerized momentarily before he collected himself from lustful thoughts. Cattily Rozelle smiled.

"Where is this Jessie, the filthy bloke you hired to do away with Rutland?"

"He's a hard one to catch up with these days. Some say he's gone mad. I myself believe it, he's as loony as that horse he rides at night." Paul brushed a speck of lint from his gray trouser leg. "Forget him, Rozelle, he's called the dark rider."

"The dark rider, hmm?" Rozelle shrugged

then. "Take me back to my place now, Paul. I'm suddenly weary of all this talk. I too have heard of the dark rider." She shivered next. "I shouldn't like to meet up with that bloke. Some gossips say he looks headless mounted on that beast, Moondust. We'll take care of Mark Rawen ourselves, in time."

With the night a dark pall around her, Moondust, cantered along the Hounslow Road. She was moving swiftly now, a fleet ghostlike apparition in the night filled with eerie, clinging mists. The moss and grass absorbed the pound of her bloodied hoofs as she swerved off the road.

A tawny owl hooted mournfully. The mare paced under the moon dappling the leafy oaks that overhung the brook. She halted there, and shook her moon-white head, blowing, content, free at last, swishing at her quarters with a long, silky tail.

She had been chased, but to try and catch Moondust was like chasing a will-o'-the-wisp off the Hounslow marshes. She had felt those mists, felt them thicken to close around and protect her while she met the fog that came out of the woods. It was as if she had been endowed with human thought, for she sought the gloomier hiding places of the moor, galloping on beautifully toward the stretch of dark forestland that sprawled between Oakhill and Heathcliff.

She took up her flight again, her silken nose homeward bound, moving east, now north, her long tail streaking out behind as if part of the mists. The owl *ke'wicked* again, mourning the dead.

Chapter Twenty-seven

Rosette woke to the tug of frenzied fingers on her arm. Rolling her head back and forth on the pillow, her eyes opened to the bleary sight of Jayne bending above her, her hand shaking Rosette's that lay bare outside the sheet.

"Wake now! You must, my lady."

"What is it?" Rosette managed to sit up, groaning over a nauseous headache.

"The h-horse, my lady. She's come back, like a blooming Pegasus, flashing her hoofs and flying about the yard as if indeed she had wings! Listen, she's out there calling for you!"

Again Rosette moaned softly. Am I dreaming,

she wondered. Then, as reason began to flow into her, she lifted her sleepy face to stare at the woman. "Horse? Here?"

Viciously the maid nodded.

"Moondust?"

She cried as her hands moved fitfully. "Yes! She's going to wake the dead. Up with you, and let me wrap a robe about you!"

With a hand she tossed aside the sheet and slid her white legs over the edge. The swiftness of her rising made her shudder. "Oh damnation, to be with child now! The curse of woman's lot!"

Gaping, Jayne could only stare. "W-with ch-child, my lady?"

"That's exactly what I said, dear Jayne. I am going to have a sheik's bastard."

Knowing she was going to swoon, the maid clutched the bedpost. A hand clutched her thin breast. "Oh dear lord, and us not knowing where the next penny's coming from. No crops, no savings in the coffer, what're we to do, dear lady?"

Already at the window, Rosette stood like a statue staring coldly down at the streak of Moondust in her garden. Hoofs came up to flash at her in a triumphant salute, nostrils flared widely, and Moondust tossed her huge, gilded head as she lowered her forelegs. With her head out the window, Rosette spoke over

361

her shoulder to Jayne, "We shall manage, you'll see."

The young Baron Rawen reluctantly dismounted from his horse and strode with high, polished boots through the mud to the Brentwood Inn. The wind was wet and cold out here, bringing a touch of sanity to Mark.

The inn was quiet this time of night. The collar of his coat was turned up to protect him against the light drizzle that still fell and the low-brimmed hat shadowed his features as he entered the inn and went directly to the taproom. He was not a drinker by nature, but a brandy he knew would feel warm in his middle. He chose a seat at the back of the room, near the fire.

For the past two days there had been a hard core of anger in Mark Rawen. He cursed himself for the weakness that had pushed him into proposing to Rosette Forrest. He sighed deeply, looking around the room. There were few customers in the Brentwood Inn at this late hour, and the lone serving wench's heels clattered, making loud echoes in the raftered ceiling as she waited on him.

She could see the despondency that was breeding in the man at the farthest window table. "So good to see you, sir." She smiled tremulously. "It's been some time since you last stopped for a toot."

"How would you suggest I remedy that?" he asked the serving wench, trying to be civil while inside a storm raged.

"Why, sir, have a good stiff one or two."

"Bring me two then, girl."

She bobbed as graciously as she could. "Yes, sir!"

Mark Rawen sat back, relaxed, watching the twitch of generous hips as the serving wench went to fill his order. He smiled a dangerous smile. More and more, he was discovering the character of the woman who had made herself a partner in Paul Moreland's crime. He had thought that the marriage be set aside, but had finally been convinced that this could not be the case. Then he turned his mind to punishments and he decided that marriage to Rosette Forrest would be the most satisfactory kind of retribution because this would make her his thrall. Oh yes, he was in love with the deceitful vixen, and all the better to have her under his palm for what he had in mind for her. He smirked cruelly in anticipation of getting his hands on her. She was going to pay for the scheming act she and Moreland cooked up.

At the same moment these thoughts for punishment ran rampant through his mind, he remembered her soft woman's body, her sweet

voice, throaty but soft and full of feminine wiles.
Ha. The bleeding rose, what an act she pulled.
He would have fallen for it had she returned the
next day to begin plans for their wedding day.
But she was gone—two days—so that
plain-faced maid had informed him. Rosette had
tricked him once again, first playing the part of
his sister, and now continuing with this plan with
Moreland, whatever it was.

Just as the serving wench came with the tray of
drinks, Mark shot up from the chair, turning it
over. By God, he thought, as the scar throbbed
along his cheek, they mean to kill me. Why
hadn't he thought this before. Fool that he was to
let the phony innocence of the woman cloud his
sensibilities.

Only for a moment did the serving wench see
the hot hate flaming in the dark green eyes of the
baron. That was enough for her to turn tail and
flee back, retracing her steps.

Mounted on the black, a curious smile played
about the baron's mouth. A third one they had in
on their dangerous game—the bloke that mounts
the gilded mare by night. A gleam entered his
eyes, reflected by not only the moon but by his
thoughts. Well, my friends, four can play this
night game.

Midnight, and the English countryside was

still and fantasylike, filled with swirling graveyard mists. But, moonlight, falling in dappled patterns across Hounslow Road, touched neither the dark rider concealed in the shadows nor the silver pistol with pearl handle held deftly in a small, gloved hand.

Garbed in black, from the cowl that shaded the masked face to the sweeping cloak that fell from the narrow spread of shoulders to the loins of the golden mare to the high boots of slim legs. A faint breeze came swirling down from the heathered hill, rippling the long cloak, and the slim crescent of moon touched the heather with silver radiance.

Black saddle leather creaked as the rider waited impatiently for the sound of carriage wheels that would most likely approach from the east where London lay. The creaking lantern lights now winked in the night, the huge conveyance sweeping along the road toward the dark rider whose fingers tightened on the butt of the silver pistol.

"Well, here we go, my beauty," the lone rider whispered to the mare. "They'll not easily forget you. But we shall hide you well when the deed is done."

The creak of coach wheels drew ever nearer. Who would be in that coach, the rider couldn't know, but still smiled in anticipation of the night's adventure. It was worth it, rather, this highwayman thought, it had better be.

The creaking grew louder and the vehicle, whatever it was, the nightrider could hear the pound of horses' hoofs on the hard-packed dirt, and kept eyes trained on the bend in the road. Nearer came the horses, and the moon-bright mare was sent into a walk that merely minced.

As the lead horse swung around the corner, the dark rider saw that it was a travelling carriage. "Now."

Coming out of the shadows into the moonlight, the highwayman levelled the pistol at the carriage. "Stand and deliver!" called the small but determinedly strong voice; then more harshly, "Halt, or this gun fires!"

Aimed at the driver now, the pistol urged the coachman to roll to a stop drawing up in drifting dust powdered into silvery moon-motes. The driver leaned over, brakes grating and squealing. "Who are ye, and what be ye wanting?" cried the driver before finding himself staring into the ominous little pistol. "Ayy, what is this?"

"A robbery, what do you think?" said the highwayman. "Toss down your arms!"

"I ain't got weapons. A-are you going to be using that barker?" stammered the driver.

"If there is a call to use it, yes." The dark rider dismounted, walking the mare to the coach door.

"A highwayman!" a voice cried from inside, seeing the dark figure just outside the door just before it was opened. The passenger stepped out as ordered by the highwayman. "I am the earl of Kingshampton, and I've influence at court I warn you. Now, what is it that you want of me?"

The highwayman stared down at the diamonds, the rings on the earl's fingers worth a small fortune, the masked eyes drifting in an anticipatory gleam toward the bulging coin pockets. "Just give me everything you have there, and that should do," said the dark rider with a satisfied smile concealed in shadows.

A pistol roared, and Rosette came flying, screaming, "Moondust! They have killed you . . . nooo!"

Rosette woke from her dream, sobbing softly, being rocked back and forth. Jayne whispered, "You've had a bad dream." She was glum as she shook her head. "Your Moondust is in her stall, and still alive."

Rosette stared over to the wide oriel windows, moonlight falling across the thin sheet with which she had covered herself. "It's hot," she said, kicking down the cover. "Silly things, dreams," she murmured, her breasts trembling as she stirred restlessly.

Noiselessly the maid tiptoed away back to her room, leaving the young woman to go back to her sleep, and, she hoped, no more nightmares. What could she have been doing out there riding in the mid of night? Jayne wondered, hoping no ill would come of Rosette's night wanderings.

The swift highwayman struck again and again, a hauntingly beautiful sight even to those who lost purse, and gathered one of the largest plunders the south of London had seen in the nineteenth century. "Dark Rider" was spoken of throughout the countryside but, the only trouble was, with noticeable regret, the description of the small, daring man answered that of no one in the coffeehouses or in the court circles.

The Dark Rider robbed with a charmingly low chuckle behind the anonymity of the black mask, astride the mare that ran like molten silver in the moonlight, the holdups stunning the police and society alike.

Chapter Twenty-eight

The coach was moving at a good clip in the swiftly fading light, the occupants anxious to enter London before night fell in earnest. The female occupant was afraid of the dark, and would be indoors before the ruffians and robbers came out of their hiding.

"Oh, what if that frightful little highwayman catches up with us?" Rozelle said in a whiny moan. "I don't want to lose my brand-new gold bracelet." She held it up in the winking light of the lanterns shedding their pale yellow glow over the fast-growing dark. Alarmed, Rozelle looked up. "It's almost night!" she cried, wringing her hands together in her red velvet lap.

Paul Moreland groaned softly. "So it is. Lord, but you are the shivering coward."

"I am not." With false bravado, Rozelle pulled back the hangings and peered out. She hid a gulp next to the window. There was not much she was afraid óf, discounting the dark. Even the name Dark Rider had given her the shivers when first she had heard of the nightly robbings.

Now the dark had settled in, and suddenly the coach slowed, the lanterns Rozelle had ordered lit long before swinging crazily in their holders.

Pulling her wrap about her more securely, Rozelle gave a satisfied sigh. "Ah, we are here, finally."

When the coach halted, Rozelle already had her hand on the latch, prepared to make a dash for the town house. Paul brushed her hand aside and was about to open the door himself when it was thrown open violently.

"What the devil is going on—" Paul stopped abruptly, having been ready to give a sound thrashing to whoever had dared open their door before the driver was even down.

"Stand and deliver!"

The nose of a long pistol came into view and the highwayman laughed softly at the sight of the wide and frightened eyes. A gasp was released, but none actually realized who had made the sound for all the noise Rozelle was making herself.

"Oh, oh, the highwayman," Rozelle said, cringing and swooning against the seat.

"What's the meaning of this?" Paul asked, pale green eyes moving from the dark rider on the golden mare to the driver prone in the road.

A stiff smile appeared below the mask, and the voice was very low when the highwayman spoke again. "If you will remove yourselves from the carriage . . . and keep your tongue quiet, or I shall put a bead in your mouth." The low voice ended in a slight quiver.

To Paul it seemed the infamous highwayman was just as nervous as himself and Rozelle, she who lay still in a dead faint across the seat. "I will stay right here."

"So, it is the Baron Rawen," said the highwayman with an audible smirk in the voice. "Or are you only posing as the baron?"

The Dark Rider leaned forward in the saddle, the pistol close to Paul's face, and spoke in a calm and soft tone now.

"Hand over all your valuables at once!"

Something in the set chin of the small robber told Paul he would live only as long as he obeyed the commands. Paul slowly removed his purse and tossed it up, the robber catching the meager purse easily.

"Hmm, well, Baron Rawen, for one so titled I

find this a very sorry purse indeed." The pistol went to the young lady still in a dead faint on the cushion. "There's a pretty trinket. Come, let's have it."

After unclasping the gold bracelet from Rozelle's limp wrist, Paul tossed that too up at the rider. "That's all there is."

"I believe you." The pistol returned to Paul's nose. "Now, tell me the truth: Are you the baron or not?"

"Just between us, little man, I am many . . . very many indeed."

With that, Paul laughed a demented sound that made even the Dark Rider shiver from the ripples pouring forth.

The pistol shifted, the low voice inquiring, "And who might the faint-hearted young lady be?"

"My sister, if you must know."

"Her name, you simpleton!"

After starting from the harshness of the question, Paul rapped out, "Rozelle Modestia Rawen."

"Your name!" The pistol prodded. "Your whole name, so help you God."

"Paul Moreland."

"How is that? She is your sister, no?"

"Half-sister," he gritted out. "My last name is my mother's. Damn you, be on your way now! You've what you wanted—and more!"

The coach door slammed, with Paul sitting back into the plush cushions to await the sound of hoofs retreating. When it came, he stepped out just in time to catch the flash of a moon-silvered tail disappear across the lea.

He had no worry, and he said this out loud, knowing there was none who could hear him. "Matters not what secrets I revealed — that hightoby rider will soon meet his death. His luck has run out."

Badly shaken, trying to soothe his frayed nerves while hearing Rozelle Modestia in the next room slumber restlessly, Paul read the London paper, of the Ashanti War, in the Gold Coast, that had been concluded by Sir Garnet Wolseley, by the burning of the capital town, Kumasi.

Reading further down: A badly decomposed body had been discovered, the man identified by his sobbing wife as one Jessie Black of Hounslow, the killing wounds had been inflicted by sharp hoofs.

Alerted by the acceleration of his heart, Paul stared a burning hole into the paper that blurred before his eyes. Of course! The dark rider had not been Jessie — who then? Paul tossed the crumpled paper aside, staring now into the fire he had lighted against the new chill London was feeling.

The horse, Moondust, belonging to none other than Rosette Forrest. Paul rubbed his newly bristled chin and reflected back. The voice had indeed been a bit familiar to his ears out there in the night — but Rosette? No, he shook his head. She was too tender, too delicate and womanly.

Paul shrugged after a time. What mattered? Jessie was out of the way, he would never open his mouth to involve Paul in Rutland's murder — that was all that mattered. Let the hightoby rider get into all the trouble he could.

With far less courage, Paul wondered ahead. What if this robber did spill the beans, and named him the phony baron? Ah, the bloke had not been caught this far, so why should he gossip and put himself in danger. No, the bloke was hiding out real good. If nothing else, Paul was grateful for that one thing.

Moondust rode at an easy pace while one slim, ungloved hand guiding her expertly turned mare off the road above the main one below. She rested there, sliding a boot free of a stirrup.

Rosette's head throbbed and pulsed; her belly ached making her bend double. Small pearl teeth gritted in the effort of will that finally lifted her from the saddle, down into the moist grass while Moondust nickered softly down to her. She lay there, for how long she couldn't tell, feeling the wet stickiness between her thighs. She was losing the poor babe, and the thought made her grimace.

Another pain twisted her insides into knots. Fate again had seen fit to deprive her, just when she was getting used to the idea of becoming a mother. At least, she laughed wryly, none knew of this but for Jayne.

She groaned, forlorn and yearning for something she couldn't name while her blood and the wee others flowed onto the grass. She owned no treasured girlhood memories, and owned nothing still, but a partially filled chest of stolen goods, of diamonds and emeralds—symbols to her of the cold emptiness of her life.

She cried out, but only once. Look what these daring raids had cost her. Hasan. Love, where are you? She smiled tremulously, and the fingers of one hand clung a little to her belly, as though afraid to lose what she had left of Hasan. So good . . . to sleep at last.

September cast her chilly fingers across the lea; two weeks had passed. Rosette was feeling stronger and healthier than ever, and it was as if a new grit and invincibleness had been born in her the night she lost the wee human.

She sat in her sofa with lyre ends, a revival of the Greek style. A smirk crossed her even lovelier countenance, marring it not a bit but only displaying her new indomitable spirit. Jayne watched the young woman covertly as she dusted the room. Soon, Rosette had informed her, there would be new servants arriving to aid her in the tasks. Jayne considered how Rosette had changed in the past few weeks, and the maid didn't like the looks of it one bit.

For one thing, to add more grease to the fire, Rosette had been going into town to convert her jewels into money to pay the Baron Rawen her father's debt. Twice now Rosette had sent him great sums, and luckily enough the baron hadn't sent back a reply or even a thank you. He must be satisfied. But for how long, Jayne wondered, for it wasn't the money the Baron desired, but Rosette herself.

"You've been swiping those jewels on your nightly escapades, haven't you, my lady?" Jayne finally got up the courage to put the question to the young woman seated gracefully but lonely-looking in the huge sofa.

"You are searching for proof of where the money's coming from, Jayne?" Rosette sighed then. "Well, I can't say that I blame you for your curiosity, dear Jayne. Someday I shall tell you all there is to know. But for now, be content that we are not in the poorhouse, or heaven forbid, in the clutches of that lecherous Baron Mark Rawen."

"He's come."

Whirling to glance over the sofa, Rosetta asked the maid, "Who has come? What are you saying?"

"I can see him out the window. See there, he's ridden over on horseback, and is just dismounting. Allan is coming to take his horse."

"Jayne, why don't you go out to the stable to visit with your husband?"

"I have work to —" Jayne nodded over the sage request and went to let the baron in.

Unaware of her trembling, Rosette perched prettily upon the sofa. Nearly a month had passed since she last saw the Baron Rawen. How angry he must be that she had avoided him since he asked for her hand. What would he say? Worse, what would he do? Pooh, he couldn't do a thing, that's what. She had decided not to marry, and he should certainly have realized that by now, after she had cold-shouldered him time and again.

Upon his entry, Rosette felt her heart give a leap. He had trimmed his beard, and she couldn't believe her eyes. He was even more virile than she remembered. He sported a new leanness, but his trousers must have been taken in at the same time, for they fit close to his manly thighs. Rosette blushed, willing her eyes to remain on his upper half and not be caught glimpsing his lordship's maleness.

She is like a damask rose, the baron thought

ardently, the rose from which comes the perfume attar of roses. Nothing could diminish the vibrations of desire that were shooting through him like knife stabs. At his leisure, Mark studied her. She didn't appear very destitute. She was not in want, which left him believing that Paul, alias Pierre Maudet, was supporting her.

Dark eyes followed the turn of her head as Rosette looked to the window to see who else could be arriving. "Did you bring someone with you?" she asked, still avoiding his eyes.

Or else, Mark kept on with his serious train of contemplations, or else Rosette could be supporting herself.

"Yes, I did. Do you mind?"

A fine nose went in the air. "Even if I did, that would not stop you, Your Lordship."

Elegantly Mark bowed slightly from the waist. She still bore for him a strong aversion, eh?

"But I do mind what you think—and feel. Rosette."

A lack of honesty, to boot, Rosette added to her collection of base charges reserved solely for the Baron Rawen.

"Sure you do," Rosette returned in a doggerel tone. "Well, who is it that you have invited without my permission into my home?"

Mark expelled a breath, slowly, as he gazed about the drawing room again filling up with fine furnishings. Where were the others? He couldn't recall if she had — He shrugged, whatever.

"He is one whose business it is to trace wrongdoers." He coughed in affectation. "Like perhaps a hightoby rider?"

The color draining from Rosette's face, Mark left her standing there mutely staring after him as he took it upon himself to open the door. He returned shortly, a cretaceous-faced man close upon his heels.

"May I introduce you to Detective Officer Mr. Worthley. Rosette Forrest," he said, sweeping his hand between the strangers.

"Harrumph. *London* detective, Your Ladyship."

"Ohh-hhh," Rosette murmured, waving a nonchalant slim-fingered hand in the air. "I am not . . . just call me Miss Forrest, sir, ah, Mr. Worthley . . . London detective." Rosette nearly choked out that last title.

Squinting an eye about the room after having been mesmerized by the slim hand traveling in the air, Mr. Worthley cleared his throat in order to speak as to his visit.

"There are villains who seem to — harrumph," he cleared again, going on, "to combine with base desires and notions a persistence in the expression of them which never wearies . . ."

Now she herself mesmerized and wide-eyed, Rosette nodded to each word as if giving emphasis to his important-sounding speech.

"And they pursue their objects—baser ones—with a tirelessness which would be most admirable in a good cause."

Now it was Mark's turn to grimace and send a jaundiced look in Mr. Worthley's direction. If one perchanced to be spying on the scene, it would no less appear to be the funniest scene from a comedy, a play of the ridiculous side of human life.

"There seems to be a romantic impulse for some in the very trials that beset the path of crime." Again the deep clearing of the throat. "The more hair-breadth escapes to be made, the more eagerly do these villains seem to enter upon their course."

"Ah!" Rosette interrupted. "You are speaking of none other than the highwayman. Quite a fellow, he."

The chalk-white face lowered to peer with an ironically sinister cast into Rosette's face. "Have you noticed anything hereabouts yourself? I have spoken to the earl of Kingshampton, who was robbed not so long ago himself, and he said the Dark Rider took his leave of him and headed in this direction. Miss Forrest, have you seen the white horse?"

"The horse is gold . . . sir," Rosette slowed to a hiss on the "sir."

"Oh, yes, yes, of course, that was the description in the paper."

"Also fits the description of your mare, Moondust, the horse that ran away, when was it?" Mark asked, watching her reaction closely.

"Why, I guess it does." Rosette again waved a hand in the air, and again the detective followed the appendage very studiously.

He caught her hand and, turning it in his palm, looking for a clue it seemed, he said, "The hightoby rider has small hands, almost . . . like a woman's." He let go of her hand, and took up staring into her face. "How long would you say your horse has been missing?"

"I am not sure. I—I was away, to Africa." Shifting her gaze, she found Mark staring at her with a melting gaze. Delicious shivers of delight shot through her, and strangely an ache began deep inside, again not unlike intense desire.

"Do you have a stableman I can question then?" Mr. Worthley rapped out, seemingly uninterested in her presence and scouring the room with a thorough eye.

"Of course," Rosette said, indignation piercing her. How dare the puny detective insinuate she wasn't well enough off to have servants employed!

"Good enough." Mr. Worthley, sniffing into a handkerchief now, turned to go. "Speak to you later, Baron. Might be I'll have learned something by then."

"No good luck to you, sir," Rosette shot at the

man's back as he showed himself out. She would have stuck out her tongue were the baron not standing there. "Well, what are you staring at?" she asked him, defying all rules of graciousness.

"At what a bitch you've become, Rosette Forrest."

With that he turned and left her gaping at the wide spread of his manly shoulders, and at his elegantly trousered legs moving swiftly as he too let himself out the door.

More determined than ever to resume her nightly raids, Rosette climbed the stairs, her momentary fears put to rest. She had hidden Moondust well into the old, vine-covered gazebo. And the baron, he wouldn't be bothering her anymore, their engagement was as good as null. His manner this afternoon had told her as much. But how long before he would demand the payment of the debt in full?

Chapter Twenty-nine

Staring ruminatively into his morning cup of black India tea, Mark stretched his long legs encased in tight, black broadcloth trousers beneath the table. His plans had not yet reached fruition, but he was getting close to something, very close. He could feel this in the pit of his stomach. Soon, very soon . . .

"Say, Yer Lordship, this just come for you," Milly announced, curtsying as she placed a silver salver with a note beside him.

"Thank you, Milly."

Curiosity for what the note contained surged through him, but he waited until the maid had smilingly exited the breakfast room. He too wore a lazy grin. Milly had not turned out so bad after all, despite her crude mannerisms and much less than refined speech.

Now for the note. Who could it be from?

Mark spread the paper, and stiffened while he read:

Sir, you had Better check into a Very Important Matter. Go to Heathcliff. See whoever there is the Eldest. Work on this ones Memory. You Should find Something quite of an Enlightenment there.

Unsigned. Now Mark Rawen rubbed his chin more vigorously than before, watching a dark-brown bird spotted with white perch on the low window sill. Another bird, a wood lark, disturbed the first of the sill and took off, singing as it soared into the blue, cloudless sky. Mark burst out laughing, the deep throaty tone sounding ironic to the maid bustling in the hall.

"A little bird told me," Mark said with a chuckle. Then, his countenance turning stone-cold hard, he rose abruptly from the table and went to fetch his fawn-colored short coat.

The team of blacks pulled the smart, new chaise up the lane, the sloping lawn flanked on either side by great oaks spreading welcome and shade to the visitor. Hauntingly beautiful Heathcliff, Mark had to pause in admiration, for he had never seen the facade shining in the light of day, nor had he ever seen a lawn that more resembled velvet. He had to tip his hat to their gardener.

They, Mark wondered, just who they were he intended to find out. Following that he would search until he discovered the one who lets out secrets, the one with the lazy scrawl of handwriting.

Alighting from his chaise, Mark experienced a bittersweet sensation as he stood immobile beside a hawthorn shrub, gazing up at the house, very white basking in the sunshine. Over the walls climbed late-summer roses, mingling with honeysuckle and jasmine, and the air was heavy with their perfumes. From a bed below the terrace walls wafted the smoky scent of lavender. Moving his fawn-colored head, Mark took in flagstone walks that ran between riotous-colored flower beds, and, looking up, felt the cool shade of solemn, old trees. Stretching his vision, he saw cool woodland that lay beyond the stately mansion.

The house itself seemed to speak to him, until he turned and encountered the curious stare of a weathered old man.

"I asked ye, what can I be doing for you, sir?"

"I am Baron Rawen, and who might you be?"

For the second time in two months, Pickworth's jaw sagged down to his jowls. "B-b-baron?"

"That's correct. Now, might it be possible to speak with Paul Moreland—" he paused—"or is it Paul Rawen?" Mark narrowed his eyes to match the suspicion in the other's.

"Could there be two barons then?" Pickworth asked, scratching the gray twigs of hairs sprouting from his left ear.

"I am here bearing several questions I might put to you. Your name first?"

"Pickworth, that's me."

"Pickworth, are you the eldest here?" Mark pressed.

"You could say so, I suppose. But then there's Harriet and there's Barbara." Pickworth's telling halted as he stared at the darkly handsome stranger. Then he looked down, staring back in time. Oakhill had harbored generations of Rawens. Baron had followed after baron and had reigned foremost. For long there had been no baron living there or here at Heathcliff. No one had known where he had gone off to, the youngest survivor. For fifteen sad years he had been absent. Then there had been the bastard, and none dared breathe his name, for the old baron had cast him off, forbidding all mention of him. He had been a feckless lad, Pickworth recalled now. Why could he not remember the bastard's name?

Ah, then the other, the young baron. As Pickworth pondered standing out here in the sun with this handsomely attired gent, he began to summon memories he'd long thought forgotten, tales of the young baron's reckless courage. Ah, that one had had a sweet smile for Pickworth—and Harriet too. His never-failing kindnesses to the servants, and of course his good humor. What a rider he had been at the small age of only six!

"Ah, he was a one, was Master Mark." Pickworth's seamy face lit up. "Mark, that was he. How his eyes sparkled, and how he did laugh, ah, just for the sheer joy of living." Pickworth halted again. There were deep lines on his face, and his eyes bore a haunted, care-worn look. Pickworth glanced up, his eyes curiously damp.

Mark caught the old man by the hand.

"My Mark, 'tis you. At last, lad! I have been awaiting this minute. . . ." He hung his grizzled head and cried, while a strong arm came around his thin shoulders. "Ye've come home."

Harriet, Barbara and Pickworth, all three stood staring at the young baron, staring as if they couldn't get enough of the sight of him.

"Sure wish I would have been at that ball

now," Harriet was saying musingly. She turned a chiding look to Pickworth. "Why did ye not tell us he was there?"

Pickworth shrugged. "Did not know him from the others, there was so many. The lot of them—pardon, sir—strutting about like so many penguins with their white shirt fronts sticking out. Ah, but there was one who stood out, like a fairy princess, she was."

Barbara put in, "You told us, and she could only have been the Lady Forrest, such a sweet, pretty lass. There's one who could do no wrong, as sure as my pie is bubblin' in the oven."

"I don't know about the doing no wrong, but indeed Rosette Forrest is fast becoming famous—" Mark cleared his throat—"for her beauty, that is." He would say no more.

"So what wrong would such a lass like Rosette be doing?" Harriet wondered out loud.

"That remains to be seen." Mark pulled up a chair and straddled it. "Now, tell me all you know, and then I'll be needing some aid in finding some items." He sat down.

That very same day Oakhill was boarded up and the servants made their move to Heathcliff. Several pieces of furniture were moved to the attic at Heathcliff, while the newest purchases were transferred from the rooms and brought to the halls of Heathcliff. Mark discovered that some of the finest appointments at Heathcliff had belonged to none other than Lady Forrest. Walking through the halls, Mark admired what had been housed at Southend, and ran his fingers lovingly on a dainty spinet she must have played upon at one time.

That very same night, after the needed items had been found, Mark Rawen rode out on a black steed, his long cloak billowing out behind, his matching mask in place. In his belt he sported a long-nosed pistol; Mark prayed there would be no need to use it.

Chapter Thirty

Watching her hands move in the mirror, Rosette dexterously wound her auburn curls and pinned them atop her head. Next she reached for the dark, concealing hat.

"I promise, Jayne, one more night of this nastiness and then we shall be settled up with the baron, and able to live comfortably without another worry to plague us."

"But, dear Rose, you are not a criminal at heart. Why do you not quit now, while you are way ahead?" Jayne shook her head, besieged by worrisome thoughts. "You might get caught, then all will be for nothing. You'll lose Southend for sure then to the baron."

Strange, Jayne mused, why the baron had forsook their wedding plans and seemed not to mind at all that Rosette had been giving him the cold-shoulder treatment.

The cape swirled as the once-lovely young woman transformed into a small, dashing highwayman. A pearl-handled pistol rode at a slim hip; a high, black shine had been given to the soft hide boots; there was not a single auburn curl visible about the bowl of the hat.

But in the back of her mind, Rosette realized this was to be the riskiest ride of all. Her cheeks were flushed a becoming hue of pink, and she felt very excited. Knowing the danger that lurked out there, still Rosette went.

Autumn had touched England with rusty browns, and the oncoming night mingled lavender and soft grays with the autumnal landscape. Rosette's eyes searched the shadows for any sign of those lurking to catch her as the Dark Rider. She had heard tales that day from Allan that the sheriff and his posse were as thick as thieves in the area, so she would have to proceed with extreme caution.

Patting Moondust's neck affectionately, Rosette spurred the mare to the cover of brush and trees that bordered the road. Keeping to the shadows that the trees provided, she rode until a spot was chosen where she could observe the fork in the road without being seen herself. She settled into the creaking leather and waited.

There was fire in her eyes and in the tilt of her chin as she listened to the whisper of the wind in the ash trees overhead. She waited, but still no sign of a conveyance along the road.

Suddenly her face whitened in shock. Directly before her, on a small rise, stood a huge, black horse mounted by a cowled and masked figure. A gasp caught in her throat. No sound had warned of his presence. Could he see her too? And just who was this nighthawk invading her territory?

The moon made its first appearance then, a thin crescent that had lain hidden beneath the night-gray clouds. Rosette started trembling, shaking as an aspen blown about in a high wind.

There was no time to think ahead. It was now or never. She had to get away. As if he read her thoughts, the strange highwayman laughed softly across to her. A tight smile nevertheless lay on the crisp mouth below the mask and Rosette stared in shocked amazement. He spurred his mount in her direction and Rosette froze to the spot.

"Your pardon, ah, Dark Rider. I won't hold up your game for long. If I might just have a word with you?"

The nighthawk held her mesmerized, half by the long-nosed pistol in his hand, half because of the grim, sobering figure he made on the walking black horse.

Sport? Rosette blinked under her own black mask. He thinks this merely sport? "C-could you put the firearm away, Sir Nighthawk?" she stammered out, still staring at the ominous bore of steel.

"Ha, ha, Sir Nighthawk?" he said with a deep laugh. Again the tight smile appeared.

The pistol hovered as he kneed his black mount closer, and now the muzzle was aimed at her heart. The large highwayman grinned coldly.

"At this distance, I could hardly miss — Dark Rider," he said with a snicker in his voice.

Almond-bright eyes were fascinated by the handsome jaw line she could see below the mask. It had never been her misfortune to meet up with this strange rider, and Rosette found herself oddly excited and perturbed at the same moment.

"What is your business with me, you huff!" Her voice dipped low as she tried to sound dangerous and threatening. "Name it. I am in a hurry, you see."

"And so am I," came the deeper reply.

Now that Mark was closer, he saw that he had been correct about the eyes — they revealed sheer terror. His measuring gaze dipped lower, to where a button had been left opened by a carelessly hasty hand.

Rosette followed where the dark eyes searched, and she almost swooned right there. In her rush to be done with this night's folly, she had forgotten the top button in her overlarge blouse. The mound of creamy breast rose above the cotton and gleamed with feminine lure in the moonlight.

"Aha," the other tobyman murmured. His turn had come to leave her wondering after a night of ecstasy. Not Jamila, but Rosette. Again, not the Dark Rider, but Rosette—he had surmised correctly.

Backwards stepped the light mare, as the dark stallion crept forward. "Run," was all the Dark Rider whispered into a flickering ear.

As if Moondust understood the word and the slackness of the reins at her ring bits, she whirled. Her hoofs clacked on the stones and she was off like the wild north wind. Rosette was bent low over Moondust's mane as the mare settled into a steady pace, her white fetlocks merely a flash in the moonlight. In her headlong run, it was as if the mare's hoofs flew over the ground. They had left the rocky area and now brushed the soft turf that stretched from the roadside into the forest beyond.

"Careful . . . carefully, Moondust," Rosette shouted over the wind rushing by her head.

But they went swiftly, while a steady hand on the reins took the mare deep under the sycamores and elms and oaks. The hank of auburn hair had come loose, the hat gone now, and the strands whipped her flushed cheeks and tickled her lips. Rosette laughed triumphantly and tossed her hair to the wind. "You won't catch me now, Sir Nighthawk!"

Mists were climbing higher now, like puffs of gray smoke as the chilled night air swept down. Behind her the sounds of pursuit grew steadily fainter. Rosette relaxed in her saddle with a deep sigh. But if he came or not, she told herself that she would not be tricked by any sense of false security. She kept Moondust at a neat run, weaving in and out of the thick boles of trees. She spent an hour going one way and then the other, evading being tracked by the nighthawk. Finally she turned the mare toward home and the gazebo that was concealed by high weeds and brush.

When she saw the hidden place up ahead, she reined Moondust back with a small cry of dismay.

Right there blocking her path was the nighthawk. How?. . . .

The huge black horse pranced threateningly toward her. "Checkmate," murmured the nighthawk.

Moondust was tired. Her head drooped and

her lungs heaved. Rosette stiffened as a gloved hand shot out and ripped the mask from her face. The dark eyes assessed the fine nose and the curving pink mouth, and his head swung in the direction of the hidden spot she had been heading toward.

"Ah, your secret sanctuary," he said low, the hunger that his body realized for her making his tall frame shiver. "I knew you were female, and have dreamed for weeks of a scene such as this."

"Y-you are a dreamer, Sir Nighthawk!" Rosette said, her bravado belied by the stammer in her voice.

The larger highwayman laughed softly and hooked an arm about her waist, dragging her from the weary mount. He placed her none too gently across the pommel of his leather saddle, and laughed again. Rosette heard the mocking laughter, mixed with a queer bitterness, and gasped when he brought her about to sit across his hard thigh. She was shockingly aware of his hard muscles and great length, not to mention the steely grip of the arm that held her tight as he moved the black in the direction of the secret hiding place.

"I too have been here before, sweet lady rogue," he said into her ear, tickling her neck with his warm breath.

The stallion moved beneath her with strength

and agile grace. She would have never thought another horse would outdistance Moondust and beat her back here. But she had taken a longer time than usual with tactics to shake the nighthawk. Checkmate, he had said. And so it was. Rosette could laugh at the situation, if she wasn't so frightened.

Seeing where he was taking her, Rosette began to struggle against his hip and ribs, trying to kick back at his shins with her booted heels. He only tossed back and laughed at her futile attempts at escape.

Curiosity overcame caution as Rosette reached up swiftly to try and unmask the nighthawk. His fingers flew to her wrist before hers could reach their destination, and he laughed with an ironic gentleness and lowered his head to plant a tingling kiss at the corner of her mouth.

"Not so hasty, my love. I realize you are in a hurry to spend a blissful night in there." He tossed his head as they neared the opening in the brush large enough for a horse to enter while dipping down its head. "But we'll have plenty of time. You will see."

Rosette tossed her head defiantly. "You shall not rape me. I—I will fight you even if it kills me!" She snatched her face from staring at him to looking straight ahead as they entered the gazebo after the black had clambered up the three steps.

The deep voice fell over her, shrouding her at the same time the dark of the sanctuary did: "Never rape, my love, never."

Chapter Thirty-one

The dense shrubbery in front of the gazebo shut out the moonlight and the rest of the world.

Still seated on the black horse with the nighthawk—for that was the only way Rosette could think of him—she barely had the strength to fight against him as he bent to kiss her on the mouth.

"Don't you dare," she managed to get out in a whisper after the kiss that was not returned by her ended.

"I dare anything I want, Rosette Forrest," he shot back low.

She gasped, wishing she could see him looking

at her as she knew he was. The hard, passionate kiss came again, one that pushed back the mists that had all week long befogged her senses. Her heart was fluttering wildly as she tried to figure out what it was about this nighthawk's touch that was so very familiar.

Now his silence frightened her and, moistening dry lips with the tip of her tongue, she wondered what he would do next. This dangerous situation was becoming more than she could cope with. Just when she thought to bring up her pistol should he try to take her, even though he had said he wouldn't, he seemed to read her thoughts and very swiftly and easily lifted the pearl-handled weapon from her belt.

"You won't be needing this, milady bandit." After he had stashed the weapon, he lifted her from the saddle and placed her on her two feet.

"What d-do you think you are doing?" she said to the man in the dark. She could not even see her own hand in front of her face, for she had tried several times, much less see the figure that had abducted her. She had finally been caught, but by another highwayman. He wouldn't turn her in, so what did she have to worry about? He might just steal a few more kisses and then let her go. Was this too much to hope for?

"I am going to take the horse outside, and then, my sweet, we are going to get better acquainted."

"Oh, no, not if . . ."

Try though she might to sweep past him, he was quicker than her attempt to flee and caught her around the waist. Holding her thus, he dragged her along while he turned the horse around and, with a slap on the rump, left the black to roam at his will.

Rosette felt a thrill of apprehension when she realized he was serious. She was trapped like a hare, and there was nothing she could do about it. He seemed to be able to see in the dark, giving her to wonder just what sort of man he really was.

No more than a minute had passed since he released the horse, and now he was turning her in his arms, slipping a hand down over her back to hold her imprisoned against his hard frame.

"I have waited a long time to hold you like this," he murmured.

"Y-you don't even know me, but for what you have heard."

"Ah, but I do know you. You see, Rosette, I have loved you forever."

"F-forever?" she stammered her confusion.

Before she could hope for an answer, his mouth was claiming hers once more, and this time the kiss left her breathless and panting. His expert fingers stroked her in places she didn't realize could excite her. The scent of him, too, was leaving her dizzy. This was no ordinary highwayman, this was a man she could easily fall in love with. She was moonstruck, she decided, that had to be it. What else could explain her abandonment to his lovemaking. Only one other man had made her feel this way. His kisses and caresses were leaving her without any will of her own.

"Hasan . . . Hasan," she murmured as the love began to flow into every part of her being.

"Hasan?" he questioned softly, lifting his head. Then, he asked, "Do you love this Hasan?"

"Oh, yes. Yes!" She swooned in his arms.

Before she could surface from her muddled desire, he was lifting her and bearing her to a bed of hay. She stirred restlessly as he laid her down and left her for a few seconds in time. Then he returned, groaning his need as he began to peel off her highwayman's outfit. After his hands had completed their task, they returned to caressing her tenderly. His mouth, coming close to her ear, nibbled gently without the bite of his teeth.

"Rosette, do you want me?"

As if of their own volition, her arms crept up to wind about his strong neck. "Hasan, you are Hasan," she cried. "Please, please, tell me that you are."

"Whatever you wish for this night, dear heart. Hasan I will be, ask no more."

She held fast to those words as he began his splendorous lovemaking, giving her sheer delight while she gave this stranger free rein. Warmed by his potency, nothing could surpass the ecstasy that shivered through her. With daring abandon, she parted his lips with her darting tongue and was rewarded with a deep groan as he penetrated her own sweet mouth with his thrusting tongue.

Manfully he moved over her and parted the soft thighs and, mounting her, he drove deep within. The hot blade teased and an ecstasy almost unheard of in her wildest imaginings washed over her. She swirled ever closer to the highest bliss, rooted and grounded in love, to make her woman's calling sure. He plunged her into the sea of love, and the endless night had only begun.

"Precious treasure, you are mine," he murmured as they attained that deepest joy together.

The top of her head felt the warm wind of his heavy breath as they lay silently spent, legs entwined, hands yet caressing as the throbbing ache of the aftermath gently subsided. They slept for a time, only to awaken and renew their kindred passions.

Close to dawn, Mark shook Rosette awake, tenderly cupping his hand to her shoulder. "I must leave you now. Your horse is waiting." He pressed a finger tip to her protesting lips. "Shh. Stay where you are until I am gone."

Her eyes were wildly round. "W-when will I see

you again?" She was trying to see his unmasked face, but he averted it as he slipped quickly into his clothes.

"Soon," was all he said as the first bird of morning began its song.

Rosette came to rest on her elbows. "How will I know you?" she asked as his tall frame moved out the opening.

But he had already vanished before she came fully to her feet. Dawn stole into the love nest, and Rosette's tears began as she looked around. Enlightenment washed over her in the next joy-filled moment. She had lain with Hasan; she just knew this for a fact.

Mark Rawen was not all that pleased with himself. He rode in the direction of Heathcliff, with the morning sun now warming his back. What had begun as an act of revenge had ended with him loving Rosette Forrest more than ever. Now she was firmly rooted in his blood and there was no way on earth he could ever put her from his heart. He began to doubt seriously that she had ever been far from his heart to begin with. Before she had come along, though, he had never known what it was to love someone. All his love and adoration had centered about one woman, his sister, Rozelle Modestia. She had been made in the perfect image of his one true love. No wonder he had been tormented, believing himself strange for longing for Rozelle's company. He still didn't cherish the idea that they, Rozelle and Rosette, were so alike. Even if his sister was dead and buried.

He slowed the black to merely a trot as he neared the line that separated Southend from Heathcliff. Suddenly it dawned on him like an explosion in his mind. He had only been nine or ten at the time, and now he was just realizing that his mother had never been with child at all. He could only remember the little girl being shifted back and forth between relatives. My God, Rozelle was not his sister, and it could be that she was no relation at all.

He spurred the black faster now, determined to get to the bottom of this mystery. Perhaps, if he picked the old man's mind, Pickworth could come up with some sorely needed answers and put an end to all his misery — and Rosette's. One thing was certain, that being that he must put an end to her nightly robbings. Indeed he had to save her from herself, if she was to be his wife. And wife she would be — soon.

Chapter Thirty-two

The Smuggler's Inn had been built in the days of the excisemen, and its sprawling walls were once used by those smugglers who had brought silks and satins from France and Spain.

Inside the inn, along one of the labyrinths of halls, a young woman moved into the room and went directly to the oak rosette, and, turning it, caused a section of the panelling to slide away revealing a spacious room hidden in the wall.

"Heavens! It's about time you came," Lucie said from a high-backed walnut chair, looking longingly toward the paper parcel that Rozelle Modestia carried.

After closing the panel from the inside, Rozelle Modestia stood staring, shivering a little before she turned to face the maid. "I do so hate these closed-in places," she said to herself, feeling only slightly secure with the lantern atop the walnut stand throwing flickering shadows across the thick Persian rug.

"I'm starving. Give me the bag, now will you?" Lucie hated begging, but she had starved long enough since the last meager meal that Paul Moreland had brought to her.

Rozelle shook her head and forced laughter as she whirled about, teasing and taunting the older woman while she held the parcel of food high in the air, her thick auburn hair flooding and spilling over her bare shoulders. "Ha, just try and get it from me," she challenged, knowing the other woman owned little strength.

"I'd rather die of starvation than touch the likes of you, Rozelle Modestia. . . ." She left off what else she'd been about to say.

Rozelle was across the musty carpet in a flash, catching Lucie's arm at the elbow and spinning the maid to face her. "Don't turn your nose up at me, old woman, or else we shall be digging your grave—" Rozelle had been about to say "at night" but changed it to—"in the morning."

Lucie snorted. "It'll be your grave they'll be digging, missy, not mine. You've kidnapped me, kept me here in this Godforsaken hole God only knows how long. And I know you mean to do away with your—with Rosette Forrest, if you haven't done so already!"

Moving back with a rustle of silk, Rozelle said, "Ah, so she is a relation of mine. Is it her mother's blood I share with Rosette then?"

"I never knew her mother's affairs," Lucie said stiffly, hoping she sounded convincing. Her stomach began to growl its hunger as she looked again to the parcel, on the floor now. "Please," Lucie begged, hunger overcoming pride.

Laughing in a taunting voice, Rozelle kicked the parcel all the way to the secret door. "Not," she tossed back, "until you give me some answers, old woman."

"I am not an old woman!" Lucie shouted, having gained surprising strength of tone despite her weakness.

"No," Rozelle said, bending to pick up the parcel, then turning before going out with the wrapped food, "but you soon shall be—" she laughed—"a bag of bones, weak, sick, unable to even lift yourself from that chair. Your beloved Rosette will not even recognize you, that is if you ever gain the chance to be released."

"Please," Lucie begged, but all she was left with was a cruel, mocking laugh, the panel shutting her off from the world once again.

Later that night, Roselle sat in a favorite velvet-cushioned chair, trying to decide what color to recover it in when she had enough money to take it to the upholsterer.

"What do you think, Paul?" she asked him, peering at him over the rim of her glass of sherry.

"That's not what's important right now, what color you do the chair in! I've told you: We can't go back to Heathcliff. That damned half-brother of mine is there. He always gets everything, now the bastard has Heathcliff, and Oakhill is sniffed about by those guards he's posted there." He smacked a fist into a palm, while staring narrowly at a painting by William Muller, one of the first English artists to do Arabian scenes. Hasan al-Shareef came to mind. If only there was some way to get Mark Rawen back there, to the Sahara desert. "Where he belongs!" he added, this out loud.

"Where *who* belongs, Paul?" Roselle perked up, interested in the nasty gleam in the pale green eyes.

"The baron, that's who!"

Standing up, Paul began to pace to the fringe of the carpet, his heels loud on the wood floor and then muffled as he returned to the plushness of carpet. A sick core of dismay lay heavy in him. The happiness he could have known with Rosette Forrest, and the dreams that could have been theirs. All ended by one devil of a man!

A sneering smile crossed Paul's thin mouth. He whirled to face Rozelle. "You begin to see for yourself what troubles me so much, eh?"

"The will, we could get that which Tremayne left to Mark Rawen!" A momentary silence followed her sudden idea.

"Yes, a will that names me as successor to the estate! I could forge a different one, a will that disowns him and names me as heir to the estate in his place."

Rozelle sashayed before him in a rustle of silk, silk that she'd paid dearly for. One night with a drunken lord in order to purchase this gown she hadn't been able to afford. Their funds were running out, for Paul hadn't been in the mood for picking pockets at White's. So he said, but she believed otherwise, that he had Rosette Forrest on his mind again.

"Yes, Paul, you think about it. You do realize you have to do away with the baron first of all."

Paul waved her away with a negligent hand. "Find something to occupy your time for a while, will you?"

"Don't worry, I shall. And in the morning I'm going to visit that reb maid again. She knows something, and I'm going to starve it out of her, if it's the last thing I do!"

"Starve her then," Paul said indifferently. "Just leave me alone to my own devices while you do."

At first light, Rozelle left the town house and made her way to Smuggler's Inn. After alighting from the carriage and asking the driver to wait, she went directly to her rented room and confronted Lucie once again. The maid was lying weakly upon the mussed pallet, badly in need of fresh air and sustenance.

Rozelle wrinkled her nose in the airless chamber, nearly fainting herself from the stink coming from the chamberpot stuck into a crevice in the stone wall. "Hasn't that hunchback come to empty that thing? What are we paying the bloke for anyway?" she asked herself. She whirled on the maid who was struggling to rise to her elbows. "Hungry, are you?" Rozelle again waved the parcel, a fresh one made up earlier, and taunted the woman with what was inside.

Whatever it was, the odor of food was making Lucie drool at the corners of her lips, and she didn't care by now if the bag contained warmed-over garbage. Lucie sagged on the bed, hungrier and weaker than she could remember ever being in her entire life.

"Please, what is it you want from me?"

"All you know about Rosette Forrest, her past, her parents, her likes, her dislikes . . . everything. Right down to the hair fashion and her manner of dress."

Eyes narrowing, Lucie asked, "What would you be wanting all that for? Do you plan to take Rosie's place?"

"Why not? She took my place not too long

ago. It was a bad mistake, but I didn't realize it at the time. I even went so far as to fake death to get what I wanted. Huh, look where it's gotten me — nowhere! But now, now that I have you here, you had better start talking. Or else your beloved Rosie is going to die, I promise you that, old woman!"

"I'll only tell you if you promise not to touch a hair on her head, and the food?"

"The food, yes," Rozelle said with a promise in her voice.

Lucie shook her head, fearing that she was beginning to hallucinate. She could see two of Rozelle Modestia, but they were both the same, both evil, conniving, ungodly women.

"Please, just a bite," Lucie begged. "Otherwise I won't be able to tell you all you want to know. Please?"

Rozelle did as she was begged. After the crust of fresh-baked bread, the maid felt a little ill, for she hadn't eaten a morsel in nearly five days, she believed.

"Rosie's mother, she had twins, you see." Lucie faltered, her stomach returning to its normal flow of juices. "She didn't want the trouble of raising two girls, one was enough."

"Who?" Rozelle Modestia questioned fiercely. "What was her name? And why didn't she want to raise two children?"

Now Lucie was growing dizzy, and the food

hung temptingly between Rozelle's fingers.

"Lady Louise. She had a lover, she always had a lover, and she run away . . . away with a Frenchman at the last."

Rozelle waved her hand impatiently. "I want to hear about the twins, not the lovers!"

"Lady Louise had two girls." Lucie belched and her face reddened in embarrassment. She felt a bit tipsy, for the younger woman had given her sips of ale between the crumbs of bread.

"Never mind that!" Rozelle almost shouted. "Tell me more. What became of the one that Rosette's mother cast aside?"

"Tamara took her. That would be Mark Rawen's mother. When the Lady Louise, that's Rosette's mother, heard wind of the other lady wanting a child, especially a girl-child, you see, Tamara was unable to bear any more children after Mark."

"Stop babbling! Go more slowly. Here, take a bite, and a sip of this." Rozelle pursed her red lips in frustration. This was all taking too long, and the woman was exasperating.

"Thank you, you're very kind."

"You're drunk!" Rozelle said with disgust.

"Your fault, Roz'lle Modesty."

"Go on, damnit, and hurry. I haven't all day!"

"Tamara was unable to bear more children." She hiccuped again.

"You already said that!"

"So sorry . . . if you ask me, Tremayne's wife was already ill when she took in that little girl."

"Tremayne's wife is Tamara?" Rozelle received a wobbly nod of the maid's head. She stood then, spilling the ale over the pallet, but Lucie didn't seem to mind this a bit.

"I know the rest," Rozelle seemed to be saying to herself dazedly. "Tamara was ill, then she sent me away. Tell me, what is the name of the woman Tamara sent me to?"

"Oh, that would be Margaret, Tamara's cousin."

Rozelle began to pace the floor like a caged tigress. "So, Rosette is my own flesh and blood. Paul is no relation to me at all. Tell me now: Why did I end up back with Tremayne, Mark's father?"

"That's easy. Tremayne found out and went to fetch you back. He then took you and Mark Rawen off to the desert."

Hysterically, Rosette began to laugh. "Paul is the sailor's bastard, not I!" She returned to feeding the bread to the maid now, forcing herself to ask her questions gently. "Now, tell me all I want to know of Rosette. Then you can have the leg of chicken too."

Chapter Thirty-three

Brusquely the doctor wiped his rinsed hands on a fresh towel, and faced the pale young woman seated in his examining room. "I have good news for you, young lady, and fortunately you came in just in time with what you thought was a case of food poisoning." He handed her a piece of paper. "I want you to have this filled at the apothecary."

With mildly shaking fingers, Rosette accepted the scrawled-on piece of paper. "What is it for?" she asked the doctor.

"It's a prescription for a vitamin-herb powder. I want you to take it twice a day mixed with warm water. You haven't been eating very well, I can tell by the tinge of gray beneath your eyes."

Eyes, velvety and sad, peered up at the white-haired man. "I—I haven't been sleeping very well, either, doctor," Rosette murmured, truly unhappy the past week with wondering when she would see Hasan again, and all the "whys?" she had been plagued with. Like why he kept himself from her?

"That should help." The doctor flicked his hand at the prescription. "And once you've begun eating well-rounded meals again, you shouldn't need the herbal remedy. But, I urgently press this point, you must eat and rest well otherwise you will either lose your baby or—"

Lose the *baby?*" Rosette blinked incredulously at what he said.

"Of course." He blinked back at her through his horn-rimmed spectacles. "That's why this visit, isn't it? To make certain your—" he cleared his throat—"Lady Forrest, tell me, you're a new patient, but are you married or not?"

Blanching first, Rosette followed with a shake of her head, choosing to ignore his question. "But what about all the blood I lost, not two weeks ago? I—I was sure the baby was no more."

"What were you doing at the time?" he asked interestedly.

"R-riding . . . a horse," she sputtered.

The doctor merely shrugged, unable to explain

the profound mysteries of pregnancy and motherhood. Perhaps some day in the future more will be known, he sighed, but for now he smiled kindly, only offering, "Be grateful you still carry the child." He stood, his action telling her another patient waited in the outer office. "Check back with me, Lady Forrest, and immediately if there's any sign of blood again."

"B-blood, yes," Rozette merely muttered vacantly, leaving the doctor's little office, unmindful of the sharp-faced nurse staring after her.

To the young woman in rustling silks just traversing the cobbled streets, the sight of her twin emerging from the doctor's was enough of a shock to make her steps slow, so much in fact that a rushing conveyance had to swerve to avoid knocking Rozelle Modestia down.

But Rosette was too elated and still in shock to notice Rozelle Modestia staring after her as she walked down the street in a daze.

A knowing smirk crossed Rozelle's sly features as she watched until her twin had rounded the corner and was out of sight.

"Well, we'll just see about this," Rozelle muttered to herself, casting a last glimpse toward the doctor's office and then hurrying back to the town house for a quick change of clothes. She should be able to find a dress that closely resembled the one her twin was wearing. Then, she shrewdly told herself, all she had to do was to pay the doctor's a quick visit for what information she needed to glean.

"Simpleton!" Rozelle Modestia faced her glowering companion at the table. "I said Rosette Forrest is going to have a baby!" She lowered her voice then upon seeing she was drawing curious stares in the refreshment room of the cheap London hotel where they dined this evening; they were close to financially bereft again.

Reaching across the table to painfully grasp Rozelle's wrist, Paul snarled into her freshly painted face, "You'd better be telling me the truth, Roz, that she carries the Rawen heir!"

Rozelle viciously yanked her arm back. "Who *else* would have gotten her with child!" she retorted sarcastically. "Time is of the essence, in order for her to be three months gone, you dolt!"

"How did you perchance get the information from that nurse?"

Paul's green eyes shone feverishly bright with what he'd learned this evening.

"First, I easily extracted what I wanted to know, and then like an afterthought asked her what the doc had written down for the approximate due date. She returned after a minute to give me all I wanted to know." Rozelle finished, and sat back in smug satisfaction.

"She didn't ask who you were?" Paul's discontented face twisted dubiously.

"I've already told you," Rozelle expelled a heavy breath, smelling of mint, "I saw *her* coming from there and went home to change into a dress like the one she had on, and of course—" she laughed—"let my hair down in back, to hang in the simple fashion she was wearing."

"Damn, the bastard!" Paul wrung his fingers as if there was a neck between them. "I'll kill him for this for sure."

"No!" Rozelle said between clenched teeth. "I've a better plan, much wiser. First, I have got to tell you all I've learned from that simple maid of hers, Lucie."

Several drinks later, the pair mildly tipsy, Paul sat glaring and glowering in turn across the table at Rozelle Modestia. But all he'd learned didn't make a shred of a difference to him. He still would have Rosette Forrest—there were ways later he could do away with the child before it was even born. The pain of learning of his poor background had lessened, the memories of Margaret were dimming; in their place was a burning desire for revenge.

"You are right, for once," Paul finally relented. "The changing of the will is out of the question—for a time anyway. We'll proceed with your plan, and get Rosette out of the country first, then you with my help will be tutored in all of Rosette's mannerisms and aspects of her character and personality," he said, his elation making him excited. "Yes, you will seduce and get Mark Rawen to marry you, and later rub him out of the picture. I'll take care of Rosette, once I get her back to the Sahara. That shouldn't be too hard to accomplish, especially if she still fancies herself infatuated with Hasan al-Shareef."

Loosing a relieved gasp, Rozelle said, "Paul, look who just walked in—moneybags herself." She began to purr now. "Know what I'm thinking?"

His old mistress, Paul saw and at once caught onto Rozelle's bright idea. She, Cynthia Bolingsbroke, would give him a loan, and all Paul would have to do was entertain her for a weekend. Deviously Paul grinned over to his partner in crime and then, with a charming smile, called Lady Cynthia over.

Cynthia needed no more persuasion; she was delighted to catch her old, fair-haired Don Juan here, and anticipated by the devilish gleam in Paul's eyes a few thrilling nights to come.

For long minutes after she'd returned to Southend, Rosette sat on the edge of her bed breathing deeply, in and out, not knowing how best to cope with this intensity of feeling that began when the doctor informed he she was still pregnant. No more nightly raids, she was a mass of quivering emotions as it was.

Entering the bedroom and seeing Rosette curled up childlike on the bed, Jayne stared frowning at the rapt face.

"What is it?" Jayne asked, to break the spell Rosette was under, it seemed.

"I'm only tired, Jayne. You go out to the stable and visit your husband—" she smiled—"and bring him some of the chicken pie you made."

Peering closely at the flushed face, Jayne said, "Sure you'll be all right?"

"I'm sure."

Alone now, suddenly despair caught hold of Rosette fiercely as she was forced to acknowledge Hasan's cold rejection. Why had he not come to her? He said she would know him next time they met, hadn't he? Had she actually lain with her love? Or, she paled, had the man been a stranger in truth? No, this could not be the case. She would know Hasan's intimate caresses and loving lips anywhere. Clearly, whatever the purpose of Hasan's making secret love to her under formidable disguise, it wasn't to make her his own. Had he been paying her back, then, for posing as Jamila?

Rosette's heart sank with hopeless despair as slow, hurtful tears traced a desolate path down her flushed cheeks. Her hand slid down and smoothed over her slightly rounded tummy. Then faint resentment stirred in her that Hasan had used her so selfishly. He must be congratulating himself right now, Rosette decided bitterly.

A frown creased the smoothness of her brow as she tried to summon up the image of her lover in the gazebo. Why was there nothing about him that she could remember clearly? All she had to go by was his lovemaking. Like the first time, he had filled her body and soul with boundless rapture.

Where is he? Rosette felt a flash of the old spirit she'd thought lost to her forever return now. If Hasan al-Shareef had only returned to England to cruelly seduce her, thereby gaining his revenge and expecting her to become heartbroken, then he had better think again!

"He is only a ruthless savage!" Rozette cried, bounding from the bed. She swung about, staring at her profile in the mirror, searching for evidence of the child she carried. Her gaze wandered over to the window, the whispering wind outside seeming to call her, as once before, beckoned by the same silken threads that had drawn her inexorably to the desert.

But how could she go to the kasbah? She didn't know the way, nor did she even know if Hasan was back there.

Minutes later it seemed almost like a dream come true when Baron Rawen arrived. Jayne, having returned from the stable earlier than usual, met him at the door. She rushed into Rosette's bedroom now, all excited, saying that the baron was going on a journey and wondered if Rosette was up to joining him.

"Oh." Rosette's face fell. "Where would the baron be going that he would want me to join him?"

"I'm not sure you want to go back *there* so soon," Jayne said, after thinking it over.

"There's nothing but sand and—"

Spinning about, Rosette exclaimed ecstatically, "The Sahara!"

Chapter Thirty-four

Jayne paused indecisively before going out the door and returning to her warmed kitchen. Should she warn Rosie there was something different about the baron? Ah well, Jayne shrugged. She would leave it for Rosette to discover for herself. After all, Rosette was a big girl now.

After donning a fresh gown of honey brocade, Rosette went down to greet the baron. Entering the drawing room, she found herself alone, looking this way and that, wondering where the baron had wandered off to. She was about to leave the room and go in search of him—perhaps in the library—when a sound brought her head back around and she caught a movement in the high-backed chair that faced the window.

"Baron Rawen?" she said tentatively, moving in the direction of the chair.

The tall shadow rose from the chair, turning to finally face her. The frail light was to his back, making it difficult for her to read Baron Rawen's expression or mood. He was behaving most mysteriously, though, and she wondered at it.

She was unaware that he watched her closely as he said pleasantly, "Rosette." Like a caress. "Come closer."

She felt a fire like lightning travel through her veins as she went to stand before him. Her fast-beating heart refused to slow to normal while her eyes traveled from the highly polished black boots, on up to the chin she could see was beardless, further up to the eyes that flashed a dark fire. Her gaze went straight back to the firm jawline, noting the long, thin scar and she stared, mesmerized with incredulous surprise.

"Remember me, my sweet?"

The room and everything in it, even the man, began to fade abruptly as she stared. With a small sigh, Rosette knew no more.

Recovering consciousness, Rosette was not immediately aware of her surroundings. When her vision finally cleared, she was amazed to see Hasan bending over her with a concerned light in his dark eyes, his hand a soft coolness resting on her forehead.

"I'm truly sorry I shocked you that way," he murmured, hunkering down beside the sofa she was stretched upon.

Rosette couldn't believe what her eyes were telling her. "Hasan . . ." Wide-eyed, she gazed at him tremulously.

His firm mouth quirked sheepishly. "I am Mark Rawen now. Hasan al-Shareef is a man of the past."

Pushing his hand aside, Rosette struggled to rise to her elbows. "You deceived me, you heartless cad! How could you? How easily you lied making me believe you were the baron. Oh — " she hid her face between her palms — "and you, you were the nighthawk, using me only as an object of your amusement." She stiffened angrily when he began to laugh.

"The rose, the lovely rose with the sharp thorns, the very same that I discovered in the Sahara. I was of the belief that love did not exist until you came along like the freshness of the early dawn. Are you so blind that I must speak the words?"

Rosette moaned, a tiny sound caught in her throat. "Why didn't you tell me, Hasan?"

He tilted her fine chin up so that she was forced to look into his dark, compelling eyes.

"Dearest, I am Mark. Say it, please?"

"M-Mark," she stammered, peering up at him shyly. "Do you *really* love me?"

He gathered her close to his thudding chest. "With all my heart and soul, believe me, forever."

"It took you a long time, M-Mark." She said his name tentatively, sighing happily against the clean smell of his white-linen shirt front.

He captured her dewy lips, kissing her long and deeply, his lean fingers buried in the curling, auburn tresses. He moved on the long sofa, bringing her against his chest, his roaming hands caressing her tenderly. Between kisses, he murmured sweet love words into her ear and against her throbbing throat, telling her gently and carefully of the sweet revenge he had sought, of the tortured nights he had spent believing her in love with Paul, until she had enlightened him of her love for Hasan al-Shareef.

"I wanted to love you and punish you, at the same time, for what you made me feel and the torment just the thought of you put me through. I went insane with jealousy, dearest Rose, thinking that if I could get you to marry me, then—" he laughed with the irony—"I would have the sweetest revenge of all, with you under my roof and in my clutches, like a hawk with a dove."

Her moist, clinging lips left his to speak at

the pulse pounding madly in his throat. "Indeed, nighthawk, now that you have me in your talons, what will you do with me?" she asked, with a smile curving over the taut scar on his cheek. She brushed her lips over the long scar and delighted in his shiver of pleasure.

"Intend to make love to you all through the night, I do, sweet lady bandit. Are you up to it, my darling?" he murmured into her burning earlobe.

"Bandit!" Rosette straightened in alarm. "Oh, Mark, what am I to do with all the loot that I stole?"

He silenced her worry with a slow-moving kiss slanted across her lips. "Let me take care of that, and Mr. Worthley, will you?"

She curled back into his arms, feeling secure and happy for the first time in a long time. "If you say so, Baron Rawen."

He looked deeply and longingly into her dreamy eyes, feeling the familiar ache in his loins, as he did whenever she was near. He took the liberty of cupping a breast gently, and, moving slightly back to make her more comfortable, he was also better able to stroke her in places he yearned to reach.

Nothing could surpass the joy of love's free rein, and the good-humored ease with each other they had found at last. A question was put into her ear, softly urging, not demanding, and Rosette, looking up at her lover and soon-to-be husband, acquiesced. Shyly, tentatively, she searched with her hand, still staring up into his hot eyes. She found the long, pulsing length against his thigh and did as she was gently bid, stroking and learning his hard shape, until he groaned for her to cease.

Beneath her skirts, he found the inner softness of her thigh and then discovered the moist cleft and stroked and discovered new places to bring her to the height of ecstasy. When she was shivering in readiness, Mark swooped her up, but with a question curving his lips, he halted at the foot of the stairs.

"Will you come to me, only once, before our marriage vows are spoken?"

"Once, milord," she said, love shining in her eyes. "But once only."

In the middle of the night, Rosette woke to find Mark gone from her bed, and she fearfully wondered if it all had been merely a wonderfully delicious dream. Then, looking to the spot where his head could have been not long ago, she knew indeed she had not been dreaming. There, on the pillow, dusky red in the moonlight falling there in streamers, she discovered the single bud of a blood-red rose, one shy petal just beginning to unfold.

*　　　　*　　　　*

The baron arrived home shortly after midnight, surprised to find as he pulled the phaeton around that a light still burned in the front room. All the servants were usually abed by now, which started him thinking about detective Worthley and his promise earlier that week to pay him a visit soon. But, surely, not at this indecent hour of the night?

Mark was only now beginning to cool his ardor, for he would have stayed longer with Rosette had she not fallen into a deep, satisfied slumber. And a promise was a promise, only once had he gone to heaven and back with his beloved. She had been all that he dreamed she would be, and more. He couldn't wait to make Rosette his bride and begin making a family with her. Who knows, he thought slyly, if the last time or this he had not made her with child.

His nightcap askew on his head, Pickworth met the baron at the door, breathless and excited as he held out a note he said had arrived only a quarter of an hour before. The messenger had pressed the urgency that the note contained.

In a heart-stopping moment, Mark scanned the note, unable to credit the words he was reading. It was written in a neat hand, signed by a woman. The beloved name reached out to him in a caress that was almost tangible. *Rosette*. Having just come from her, how was it that she wanted him to meet her at the fork in the road leading to London town?

Chapter Thirty-five

Rosette's wracked body inside the thin rug hunched, and she hugged her knees to warm herself. Drearily she guessed her abductors must have taken her somewhere quite isolated, miles from civilization.

Since late last night—it must be near noon for they had long ago stopped for the first meal of the day—she had lain inside the rug. Only once had her tormentors given her what she had guessed was breakfast. Yes, they must be well into another day.

She hated lying here, not knowing what the coarse-speaking men had planned for her. The wagon she was in bumped and jostled over the rocky road in a bone-crushing ride, for the thin rug did little to alleviate her discomfort.

In her pregnancy, Rosette's qualmishness had returned. A lot of it she put down to fear of the unknown and why she was, for the second time in her life, being abducted. And, of course, the poor fare didn't help any.

She hated the foul odor of the men who had whisked her from her own home, in the middle of the night, while her servants slept unknowingly. Right into her bedroom they had crept to gag her! And rolled her up in this rug she'd come to detest with all her being.

Rosette was afraid and cold and thoroughly tired, while the rough men alongside the wagon joked and laughed. A feeling of foreboding washed over her and, in that, she knew the worst was yet to come.

Days undeterminable had passed, and there wasn't a soul to talk to. Frantically Rosette began to wonder how much longer she was expected to bear this torture. What did these abominable men care — they must be getting paid well for this evil deed.

Now she had been blindfolded and trussed up like a turkey, allowed to come up for air from the musty-smelling carpet. It was salt air she discovered, and once in a great while the sea breezes cooled her cheeks. For certain the ship—she finally realized she was on one—was no luxury cruiser.

Would she ever see Hasan—Mark Rawen to her now—ever see him again in her life? Was he worried sick, and searching for her at this very moment? Oh, God, she prayed it was so. He would be back in England, never having realized she had been taken from the country. Taken yes, but to where? Where were they headed?

Her knees pressed against her sore breasts, Rosette thought, "I am going to die, I'm sure of it."

A procession of faceless men passed before her bound eyes. Jack was the most aggressive of these her abductors. Philo was violent and lustful, yet thank God he left her alone. Then there was the third man. A mystery. Silent, but his dangerous presence felt nevertheless.

In the dusk before dawn of what she guessed was approximately ten days later, she heard the scuffle of feet aboard, the subdued voices of sailors preparing to leave the ship. To disembark. She was grateful for one thing, that being she would probably be taken from the ship now. But to God knows where!

She shivered in the thin rug, and wished someone, anyone, an avenging spirit would even do, would come to set her free of her agony. The thought of death was beginning to seem somewhat more pleasant compared to the discomfort that was growing worse with each passing hour.

Later that afternoon, carted from the ship like so much useless baggage, Rosette began to suffer badly, and even feared she might lose the child. Guilt began to gnaw at her, wishing she'd told Mark about the new life begun between them. A sweet little boy, she hoped, that would be the image of his father. Now Mark would never know. What a fool she'd been! Like a shameful secret, she had kept this from her love. What a *fool*!

A sense of familiarity nagged at her several hours later while she again bumped along, this time in what she guessed was a road cart, feeling that they'd been passing through towns and villages. Sometimes she felt the cart resembled a brick oven. Where, she wondered, had she experienced this before?

Time passed. Where they had been Rosette had no idea. Where they were bound she had even less of one.

Finally, freeing her face from the cavern of hay bales surrounding her, Rosette could see by working the blindfold down over one eye. She bit back a gasp then upon reaching the village.

She had never seen anything like these men before. Dark, thin, intense faces with slits of cruel eyes, three strangers met the cart. She knew then: They are Berbers. Now the silent one spoke up — in native Arabic. The *Sahara*!

"Oh dear God," Rosette moaned. "My wish . . . my fate has been sealed. Here I am, but without my beloved." What was to become of her next?

The answer came quicker than Rosette anticipated. The silent one spoke again, joining the Berbers now. He spoke to one, mostly in French.

"We will take her from here."

Rosette could hear Jack clearly now: "What will become of her? The lady said this one was never to return to England's shores."

"We will make sure she does not, ever," said the silent.

"Best do that, elst we won't get our other half of what's due!"

Rosette could imagine the silent one shrugging at that before he demanded, "Be on your way now!"

It wasn't long before Rosette discovered the name of the silent — he was called Arek. He was, she also learned, to take her to her final destination. Rosette felt faint when Arek spoke in perfect French to another of his kind, saying the young woman was destined for a nomadic chieftan who paid highly for white woman flesh.

"He likes to use them first, and then beat them." Arek seemed to be cruelly taunting Rosette, as if he knew she overheard. "At times a captive white woman will feel both at the same time, you know what I mean," Arek was telling his companion, "and sometimes, they will die mercifully before he has finished with them." With a nasty ring, he chuckled deeply.

"Do you think she can hear and understand you?" asked the other.

"This does not matter."

At that moment Rosette was curled up in a tight ball of fear and apprehension on the hard floor of the cart. Hay needles pricked her soft cheeks, the chaff nearly choking her.

Just when Rosette had resigned herself to curling up in hopes that death would soon take her naturally, she was being transferred from the horrible cart to the high back of a dromedary. *"Mareh,"* had been shouted as she was pointed to.

Miles around all she could see from this vantage point was sand—nothing but sand under the immensity of desert sky.

Arek's eyes, with a dark, lustful glint, followed as her ragged dress displayed the thin laces of her see-through chemise. So, she thought, the silent one runs deep. Here was trouble, perhaps. Maybe, if she summoned enough strength and courage, she could use it to gain an advantage. But who was there to help her escape across the vast, burning sands? Surely not Arek himself.

What Rosette didn't know was that her unbound hair gleamed like dark fire in the sunlight, and had she caught the many hungry stares resting on it and her pale beauty, she would have been triply alarmed. As it was, Arek proved the boldest, allowing the beauty to catch him absorbed in studying every inch of her figure and face.

Thankfully, she had been given a length of black fabric to twist about her head, thus concealing her hair, and she guessed this to be Arek's idea. In part, she knew, to keep other wandering tribes with their searching dark eyes from discovering she was a very desirable woman.

From below, she knew, all they could see was the top half of her black turban swaying to and fro in the pavilion high atop the camel's back. She needed to lean to the side and look over in order for anyone to see her face.

Arek continued to ride guard beside Rosette's dromedary. She gave this matter considerable thought, coming to the conclusion that Arek was quite taken with her. Hadn't his dark eyes gleamed with blatant desire when she leaned over and lifted an eyebrow coyly? Hadn't she seen him shift in restless discomfort when she kneeled in her pavillion and with fluttering fingers bared a soft, ivory-white shoulder to his already openly ardent gaze?

Yes, Rosette smiled lazily, perhaps Arek was the answer to her much-sought freedom. She would do anything, *almost*, to save her unborn babe and find her way back to her beloved sheik.

Chapter Thirty-six

Her dress was an almost-black poplin, with a floppy bonnet of black net tied beneath her chin in a bow. A black parasol festooned with red muslin—the only bright splash on her—was held aloft resembling clouds awash in sunset. The dress had been supplied at two hour's notice by the costume rental on Regent Street.

Rozelle Modestia, the perfect image of her by-minutes younger sister, adjusted the dainty bows on her black kid slippers and waited. The driver of Rozelle's rented landau was becoming impatient.

"We have waited for two hours now," the

young driver said. "I'll not wait much longer." He sat back, disgruntled.

"Don't worry, I shall pay you for the extra time." She caught his eye then as she posed mischievously. "There will even be something added in it for you, if you know what I mean," she said coaxingly.

He sat straighter, thinking this was no haggard lady, but one who could dance to any tune he played. Feminine and fetching, even in her widow's weeds. Unlike the cantankerous old babes who paid him and sent him along his way without even an extra coin. But this here beauty was offering him something that was more to his liking. Later, all he had to do was get rid of the gentleman she was meeting, and then they could have some fun. He, Carlton, would not pass this up. No way!

This had better work, Rozelle was thinking. If she failed in this scheme, she might as well throw in the towel.

Rozelle felt her forehead. It was burning, and her pulses—how they beat. Like hammers. She must get a hold of herself before Mark Rawen showed up.

"Why are you meeting here so early in the day?" Carlton asked his passenger.

He spoke suspiciously, Rozelle noticed. "Is such a thing so unusual?" she asked the handsome, blond-haired giant.

"No, I suppose not so unusual. But does he ask for anything?"

Rozelle frowned, then laughed lightly as she caught on. Coyly she said, "Ask?"

"Will you offer him—something?" he wondered.

"Naturally."

Carlton shifted in his seat, crossed one leg over the other, and stuck a finger inside his hot collar. "It's rather hot for this time of year," he said, making a go at conversation.

She was silent, looking toward him with her bold, steady eyes. Carlton would love to lay his lips on hers with passion, hot, burning with force and fire. As far as Rozelle was concerned, she was just flirting with a jolly, big and rather rowdy boy rather than with a cabbie. Easily she could put him off later, she decided, unworried over this.

"Who're you waiting for?" he boldly asked the young lady in black. "Are you in mourning?"

"Oh," she laughed, "not so fast. First, I am waiting for—for an old friend I haven't seen in a long time."

He grinned hugely. "Going to make up for lost time, huh?"

"You could say, yes, that is what we will surely do!"

"Well, who died then, you didn't say?"

441

"My sister, she will no doubt be drawing her last breath any day now."

His eyes widened. "You mean you're already mourning her death?" He shook his head when she nodded. "Incredible!"

The clop of hoofs drew them both around as the carriage, with its lustrous equipage, came up the wide dirt road. Rozelle straightened her skirts while Carlton sat stiff and obsequiously.

Mark Rawen could see the landau up ahead now, and as he drew nearer his bemusement grew apace. For the hundredth time he asked himself the reason for Rosette meeting him like this. Was she in trouble? Had Worthley found something out? No, that couldn't be the answer. At least he hoped this wasn't so. He had sent Worthley and his detectives after the "man" he had described as the dark rider. Too bad for Paul Moreland, but Mark really couldn't say he felt any sorrow for the man, or any guilt for sending the hounds at his heels. The man was a liar, a thief and a troublemaker to boot. He would soon be behind prison bars. Mark sighed. So much for Paul Moreland. Now to see what Rosette was up to. He was eager to get under way with wedding plans.

The brasswork on his carriage gleamed as Mark pulled up alongside the landau. Seeing the dark head with its net bonnet peep out demurely, Mark had a sudden flashback. He was possessed by a feeling of *de ́ ja ́ vu*. Haunting, stamped on his memory. She tilted her head and smiled beautifully, showing pearly white teeth in that face he loved so dearly.

"Darling," she purred. "Are you late?" she laughed. "Or is it I who is late?"

Mark racked his brains in an effort to remember something that nagged at him persistently. He tried to make whatever it was rise from his subconscious, but try though he did the image would not clear; it was lodged too deep in his mind.

"I suppose —" Mark shook his head — "it's my fault. I'm sorry," he said, looking down at his watch, "I am a bit late."

Tossing her head, Roselle chastised playfully. "And so you are, darling. But now that you are here, should we go on to the inn up ahead? I am famished, and we do so have much to discuss, don't we, darling?"

Frowning lightly, Mark stared down at the leather held loosely between his long fingers. Something was wrong. He just knew this. For some reason unfathomable, he was disappointed. What was it? Why couldn't he see the writing on the wall?

"Very well, we'll go to the inn. There shouldn't be too many people there at this hour of the day."

"Good." She tossed her head in its floppy bonnet. "Lead on."

Pulling ahead, again Mark frowned to himself. Something about Rozette disturbed him intensely today. There was about her an air of mystery, and she seemed to be secretly laughing at him for some reason. For a woman who just last night had lain with him in ecstasy's embrace, she seemed odd, strangely excited. He was further puzzled. She was gowned all in black, as if in widow's weeds.

Steep roads ran down from the small-fronted, eighteenth century Leigham Court Inn, and it was here at the entrance that both carriages drew up together. Like a bolt from the blue into his brain, Mark Rawen stiffened as the lady in black alighted from her carriage first, bringing back to his memory what it was he'd been unable to remember.

Mark frowned darkly. Someone had made an ass out of him. No, two had fooled him to the top of his bent. Now was his turn to lay a trap for his enemies. In truth, only one remained.

Devastatingly compelled in his embroidered waistcoat and matching gray broadcloth trousers, Mark swung down from his seat. Taking the lady in black by a crooked arm, he smiled gently into her upturned face, saying, "Has someone died, my love?"

"No, darling, not yet."

"Well then, shall we go inside and see about a room?"

Slightly taken aback by his instant ardor, Rozelle recovered and purred up at this debonair man who she had at one time thought her brother. Instant success — she cheered for herself for being so coy and smart. Soon, ah yes, soon all would be hers. With Rosette Forrest out of the way, all three estates would be joined. She was free to become Mark's wife. She had hoodwinked him where Paul had failed miserably. He would never learn her true identity, and how fortunate for her she had discovered just in time that Mark Rawen was no relation to her at all. She had put on a good face indeed!

"A room, yes, darling. I can hardly wait."

Neither can I, thought Baron Mark Rawen.

Chapter Thirty-seven

Her cheeks pink with confusion, Rozelle looked aside. The Welsh rarebit had hardly been touched, the wine was yet three-quarters full. But Mark Rawen sat back as if sated by the little he had eaten, his chair tipped back as he considered her, his tawny brows drawn together, threateningly close.

"You are not hungry, darling?"

Warily Rozelle watched him as his countenance altered, lips curled in a devilish smile. His broad shoulders moved laconically.

"Not very. I've more serious matters on my mind, other than feeding my hunger." His eyes flicked the rounded curve of one profiled breast, then leapt to her face. "Do I detect the hint of a blush? Really, love, after last night I would have thought to see you less virginal." Mark smiled faintly. "Ah, how you responded to me, sweet." His eyes darkened almost imperceptibly, and he leaned close to whisper, "Do you remember how you loved to feel the . . ." He grinned when her eyes widened in alarm. "Ah, the memory of the yielding of your sweet flesh under my thrust."

Rozelle started, feeling the flush rise up from her chest to settle in her throat. "Y-yes," she muttered inanely. Fear was beginning to take hold now. There was something of a dangerous nature in his compelling eyes.

"Come upstairs with me now," he said urgently.

"But Mark . . ."

He gritted his teeth, then barked low, "Now, Rosette. I mean to have you now, as I've waited long enough this day. What is the matter, love, getting cold feet at this late date?"

"N-no, it's not that. I just — couldn't we sit here for a while longer?"

"No."

Rozelle felt herself being pulled up from the chair, tingles of shock running through her blood at the contact of his hard fingers cruelly pinching her arm. "Mark, why are you hurting me? Are you angry over something I've done?"

"It's what you haven't done, my love."

"Whatever do you mean?"

Something had gone awry, and Rozelle could feel again a sense of foreboding arise within her. All of a sudden she was quailing, with no stomach for this game. He seemed overeager, and rushed to get this over with. She had a feeling, too, his plan had nothing to do with making love to her. Just what did he want? Had he already found her out? What was she to do now? Sickening disappointment raced through her, of ridiculous hopes destroyed. All the happiness and wealth she could have known. Why was he frightening her this way? Was this the manner in which he treated his twin? If so, she wanted nothing to do with Mark Rawen.

She turned to him as he was taking care of the bill and obtaining the key to their room on the second floor. "I'll be just a minute, darling. I left something out in the carriage—a reticule that I shall be needing. Do you mind? I'll not be a minute."

Brusquely he faced her, stuffing change into his trouser pocket. "I'll go with you."

"That won't be necessary, dar—"

"But I want to accompany you outside," he said, seeming to deride her as he emphasized his desire.

Pricking her anew was an intense fear of what he would do should he really find her out. She was scared out of her wits, for never had she seen Mark Rawen so intimidating. He struck terror into her with the slightest burning touch from his hand.

"You are shaking, dear Rosette. What is it?"

Rozelle could swear she was perspiring from head to foot. She put on a bold front, every inch of her intent on escaping this fearsome man. The look in his eyes just now made her want to slink away and never set eyes on Mark Rawen again! How could she have lived with this man for so long not knowing his true formidable nature?

"Don't spurn me now, sweet. We are halfway to our lovenest," he said, with a mocking inflection in his tone.

Slowing she turned her head and looked at him, but Rozelle could find no glory in her triumph. She could kill him now, for he had robbed her of her strongest weapon: hate. That hate had been replaced by unreasonable fear.

"I think — yes, I do want to return home now, Mark. I — I feel a bit faint, and need to lie down." Daintily she lifted her skirts above the hard-packed ground.

Mark's dark eyes looked her up and down as his lips sneered over her. Suddenly he caught her arm and drew her up, pinching fingers torturing the soft flesh of her upper arm in his grip.

Pain made her whimper. "For God's sake, darling, what are you doing? Whyever are you hurting me this way?"

His voice rasped in her ear. "Forget the damn reticule! We are going upstairs this very moment." He jerked her against his hip. "Come along now and heed this warning: Don't make a scene." Askance he saw that she nodded. "Good, then."

Rozelle's tongue nervously licked her upper lip. Her legs trembled as he led her up the narrow-railed stairs to their room. Inside, frantically her eyes scanned the big, wooden bed and the tiny window flanking it. There was no escape. Her steps faltered, and it was then, after he had secured the door by using the key, that Mark put a hand to her elbow as if to steady her.

"No need for alarm, my dear." He pushed her to a high-backed chair. "Ah, now, be seated."

Bemused by his change in behavior, she sank into the chair and clasped her hands together. Her skirts clung to her trembling legs, her eyes hypnotized by his dark gaze. He showed his back to her as he strode about the room. Suddenly he halted and swung about to face her sternly.

His smile grew tight and cruel. "So, tell me where you have sent your twin? Don't appear so surprised, sweet. If I should happen to go, at this very moment, to visit the woman I love, don't you think I realize she will not be found anywhere in the vicinity of Southend? Perhaps not even in England?" He gave her a withering look, full of contempt. "To think I would have given you the moon had you so desired it, and to think my world revolved around you. That is, at one time."

Rozelle's body convulsed under the whiplash of his tirade that went like tongues of fire through her nerves. "Please, you do not understand. Mark, can't you see who I am? Truly I am Rosette. Rozelle Modestia lies dead in her grave in Morocco! Please believe me!"

He snorted in disgust. "Believe you? You lying bitch of a slut, planning my demise with that good-for-nothing Paul Moreland." His face turned into a fixed, hard mask. "How many men have sampled your charms? You are beautiful, you know, almost as perfect as your twin. Almost. Where she is like sweet wine, you are like sour grapes. You turn my stomach."

Like one possessed of the devil, Rozelle went crazy next. When the scream would have come ripping from her throat, Mark reacted like lightning and clamped a heavy hand over her mouth. Her lush body flailed as she tried to fight him off, nipping foul curses muffled between his fingers. While his fingers sent maddening points of agony into her soft flesh, her finger tips could only scratch futilely at his hard wrists.

"Tell me, you Jezebel, where is Rosette Forrest?"

Her red mouth wide open across his palm, she bit down as hard as she could, releasing her mouth momentarily to hiss up at him, "In hell, where she belongs." She tried to kick out at him but he was too fast and too strong.

"So, you do not know where she is?" he ground out, his free hand coming up like a whip to strike her lovely face, making the room spin all about her.

"No, no, no!"

His open hand came down again, hitting hard against her cheek, slamming her head back and around. His palm returned to send her face flying the other way. Her knees came up, and she huddled on the hard chair, daring to touch her cheek to check if he had marred it, and wincing for the pain of its wales and bruises.

"You bastard!" she spat up at him with false bravado. *"Ha!* The sheik of dogs! The baron of bastardy!" She sat hissing and spitting in her dishabille. She flexed a slim arm up at him. "If I were a man, I would string you up by your manhood! Ha, if you have any to speak of at all."

"Ahh-hhh . . ." He shook his head, grinning at her cunningly. "Would you like me to prove that point, my dear one-time sister? If only back then your true identity would have been known to me, you would have been used well, knowing your true nature—which is nothing short of a lying whore."

Mark let go with a slap that sent her to the floor. She collapsed, moaning like a banshee, burying her lovely, bruised face in the tapestry, biting at her wrist, writhing like a black snake. Dimly she sensed him looming over her, his face wet with sweat, the insane light in his dark eyes. He kneeled on the floor, his hand twisting in her loosened auburn hair and he pulled, tugging her head back until she was forced to come to her knees.

Minutes passed, and after a time Rozelle realized it was her own voice that was sobbing and babbling incoherent words, and that she lay across the bed where the baron had slung her. Before she knew what was happening, he was ripping her skirts from her lower half. She moaned, trying to pull her body away from the hard, insisting fingers. Unceremoniously she was flipped humiliatingly onto her stomach. Looking over her shoulder at the seemingly demented man, she whimpered.

"What are you doing? Are you mad?"

"Indeed, I thought as much."

She peeked up at him through swollen, squinting eyes as he brooded down at her, and there was quiet triumph in his face.

"Be grateful that I did nothing more to mar your pretty flesh other than bruise it a little." He let his eyes roam over her bare waist and hips.

Frenziedly her head shook. "What are you going to do now? Now that you have me bared, will you ravish me, Lord Rawen?"

Deep laughter rang out, mocking and cruel. "Touch you? Never!" He slapped her soundly on her bare buttocks. "The talented rose." He backed away, putting his ruffled shirt front to rights.

Twisting about, Rozelle surveyed the spot he had smacked. Her rose, her birthmark, he had dared one further to degrade and humiliate her. "You really did know, didn't you?"

"Of course, Rozelle Modestia," he said tauntingly.

"One thing you do not know!" she spat.

Cocking his hands at his hips, he mustered a pleasant tone of voice. "What would that be?"

"Where your whore is at this very minute!" Rozelle sat up in the middle of the mussed bed, straightening as graciously as she could her torn skirt. "Hah! Try to figure that out, you bastard!"

"You are wrong, Rozelle Modestia. It is you who bears the name bastard. Your own mother put you out. Do you know why? Well then, I'll tell you. The Lady Louise realized which of her twin daughters was the evil one. Like my own Spanish mother, she had the sight and put you out for the evil eyes you possessed."

Long fingernails bit into tender palms as Rozelle screamed low, "No, it's not true. If so, why did you not realize my evilness —" she went on in a clipped voice—"Hasan al-Shareef?"

"Ah, but I did. You see—" he held up a finger—"you are a witch, Rozelle Modestia, afraid of the dark—*a djinn* as the Arabs call them."

Forest-dark eyes narrowed.

"Lucie has informed me well."

"Oh! You have found out where we have hidden her. You have tricked me again, you bas—"

He held up a finger to interrupt. "Tsk, tsk, no more of your foul language. No, I do not know where you have concealed Rosette's maid, nor did I know you really had her." He shrugged nonchalantly. "It was merely a hunch. But now, thanks to your quick, waspish tongue, I do believe I know where to look. I've had you followed, if you didn't know, Roz. Oh, you flinch. Do you know a fellow by the name of Worthley? *Detective* Worthley?"

"Ohhh . . ." Rozelle raked her nails across the coverlet, leaving ragged tears where she had rent the thin material.

"Well," Mark began casually, "I must be going. You see, Rosette and I are traveling to Morocco and from there a visit to the kasbah. I've some things to pick up there. Is there anything you want me to bring back? Your Moroccan dresses, shifts, ah, you must have something you left behind?"

As if she'd seen a hideous monster come alive in the room, Rozelle stared aghast, trembling like a newly opened leaf. "You—you beast. Again, you tricked me! All the while you had Rosette . . . she never did get abducted. Oh! I hate you! Hate you!" She pounded furiously upon the bed with balled fists. Wretchedly she faced him once again. "Wh-what are you grinning about, you fool?" He curled his lips maddeningly, and she narrowed her eyes in horrible suspicion.

"Thank you, sweet." He made a mocking half-bow from the waist. "I do thank you for that bit of information. You see, now I must make haste and follow my love to the Sahara." He sighed as if pained. "Roz, Roz, you have put me to great trouble." He shook his head. "All the way to the Sahara."

He turned briskly after saluting her with an imaginary tip of a hat, then showed her his long, lean back in going out the door.

"What is going on!" called the alarmed voice outside Rozelle's door. "Open up in there. All right, if you won't, I'll do it myself!"

And what the proprietor came upon in that room in his Leigham Court Inn he would never forget. He gaped and gaped, scratching his balding pate. The lovely young woman clung to the edge of the bed, a wide-eyed, tear-eyed expression as she too gaped at the handfuls of long auburn brown hair gleaming between her bared claws.

"Ye did that to yerself, ma'am?" the proprietor

asked, dumbfounded that such a lovely head of hair would come to ruin.

Rozelle snatched up the nearest item she could find to throw, which was the urine bucket, and heaved it with all her might, screaming, "Go away! Oooh! Just go away and leave me alone!"

Part Six

Wind, Sand and Stars

"I am my beloved's, and my beloved is mine."
    —SONG OF SOLOMON   6.3

Chapter Thirty-eight

The Sahara — The black, well-knit eyebrows rose as the eyes beneath savored the beauty of the English girl.

"*Cherie*, how did you like the food? Was it to your liking?"

"*Oui*, very much so," she said to Arek while his dark, unrelenting eyes rested on her white throat. With the few feminine items she had, she tried her best to look alluring. Her polished copper hair was artfully and femininely drawn up, to a topknot allowing a fall of heavy waves to sway below her shoulders. Wispy tendrils hugged her temples, some resting beside her ears. Like two polished agates, her almond-gold eyes glittered.

Like the sands of time in an hourglass, Rosette knew her time was running out.

"The Touaregs have a proverb. Would you care to hear it?" he said, reclining on strewn pillows in the hastily erected tent.

"Of course," she answered sweetly, while making plans of how best to persuade Arek to take her back to Morocco.

"The further tents are separated, the closer hearts are to each other," he quoted.

How odd, Rosette thought. Mentally she shrugged then. Indeed she had noticed how widely dispersed the tents had been erected. "Will your tent be far from mine this night, Arek?" She shivered to think of his answer before she had it. Was she being overly bold in the presence of this dangerous man? She didn't care, all she desired was to get away before that nomadic chieftain got his hands on her.

"If you desire it so, mademoiselle," he let it lay.

She didn't feel much like she'd been abducted and was now a captive. Arek was being kind, which showed he liked her. Or was he only playing the same cat-and-mouse game she was?

With true feminine guile, Rosette said, "The language of the Berbers is very beautiful. Are you one yourself?"

"I am a Touareg. *Targui.* My native language

is Tamahag, and it is much like the language of the Berbers."

Arek caught her staring at his sword hilt, and he grinned proudly, his deep caramel tone flushing darker. "There is a legend, that our people have come down from crusaders who escaped from the Saracens, and made their way into the Sahara."

"The hilt," she said, still studying its shape. "It is like a cross."

There are tales that the Touareg went through a time in which they were Christian."

She supplied, "Before the Arab conquest."

"*Oui,*" he still spoke in French for her benefit. "You are well informed, mademoiselle. Then they were converted to Islam and they have — we have been such in name only."

Unrestrainedly she said, "Mohammedan."

· He shrugged, allowing his scrutiny to rest on the full circles of her breasts outlined in the cool drapery he'd found for her to wear. "Of course," he murmured.

With vivid lights in her eyes she ventured boldly, "Do you have a wife, Arek?"

"A *Targuia? Non,*" he said, dark eyes aglow with mystery.

Languidly she reclined on the exotic-colored, if not a bit dusty, pillows. "Tell me about the Touareg women, please?" She smiled radiantly with her pearly teeth showing.

On this subject, suddenly his eyes lit up. "She is more independent than European women," he began, watching her closely, but Rosette did not flinch once. "And she is greatly looked up to. The Hoggar still live like medieval noblemen, and their women do only the lightest household tasks."

"Who then does the manual work?" she asked with a slow, husky purr, not overhasty, knowing full well why he treated her not like a captive but an honored guest. He wanted her; it was in his lazy, hooded eyes. But she abandoned her initial deductions, for, somehow, in the short time she'd been imprisoned along with him, she'd read that Arek was self-enamored. True, Arek admired her—as he admired himself. He wanted her in the way a pirate desired a treasure—pretties to gaze at and compare with other treasures. Then she wondered: Was Arek a little . . . fluffy?

"The Haratin," he was saying, "or Negro slaves do the hard work. They are fed and clothed and treated as part of a family."

"Are they paid then?" she wondered, warming to the subject, forgetting for now that she was a very frightened woman bound for the tent of a no-doubt very cruel, sadistic nomad. Rosette suppressed a shudder at the mere thought of fat, greasy fingers crawling over her soft flesh and tender parts.

"They are not paid," Arek said abruptly, this time causing Rosette to flinch.

Night came and campfires flamed all about. The sands had cooled quickly, and the spell of the desert night was upon them with the blood-red moon rising enormous. Arek rose, unwinding his tall, lanky frame.

"I must go inspect the camp now."

He bowed from the waist most graciously.

"Belafia, mademoiselle. Good night," he said.

That was it? *"Belafia,"* Rosette returned. She stemmed what she'd been about to say to him in a gentle flirtation. He had only been nice; it was plain he had no real interest in her. He hadn't been unkind, though.

But the Targui disappeared, walking slowly into the dark.

"Whew." Rosette drew the back of her forearm across her forehead. Staring at the closed flap for several more minutes, she murmured forlornly, "Good night, beloved sheik, Mark Rawen, wherever you are."

But no sound, no voice of her beloved came to answer Rosette. After a while only the long-lost song of the wind kept Rosette company. *Love comes but once and never again,* it sang mournfully. Would there ever come another night in paradise for her and her beloved sheik again? If only. How much she wanted his manly, sensuous passion.

*   *   *

Rosette awoke, glancing rapidly around the dark, breathing walls of her tent. Breathlessly she came to rest on her elbows, wondering at the sound that had rudely awakened her from dreams of her sheik. Was it only the desirous thudding of her own heart she'd heard?

With a savage leap to her bare feet she searched for the borrowed robe. A hand groped out of the semi-darkness to hand it over to her. She gasped as flesh contacted flesh.

"Here it is, mademoiselle."

Unwavering, Rosette stared at the hand she could barely see but knew was caramel colored, as the half-moon rode across the desert sky—a rapturous moon meant for a night of bliss. But her romantic ideas were unsafe at the moment—a dangerous atmosphere pervaded.

"Guns," was all Arek murmured hastily.

"Oh, was that sound I heard earlier rifle shot?" she timidly questioned Arek, her eyes fixed tensely on the glittering orbs of his eyes.

"Yes, I believe the guards posted outside the camp have been executed. We will soon be under attack."

Chapter Thirty-nine

Ominously, Arek held something that gleamed in his hand. "Now you know what must be done? No one else must have you."

Arek's words were like a sigh.

"No." Rosette stepped back. "But why? By whose orders are you to slay me in case of attack? Who would wish me dead?"

With a side glance to the ominous blade she could barely see, Rosette waited for the insidious Arek to answer her. Oh God, had Mark himself sent her away? How well did she really know Mark, she had asked herself hundreds of times. Was Arek acting merely as Mark

Rowen's — Hasan al-Shareef's — mediator? Arek was to do the dirty work while Mark washed his hands of her? In the meantime Mark returned to his former love, whoever she was?

"I'll kill her!" Rosette snarled, without thinking Arek had this very same planned for her.

Arek advanced, his black-orbed gaze unwavering and inscrutable. Rosette pretended to be dauntless, even though she was almost petrified. "This was not accomplished in a fortuitous manner, I take it?" she said, stalling while the moon outside followed its nocturnal course.

"You are right, this is not happening by chance."

Rosette gulped, for Arek was proving to be an insidious enemy. "I asked you, please, Arek, who would wish me harm?"

"*She*, that is all I will say. She paid us well to kill you and let the ever-shifting sands of the desert bury you. But of course we discovered our own plans for your future. But now —" He left off.

"Was the woman mad?" Rosette wondered out loud.

She stalled for time. "How did she pay? Who was she?"

Arek had stepped so near that their faces were only a foot apart.

"She says she is your twin, I can tell you that —" he shrugged — "because soon you will have to die, mademoiselle. I'm sorry."

"Rozelle Modestia," she murmured as truth was a blinding flash in her brain. She, who had been her image that night she held up Moreland's coach, was in truth her flesh and blood. The other half of herself she had always thought missing, the puzzle, her loneliness. Rosette's lashes fluttered. Had it all been a scheme to get rid of her? Mark as Hasan; Rozelle Modestia playing the part as his sister? Then she herself had been drugged by Hasan's man into believing she was Rozelle? But for what reason? Had they planned for her demise, Rozelle and Mark together? Then why had it taken them so long to lower the *coup de grace*?

"Mademoiselle, I am sorry."

The blade — as it lifted high in the air, Rosette could feel and hear its deadly passage. "No, please, Arek, I am too young to die," she begged, her voice fraught with tears.

The steel of death hovered in the oppressive air of the tent. Arek hesitated then, nonplussed by her tears.

"I am going to have a baby, Arek. Hasan al-Shareef's baby." She saw his face twist at that in a grotesque fashion. "Would you slay a woman in this delicate condition?" Suddenly the smooth features of his youth turned to the haggard face of a worn-out old man. "Think of it, Arek, haven't you ever desired children of your own? I am sure you have, for your face softened when you spoke earlier of the Targuias of the Hoggar." Rosette was conscious of a feeling of unusual weariness, uneasiness, even dread now for the future — future? Would she even have one?

Another shot, closer this time, and Arek flinched and stole a glance to the tent flap. Arek seemed to be yielding to an inner frustration of mind and soul. Rosette shook her head. Arek was certainly a paradox. Did he want to kill her? Or did he want to save her for something? Something, or someone.

"Arek, who is this nomadic chieftain you were to bring me to? Is this perhaps who is raiding the camp?"

"No!" he said vividly, sweating profusely.

This was the momentous decision. Would he use that devil blade on her tender flesh?

Suddenly an intensity of life permeated and startled Rosette. It was as if the fluid of life were being poured into her out of unseen vials. Precious liquid. As if her bittersweet bondage was over. For all time. Perhaps she was dying now. Had she already been stabbed by Arek's descending blade?

A discordant sound reached her ears. Another voice? One that sounded very angry, prepared to slice open whoever got in his way. Screams of dying men came to her—high pitched . . . horrible.

"I am sorry, it must be now." Arek modulated his voice to a low growl. "The camp raiders are killing all my men. It must be—"

That movement, slight though it was, seemed to remove a veil of darkness that, like death, had hung over her and allowed in upon her a flood of light.

It was all over. No need to worry any longer. That light was a bright angel coming to claim her to paradise. What was that tune out of harmony being played? Merely blades clashing by night?

Like a somnambulist, Rosette caught hold of the canvas of the tent. Had she been stabbed? Was this the reason for her sleepiness of a sudden? Had a whizzing bullet struck her?

Spasmodic coughing took hold of her. "Oh . . ." For a moment Rosette felt weak as a babe, then strong as an Amazon. She stumbled outside, the flap having been thrust aside impatiently as a low growl like thunder reached her.

"Rosette!" A deep voice fell over her solicitously.

"Why?" She coughed again. "Why do you sound so distraught, lord of thunder?" she asked the stranger, spasmodic in her speech, staring wide at his drawn, bloodied blade.

In a sinister fashion, Arek melted back into the shadows of the tent. Arek, too, had seen the flash of red-dipped blade.

The skirts of Rosette's robe tumbled about her ankles. She curled her bare toes into the sand, then gave a whimper of pain.

The handsome sheik, his caftan a moving whiteness upon the dark, reacted swiftly to catch Rosette before she fell. Bended upon one knee, he caught her up into his arms and then hefted his weight and hers as he stood tall. He tossed his blade to his man.

From inside the tent, Arek threw a furtive glance out the tent flap. Slyly, he straightened and withdrew into the tent.

Catching the modicum of movement, the sheik snarled angrily, turning to a black-robed figure behind him. "Take him!" He lifted the hand that held his feminine armful to indicate the stealthy man therein. "I've no more taste for blood, not now—or ever again!"

Her avenging angel was a man, Rosette thought through her haze with ecstatic joy. The glory of warmth and security rushed upon her as a flood of gold. She felt him, even in her numbness, caress her unbound hair in a tender fashion, and that gold of the sun which was her love burst, and thousands of illuminations danced in her head. Her angel was giving her back her life!

"My love, how you had me worried!"

He speaks! But as the blackness invading her mind drew nearer, Rosette saw dimly that it was not an angel, but a sheik, walking steadily away from the tent with her in his strong arms. The man owned Hasan al-Shareef's gait. Oh, she should have met him at the threshold of their wandering home! If only he would speak again!

"Taleb, she is delirious! Bring my horse! My God, she has been wounded!" He stared dolefully at the additional blood wetting his white caftan. Hers was mingling with that of his victims.

Rosette smiled. He does speak, and oh! how perfect he sounds! But why is he spattered with blood? Was it blood, truly?

"My love?" Rosette mumbled between slack lips. "Why did you deceive me?"

She could feel herself floating above the ground, something hard wound about her shoulders, one warm tentacle beneath her knees. He smelled of sweat, horse and the blood of many men.

"Deceive you?" came the harsh reply. "Never!"

With a desperation born of love that bears frustration, a kiss, long and tender, was given to her by this agonized man in her dream. Darker, growing darker. Rosette moaned as at last he took his lips from hers. "Am I dying . . . Hasan?"

"No, never will I let you die!"

She was still being carried, but now by the wind that dug its fiery heels into the sand. The desert moon flouted the dark, mounting ever higher. The gouge in her shoulder began to burn and ache now.

"Have I been hurt?" she asked the face so near her own.

"Yes. But stay still, my love."

She sidled closer to the life-giving warmth, and he stayed her with a gentle, restraining hand. "Please, don't move," the deep voice begged her.

The dryness and barrenness of the desert swept by in a blur. But Rosette sighed in peace for the moment. What is woman's great joy that stars the desert with flowers and makes the dry, barren places run sweet with water? Paradise, all around her, enhanced by the man whose arms were wrapped securely and tenderly about her.

"Hasan, can you tell me?" she murmured incoherently.

Now, the moon—it must be the moon—that was making her hero's face appear odd somehow, like in this dark face the eyes glittered with feverish light.

"What is it?" she asked again of the white phantom that was all a blur now.

She felt his comforting hand encircling her wrist, firmly and gently at the same time.

"Rosette, do you hear me? Rosette!"

Ah, now she could hear his deep male voice again.

"Are you . . . my beloved sheik?"

"Yes!" he shouted. "I am anything you want, my sweet, yes, I am your sheik. Is that what you want?"

"Hasan?"

Mark Rawen turned to the black-clad rider flanking his white stallion. "Finally, Taleb, she is speaking to me."

"Can you tell how bad is her wound?"

There was agony in his voice now. "No, but there is much blood, an alarming amount that cannot be stemmed by this cloth. We must hasten to the ruined castle."

"Ahh, Lord Hasan, that is a bad place where the old Roman buttress and walls still stand. There are ghosts of *djinns* there!"

It was hard to dissuade Hasan from doing what he planned. "Will you come with me, I am asking, Taleb? I need your aid in this. You can hasten to your camp and return with the needed items. She must not die from this knife wound. I shall not allow her to!"

"Perhaps it is not so deep then."

The voices drifted out of range of her hearing. Against the rough material of the caftan she muttered, "Hasan . . . Mark . . . I love you, love you so much. . . ."

She whispered the endearment over again and

again. Strangely, the numbness began to pass away.

"And I love you. Ah, my dearest rose, you cannot know how much!"

This returned sheik stood at the entrance to the four roofless walls, drinking in his beloved's unparalleled beauty. He was wearier of bone than he could remember ever being in his entire life. Not even months of warring with nomads and constant skirmishes with neighboring tribes had so sapped his strength.

Ah, the silence of the night is long. Mark stared down at the rubble and sand where once soldiers' boots had trod. He looked up again. Taleb had come and gone. He and the young Arab had done all they could to stem the flow of blood from Rosette's deep shoulder wound.

Arek would pay dearly for this. Indeed, Taleb had gone to see to the man's fate — as it should be seen to.

How in the world, he wondered fiercely, had Rozelle found the skinny little bastard to do her dirty work? Ahhh. Now Mark suddenly knew. Arek's sister had married defiantly to an Englishman, a knavish lad, one Arek would have liked to have slit the throat of. That explained why Arek had been visiting in the south of London. Arek, born from the illicit union of a

Touareg chieftain and the comely daughter of one of the descendants of Negro slaves brought up from the south.

Mark clenched the fingers of his swiftest fighting hand. If he had touched Rosette in any lecherous fashion . . . Mark shrugged. Arek was being well taken care of, for sure!

Even as the moon waned, a faint, cool breath of wind stole over the sands among the protruding stubble of rocks and stone in the abandoned castle site, one of the lost cities of the Sahara.

Mark propped himself against a massive, crumbled pillar. He rested a little now, seeing that Rosette slumbered peacefully at long last. He took the time to look at the surroundings, rolling his turbaned head to make certain the borrowed stallion—offspring to El Barq—had been given enough feed by Taleb. Taleb was an old friend, as old as these landmarks, Mark chuckled. Tried and true, Taleb was to be trusted at any time, unlike some other Arabs Mark could name. He snarled at the thought of them here and now.

Would Hadji-ben-Haroun be back at the kasbah now? By now, Tarek must have taken over as chieftain of El Taj. Let him. Mark looked adoringly at his sleeping lady. He was done with that past life. Let the Arabs and the Touaregs have it all. He had been led to the

Sahara—though Tremayne had brought him, true—led here for a definite end.

And now Hasan al-Shareef, Mark Brandon Rawen, acknowledged what that end was.

He closed his eyes and curved his lean buttocks into the sand, stopping to pluck a stone from beneath his thigh and toss it aside. He burrowed deeper and found a comfortable bed finally. He peeked at Rosette with one eye, then satisfied, he shut his eyelid once again.

It seemed to Mark that before Rosette had been wounded she had never really known what it was to love. Even in his arms at Southend—ah, but what a night!—she had not fully abandoned herself in love's joys to him, not perfectly as he would have liked. The missing link of Rozelle Modestia, and the lonely childhood Rosette must have felt knowing all along some integral part of her was missing—fear, hate, bitterness had finally been mingled with her love. She must have not long ago discovered Rozelle Modestia to be her flesh-and-blood twin.

It was as if Rozelle Modestia had been the one to be stabbed back there—but fatally! Was it true what they said about twins being so close in soul that they felt what the other was going through? Could one die and the other still live on with a fruitful existence?

Ahh, but how Rosette would love him perfectly, because she would love freely, unfettered by the bitterness that had clung to her. She had finally shed the mystery of her life—the cocoon that must have imprisoned her all along.

Indeed Rozelle Modestia—cowered now forever—must have hated her twin thoroughly, once she discovered she had one and that that one had not been cast aside as she had.

What else, he wondered, had caused Rosette to have that sad, haunted look on occasion? Who else, and how many, had caused her heartache?

"Good lord, all those years thinking Rozelle Modestia was my only living kin, my beloved sister!"

The twins, both named after the rose. Each had a flower on her buttocks. While he'd been ministering to Rosette's wounds, looking her over for any others, he'd found the perfect rose. Where Rozelle's was on the left nate, Rosette's was on the right. A more perfect birthmark he'd never seen.

"Good lord," he shouted again, shaking his head.

Now Mark had no one to call his own, no one but that adorable, beautiful, ah yes, and tempting woman lying there, while he lounged here wishing to make wild love to her.

Rosette, she had come to his soul like fire in the desert. In this same way he'd been able to find her this time. Ah, his bittersweet love—sleep now, my lovely bride-to-be. He could hardly wait to make her his own, in body, soul and name.

Chapter Forty

She could see and feel herself running laughing through springtime's gloriously blooming wildflowers and the tall grasses bordering the meadows of Heathcliff and Southend, and, yes, she could see Oakhill in the far reaches of the picture too.

Sweet as cherry pie and pretty as a painted French doll, with vivid curls that tumbled below her hips, the little girl climbed upon her mother's lap, leaned her face against the ample breast and cried, her soft, rosy lips pouting and trembling. "Why, Mama, don't you love me?" she asked her mother.

She was cast aside like a forgotten, discarded rag doll. "You can see, daughter, that you muss my skirts! Now go, as I have an afternoon tea to attend to."

Pushing open the door to her father's study, the little girl climbed upon her father's lap, leaned her porcelainlike face against the firm chest and cried.

"Papa, do you love me?"

"Yes, yes!" he grumbled. "Go away, Rosie, I am busy. Can't you ever see that, naughty girl?" He put her down and, patting her bottom, told the child it was bedtime. But it was not.

A contraction of pain shot through her closed eyes, and her pink lips tightened in dejection. Why didn't they love her? Why didn't Perry Marland love her, she choked, anymore? Hasan! Mark! Oh, please love me . . . love me . . .

"Mark!"

Rosette whimpered, stirring awake in her now-restless slumber. She knew an active, gnawing hunger tearing at her heart.

"Rosette," the solicitous voice belonging to the face hovering over her murmured, "you are not alone—I am here to love and protect you—forever and ever." He caught his breath as his heart went out to that lonesome little girl she must have been.

"Hasan!" Her lucid tones reached his heart, burrowing their sweet barbs into his soul.

"Hmm—yes."

"Mark?"

"Yes, I am he too."

"Oh, hold me, Mark!"

He caressed her gleaming head, the disheveled hair betraying the crisis she'd just been through. Her long auburn hair hung unbound to her waist and the dawn's light caught its fiery-red highlights, making it gleam like a scintillating ruby. "Not too tight, though." He climbed carefully into her blanket, taking caution not to bump her bandaged shoulder. "You have a wound, my sweet, and—"

"I feel it, Mark," she interrupted softly. "But my heart hurts more, why did you send me away to the Sahara? Why did you and Rozelle do this to me? I thought you—that you loved me."

"Shh." He placed a finger over her moving lips. "Would I ever do such a terrible thing to my beloved? Tell me, would I?" He hugged her gently. "You must know my intentions by now better than that, Rosette."

"I—I don't know."

"Of course you do. You see, you've just lately realized the chains are broken. Your parents were heartless to reject both of you, but Rozelle no longer is a part of you, in fact she never really was. Evil and good cannot share the same place, even though you shared part of your life—nine months to be exact, in the same cubbyhole." He smiled, tracing a finger from the tip of her nose down to the corner of her sweet mouth. "Later, after I discovered your true identity, you made me think of a bird in its gilded cage, wishing it could sing but unable to do so. Caged, though you watched the larks and doves winging their way high in the sunshine, while you sat and watched from your cage. You were afraid to reveal your feelings, because exposing yourself, opening up to love might be painful and bring rejection."

"True, Mark, so true." She smiled wistfully up at him. "What about yourself? What were your dreams, Mark?"

"Night after night in the desert I dreamed of joys — those which I dared to even think of — and Rozelle Modestia was in those dreams. On the one side I thought of her, and then when you entered the picture — believe me — I was damn confused. I thought there was a dual nature to this auburn-haired lady, with the dulcet tone of voice. I could not gainsay what went on inside my heart, Rosette." He stared deeply into her limpid, tawny eyes and saw the sheen of love in all its brightness there.

For a minute Mark remained silent, staring back to several weeks ago. How he had felt Rozelle Modestia's badness reach out to him as soon as she had leaned sensuously from her landau, but he wouldn't tell Rosette this now.

Nor did he believe he should ever relate to her the manner in which he had frightened the dark twin and cowered her to a jelly. With Rozelle, beside that bed, he had felt apart, like a male without sex, a male minus those strivings that motivated a man to lust or to love.

"I suppose you thought she was more beautiful than I?" Rosette ventured softly now.

His answer was spontaneous. "She possessed a physical charm, yes. But never once did I know that charm after you came along."

His voice made Rosette's flesh tingle, all around, as the warmth spread throughout her body. Such brand-new, exquisite emotions were coursing in her blood, throughout her being, as she knew he wanted her with desire mounting just as hers.

"She was not a good woman, Rosette." He had plucked all of Rozelle's pretty feathers, he would not add, for now. "She lived mainly for pleasure, for self-focused gain, and she allowed many men to make love to her. A man knows these things instinctively like a woman knows many things about a man."

"Did you ever want to?" she ventured shyly.

"Want to what?"

"To—make l-love to Rozelle Modestia?"

"My God, Rosette, she was supposed to be my sister. How could I—" He cut himself short. He sighed deeply before going on. "I realized there was a part of her that I desired deeply. Do you know what part that was?"

"No," she muttered, afraid to hear the truth.

"You."

"Me?" Rosette blinked up at him, only half-believing him.

He paused, then continued. "I felt ashamed, for wanting to be with her so badly, the feverish moment recalled now when I awaited her return to the kasbah. Hadji was supposed to have brought her to me. He had failed. The feeling was, was that you, my real true love, was so near, so agonizingly near that I could almost reach out and feel and grab you." Astutely he smiled here. "You were on your way, sweet, your dainty feet had already touched the soil in Africa."

She wanted to hear more about her elusive twin. "Is Rozelle Modestia a woman that men love but do not marry?"

Mark's crisp mouth grew taut with disdain for Rozelle Modestia's kind.

"Yes, a woman who is desired by husbands and rogues alike."

"Had there been no others after me?" Rosette quizzed tentatively.

Mark disappointed her by keeping on the same track, with Rosette wondering what would be his final destination.

"All other women, you see, had ceased to exist for me. God, I had become her slave! I was insanely jealous of all the men who had been in her life, who might be in it again. I was tortured by loving her—a woman who was my own flesh and blood!" He lowered his head. "So I thought. She could have deceived the devil himself."

"But Rozelle wasn't your own flesh and blood, so now how do you feel about her?" Rosette wondered painfully, with worry lingering.

"She is the bad seed. Hers is the passion of one body for another. Bodies straining with animal lust, nothing more." He clasped her chin between thumb and forefinger. "I love you, my sweetest, defiant little rose. I never loved any of those other women, not one of them: not Shamara, not Jamila—" he grinned here—"they were in my life but for a moment only, at the time of pleasure and release. But no love, ah, never that!" He traced a long, brown finger over lips that had blistered and were healing now. "I shall make you understand, my love—as soon as you are healed—as you have not understood it before."

"Oh, Hasan Mark—" unknowingly she had said Handsome Mark—"without you my life would not be complete. One half of a heart without the other half. God must have sent you to fill the hunger in my soul for love. I believe you are a gift from the Almighty."

He hugged her with a virile cheek pressed to a feminine one. "That was beautiful, love." He smiled happily when her laughter broke like a sunshine-clear, babbling brook. "You are delightful, do you know that?"

She sighed and snuggled against him, preparing a question of her own.

"Are you really prepared to yield your self under the yoke of matrimony?"

He chucked her fine chin. "Does my heart pound madly when you are near for no reason? Why does the very sight and sound of you bring fire and longing to my heart? To my body? You are no mirage, sweetest rose, I see you here, there, everywhere. You are real, you are the essence of life to me, the air that I breathe. Now, have I answered your question well enough?"

"No," she giggled soft and feminine.

"May I show you just now? If I am careful with your wound?"

He eased his arm beneath her wounded shoulder, bringing her willing body gently against him. He was suddenly seized by a savage desire to make love to her. Covering her mouth, he kissed her with such tenderness, piercing sweetness, that it was all Rosette could do not to break out in tears and sobs.

"I like you this way, Rose. Unafraid to love."

"How I have missed you," she said with a wistful little sigh into his mouth.

Beads of body-heat perspiration formed on Mark's upper lip. A miniature swordplay of tongues ensued. "I love you," Mark exclaimed, removing his tongue after a full thrust that sent thrills throughout her entire being.

Rosette thought she would surely die from it next as he kissed her with such tender hunger, such sweet ecstasy, such naked desire in his smoldering, love-slitted, roving, dark eyes. His eyes made love to her eyes as he bared her breasts, massaging and stroking the full circles of plump, soft flesh. His eyes glittered over the new, heavy roundness attesting to her pregnancy, but he couldn't know this—yet.

In the intense moment of love, Rosette shivered as the heat and hardness of his throbbing manhood lay against her thigh, boldly rigid and animated. Her warmth and softness ached to open up for him, to feel him driving deep inside her.

His eyes delved deeply into the limpid pools of hers. Ah yes, she discovered, emerald eyes now, emerging from the darkness into the light of dawning love. A wild surge of elation shot through Rosette while he held her gaze, sensuous pleasure surfacing from deep within her as she realized their mutual need was great.

Now she melted with a gratified murmur against his iron-thewed chest, giving herself up to the next thrilling kiss. While he was still kissing her, his hand found and palmed her softly rounded belly. Abruptly he lifted his tawny head; his eyes narrowed down over her.

"What's this?"

Mark continued to examine her while tingles of desire racked her lower half. She stared up at his lips, dew-kissed from hers, that had clung and not wanted to let go.

"All yours, my darling husband-to-be." She grinned impishly, adding, "It seems, my virile sheik, you left a gentle reminder of your passion with me?"

"Mine?"

She smiled secretively. "Remember Jamila?"

He chuckled. "Ah yes, the one with the resistant thighs, the virgin who bewitched my poor, befuddled senses—" he hoisted an eyebrow—"surely not one time?"

His hand continued to caress the gentle bulge of tummy, knowing the babe was indeed his.

"Yours, all yours, darling."

Mark grimaced in distaste. "Please, never call me 'darling' again."

Unhappily she pouted. "But why not? Can you think of a more appropriate endearment?" She peered up at him and waited.

"Hmmm." He rubbed his scarred cheek in deep thought, dark eyes twinkling down as he revered the woman he loved. "A while ago you said 'beloved sheik.' I think that should do. Yes, beloved, that should do very well. What do you think?"

"Beloved, oh yes—forever and ever!"

He kissed her with passion's fire unbridled, devouring the sweetness of her nectar. "Rosette, my love, wilder, sweeter than a field of roses."

She laughed in pure delight, snuggled securely in her sheik's arms. "Are you happy too, Mark?"

"Happy? Need you ask?" He joined her and chuckled in mirth. "You shall only give me happiness, for sure, from this day on." He fondled the new life within her. "No other shall place the seeds of life where I have planted mine. Your body shows what your heart feels," he said suddenly, his eyes smiling into hers.

"Mark?" She dropped her eyes and flushed.

"Yes," he said, smiling knowingly.

Her eyes flew to his smiling, waiting ones. "Make love to me, right here, right now, please?"

"All the way?"

She nodded yes.

"Are you sure, Rosette?"

"Most sure!" she giggled, emboldened in her intense need for her man.

"Positive? Recall what you said before?"

"Positive?" She stared hungrily into his gaze. "My God, Mark, I'm the one who's almost raping you!"

He leaned back his head and roared. "You have indeed changed. For the better!"

"Since I fell deeply and irreversibly in love with you, my beloved sheik!" She touched his hand gently, drawing the long, hard flesh to her swollen breast.

"Hmm, I see that—I mean I feel that you indeed want me. Oh yes. Indeed!"

"I do, with desire that overwhelms me," she insisted boldly.

Their eyes met, instantly set ablaze. Mark knew he could not extinguish the fires now, even had she begged him to. He chuckled low, for the long, thick hardness between his thighs was too growing most insistent.

When she touched that pulsating member, Mark sucked in his breath and his eyes widened in passion's fury.

She squeezed his biceps in a womanly movement, as old as love itself. "Do you want to be the first man in the Sahara to be raped by a woman?"

She arched and purred like a love-starved kitten.

"You are as well as my bride," he began deeply, "for what remains of this night!"

Like a sunlit dream, they began to love amidst the pillaged and ruined temple, amphitheater and public buildings of Roman time. When he opened her long legs and mounted her she was ready for the first knobby bit of him. Before entering that source of heat, his lips sought hers once again. Now the long, straining hardness probed at her golden burrow, then slid smoothly, with ease, into it. Soon they were completely joined.

He looked down at her, whispering love words as he moved in slow, rhythmic strokes, withholding bringing her to that stunning end.

But the pressure built and rose until she could stand it no longer and she needed to beg Mark to strive and accelerate his speed to bring her to that peak of release.

Now the whole of his strainings pulsated within her. "Mark, oh Mark!"

"Dear God, you're as beautiful inside as outside," Mark deeply echoed her fierce joy.

He quickened the tempo, his lustily unabashed love words making her cheeks burn. But his harsh breaths were like music to her ears, and she met every savage thrust with eager, arched hips, her own gasps and cries becoming louder, faster notes of ecstasy unbounded. Then his hands grasped her firm buttocks to bring her closer, if possible, and go deeper.

Caught in the storm of climbing, whirling passion, she held nothing back this time, loved with her whole being, her heart and blood pounding wildly. Nothing more was wanting. At last every veil had been lowered between them, as they had long been one flesh they were now becoming one in love's spirit. Their loving was like a dance, undulating to that glorious moment of ultimate mating.

The storm of passion intensified threefold. The last thrust was more animated than before. It happened then.

The sweetest ecstasy suddenly surged and shattered her very sense of being, spasms convulsing her, as beneath the Roman columns and cornice stones together they met and pulsated to a blinding, glorious, whorl of ecstasy.

Romans, Turks, Arabs, Spaniards, French and Italians had all left their imprint on this Sahara. But it was a superficial mark compared with the one Rosette and her sheik left behind as the sun burst, bloody-hued and romantically, to flood the ancient castle walls and the lovers therein.

Neither spoke in the magic of the moment. Their eyes met and held, emerald and amber melding in love's soft afterglow.

No ghosts, here or forevermore, would ever come to haunt these lovers again. As surely as the sun followed its diurnal course across the desert sky.